THE
SAFECRACKER

JAMES GARRISON

Relax. Read. Repeat.

THE SAFECRACKER
By James Garrison
Published by TouchPoint Press
Brookland, AR 72417
www.touchpointpress.com

ISBN-10: 1-946920-76-2
ISBN-13: 978-1-946920-76-8

Editor: Kimberly Coghlan
Front Cover Image: Geoffrey Garrison
Cover Design: Colbie Myles, ColbieMyles.net

Connect with the author at https://jamesgarrison-author.com/

First Edition

Library of Congress Control Number:2019948861

Printed in the United States of America.

Other titles by James Garrison

QL 4

A fictionalized story of the author's year as a drafted MP in Vietnam during the war.

Awards

2017 Silver Medal in Literary Fiction from the Military Writers Society of America
2018 Montaigne Medal, Finalist
Distinguished Favorite for military fiction in the 2019 Independent Press Awards
2019 Independent Book Award for literary fiction and military fiction

For my lawyer daughter and the women attorneys I've known who paved the way over the last half century.

Part 1

Chapter One - Billy Angel

HOW THE HELL DID IT GO SO WRONG? A fast food joint should've had an easy safe to take out. Now he was in Central Prison, Judy Kay was in hiding, and Lazlo was deader'n the block of concrete that safe was set in.

The guard jangled the keys on the other side of the steel door and Billy watched for it to open. Taking him to meet his new lawyer. A freebie since they thought he didn't have any money, certainly none in a bank anywhere. Standing to receive his jailer, he chuckled. Safecrackers don't use banks.

All the other jokers in the cells here, the highest security area of the prison, the state even, were in a bucket of shit a lot worse'n him. Unless, God forbid, the D.A. went for a murder rap. But that didn't mean the death penalty, not with the cops shooting that guy. Or did it? Still, he'd be in the slammer a long time unless this shyster was worth his salt. Maybe he should tap into his stash, get a real lawyer. But he'd need Judy Kay for that, and with the heat on, she might just lead the cops to it.

They had brought him here because he was good. A regular fucking Houdini, that's what Judy Kay called him. But they'd have to take him back to the McFee County Courthouse for trial. He gave a low snort. Then he'd show 'em some real magic—leastwise if this lawyer couldn't do any.

He waited quietly, maintaining his harmless hangdog look while the guard placed shackles on his wrists, then ran the link through a loop in his belt. Not the worst bracelets he'd ever worn, could even lift his hands past his waist.

He eyed the bulge in the guard's shirt pocket—a cigarette pack resting comfortably on a bulging belly. Reckon they'd let him have a smoke before they brought him back? He looked hopefully at the guard's square face. Hard, hard, hard. With narrow, yellowish eyes. Not someone to give you a break, have a little pity on a man. He wasn't going to give the sonuvabitch the satisfaction of saying, "Hell no!" so he didn't ask.

After all this time, his knees and hip still ached from when he'd hit the ground. They'd laughed at him when he asked to go to the hospital. Ignored all the pain a fellow man was suffering. Said he deserved the Lord's vengeance for what he done to that poor jailer. Shit, that poor jailer had almost a foot and more'n a hundred pounds on him.

Going down the gray corridor—gray concrete floors, gray cinderblock walls with serial doors like tombstones—he peered at the evenly spaced slabs of blank steel, their judas windows pulled tightly shut. Only a few muffled noises came from within these cells: no rattling of tin cups on bars or shouting in this place, only the sound of buzzing lights in the high ceiling.

If only he could get to his stash, he'd get him a good lawyer, get his sentence down to twenty so's he'd be out in eight, maybe five. How could he work his defense? Why, I was just lyin' in that ditch 'cause of all the shootin'. That kid on lookout, damn his hide, so spaced out he didn't know shit from Shinola.

Billy ran back through it for about the thousandth time.

Fisheye had rapped twice on the doorjamb and yelled, "Cops!" Then he was gone.

"Move it." Billy's voice was low and calm. He started grabbing the tools and stuffing them into the canvas bag.

Lazlo was already at the door when he stopped and came back, on the way yanking the plug out of the socket and adding the drill to the bag.

Billy heard something outside. A cop car? Voices? Or Fisheye on the run?

"Leave it," he told Lazlo, pointing to the drill. "I got what I want. When we get out, you go right, I go left. Stay in the woods 'til you reach the car. Keys are under the seat." Now Billy could clearly hear movement. It wouldn't be Fisheye. He was long gone.

They bolted through the back door of the Taco Pal, Billy first, then Lazlo. Voices yelled for them to stop. Then the cops were behind Billy, chasing him through the woods. Two shotgun blasts sounded on the other side of the Taco Pal followed by bullets whizzing over his head.

Billy dove into a ditch and flailed about to pull dead sticks and leaves over him. He had dropped the bag, but it didn't matter. Tools were easy to get, and nothing was in the bag to I.D. him.

JAMES GARRISON

Jerking the leather gloves off his hands, he shoved them deep into the muck. Small and wiry like a weasel, he was good at this, playing hide and seek with cops. No panic for Billy Angel, icy calm and muscled like a high-wire artist.

Reality crept in. They'd never buy it, him lying in the ditch. But hell, any fool would've been eating grass with all the lead flying, bullets whizzing over his head, leaves and woodchips falling like snow. That fellow at the apartments, look what happened to him. And poor ol' Lazlo.

He started thinking about the dead man at the apartments. Somethin' mighty funny about that. He and Lazlo were clear on the other side of the Taco Pal, and the kid must've hightailed it soon as the cop car came up the street. That damned Fisheye gave the signal, then he vamoosed, too.

Maybe if they hadn't stopped for the tools? He and Lazlo split like they'd agreed, out to the sides. So why'd the cops start shootin' up the hill and hit the guy at the apartments? Unless they were shootin' at each other, 'cause he and Lazlo didn't have no guns.

Yeah, they must've been shootin' at each other. Or at Fisheye.

He grimaced and shook his head as the guard herded him toward the end of the corridor. They sure nailed poor ol' Lazlo, while that mother got away. Good thing for Fisheye, Billy Angel ain't a snitch.

Opening a pair of double steel doors, one after the other like an airlock on a space ship, the guard led him into a large, high-ceilinged room. A sturdy wall, the top part thick glass halfway to the ceiling, divided the area into two parts. Sunlight, the first he'd seen in days, splashed the walls and, dispersed by the glass divider, cast dusty rainbows to the far corners of the room. Down the center ran a solid barrier of open-sided booths—all empty—paired with their mirror images on the other side of the glass wall.

God, he wished it was Judy Kay coming to see him. But they'd never let her; she came anywhere near here, they'd lock her up, too.

He sighed as he turned into a booth, the guard steering him by the elbow. Then he froze.

Oh shit! They sent me the high school debate team.

4

Chapter Two – Patricia Egan

THE SKYSCRAPERS ROSE ABOVE THEM IN BLACK, rain-soaked shadows. Standing on the curb, Patricia Egan watched her boss, Dick McFee, pay and over tip the yellow cab driver, Dick still rambling on about some Mets baseball player. Impatient to get inside, she glanced up at the foreshortened grid of windows, then quickly ducked her head before the mist smudged her makeup. She eyed the wet street beyond the pointed toes of her new black pumps, the rainbow slick by the curb and, in the slick, a dark cigar butt nudging a cellophane candy wrapper. Up and down the street, black limousines with darkly tinted windows waited for bankers and lawyers to stream from the cavernous entrances of the buildings.

She had been here before, when she was in high school and her father brought her along on a business trip. Before the family came apart. She didn't remember the City being this dirty then, or as dismal.

Dick finally joined her on the sidewalk. Their appointment was at four o'clock, the only time Elroy Bell could see them: the senior partner in the McFee law firm and his new associate who had just flown up from Carrville, North Carolina.

The offices of Becker, Bell, Jones, and Boyd occupied floors forty through forty-six in a building whose granite façade had blackened with age. *Probably built by robber barons,* Patricia thought, *buried in raised sarcophagi in the lobby, their stone arms crossed over ancient railroad bonds.* Dick reached above her head and gave the revolving door a shove, then stood back for her to enter. Going past him, she vowed to tamp down her cynicism.

The windows of Elroy Bell's conference room on the forty-fifth floor looked out over the darkening street to a newer and taller building of smoky glass on the other side. The room's low lighting, the shiny dark wood of the furnishings, the mahogany paneling, all seemed designed for mellow assurances of competence and stolid respectability. They only served to heighten her foreboding about the meeting.

Neither Elroy Bell's warm greeting nor the hot tea in a gold-rimmed cup dispelled her gloom—nor did the praise he heaped on Dick for selecting the choicest associates from the top law schools. She smiled at Elroy without blushing and tried to suppress the thought that he was looking her up and down and had no idea where she went to school. A few inches shorter than her, he was a dapper little man with a comb-over of thin, white hair. Bouncing about to make them welcome and show off his office, Elroy Bell came across as a bit pompous, with a sharp, sarcastic voice tempered by a slight southern drawl. But it was a voice that drew you close and commanded respectful attention.

Instead of tea, Elroy offered Dick a scotch. "Like a little Dalwhinnie's?" he asked, extracting a bottle from a well-stocked liquor cabinet inside a credenza.

"Yes suh, if you please, suh." Dick had lapsed into Southern speak as soon as the two shook hands. He waved a nicotine-stained finger in Elroy's direction. "Just a splash or two, no ice."

Her father, from old South aristocracy, never spoke like that, with an affected Southern accent. Elroy poured more than a splash or two of scotch in a tumbler and extracted a bottle of Perrier for himself from a small refrigerator. Watching the two go through their ritual, she couldn't help but compare Dick to her father, how different they were, but in some ways alike, both eminent lawyers in mid-size Southern towns. Or so her father had been, before his decline.

Once they were seated around the cozy little conference table, she nursed her tea and listened while Dick swilled his scotch and Elroy sipped at the Perrier, the two of them conversing without coming anywhere near the purpose of the visit.

Finally, without preamble, Elroy asked, "Dick, how are we going to give the bankers some assurance this thing's actually gonna fly and all their work won't be for naught?"

Dick plunked his empty glass down on the table and jutted his chin out. "I wrote the damn statute, and the legislature passed it *just* like I wrote it."

"My people tell me it's not clear you can do all this." Elroy raised his hands, palms up. "A huge research complex, experimental prototypes for all kinds of new energy facilities, partnering with the private power companies. This looks like more than the legislature contemplated. And the power companies are going to throw up roadblocks."

What he was saying sounded like her memo from before the bar exam. But she knew Elroy hadn't read it. Dick had kept it to himself and Leslie Sharp, the firm's junior partner, and he had admonished her not to mention it to anybody. She hadn't—except to the firm's other new associate, Jack Alexander. He had proofed the memo for her.

"Bankers don't like last-minute legal challenges," Elroy added. "It gums up their being able to place the bonds—and get their cut."

There was a knock on the door, and it opened at once.

"Ah, here's Aaron," Elroy said as a stooped man with an unruly shock of graying black hair entered. As if presenting a sacrifice, the man held out a thick document in a plastic cover, along with a loose stack of papers on top of it.

"Here is what you requested, Mr. Bell."

Elroy rose and accepted the offering. "My assistant, Aaron . . . Harvard Law," Elroy said, dropping the binder in front of Dick while retaining the papers.

Patricia clenched her teeth. *Harvard like both of you and I'm not?*

They stood for the introductions. "Aaron's a senior associate," Elroy said, parceling out the papers among them. "He's putting together the prospectus for the bond issue." He gave his minion a magisterial wave of the hand. "Thanks, Aaron. That's all we need."

Aaron made his farewells and departed. *God*, Patricia thought, *he can't be much older than I am, yet he looks fifty.*

"Aaron works long hours," Elroy said once Aaron was gone and they were seated again. As if he were reading her thoughts. "But he's paid well." His eyebrows went up. "Bond counsel reap the benefits of being associated with huge volumes of money."

"Justly and well earned, I'm sure," Dick said.

"The reason partners in a municipal bond practice do so well isn't because we work hard." Elroy's eyes were unblinking, fixed on Dick McFee. "It's because we put our reputations on the line. We stand behind

7

the legality and bona fides of the bonds." He shifted his gaze to Patricia. "It is a reputation we earn over decades. We earn it by never being wrong."

This guy didn't get here by being anybody's fool, she thought.

"I hear you, Elroy," Dick said, "and I can assure you this project is one hundred percent legal. Your reputation's absolutely safe."

"The papers in front of you contain a précis of the bond issue with the details we have so far about the project." Elroy's eyebrows shot up. "And where the revenues will come from." He held up his hand before Dick could speak. "I know, I know. The cities' electric and gas revenues are pledged to back the bonds. But there are questions about the cities' authority—"

"The statute says the cities—"

"I know what the statute says, and Aaron has written a little memo that *points out* a few concerns on whether it says the cities can do what you're trying to do here." He hit the table with his hand. "We've got to have some imprimatur of legal authority to get the bankers to pick up these bonds, Dick."

Patricia gave a start, then tried to hide her reaction. *So this isn't the done deal Dick's been telling the cities it is.* What Leslie Sharp, Dick's junior partner, and the Carrville mayor were so confidently telling a whole slew of city officials, consultants, and private investors this same day back in Carrville.

She kept her eyes down, skimming the précis. *Mr. Bell and company have the same concerns I had. Have.*

"We'll get a court order that it's legal," Dick said.

Elroy leaned back in his chair and stared at him. He didn't say anything. She could almost hear the gears working.

"A declaratory judgment?" Elroy said finally. "And how many years will that take? And where's the *real live* controversy that makes it justiciable?"

Dick gave a dismissive wave of his hand. "Xeco and its allies have been popping off in the press—and every goddamn where else. Sayin' the project violates the constitution, sayin' it's not authorized by the statute I drafted. CEO even blasted us in a Kiwanis speech last week."

Dick had said it was all "just puffery and nonsense," or so he told the clients. She stared at him, then looked over at Elroy Bell.

"That's a start," Elroy said. "But how far does *that* get you?"

"We file against Xeco, get a superior court to say it's all authorized by statute—and constitutional to boot. Once we get a lower court ruling, the supreme court'll go with us. Half of 'em are old friends of mine." Except for Dick's reliance on his old friends, this was all straight from her memo.

Elroy Bell nodded slowly. "That might work. You got a lower court judge in mind?"

"Larkins over in Sniderville." Dick smiled. "Like our dear ol' Professor Ames always said, the judge is more important than the law 'cause it's the judge who says what the law is."

"He was a cynical old bastard at that." Elroy didn't return Dick's smile. "You have to move fast. We need a favorable decision by January, *if* we want to get the ball rolling next year. And we don't know what will happen with this energy thing if Reagan wins."

"We can do it," Dick said.

Patricia wasn't so sure.

Stretching out one leg, Elroy extracted a pocket watch from the top of his trousers and glanced down at it. "We'll go over to my club for drinks," he said, putting the watch back. "One of the bankers wants to meet you, so he'll be joining us." Elroy gave Dick a devilish smile and then winked at Patricia. "Said he wanted a face to go with this pre-e-posterous idea before he goes trying to foist off any bonds on his rich-ass friends. Needs to look you in the eye and make sure you didn't come out of the funny farm somewhere."

Elroy laughed and Dick laughed with him. Patricia didn't join them, and she saw little humor in Elroy Bell's eyes.

While they waited for Elroy at the elevators, Dick gave her a light pat on the arm. "That was a fine memo you wrote." He momentarily stretched to his full height, tall and thin in his battered gray fedora. "A big help," he said, looking down at her. "Especially the declaratory judgment bit."

"Thanks." She hesitated. "But it's a long shot. Any careful judge could say it's premature. Some press releases and speeches—"

"Don't worry, my dear. I know my judges. We'll have one who loves us—and who's not so careful." A watery eye winked at her from behind his glasses.

9

She cringed but didn't say anything. *A case like this might provide fodder for a law review article, but as a strategy on which to base issuing millions of dollars of municipal bonds? Millions that might not be enough? Or might be for naught—was that how Elroy phrased it?*

"I want you to start working on the petition to the court and affidavits soon as we get back," Dick said.

She bit her lip to keep from shaking her head and repeating that it might not work, not in the time they had.

"And I want *you* working full-time with us on the project," Dick added, placing his hand on her shoulder and giving it a squeeze.

"That's great!" she said. "I'd love to." And she meant it. It would be interesting legal work and a lot of exposure, both with the clients and in court.

Her second thought was Jack. *He'll hate me for this.*

Chapter Three – Jack Alexander

HE HAD TAKEN THE JOB ON A WHIM. Rather than New York or Atlanta, here he was in podunkville North Carolina. Five offers from big firms in real cities, and he'd gone with the McFee Law Firm. Colin, the prick, was the only reason he even came here to interview, and Colin had left months ago.

Still, this was a chance to make some real money, do exciting stuff. Not stuck in a mega-firm library doing research and drafting memos all day, maybe not seeing the inside of a courtroom for years. But here . . . here he was in on the ground floor—the energy revolution, as Leslie Sharp called it.

He swiveled his chair away from the window. As tempting as the view was four floors up in the McFee Savings Building, the highest structure for fifty miles, he needed to finish reviewing the black notebook on his desk. He looked at his watch. Less than half an hour to the big meeting.

Joe Mayes was already down the hall with Leslie. Going for coffee, he'd heard the two of them behind Leslie's door, Joe's braying laugh and Leslie's booming voice. Probably telling jokes and debating the Braves' chances at the pennant. No matter, the meter was running.

He stared down at the ancient wooden desk, incongruous in this modern office with all its tinted glass and chemical carpet smell. On returning from the bar exam, he'd found a lot of things to be incongruous in this place—and him and Patricia the only remaining associates. At least now he had a seat on the center ring. Opening the notebook, he flipped to the list of attendees.

Mayor Fisher, leader and primary booster of the cities' renewable energy project. Smart, Leslie said, and suave, a smooth politician. Very smooth.

Joe Mayes, one of Dick McFee's old friends. A high-powered trial attorney from Atlanta—and a major pain-in-the ass for the power companies.

Then the Carrville city attorney, another old friend of Dick's, and a number of other city attorneys, mayors, city managers, city controllers, and members of the city councils of the twenty-one municipalities that made up Cities Renewable Energy, Inc., or the "New-Energy" group as Leslie had dubbed it.

Near the top of the list of city council members was Allie McFee, Dick's ex-wife. That should be interesting. Maybe that was why Leslie was running this big summit meeting while Dick was off to New York. With Patricia.

"Let's go, Jack!" Leslie Sharp banged his hand on the inside of the doorjamb. Still moving, he banged again on the wall outside. Jack closed the notebook and pushed his chair back just as Joe Mayes slipped through the door.

"Hey, Jack, my boy. You ace the bar, ready for the big time now?" Joe's extended hand exposed a gold cufflink and crisp white French cuff below a dark blue pinstripe coat sleeve.

"I'm always ready," Jack said. Standing to shake hands, he grinned down at the square, ruddy face and squinting eyes. "So, Mr. Mayes, is this it?" He waved toward the conference room down the hall. "The big time?"

"Hell yes!" Joe paced in front of the desk. "We're gonna do the biggest goddamn project . . ." Stopping, he pointed a finger at Jack. "Biggest goddamn *new*-energy project this country's ever seen. Billions of dollars."

Jack grabbed his suit coat off a hanger behind the door and started out. *Billions of dollars?* He doubted it, but that was Joe. As they exited, Joe slapped him on the back.

"Billions of fucking dollars." He put his arm around Jack and pulled him close. "The fun part, bub . . . we're gonna slap the livin' shit out of the power companies and make 'em love us for it."

"Looks like we'll have to keep 'em from stopping us first." Jack slipped from his grasp. "Law doesn't look all that clear to me." At least that's what Patricia said in her memo. The one that hadn't made it into the notebook.

"We'll kick their butts. It ain't what the law says; it's what the times demand. Shit, my lawn boy had to siphon gas out of my wife's Mercedes to mow the grass last week." He grabbed Jack's arm. "The cities are a natural for all this energy crap. They got locked-in customers and their own fucking electric and gas systems."

Jack tried to pull away, but Joe held him back. At the far end of the hall, several men in dark suits filed into the open door of the conference room.

"Most important, my friend, we raise money, lots of money. And the power companies are gonna see it's to their benefit to tap into it." He yanked Jack's arm. "And us lawyers are gonna make a ton of money."

"*That* I'm looking forward to." Jack finally managed to shake loose from Joe's grip, but he was thinking, *Leslie and Dick are doing quite well already.*

They started off again, Jack shortening his strides to allow Joe to keep up. As they passed an empty office, Joe veered off to peer inside. Jack came back to join him.

"Say, what d'ya hear from Ray?" Joe asked, switching on the light.

Jack looked around. The office had never looked so bare: big empty desk and a swivel chair, its back broken by the rocking of the firm's former senior associate, Ray Malloy. Leslie's longtime friend.

"He's okay, I guess," Jack said, switching the light off and exiting to the hall.

"Yeah, but what d'ya hear from him? You think he'll be here today?"

"He's not on the list." They had reached the conference room.

"Hope the hell he doesn't screw things up." Joe's hoarse whisper came over Jack's shoulder as they went in.

Turning, Jack started to say that Ray wouldn't do that, but Joe had spotted a more compelling target.

"Mr. Mayor, your honor, sir!" Then the braying laugh.

A tanned, silver-haired man broke off from waving his finger at a mid-sized giant and hurried toward Joe. Shaking hands, Joe and the mayor each clutched the other's arm.

"Glad you're on board," said the mayor, shifting to wrap an arm around Joe's shoulders. "How's your game?"

The man who had been talking to the mayor shoved past Jack, headed for the door. Broader and taller than Jack, the man was dressed in a polyester olive-green suit, gray shirt, and no tie. Not the standard uniform for a meeting like this.

"Better'n ever," Joe was answering the mayor. "Play twice a week."

The mayor ushered Joe toward a corner near the window. Their heads came close together and their voices were lost in the general din of conversation.

The conference room was baronial in size, three massive windows long, and full of people. Stretching three quarters of its length was a conference table: polished dark maple with a gentle curve. Almost leaping off the near wall was a full-length, bigger-than-life oil portrait of Richard C. McFee, Dick in his younger days: a full head of blond hair, an unlined face, and no glasses or moustache.

Once he had networked and provisioned himself for the meeting, Jack settled into a seat near the entrance. Poised to attack a Danish, he glanced up as an attractive woman with short, platinum blonde hair pulled out the chair across from him.

Smiling, she held out her hand. "You must be Jack Alexander."

Dropping the Danish, he jumped up, brushing off his hand on his pants, and stretched across the table. "Yes, ma'am. Don't believe we've met."

"Allie McFee. Dick's told me a lot about you." Her grip was firm, her hand warm in his. "And his other new associate, Patty. She's in New York with Dick, isn't she?"

"You mean Patricia." Jack released Allie's hand but remained standing. "She doesn't really like to be called Patty."

Allie McFee burst out with a clear, melodic laugh. "Dick would do that, wouldn't he?" Her eyes shifted to Dick's portrait to the left of Jack's shoulder. "He has a tin ear for people's sensitivities."

Jack raised his eyebrows. The ex-wife would know about that, wouldn't she? He changed the subject. "I understand you're on the steering committee."

"Advisory committee they call it now." Allie sat down and pulled the chair closer to the table. While her face exhibited the smooth hauteur of moneyed aristocracy, her eyes had a sparkle of humor. "It's the mayor, the city attorney, and me," she added as Jack resumed his seat.

"If you need anything, just call me," Jack said. "I mean us, the firm. We're here to help."

"I'm sure." The words came out with another laugh. "At Dick's and Leslie's rates, it'd save us money to call you—or Patricia." Her smile took some of the edge off the response. "I know what Dick and the firm are doing is essential. Unless we get the legal clearances, this thing will never fly." She gave a sigh. "And it *is* important, not just for this group," she gestured around the table, "but for everyone in the country. We must have substitutes for foreign oil, and not just coal . . ."

She stopped as several of those nearby stared at her.

"Sorry." She put up her hands. "That sounds like a campaign speech, but I believe in what we're trying to do."

"No, no, Allie. Go on, go on." Coming up behind her, the mayor's bass carried over the waves of other conversation. He patted her on the shoulder as he went past. "That's a good opening to start the meeting."

The mayor reached his place next to Leslie, who was rapping on the table and bellowing the meeting to order. "Everyone be seated." Rap, rap, rap. "We have a long agenda."

With the hubbub subsiding, people drifted to the conference table and started pulling out chairs. Jack glanced around. From behind him, the big man in casual attire slid into view. He handed the mayor a file, then sidled over to a nearby food table for coffee. As he settled into a chair in the corner with his coffee in one hand, his coat fell open. Before he pulled it closed, a gun butt appeared, protruding from a holster on his belt. *That's weird*, thought Jack. *A bodyguard for the mayor?*

Mayor Fisher patted Leslie on the back, and Leslie, pallidly cherubic next to the elder statesman, obediently took his seat. Notebooks slapped open, papers rattled, and a few coughs replaced the dying murmur. Smoke from several cigarettes wafted up to form a thin haze under the lights, and one city manager fiddled with a lighter over his pipe. At the far end of the room, Lacey Lippard, Dick's secretary and quasi-valet, as well as the office administrator, began running the mayor's slide presentation on a portable screen.

After the first slides, the mayor paused to introduce several non-members in the group. The first was a rotund investment advisor who handled Carrville's municipal bonds and, beside him, the senior partner in a big engineering firm. On the other side was a sleek-looking man who described himself as a private investor interested in the energy project. Jack remembered Dick mentioning him: Evan Fitzhugh, recently come home to Carrville after years away making a fortune in perpetual-care cemeteries and retirement homes. One of Dick's dear old friends and evidently the mayor's, as well, from the effusive praise the mayor lavished on him.

The final guest was Leon Hayes, one of only two dark faces in the room and a prominent African-American lawyer in town. Not a dear old friend of Dick's—and certainly not one of the mayor's from his cursory introduction.

Past the preliminaries, another slide went up with the bullets: "Strategic Planning; Engineering Studies; Legal Approvals."

While papers rustled up and down the table, Jack found his gaze wandering to the big man in the corner by the refreshment table. The man didn't fidget, he didn't move at all. He just looked out at the room with a blank-faced stare. A broad face, crooked nose, dark slicked-back hair. Something funny about the eyes, one of which seemed to shift to him.

Jack looked away. The guy's presence irritated him, but he couldn't figure out why. Maybe it was the gun. Or the eye that stared off to one side.

"In broad outline," the mayor was saying, "we build our research facilities; we staff them with the finest scientists in the country; then we do several prototypes—standard stuff like synthetic fuels but also brand-new technology, wind and solar, whatever the scientists want to try. At the next stage, we can create partnerships with the big power companies." He cleared his throat and took a sip of water from a glass. "And anyone else who wants to join us."

"Mayor," a man Jack recognized as the Sniderville city manager interrupted. "The Feds have already proposed a research center in Colorado. Why can't we work with them or partner with the companies from the start? They have all sorts of tax credits—"

"Oh, we will, we will. But we've got to show what *we* can do. Show we can raise the money." He smiled over at the investment advisor who smiled back. "First, we have to do the engineering studies," the mayor said, holding his hand out toward the engineering consultant. "And we have to get all the legal approvals." He placed a hand on Leslie's shoulder and nodded at Joe Mayes across the corner of the table. Joe returned a broad grin.

Surveying the room, the mayor paused to meet the eyes of those who would meet his. "I've sent out a request for each city's share of the estimated costs. Yesterday, the city attorneys met—"

"Mayor Fisher, I'm okay with using the monies for studies and legal work, but aren't we going too far if we start acquiring land and letting contracts?" The Sniderville city manager again. "That's what it seems to be saying here." He held up one side of his notebook.

The mayor puffed out his chest. "We have the best legal minds in the business advising us." His hand went down to Leslie's shoulder again, and Leslie beamed up at him. "I can assure you, we won't let any contracts or buy any land until we have all the approvals. But we have to move forward—and that means finding the right site for the complex and developing a bid package." He pounded lightly on the table. "Dick McFee is up in New York, as I speak, finalizing arrangements for the bonds. Gentlemen . . . ladies," he bowed slightly toward Allie, "this is a matter of national urgency. We cannot, we *will* not give the world over to plodders."

"Hear, hear," said Joe Mayes, raising his hand in a loose fist and flashing a gold cufflink.

Leslie pushed back from the conference table. "Let's take a break, folks," he said, rising from his chair. "We can continue after we stretch our legs and get a little nourishment." He gestured toward a fresh spread being delivered by the liveried waiters from the City Club upstairs.

Half the group stampeded for the restrooms while the others made for the food. Jack ended up at the refreshment table behind Leslie, who was conversing in low, intense tones with Joe Mayes in front of him. Catching a reference to Dick and the firm, Jack strained to hear, and Joe's eyes met his over Leslie's shoulder.

Grabbing Leslie's arm, Joe stopped Leslie at, "Dick isn't . . ."

"Jack, Jack, you learning a lot here?" Joe asked, edging past Leslie. "Or would you rather be in New York with that pretty associate of yours."

"I like this." Jack gave a tight smile and motioned around the room. "Get to see what's happening with the project."

Giving Jack a brief nod, Leslie took a bite of doughnut and began searching for a clean cup on the table. Joe slipped past him, coming closer to Jack.

"Say, buddy, what's with the lady and her boyfriend? Heard he just up and left. Weren't you three livin' up there together—in that old Francis house? He got the house from his aunt, didn't he?"

Jack suppressed a start. *Nosy bastard, asking about Patricia and Colin.*

"So why'd Colin take off?" Joe asked from close under his nose. "I mean his father's firm is one of the best in town. I hear he freaked out."

"Joe, believe me, I don't know what it was." *And I wouldn't tell you if I did,* thought Jack. "Colin decided to go on active duty, and that's what he did."

"Well, shit, the old man had a heart attack over it. The boy was—"

"Gentlemen, let's get back to business," called the mayor. Leslie was already seated, a fresh doughnut on a napkin on top of the black notebook.

"I don't know anything about it, Joe." Jack shrugged and edged away.

"Must be interesting, you and that pretty woman up there all by yourselves. You two have breakfast together?" As Jacked turned away, forgetting his coffee, Joe winked at him and grinned.

Part II

Chapter Four – A New Day

PATRICIA HAD DRAGGED HER FEET as long as she could. Any hope of reversing the decision was dead, so she might as well finish packing up the files and ship them off to Joe Mayes—and consequently to Leslie. He'd know if anything was missing. She couldn't fudge by sending some and tossing the rest in the trash. Or keeping them. Just in case. So she'd make copies of the most important documents, the ones they might need again someday. Just in case.

She turned away from the filing cabinet and stared through the partially open blinds at the ancient jail up the street, three rust-colored stories high. To the left of the jail, the sun was coming up over the pine trees, a red ball embedded in a milky haze of fog rising off the river.

Over the past months, it seemed like she was always here to greet the sun in the morning and to see its final reflection in the corner windows of the jail at night. Except on Saturday and Sunday. Then it was well up in the sky before she arrived, alone, to do some quiet research or dictate a memo or brief.

Those days were past. Now that the city of Carrville had fired the McFee firm. Not just the city. The Cities for Alternative Energy Research and Development, Inc. The name change had come after Leslie left and Dick saw an article in the New York Times about an "Alternative Energy Conference." Then he started calling it the Alt-Energy group. Alt-Energy this, Alt-Energy that.

She turned back to the file cabinet and pulled a bulging file out of the drawer. Grandiose ideas and big plans they had back then. The cities still might do it, without Dick, or her. Or Jack.

"Aerial," she called to a young woman passing by in the hallway. Aerial veered from her path and swung back to wrap the top half of her body around the doorframe.

"You like my new coiffure, honey?" Aerial patted her teased-up, reddish-blond hair. Her finely sculpted features were accessorized with a gold stud in the left nostril, sunglasses, and a bright jade necklace. An expanse of rich, dark skin led down to the low neckline of a form-fitting aquamarine sweater.

You should be out competing with the hookers on Main Street, Patricia thought but didn't say it. Not now. She needed Aerial's help. "Will you copy these files for me?" she asked sweetly.

"You know, Miss Patricia, honey." Aerial shook her head, scrunching up her face in regret, possibly sincere. "I really can't," she said in her nicest, most saccharine voice, the one she usually reserved for Dick. "I only came in this early to finish those documents for Mister Jack."

She flounced out her left hand, displaying a jangle of gold bracelets and long, gold fingernails. How the devil did she type with those?

"He's not even here." Patricia looked miffed, or tried to. She found herself more amused at Aerial than angry. "He probably won't be here for another hour."

"Oh, but I promised I'd have 'em for him first thing this mornin'." She always did what she said she would and did it well, but usually for Jack. "Couldn't stay last night." Pulling down the sunglasses, she gave a wink, showing a turquoise eyelid. "Had to be somewhere."

Exasperated, Patricia dropped the file on her desk and started to argue, the usual beginning of her day with Aerial, who never argued with Jack. But Aerial only batted her eyes and ended the argument.

"I'll send Kitty down soon as she gets here." Kitty, the part-time secretary. "We need to keep her away from Jack, you know." Aerial gave another wink over the glasses. "She get her hooks in that boy, he won't be up for air for weeks. Need to save him for *you*."

Patricia didn't find that funny. She pressed her lips together and stared at Aerial with hooded eyes. "That really your hair?"

"Only one way to tell a real blond. Heh, heh." With that, she was gone.

Patricia stared at the empty space in the doorway. What a pain that woman was. Said her name came from a play her mother saw in high school. Shaking her head, Patricia turned back to the file cabinet. At least Aerial could type. Answer the phone like a real secretary, clear and crisp, and always—well, usually—she got the name and number right. The sunglasses needed to go, though, and Jack would have to help. But he'd only laugh; say, if she can see to type, it didn't bother him.

The next file Patricia pulled out of the file drawer held her outline and notes for the court argument when Carrville tried to sell electricity to one of Xeco's biggest customers. Her brief had been brilliant; Dick said so himself. That didn't matter now. It had all worked out to Joe Mayes' benefit.

She tossed the file and the next one on top of the files on her desk. Reaching for another, she jumped at the voice behind her.

"Hi, Patricia. Aerial said you needed copying done."

"Yes, thanks, Catherine." She couldn't bring herself to say "Kitty." She waved a hand at the stack of files. "We need copies of these; then box up the originals for Joe Mayes."

"Sure thing. You want me to mark which ones I copy on the original?"

"No, of course not. And give Lacey our copies. I don't want 'em back in my file cabinet."

"Okeydokey." A bubbly voice. She started gathering up the files. "Want me to put some rat poison in for Leslie?"

"Wait, don't take all those." She placed a hand on top of Kitty's. "Just the first two. I'll have more by the time you finish those. And bring me a box for the others."

"Okeydokey." Kitty bounced out the door with the files.

Patricia watched her go. No wonder Jack couldn't detach his eyes. Ray Malloy, bless his heart, had taken the bait and hired her; now he was gone, and that little sexpot was still here.

She removed the files quickly now, sorting them and putting the originals she didn't want copied in her chair. Her malaise eased with the task.

"Here's the box."

Patricia jumped and looked around. Kitty again.

"Back in a sec with the copies," Kitty said, then undulated out the door.

Patricia began placing the files in the box, carefully pushing them forward one after the other. Each represented hours, days, some even weeks out of her life. Life measured out in billable hours. God, she could use another cup of coffee. Maybe Kitty would bring her one. Ugh, she'd never ask a secretary to do that. Not even one hired for randy-male magnetism. There had never been anything like that in her father's office. Just spinster librarian types.

She heard Lacey's voice far down the hall. Lacey sure didn't look like that. She was one tough woman. But why did she have to talk so loud when Dick wasn't around? A good thing all three were so capable, Lacey more than capable. Dick would never fire any of them, even though they didn't need two and a half secretaries any more.

Lacey's voice came closer, followed by short assents from a male, "Yeah, yeah. I know." Jack. His voice and the file in her hand made her discomfort return for a different reason. He had started out with the energy work.

She looked up as Jack entered, morning coffee held out in one hand. Chin raised, he tossed his eyes at the voice behind him.

Lacey stopped by the door and leaned against the jamb. She was smoker-thin, almost gaunt, not runner-thin like herself. Fine blond hair, cut short above a narrow face and sharp nose. Sharp eyes, sharp cheekbones. Sharp tongue. No makeup, no lipstick, but Lacey's ordinarily pale cheeks were flushed.

"You have to talk to him." Glaring at Jack, Lacey clasped her arms across her chest. "We don't have the money to pay everybody, and I've put off the library bills long as I can. You have to talk to him."

"Just cancel the damn services. We know all the law we need for this petty ass practice." Jack put his cup down hard on the desk, on a stack of papers.

"No you don't. Not the advance sheets," Patricia said. She moved Jack's cup to a coaster away from the papers.

"Take it out of the trust account then," Jack replied.

She stifled a groan, and a protest. Old Gladys McFee, Dick's unmarried and filthy rich aunt, now dead, had intended her money to go to rescuing abandoned pets. No pets had been rescued, but the trustees had disbursed thousands of dollars to research IRS regs on changing the trust's scope and bringing other activities within its bequests.

"Haven't we done some research lately, drafted something or other?" Jack added, plopping down in one of her two maroon-leather client chairs.

"All been paid," Lacey said. "And Dick said to lay off for a while."

"Yeah, Jack. The legal fees have dwarfed the charitable giving." Patricia collapsed into her chair as she said it. "Better hope we don't get an audit."

Jack moved his head back and forth. "Okay. We'll talk to him."

"*You'll* talk to him," Patricia said.

Jack frowned at her, then turned back to Lacey. "Don't you have anything coming in from the city, or the group? For work we did before we were so ig-no-miniously fired."

"Dick said *not* to bill 'em for his time last month. Principle, he said." Lacey pursed her lips, like she was tired of explaining this to her inferiors.

"What about our fees?" Jack asked, pointing at Patricia.

"Billed and paid. And already spent."

"Shit!" Jack wedged his feet against the corner of Patricia's desk.

"How about your new client?" Patricia asked. "You bill him yet?"

Evan Fitzhugh. There should be some real money there; Jack had *spent enough time with the man—though much of it seemed to be male play dates: sports bars, ball games, and fishing trips.*

"He hasn't turned in his time," Lacey said, smirking at Jack.

"I need to get the documents done and go to the closing on the first properties." Jack glared at Lacey; then he looked down at his hands. "Should be, uh, maybe next Tuesday . . . or Friday."

"You could at least give him a bill for your time so far," Lacey said. "It's been a couple of months."

"Don't you have to get ready for Dick?" Jack gave her an exasperated, sideways look. "He'll be here in an hour. You can show him," he threw up a hand, "whatever the hell we owe. And close the door when you leave."

Turning on her heel, Lacey stalked out, pulling the door shut as she went.

"A little rough there, weren't you, Jack?" Patricia swung her chair back and forth, staring at him. "Try not to be so rude."

He glared past her, out the window. Patricia figured he was thinking, fuck you, but he wouldn't say it.

"Lacey's only doing what she has to," she added. "If you can get a few dollars out of that client—"

"Should we cancel the clerks?"

"This late? They'll be here in a few weeks. It's not fair to them either way."

"Well, we need to level with 'em. They can make their own choice." He scrunched his long form farther down in the chair, and his feet moved higher up the corner of the desk.

"Look, we'll find a way. Get some new—"

"You heard from Colin?" Jack asked.

"Of course. Once a week at least." She swiveled to look at a poster of *The Scream* on the wall. She didn't want to talk about Colin.

"He can't call you, can he?"

"Not where he is now . . . But he manages to get me a letter." She continued to look at the poster. "You see the envelopes."

"You even know where he is?"

"Not really. It's . . . secret. Special Forces, you—"

"Damned if I ever thought he'd go Lawrence of Arabia on us."

"Colin thought it'd be good to get away for a while," she said, turning to face Jack. Before she could continue, there was a knock on the door, and simultaneously with Patricia's call to come in, the door opened.

"Here are the files . . . Oh, hell-o-o, Jack." It was Kitty. Displaying a dental-poster array of teeth, she stopped and leaned back against the doorframe.

"Hi, Kitty. You look . . . happy, this morning."

With a lingering look at Jack, Kitty deposited the files on Patricia's desk. "Here are the copies. Have any more?"

"Not yet, Catherine. Give me a few minutes." Seeing Jack's eyes on Kitty, Patricia pushed up from the chair and started to turn back to the open file drawer.

"Lacey asked me to give you this. You got a new case . . . district court." Kitty handed an open letter with a multi-page enclosure to Patricia. "Sounds like a real doozy."

Standing behind her chair, Patricia read while Kitty leaned against the front of the desk—and Jack stared at the backs of Kitty's legs.

"State versus William S. Angel . . . Isn't this the thing at the Taco Pal last year?" Patricia flipped to the enclosure. "But this is for escape."

"That's him," said Kitty. "Paper said his girlfriend snuck in some hacksaw blades at the jail. He messed up one of the jailers and almost got away."

"God! That's awful," Patricia said. She quickly skimmed through the other pages. "There are two indictments here. Shit! They'll never pay me for all the time this will take." She rattled the pages. "Safecracking, burglary, assault. Shit, shit! They took him to Central Prison. That means I've got to waste my time going up there."

"Last time you got lost," Jack said.

"Shut up! That's not funny."

"That was my uncle who was shot," Kitty said, no smile and no bubbles in her voice now.

"Oh, no," said Patricia. "I didn't know that."

"At the apartments?" Jack asked.

"Yeah. Just getting in his car. Going to work."

"I'm so sorry," Patricia said, and she was.

Jack slid his feet to the floor and stood. "I gotta go see about Fitz . . . Aerial here? She's supposed to get the contracts done for me."

"Bright and early. She beat you in by a good hour, and *she's* working." Patricia dropped the letter and indictments onto her desk.

"You could have some fun there," Jack said, pointing to the indictments.

"It won't pay the bills."

"Guess I need to give Lacey my time sheets, huh?" He started out the door, Kitty beside him.

"Need any help, Jack?" Kitty placed her hand on his arm. Her sad face had dissolved into a smile. She looked so cute and beguiling that Patricia felt like throwing a file at her.

"You have to make my copies first, kiddo," she said instead.

"See you at lunch," Jack said. He disappeared out the door, Kitty like a too-friendly puppy close on his heels.

Chapter Five – Lunch with Dick

LIGHT AND AIRY AT THE FRONT, Plato's Cave became dark and intimate in back, with a stone fireplace that crackled and hissed during the winter meals. Plato's father had opened the restaurant as a small Greek café, which Plato upgraded to white tablecloths, real napkins, and tuxedoed waiters. A fringe of black hair and thick eyebrows made Plato appear much younger than he was.

"Congressman McFee, how good to see you!" Plato stretched out his hand as they entered. Ushering Patricia inside, Dick reached past her to take Plato's hand in both of his, leaning over to get close to the shorter man's face.

"Thank you, old friend. I always look forward to the exquisite food and most especially the wonderful host and his lovely bride." A small rotund woman, her gray-streaked hair pulled back in a bun, came up beside Plato. Reaching out a hand to her, and still holding onto Plato's, Dick leaned down and gave the woman a peck on the cheek.

Jack hung back in the doorway while Patricia lingered off to one side. *What a schmoozer*, she thought. *He greets one and all as if they were his long-lost best friends. Did he work the room like this when he was in Congress? Too bad he lasted only one term. Something's changed, though. He seems a little more stooped, more down to my height now than before Leslie left.*

With Dick patting him on the shoulder, Plato turned to Patricia and gave a little bow as he took her hand. "This way, madam, gentlemen." He nodded at Jack, who had edged his way inside. "Your table is ready."

Plato led them to a round table in a small alcove by the front window. Separating them from the other diners were bushy scheffleras in ceramic pots made to look like ruined Corinthian columns. An awning blocked the glancing spring sun but allowed in plenty of light to bathe the alcove and inscribe "Plato's Cave" in a shadow across the white tablecloth. Once they were seated, a martini magically appeared in front of Dick even as Jack was ordering a beer and Patricia iced tea.

Patricia raised an eyebrow. *Probably not his first martini for the day.*

"You remember Millicent, don't you?" Dick asked after taking a deep draw of the clear liquid. Without waiting for an answer, Dick chuckled. "Her dog bit a woman, and they put her in jail."

"What?" said Jack. "Put who in jail?"

"Princess. In doggie jail. City pound. Poor Millie's all upset about it. Nothing's getting done at my place or over at Allie's, and that makes Allie upset." *Ah, the McFee family's joint maid.* Holding up the martini glass, half-empty now, he closed one eye and stared over it, out the window. "Plato's little Mexican boy's learned well. Showed him how to make it myself, two olives."

Placing the glass on the table, he was silent long enough for Patricia to weigh bringing up the firm's finances.

But Dick snared an olive and continued. "Jack, we need you to do something about this travesty."

"Do something about *what?*" Jack lowered his Heineken.

"Why, get Princess out of jail. Something about a quar-an-tine. Dear Millicent doesn't feel safe out there where she lives without her protector."

"How do I get a dog released from the city pound when it's bitten somebody? File for habeas dog-us?"

"Oh, I don't know; you'll figure out a way. And Allie will be grateful." He finished the martini and motioned to the waiter. "*Garçon*, another of these elixirs, please." He held up the glass, then turning back to them, added, "Scuse me boys and girls, I need to visit the gents." He knocked the chair sideways getting up, but instead of heading back to the restrooms, he pointed toward the entrance. "There's Lena. I'll just run over and say hello."

He hurried toward the maître d's desk and a fiftyish woman trying to look like Liz Taylor at thirty: dyed black hair, buxom hourglass figure.

"Dick, you ol' booger you," she shrieked as Dick stumbled up to her. Her cackling laugh brought all eyes around as the two embraced and Dick supplied an overly loud kiss to her cheek.

"How many you reckon he had on the plane?" Jack asked, slouching down in his chair. Lena's voice settled into a clucking in Dick's ear, while he nodded his accordance with whatever she was saying.

"You have to talk to him about the finances," Patricia said.

"Why me? You know as much as I do."

"Lacey told you to do it." She gave him a smug smile.

"This is why Leslie took off."

"You mean the finances?"

"Finances were fine then. Leslie had to be pulling down twice what his classmates were in New York, and only five years out of law school."

"What are you talking about, Jack?"

"The martinis. He saw it coming. That fucking Leslie." Jack took a hard swig out of the Heineken bottle, leaving a bubble on the top.

"He sure as heck didn't share his foresight," Patricia said, thinking, *certainly not when he announced he was leaving and asked us to join him.* They'd take the New-Energy clients and build a powerhouse firm in Atlanta.

"Well, Leslie's in high cotton now," Jack said, slouching farther down.

Dick was now wringing the hand and massaging the upper arm of Lena's husband, the mayor. With his mane of well-coifed silver hair, square chin, and tailored gray business suit, the mayor looked every bit the part of Liz Taylor's consort.

"Mayor, good to see you, so *very* good to see you," came Dick's voice before it sank beneath a clatter of dishes and the general hubbub of the restaurant.

As Patricia took all this in, the salads arrived and Jack ordered another beer. Across the room, Dick continued to talk, and the mayor continued to nod while tacking toward the table where his wife was shrugging off her jacket. To watch, Patricia leaned to one side and peered under the bottom leaves of the potted trees.

"You gonna take pictures?" Jack asked.

She turned back to the table and scowled at him. "You trying to imitate the boss?" She tapped her fork in the direction of his empty beer bottle.

"Ha! Take more'n this to send me knee-walkin' outta here. Not so sure about him, though." He gestured toward the greenery beside them. "Leslie damn-well saw it coming and made a break for it."

"We had our chance. He won; we lost."

"He got the client; we got the shaft." Jack grimaced at her and reversed his slouch. "He had to go with Joe Mayes to do it. You reckon that was his plan all along? Teaming up with that sleazy bastard." Jack speared a layer of spinach leaves in the salad.

"You never said that before. 'Best damn trial lawyer in the South,' it was."

"Joe was on our side then." The retort was muffled through the spinach. "And you're the one who ended up working with 'em all the time. Al-l-l the big-ass cases."

A trace of bitterness in his voice. She ignored it.

"And what will you say about me if I leave?" She gave him a taut smile. "There's no reason to stay now. We're left to taking walk-ins and appointed cases."

"Hey, I got Fitz and his land deals."

"Not to mention your new case."

"New case?" He frowned, eyebrows knitted.

"Princess versus City."

"Ah, shit!" He took a final bite of spinach. "You aren't going anywhere, not as long as Colin's out playing his games."

She toyed with her salad and didn't answer. He was right. She wouldn't leave. But he didn't have to be such an ass about it. And it wasn't just Colin.

Jack shoved the salad plate to one side. "You know what he wants to talk about, don't you?"

"His grand plan to get the cities back and stick it to Joe and Leslie?"

Jack drummed the table with his fingers. "We're not gonna talk about anything at this rate." He paused. "A-ha, there he goes, off to the gents. Now the martini will come."

She shrugged and took another nibble from her salad. Jack was right. A new martini appeared, followed not long after by Dick. He took a sip of the drink as he eased onto his chair.

"Chilluns, here's the plan." He paused to down some more of the martini. "As you know, the mayor and his lovely wife are dear old friends of mine, and they can swing a few votes back our way on the council." He held up the glass to examine its contents. "And if we're nice and convincing to Allie, she'll come 'round to see the righteousness of our cause. She and I get along splen . . . splendidly. She's a great councilwoman, a real asset to the city. I helped her get in, you know." He leaned forward, his eyes on Jack. "But Jack, she really likes you, Jack. You'll need to," his eyes shifted to Patricia, "you and Patty here need to talk to her 'bout what we can do for the city. And what dem two low-down snakes in Atlanta can't do."

The waiter materialized at Jack's elbow with a fresh beer. While a second waiter replenished the water, Dick picked at his salad and ordered a Heineken.

"You see, Jack," Dick said, pushing the salad to one side, "helping Millicent with her faithful companion will give you the opportunity to stop by Allie's this afternoon . . . to see Millie of course." He fiddled with his napkin and rearranged the fork and knife on the table. "Allie's home, so you can put a bug in her ear 'bout us'ns, what we can do."

Jack scowled at him. "But Dick, I have to go with Fitz—"

Dick brought his almost-empty martini glass down on the table with a ka-thunk. "You can get back by four, can't you? This is important, Jack. Allie can bring *us* the votes we *need*—along with the ones we have in the mayor's camp."

"Yes, sir." Jack was tight lipped.

The food arrived and, not far behind, Dick's Heineken. Patricia eyed Jack, concerned that he might order a third beer. He didn't. But his fixed stare at Dick made her worry he would explode and say something rash. She needed him to stay.

"They've already voted to fire us." Jack's voice was strained, and he leaned forward over his plate. "What good's all this now?"

"That was last month. I've been calling in a few chits . . . We got blindsided. Never expected anyone'd pull a sorry trick like that."

You got blindsided, thought Patricia. *Everyone else saw it coming.*

"They're going to reverse it." Dick said, checking the glass that had come with the beer. He made a face.

Uh oh, thought Patricia. *It's not chilled.*

Dick dumped ice water into the empty beer glass, then poured the remaining water into the potted plant beside him. Catching her look, he addressed her as he decanted his beer into the empty water glass.

"Patty, I have a little matter I . . . the firm needs you to take care of." He searched inside his suit coat and pulled out a sheaf of papers. "A little mix up *years* ago seems to have caused, ah . . . some difficulties for one of our clients."

He carelessly handed the papers across the table. Patricia grabbed them before they dropped into her plate.

"A little mistake and . . . well, read the letter; you can figure it out."

While Jack and Dick ate in silence, she quickly read the letter. It was handwritten, dated several weeks before, from an Agnes Jones. Two women, sisters, had run off a tenant living in a house Ms. Jones had inherited from her father and then installed their own tenant. The sisters claimed the house belonged to them because they had a deed to it, a deed they had found in *their* father's papers when he died. The sheriff had refused to act on Ms. Jones' criminal complaint to have the sisters and their renter evicted. Something to do with "color of title."

"Dick," Jack said, looking up from his plate, "Lacey says the bank accounts are a little low."

"Just a slackening in cash flow."

"Lacey knows what's coming in, and she says it's not enough—"

"Well, I'll be . . . she never told me that."

Right, thought Patricia, half listening and trying to read the documents enclosed with the letter. *She tells him every time she talks to him.*

"We need to pick up the billing, team," Dick said, the words slurred even more than before.

"It won't pick up with this case." She'd finished skimming the criminal complaint. "I think there was a mistake on the deed, the one to the sisters' father."

"Then sue them that made it," Dick said.

Jesus, she thought, *he didn't read this. Or doesn't remember.*

"They're still around," she said. "McFee & Associates drafted the deed to the sisters' father as well as the one to Jones'. The same property description is on both, and both conveyed property from a McFee development company."

"Let me see that." Dick reached across the table, almost knocking over

32

a water glass. He quickly perused the deed, then flipped to a second deed, at which he barely glanced. Refolding the papers, he thrust them at Patricia. "Couldn't have been our fault. Probably the real estate people." He made a dismissive gesture. "Just charge her what you think's right."

"It might be a conflict for us to handle this," Jack said.

"We certainly don't want that." Dick drew back, eyebrows arched up. "Tell Miss. . . what's her name? Smith—"

"Jones," Patricia said, her lips pursed. "I'm not sure—"

"Tell the woman we'll only charge for expenses, since the deed's on our form. That's better'n she'll get from any other lawyer in town." (*Unless they sued us for malpractice*, Patricia thought.) "She'll ask you to handle it and love you for the deal you're giving her."

Patricia wasn't so sure. "This won't pay the bills," she said. Today's refrain.

"Don't worry your pretty head about that." Dick gave her an ingratiating smile. "I'll cover the firm's expenses; you just go out there and practice law. By next month, we'll have the city back. Its checks are like gold in the bank."

She swallowed a sigh. That would be nice, but the big fees didn't come only from Carrville. Something in the way she popped an olive in her mouth to stifle her retort must have made Dick realize the flaw in his plan.

"And we're going to get the Alt-Energy group back, too."

Jack gave a low groan, drawing a dark scowl from Dick.

"Had discussions with all the powers in the cities," Dick said. (*That's a new one,* she thought.) "All the key mayors and city managers, and with only one ex-shep-tion, that hick manager in Sniderville, they're ready to put it up for a vote at the next meeting. We only need to get our own shi-ity council on board. My good friend the mayor's in our corner, and Jack, it's gonna to be up to you-u-u to bring Allie 'round."

Leaning back in his chair, Jack looked out the window and said as if talking to himself, "I heard the good mayor has his own problems."

"Just nasty gossip," Dick snapped, his voice sharp and clear. He stretched to peer through the scheffleras. Lena and the mayor had gone. "Investigation went nowhere," he said, straightening up. "Something stirred up by a young fool in the controller's office."

"I don't know who started it," Jack said, still not looking at Dick, "but I don't think it's done. Ray Malloy tells me they've been checking on the mayor's dealings with contractors, like that fancy new deck—"

"Hector Grimes is a dear old friend of mine," Dick said. The city attorney, Ray Malloy's boss. "Hector's got it all under control."

"Hector's in the hospital, heart attack," Jack said, staring at Dick.

"I'll be damned! No one told me." Dick glared at Patricia like it was her fault. Then his face softened. "How's he doing?"

"Not good," Jack answered. "Ray says he'll be out for a while."

"So who's taking his place?" Dick asked. The check for the meal had arrived. Without looking at it, Dick waved a credit card at the waiter.

"Our friend Ray, mainly," said Jack. "But he's got to get some help."

Dick's face lit up. "We can help." *He's anticipating some city legal work,* Patricia thought, *and an inside track on influencing the council vote.*

"Allie told him to get a minority firm," Jack said.

"A minority firm!" Having released his credit card to the waiter, Dick brought his hand down hard on the table. "There isn't but one or two and—"

"That's right. Napoleon Hayes."

Dick looked off, drumming his fingers on the table. "This certainly stirs the pot. Leon's working as local counsel for Joe and he's part—"

"Right!" Jack said. "Part of Mayes' strategy."

"We'll just have to stop 'em from doing it."

Patricia took a deep breath. "Dick," she said, "Joe and Leslie already have the Alt-Energy business so why wouldn't the city give their local counsel this new work."

Dick didn't answer. He was focused on entering the tip and total on the credit slip, moving his glasses up and down on his nose. He signed the slip, then slapped the pen down on the table.

"Well, *we're* gonna get *all* of it back, all the damn utility and Alt-Energy business. And Allie shouldn't be giving aid and comfort to the enemy." At "enemy," he swung out a hand and knocked over his former beer glass, now full of water.

"Shit!" Jack said, jumping up, too late.

"What power has she got—"

"Now I've got to go meet Fitz like *this*." Jack was staring down, his face red, teeth clenched. The water had splashed onto his white shirt and the front of his pants.

"She's just one damn member of the council," Dick continued.

"She heads the MBE contracting committee," Patricia said. Dick gave her a puzzled look. "Minority Business Enterprises. The city has goals—"

"They could've found somebody other than that slick shyster. He's nothing but a divorce lawyer, takes drunk driving and criminal cases." Patricia felt her ears burning.

"He drives a new Cadillac," Jack said, "and he's good at what he does." Jack stood over them, blotting his shirt and pants with a clean white napkin from a nearby table. "And he's made a few strategic campaign donations."

He should be able to, Patricia thought. *He owns a bunch of land between town and the military base and keeps selling it off for trailer parks and strip malls.*

"Maybe Raymond will drop the damn thing," Dick said.

"Drop what?" Patricia asked as she slid her chair back from the table.

"With ever-thing he's got going on and all." Dick wobbled to his feet.

Ah, she thought, *he's back to the investigation of his good friend the mayor.*

"Ray's applied for a job with the district attorney," Jack said, dabbing at the wet spot on his pants. "And there's the whistleblower you mentioned—in the controller's office. He's not *just* going to shut up about it."

"I think *he* already has-s-s," Dick said. He was now afoot and stumbled against the ledge below the window. "I think he's defuncto."

Jack caught Dick by the elbow and helped steady him.

"Got shot in a robbery," Dick added. "Fast food joint or something."

Patricia moved a chair to let Dick pass. "Not the Taco Pal?" she asked.

Dick didn't answer her. He was already navigating past the tables and chairs on the way to the door.

Chapter Six – Jack and Fitz

PACING ON THE SIDEWALK, Jack glanced at his watch. Twenty minutes late. Rich client or not, he was almost ready to retreat upstairs when a green Jaguar XJS convertible whipped up to the curb.

"Hey, Jack! Hop in." Evan Fitzhugh was decked out in a flowery Hawaiian shirt, its top buttons undone to expose a shock of gray hair in which nested a large gold medallion on a heavy gold chain. The face was preternaturally smooth, with a tan so perfect it looked painted on. A fading version of James Dean with iron gray hair.

Fitz reached across the passenger seat and shoved the door open. As Jack caught it, Fitz did a double take. "What happened to you? Pee on yourself?"

"Water spill. Lunch," Jack said, pulling the door open to get in.

"Must've been some lunch. You go out for a nooner with that cute little thing in your office?"

"What? Patricia? You must be kidding."

"No, no. What's her name? That temp Ray hired."

"Oh, Kitty." He clicked the seatbelt in place.

"Here, Kitty, Kitty," Fitz said over the revving engine. "She sure purrs when I'm around." The car leaped away from the curb, throwing Jack against the seat back. He wished he'd brought sunglasses—but maybe a crash helmet and goggles would've been better.

Fitz had once been in a seminary, Methodist, Baptist, Jack couldn't remember which. Fitz claimed he'd enjoyed it, with all the rights and privileges of a man of the cloth; but he'd found more opportunities out in the secular world. He had used his native skills to exploit old age and death, from assisted living to funeral to cemetery. Only the slickest and the quickest got rich doing religion, he said, and he couldn't compete with them. Compete or not, Fitz led the good life, and in the months since Dick's "old friend" had become Jack's new client, Fitz showed him the good life. Trips to Atlanta for Braves games—on Fitz's private jet; fishing in the Keys—on Fitz's fifty-foot boat; and lavish restaurant meals—on Fitz's tab. Fitz said he'd put him on his staff, if he needed a staff beyond his secretary.

Three miles out of town, they veered onto the Old Schoolhouse Road, a two-lane blacktop with no shoulders, snaking between barbwire fences and water-filled ditches. White clouds floated lazily in a bright blue sky as a checkerboard of brown soil and light-green crops whisked by on either side.

On the interstate, it had been impossible to talk so Jack stayed lost in his own thoughts. He liked that, and he liked watching the scenery flow past. Once on the backroads, though, he had to put on his game face and listen to Fitz.

"This is farmland," Fitz yelled above the noise of the wind whipping over the car. "Agribusiness at best; poor dirt farmers at worst. Even the bigger ones struggle, depend on the Feds to throw 'em a bone, giv'em a little profit." Slowing at a row of houses off the main road, he looked over at Jack and chuckled. "I'm gonna turn all this into pure fucking cash."

Jack nodded. He'd had enough of grand plans for today. And he couldn't understand why Fitz wanted to bring him all the way out here. They had a survey that showed what Fitz was buying, and land was just land.

Fitz swerved off the paved road and accelerated down a dirt lane, kicking up gravel, then a cloud of red dust as the car bumped and jerked along the ruts. Jack cringed at the groaning chassis and din of ricocheting rocks on the undersides of the Jag.

The road ended, and they pulled onto a patch of grass facing a grove of pecan trees. Fitz turned off the engine. Silence. Then the, "chee-ter, chee-ter," trill of a Carolina wren. A mockingbird mimicked the call from a lineless telephone pole by the road.

Alighting from the car, Fitz bounded off through the grass. Stopping a short distance away, he whirled around, arms out. "Land! Land and water! I'm gonna own it all," he yelled to Jack, still at the car.

Pausing only to tuck in his gold medallion, Fitz took off again, into the pecan grove. Thirty yards past the trees, the ground dropped off in a steep embankment, down to a sluggish brown river as wide as the four-lane highway.

"Land and water," Fitz shouted again. "That's what *they* gotta have, and I have it right here." He turned to Jack, who was coming up behind him.

"What're you going to grow?" Jack asked. "You'll have a couple hundred acres once we close on the new parcels."

"Oh-h-h, corn, soybeans, maybe try some sugar cane." He winked at Jack. "What grows *on it* ain't what matters." Coming closer, he almost whispered, "It's more'n that. It's who wants it and what they want it for." He chuckled. "And what they'll pay me."

"So-o-o, who's your buyer?"

Fitz swept his hand over the river and the fields and pecan trees on this side of the river. "Energy City! Oh yes, some of it will go to crops, but that's not where the money is. No siree bob." He turned and placed his face close to Jack's. "Don't tell a soul, but this is the new Manhattan Project. A modern boomtown ready to rise up." He pumped his fist in the air. "And I'm gonna have a piece of it."

Jack stepped to one side. Fitz had said he was buying the land for an agribusiness venture to raise soybeans and corn. There had been nothing about the Alt-Energy project. He stared out over the empty fields and the grove of trees, then down at the milk chocolate river. *Why this land? Why here?*

"Jack, Jack." It was like he saw the doubt in his face. "We can do it. But we have to keep it quiet." Fitz tapped his lips with an index finger. "For all anyone knows, I'm just starting a big ol' farm . . . But look around." The arm went out. "This is what the cities need for their project, and they're gonna be floatin' on a hundred million worth of bonds to invest in it." He spread his arms in a wide arc. "This is the place. Empty land, water, wind. The research complex over there." He pointed up the river. "Solar and wind over there." His hand swung back toward the open fields. "Waste-to-fuels and recycling. And a power plant." He nodded and grinned at Jack. "Maybe, if we can swing it with Xeco," he pointed toward the sky, "and everybody forgets the damn Three-Mile-Island business . . . a nuclear plant down the river. This is the place!" He was bouncing up and down. "Buy up the land for hundreds of dollars an acre and sell it for thousands. You see, buddy, you see?"

No, he didn't see. He felt too overwhelmed to reason this out. What Fitz was describing, to the extent he could understand it, went far beyond what Dick McFee had ever talked about. It seemed implausible. But it was big, and it meant lots of money for Fitz. And his lawyers. He tried to soften his skepticism.

"How can they issue bonds for this? It sure looks like a speculative venture, no assurance of income or—"

"Not a problem." Fitz snapped his fingers. Taking Jack by the elbow, he steered him along the riverbank, to a weeping willow leaning out over the water. "Cities'll issue revenue bonds . . . the usual language for the usual type of projects, some broad authorizations to spend the money, and Industrial Development Bonds for private ventures. Money'll flow faster'n this damn river—and some of it's gonna end up right here." He smacked the breast pocket of his Hawaiian shirt. "We have the land."

"How do you know they'll want it? I mean, they could look for a better deal. Go anywhere in the state."

"They could, my friend, but they won't go anywhere else. Trust me." Fitz gave him a knowing, self-satisfied smile, and a wink.

"If you're depending on Dick—"

"No, no. Are you kidding? I know better'n that." He pressed his lips together and shook his head. "That would be nice, but I'm not spread so thin I need Dick." He jingled the keys and change in his pocket. "Oh, he can be some help. He and the mayor go way back, and his ex is on the council. But, you know, I can work with Joe Mayes, too; play golf with him all the time, and the mayor . . . I've got that sack of shit by the short hairs." Fitz clutched his hand in the air and nodded, his face smug. "He'll go our way. He has to."

"He's just one of a dozen city—"

"Hah! Those . . ." He stopped and gave Jack a sideways look, then shrugged. "Anyway, this is the best spot. Central location. No one around to complain, lots of land and water, wind and sun." He jingled his change again. "Yeah, this is what they're gonna want." He stopped and eyed Jack. "We just need to avoid any talk that'd keep those people up there from selling." He pointed over the bare fields toward the main road, where six single-story brick dwellings sat in lonely relief against the horizon. "That piddly-ass little subdivision over yonder. Developer went belly up. A McFee company. Dick's gonna sell me what's left of the land. Giving him a little more than I been payin'—and I agreed to continue using your firm."

"Uh," Jack said, "I understand." Now it made sense why Fitz had stayed with them even if he was Joe Mayes' golfing buddy.

"I've got all the other land wrapped up, but those houses over there, they proved to be a little more difficult. Got four of 'em on the hook, but the last two—that's the reason I brought you out here, that and to show you what we got going. I want you to help me, Jack. Go talk with 'em."

"Talk with them? Me?" He pulled back. "What can I do?"

"Two sharp-eyed old biddies . . . they live in one of the houses and rent out another one down the road. Damn it all, they won't sell." He grinned at Jack. "But they might go for you."

Jack shook his head. "Why would they trust me any more than you?"

"Hey, you have that fresh-faced Mormon missionary look . . . Suspicious old biddies. They know about me, and they don't know you."

Narrowing his eyes, Jack thought, *there's more here than he's telling me.* "I can try to talk to them," he said, "but I don't see how I'll have any more pull than you do."

"Oh, I don't know." Fitz nodded. "Just give it a try. If we have to, we can work around 'em—but those lots are almost an acre each, and it'd be good to have 'em. Facilitate access and all."

Jack was baffled by how he was supposed to do this—and by Fitz's ties to the city officials and their big energy project. But Fitz had tapped into it, and that could help pay the bills. He contemplated the possibilities as he watched Fitz stroll off toward the pecan grove.

"Hey, Fitz," he called and hurried to catch up. "Who's the buyer for the houses? You said they don't want to deal with you."

"Why, you are, my man. Just draw up a little agreement that you're my agent or trustee or something."

"That sounds . . . I don't know, kind of sneaky."

"You're a damn lawyer, son." Fitz stopped under a pecan tree. "Sneaky's what you get paid for. If they sell to you, and they will, it's none of their damn business who gets the property." Fitz started off toward the car again, Jack beside him. "I'll deposit the money in your account. Go on and draw up a little document—put in five percent for yourself. Knowin' fact you need the money with what Dick's payin' you."

They came out from the shade of the trees. Ahead of them, the sun glinted on the car's windshield. Nearby the wren called again. Wading through the grass, Fitz continued talking as Jack, hands in pockets, walked beside him.

"I can see Dick crumbling piece by piece. Pretty soon, there's not gonna be anything left of that firm. You and that lady lawyer . . . " Fitz shook his head. "You two are gonna have to make your own go of it." He patted Jack on the back and started around to the other side of the car. "Just you stick with me, my friend. As my ship rises, so will yours."

Chapter Seven – Princess

ALLIE MCFEE'S RAMBLING, multiform house was set back from the road at the end of a curving drive, deep in a mixed grove of pin oaks, pines, and pecan trees. A perfect rural setting within a McFee subdivision.

Millicent answered the door. Jack could tell she had been crying, and she dabbed at her eyes with a Kleenex.

"You here to see Missus McFee, Mr. A?"

She filled the wide entrance, designed to accommodate an antebellum oak door Dick had plundered from some tidewater plantation fallen into ruin. While he hadn't lived in the house for years, it still bore the marks of his eclectic tastes, from antique doors and shutters to five fireplaces, all in different shapes.

"I'd like to say hello to her," Jack said, "but I'm here to see you, Millie." He stepped inside as Millie shuffled back in her high-top bedroom shoes. Hard shoes hurt her feet, she said. She preferred doing housework in the soft, fur-lined slippers the McFees supplied her with every Christmas. Two pairs.

"Dick asked me to help get your dog back," Jack said as she closed the door.

Millie's normally pleasant face contorted into a tragic mask, and tears rolled down her cheeks. She began to weep and her broad bosom shook. "Oh-h-h, it's no good now, Mr. A! It's too late!" A wail. "They done kilt her!"

"Killed her?"

"A poor innocent dog that never did no wrong to nobody." She settled into extended sniffling. "They might as well stuck a knife in me."

"Wait a minute. I thought they were holding her at the pound for . . . what is it?"

"Oh, I don't know." More sniffles. She twisted the Kleenex in her fingers. They stood facing each other in the wide marble foyer.

"A week or so," Jack said. "To make sure she didn't have rabies."

"They was! They was! But they done hauled her off to the gas chamber, this very mornin'. Oh, poor-r-r Princess. I don't know what I'll do without her. Out there in that lonely old place . . . all alone."

She lumbered ahead of him, down the steps into the sunken living room and across it to the kitchen. As she lowered her weight onto a sturdy kitchen chair, he moved to sit near her at the butcher-block table.

"What on earth happened to your pants, son? You got some sorta stain on 'em. You need me to take care of that for you?"

"Just a little accident—at lunch." He dropped into the chair and pulled it forward under the table. "I'll take 'em to the cleaners tomorrow."

"Be glad to do it for you, darlin'. I can get a stain out of anything."

"That's okay, it's only water. Tell me what happened to Princess."

The corners of her mouth drooped, and she dabbed under her eyes with the ragged Kleenex. "I went down to see her . . . right after lunch. Took her a nice steak bone left over from Missus McFee's dinner party last night. I thought she might like something special, being cooped up like that, all them howlin' mongrels in there. Even had a hunk a meat on it . . . You know how them skinny white women eat."

"So you took Princess a bone and what happened?"

"She was gone!" Millie blew her nose on the remnants of the Kleenex, then wiped her eyes again. "They didn't even have a corpse so's I could give her a decent Christian burial." She sobbed. "They burnt her! Burnt her plumb up." She drew in a deep rasping breath. "Didn't even save her ashes."

"Okay, okay. Did they tell you what happened?"

"The dogcatcher or whatever he is out there went sneakin' around, whisperin' on the phone and such. Finally, he come back and told me there was a mix-up; they got the wrong cage. Mr. A, I can't stand bein' out there all by myself, without no company or protecshun. What am I gonna do?" She began to give low soft whimpers, her eyes closed, her chins folding and unfolding.

"Isn't that the most awful thing you ever heard, Jack?" Allie McFee stood in the doorway to the dining room. Tall, elegant, platinum blond hair streaked with gray he hadn't noticed before, pure white skin unwrinkled and untainted by the sun. As finely preserved as her ex-husband was not.

43

"Kill this good woman's dog for no reason at all. And just a mistake!" And just the right touch of indignation. She glided over to Millie and put her arm around the big woman's shoulders. "You can stay here, Millicent, in the room over the garage. Until you get a new dog."

"Thank you, missus. But I don't want no charity. I'll just have to go out there and face," a sniffle, "and face . . . whatever's out there."

"Well, you don't have to." Mrs. McFee gave Millie a quick hug. "Either I or somebody'll go out there and stay with you. Won't we, Jack?"

Jack cringed but managed to conceal it. The last thing he wanted to do was be a bodyguard for a woman who could pound him into mincemeat if he got between her and anything that went bump in the night. But he remembered Dick's admonition. They needed Allie's help.

"Yes, ma'am." He gave his most beguiling smile first to Mrs. McFee, then to Millie. "Be glad to."

"And you can sue the city—a wrongful death case," Allie said with some vehemence.

"Sue the city?" His smile faded—fast.

"That's right. I'm sure Dick would want to see justice done, especially for an old family friend like Millicent. She's been in our family for . . ." Allie leaned away, still holding onto Millie's shoulder, and looked down at the big woman. "How many years now, Millie?"

Jack felt an involuntary twitch as a small imp of sarcasm ran through his head. *How long has the old Slave Market been out of business?*

"Nigh on twenty-two years, Missus McFee. Ever since your Sally was a baby."

"That's right." Mrs. McFee nodded her aristocratic profile at Millie. "Since Sally was only six months . . . Have you met our Sally?" she asked, turning to Jack. "You'd just love her."

"No ma'am."

"Well, we'll have to see that you do." Mrs. McFee coughed and changed course. "We're going to see that the city pays for this."

"You're on the city council, ma'am," Jack said. Maybe he could head this off before she pushed it too far.

"Oh, that's right . . . Hmm. That could be a problem." Her smooth, serene face took on a perplexed look. "Guess I'd better stay out of it." She glanced from Millie to Jack and back to Millie; then she rallied. "Well, you can depend on Jack, Millicent." Her chin tilted up a fraction. "I know he'll do right by you." Then she made a show of looking at her watch. "Oh my, I need to get dressed. Have to meet the mayor at five." Her eyes came back to Jack. "You'll take care of this, won't you, Jack? We're counting on you."

Inwardly Jack groaned. *We* are counting on you? Not only was he on the spot for an idiot's task, there was no money in it.

A lame, "Yes ma'am," was all he could muster.

Allie patted him lightly on the shoulder as she swept past and out of the kitchen. He watched the vacuum in her wake, then smiled over at Millie, who was already smiling broadly at him.

"So, tell me about Princess," he said.

"She was a sweetheart, Mr. A—a real princess, one of them purebreds . . . German shepherd, maybe a little Doberman or collie here and there, but just like Lassie on TV in how smart she was. You know, that woman was *plumb* drunk. Stumbling through my backyard like that. Princess'd never allow such trash as that in *her* yard."

Chapter Eight – Central Prison

ONCE YOU'VE BEEN TO CENTRAL PRISON, you never forget it. Patricia stared at the high yellow walls of pitted stone, algae-green along the bottom, rolled razor wire on top, and at each corner closed-in towers with tinted windows and gun slits. And the moat. Filled with green grass nourished by swamp muck. The place was more like a medieval fortress than a state prison. It had been built after The War, the only one that still mattered here, spreading its long shadow across the tobacco and cotton fields, the pine woods and muddy rivers—a scourge that had insinuated its tendrils deep into the Southern soul.

Once past the portcullis, they followed a khaki-clad guard through a stone tunnel into the interior. The flagstones echoed with the rhythmic click of Patricia's heels. This wasn't a big-fee client, one for whom she could rack up billable hours, only a minor crook for whom she'd receive a stingy court-approved rate. You had to do what you had to do. But she felt sorry for Allen, their new law clerk. She'd called him, told him how low they'd fallen; he shrugged it off and asked to come along—to this. *God, what a depressing place*, she thought, staring up into the dim, arched reaches of the stone corridor above them.

Coming to another antechamber and another set of gates, their minder, an amiable white-haired man, motioned to the guard inside a bulletproof booth. Patricia could tell it was bulletproof by the diagonal line of pings across the glass and a spray of deep indentations in the right corner. She pointed to them and nudged Allen in the arm.

"My guess is those came from the riot," she said.

"You think so? That's been a few years."

"No money," mumbled the guard. He added in a louder voice, "You go on through there. Death row's up the elevator on the other side."

The first shiny metal gate slid open, into a recess in the wall. No sound of clanking chains in this dungeon, only a modern rasping of metal against metal.

They stepped inside the gated chamber while their escort stayed behind, giving them a sympathetic nod as the gate rasped shut. A woman whose square shape was crammed into the standard khaki uniform emerged from the glass booth. In swift mechanical movements, she patted them down and searched Patricia's briefcase and handbag. *How did I ever end up here, doing this?* Patricia wondered as she waited for the far gate to open.

On the other side, a guard she would've taken for an inmate, absent the uniform, escorted them up the elevator and down a hallway to a door marked "Visitors" in faded letters. Unlocking it, he admitted them into a large room with two high windows at one end and a glass barrier down the middle. No visitors were in evidence. The guard pointed to an open booth that looked like a library carrel in the middle of a row of like booths on their side of the barrier.

"You go there," he said. The booth on the other side of the glass was empty.

"Where is he?"

"He'll be here." The guard gave the nearest thing to a smile his battered face could summon and moved back to stand by the door.

Glancing at the dividers to her right and left, Patricia slipped into the booth and eased down on a low metal chair. The side panels were old, a lot older than her, heavy oak polished and aged to a benign yellow. The small desk was worn and scarred. She ran her fingers across it. Any finish or polish had been stripped away by arms and elbows, maybe even fingernails or foreheads, and the wood left naked and unprotected against the indelible stains of perspiring or weeping visitors.

She took out a yellow legal pad and pen and set her briefcase next to her handbag on the floor. Black and white tiles formed a ghostly checkerboard that extended into the shadows under the high windows. The wall above glowed an eerie yellow-green from the angle of the light.

Allen pulled up a folding chair to one side and slightly behind hers. All he'd brought was a legal pad, which he placed on the knee of a crossed leg. In the silence, she could hear the tapping of his pen on the pad.

Outside, the day was brimming with life and real sunlight, not the dust-laden remnants filtering into this bleak room, and front yards were filled with ranks of blossoming azaleas. It was almost a year since she had joined the McFee firm. Everything then had seemed as bright and promising as this day in April. Now, even John Lennon was dead and The Beatles would never reunite.

She found herself bobbing her head and humming a song from the radio in the car, "She's come undone . . ." She looked around at Allen to see if he had noticed. Blond-hair, blue-eyed, and good humored, he was a sure success at whatever he tried.

"You bring the indictments?" She felt foolish as soon as she asked.

"You have them."

"Oh . . . yeah." She opened the briefcase again and pulled two stapled sets of papers out of a side pocket. Not wanting to talk, she began scanning the top one for the fourth or fifth time. So, here she was. An appointed lawyer in a criminal case. The last kind of lawyer she ever wanted to be.

Her client was on death row even. Not that he had been found guilty of killing anyone. After his escape, if you could call it that, the county didn't want to provide him with accommodations. Then the jailer—she shook her head—it was a wonder they hadn't shot him. But death row?

Oh God, what have I gotten myself into? Never tried a case, much less one like this. And Allen—the bright young law clerk sucked into this fool's mission. He signed on when times were good, great prospects for an exciting, cutting-edge practice. Renewable energy, municipal bonds, big picture stuff.

Now she was left with crap like this. Representing a safecracker . . . accused safecracker, found lying—hiding—in a ditch, maybe a hundred yards from the Taco Pal, which, according to the paper, looked like a bomb had hit it.

She focused on the indictment. Escape. Assaulting an officer. Using a deadly weapon with intent to kill. *Jesus, what's with this guy?* And the second one. Burglary of a business. Breaking and entering. *How many different ways do they have to say the same thing?* And safecracking. *Easily ninety-nine years on the hard-rock pile.* His partner dead, shot in the back. An innocent man dead as well. *It's a wonder they didn't charge him with felony murder. And a stupid Taco Pal restaurant. Why not a bank?*

She sighed and looked up to see a man, small and wiry like a Kentucky Derby jockey, being ushered into the opposite booth by a huge black guard who dwarfed him. The prisoner maneuvered his shackled wrists around the chair back and eased down on the seat as if he found it painful to move.

Chains even in here, she thought. *They really do think this guy's an escape artist.* Placing his manacled hands on the small desk, he grinned at her—showing crooked yellow teeth, one missing on the lower right, another one on the upper left, and surprisingly direct, limpid blue eyes.

"William Angel?" Patricia asked, bending close to the glass and the small opening covered by a silver square of metal with holes in it.

"Who'd you think? Jesse James?" His grin was for real now, wrinkles like crows' feet spreading out from his eyes. A shock of strawberry blond hair with hints of gray hung across his forehead.

Chapter Nine – No Angel

A SMART ASS. NOT ONLY DO I HAVE A LOSING CASE, but I've got to deal with a smart ass. Patricia gave a wan smile at the glass partition. "Glad to meet you, Mr. Angel. I'm Patricia Egan; this is Allen Belknap, my law clerk. You'll have to speak up so we can hear you through this thing." She tapped on the metal grille at the bottom of the glass.

"You won many cases, Miss?"

"A few." *Cheeky bastard.* It was a few, sort of. There was the marijuana case, even if it did end in a plea, and she had done some successful work for the city and the Alt-Energy group. So what if it wasn't in court?

"That guard over there," he nodded toward the big khaki-clad guard who had brought him in and remained by the door. The one on their side had gone out. "He's got good ears, and he don't keep no secrets. We need to whisper down close." He dipped his head toward the grille.

She leaned forward to hear him, as did Allen—almost hugging her shoulder. Ignoring the clerk's minty breath and aftershave, she addressed Billy.

"Okay, but we don't have a choice." She pressed her lips together, not pleased at getting instructions from her client. "You're going to be tried first on the escape and assault charges, so maybe we better stick with that. We can deal with the other stuff later."

"Fine by me. Not much they don't know on that one." Billy gave her a tight smile that reminded her of someone.

Behind her, she heard Allen's pen scratching on the note pad. She was glad to have him here to take notes, but if he kept sticking his head over her shoulder, she might have to slug him. She focused on the papers in front of her.

"The indictment says you sawed your way out of the cell. Is that true?"

"Yep."

"What did you use?"

"Hacksaw blades. What else is there?"

"Hacksaw blades?

"Yep. Six of 'em."

"How did you get six hacksaw blades?

First came the smile, then he showed the crooked yellow-tooth grin, gaps and all. He shook his head, but didn't answer.

"Just tell me what happened," she said. "In your own words."

Billy's face became serious, his clear blue eyes more bemused than hard or icy like she expected from a seasoned criminal. "I sawed through two bars at the bottom of my cell—"

"Where was the guard?" Allen asked over her shoulder, a little too close to her ear and a little too loud.

"Back around the corner, on the other side. Must've been nine o'clock or so. He usually don't come back for a while after they get the supper dishes."

"Didn't the other prisoners give you away?" Allen again, his shoulder against her back. She shrugged him away.

"Ha!" Billy snorted. "They'd never do that. The old trustee pretended he was asleep, but he'd know better'n rat on me . . . You want me to tell this?"

"Yes, please, go ahead," Patricia said. She shot a warning glance over her shoulder at Allen.

"I sawed through the bars and got out into the hallway that runs around the outside of the cellblock . . . You never been in there, right?"

Patricia nodded.

"The cells are in a row on an outside hall, but I had to go back in and get the sheets. I'd already torn 'em in pieces and tied 'em together—"

"Just like in the movies," muttered Allen past Patricia's ear.

"So's I could climb down once I got out." Billy paused, and his eyes narrowed, staring past her at Allen, now concentrating on his note taking.

"We was up on the third floor, you know. I pushed them and my hacksaw blades . . . weren't but two of 'em left any good. Pushed 'em through the hole and squeezed out after 'em. There's a window a tad down the hall. It had bars, too, so I had to saw through them, but I couldn't get enough play . . . 'cause there's a shutter . . . outside. Finally, I gave it up and yelled for the guard."

"Yelled for the guard? Why did you yell for the guard?" Allen asked.

Annoyed, she looked back and hissed, "Let him tell it."

"Well, he had the keys, didn't he? Looked like that was the only way I was gonna get outta there." Billy coughed several times, a smokers rasping liquid cough, deep in his chest. "Pardon me." He wiped his mouth on the sleeve of his prison jumpsuit. "He come around the corner . . . I didn't realize how big he was 'til we was face-to-face. He took one look at me and pulled that little nigger knocker out—"

"What's that?" she asked.

"Uh, nigger knocker? One of them little blackjacks." Grinning at her, he flapped his hand up and down, hitting his manacles against the desk on his side.

"Okay, then what."

"He told me to get down on my face, on the floor. When I didn't, he took a swing. Caught me on the shoulder. That's when I hit him."

"I thought he was bigger than you," Allen said.

"A giant mothe-r-r . . . giant guy." Billy raised a chained hand as high as he could. "Hit him with the bar I sawed outta the cell. It didn't stop him." He shook his head. "Not at all. So I hit him a couple more times and told him to give me the keys. He fell down, but then I heard the elevator coming, and I ran up the hall . . . There's a door, you see, and stairs at the back, but they went up, not the down stairs I wanted the key for. Well, that door—it was unlocked. So I went up . . . only way I could go. Up the stairs. Ran around up there on the roof, lookin' for a way down, fire escape or something, 'til I heard shouts down there in the jail. So I hung from one of the gutters and dropped to the ground."

"Wow!" said Allen. "How'd you not get hurt?"

"I did some. Gimped my leg a bit, bruised my hip, my shoulder. It was already hurtin' from where he hit me. But I've taken worse'n that . . . Some bushes broke my fall, and it'd been raining, so the ground was pretty soft." His face was somber now. "I got up and started to run. Couldn't go fast 'cause of my leg, and one of those cops come out the front door and come after me. Told me to stop or he'd shoot." Billy shrugged. "And here I am."

She studied the top indictment, the shorter of the two in her hand. "Count one: escape. That's five years, right there."

"I just wanted to see the kid 'fore he . . ." Billy stopped at her raised eyebrows and held up his shackled hands. "I wasn't gonna hurt him or nuthin." He grinned. "Just wanted to talk to him, see if he'd like to take a little vacation." His whisper was almost inaudible through the grille.

Patricia frowned and looked down at the indictment. "Then count two: 'Assault with a deadly weapon with intent to kill.'"

"Look, it was self-defense. He was gonna brain me with that sap of his'n."

"Last time I checked self-defense doesn't work against a jailer trying to stop an escape." She glared at him for emphasis.

"Yeah, well, he was a helluva lot bigger'n me. I had to do something."

"Yeah, *well*. Did you intend to kill him?"

"Hell, if I'd meant to kill him, I'd a done it." He shook his shackled hands in the air as if he were holding the bar from the cell, then grinned sheepishly and lowered his hands to the desk with a rattle of chains. "Just tapped him on that fat bald head of his . . . to get him to give me the keys. Weren't none of 'em hard enough to knock him out even."

"He had over two hundred stitches. Just on the top of his head."

"Damn it all. He wouldn't give me the goddamn keys."

Allen's pen stopped scratching on the note pad.

"Wouldn't give you the keys," she said. "You expected him to give you the keys?" She took a deep breath. "All we've got is 'no intent to kill.'"

"Fine. That's just fine," Billy said, nodding, his grin gone, his eyes lacking any bemusement. He leaned forward, close to the grille. "Can you at least get my car back? It's a good car, and it's just gonna set there in some police lot and rot. My girlfriend can take care of it for me."

Patricia grimaced. "We can try. It's not going to do you any good—"

"Call the Patriot Bar down on Main Street." He rattled off the number, and she motioned with her hand to Allen, who wrote it at the top of his pad.

"Ask for Judy Kay," Billy said, his voice so low she almost couldn't hear him. "If she's not around, just leave a message. She'll call you back. If you can get 'em to give you the car—"

"I'll have to file a motion, get an order from the judge."

"Her name can't be in it."

Patricia raised her eyebrows. "Why . . . ?" Then she remembered. "Oh. She's the one they're looking for." Allen snickered behind her.

"Yeah," said Billy. He leaned back and grinned at her.

"I'll see what I can do." She squared off the corners of the papers on the desk. She was ready to go. How was she going to mount any kind of defense for this guy? Across the room, on Billy's side, a dull rap sounded on the door. The guard opened it, looked out, and started talking to someone.

Billy looked around, then leaned forward and whispered, "Find out how Lazlo got it."

"Who?"

"Lazlo. Lazlo."

"The other guy?"

"Yeah. And that other fellow. That wasn't our fault. No one was even near where he was, unless . . ." He trailed off.

"Unless what?"

"Nuthin."

"I'm your lawyer. You need to tell me. How am I going to defend you on that? You were there; at least you were caught a hundred yards or so away. And this Lazlo was a friend of yours—right?"

Billy stared at her without answering.

"The kid . . . what's his name, Jenkins, says you were there. So what's your defense?"

"They have to prove I was inside the place, don't they? That kid, he was so fu-u—hopped up on drugs he didn't know where he was from east Jesus. It coulda been somebody else he was with."

The cockeyed look he gave set the gears in her mind going.

"Was there?" she asked.

"Was there what?"

"Was there someone else there?"

He cleared his throat. Turning his head, he looked behind him again. The guard was still engrossed in his conversation at the door.

"Snitches don't make it long in here." No grin now. "Kid better learn that real fast."

"Okay." She didn't like this. "We can talk about it when you come down for trial on the escape." She flipped to the second indictment. "Burglary of a business, grand larceny, safecracking. Jesus, why were you there at six in the morning?" Behind her, Allen edged closer to her shoulder.

"We just, you know," Billy shrugged, "lost track of time. We'd been there since four."

"Four!" said Patricia and Allen together, loud enough to make an echo on their side of the glass. The guard turned away from the door and stared at them, then raised his hand and made a circling motion with one finger in the air. A faint "wrap it up" came through the glass.

In an urgent whisper, Patricia said, "It takes you that long to open a safe?"

"Nah-h-h, I can open one like that in three, four minutes. We were gonna take it home with us. It was in a block of concrete, for Christ's sake."

"Take it home?" she said. "Why would you want to take it home?" Allen pressed against her shoulder and started to say something. She held up a hand to stop him.

"Lazlo," Billy said. "He wanted to learn the trade, and we needed a safe to practice on."

Allen made a choking noise, then spoke past her shoulder. "You do that often?"

"Couple of times. We . . ." Billy stopped when the door behind him slammed shut. The guard came over to his chair.

"Let's go, Mac; time's up." He put a hand on his prisoner's shoulder. Billy gave Patricia a thin, tight smile. Now she remembered where she had seen a smile like that. The movies. Steve McQueen.

"Miss . . . ?" Billy said.

"Egan."

"Miss Egan, check on, you know . . . what I said. Will you?"

"Yeah, sure." She tried to remember what it was. Then remembering, dismissed it as ludicrous. The man's not charged with murder, so why does it matter how Lazlo got it? Or the other guy?

Part III

Chapter Ten – Billy's Moll

THREE YEARS IN LAW SCHOOL, distinguished member of the bar, and what the hell was he doing? Outside the McFee Savings Building in the midday sun, waiting for some woman wanted by the law. Patricia had conned him on this. Jack chuckled despite his irritation. The order for the car was a nice piece of work, talking that sweet blonde assistant D.A. into it. Maybe he'd go back and see her.

He stared up at the silvery wall towering over him, the sun reflected at a high angle in the glass, brilliant blue sky creased by the top of the building. If he weren't so pissed, he'd feel sorry for Patricia, up there baking a proposal for Dick to present to the city. How the McFee firm could do the Alt-Energy work better and cheaper than Joe Mayes and Leslie. *I need to get out of here,* he thought. Not even his love life was worth a damn.

He looked up the street at the old Slave Market, a raised stage of brick inside an open rotunda of Georgian arches and columns. Whitewashed brick, white columns, the South incarnate. Fancy architecture to sell slaves. Tearing children away from mothers, husbands from wives, whip-welted bodies, fear and hate mingled in anguished and tormented souls. Bent human forms huddled on the raised arena inside the columns, black faces and bodies blurred by the shadows of time. Black men and black women—like Aerial.

But not like Aerial.

One sexy woman, nose stud and all. Wonder if she has that smooth ebony sheen all over. Too risky in this town. But he wondered.

A young woman in a business suit came out of the building. He smiled and nodded hello. She smiled and nodded back, but she was gone before he had time to form more than an impression of cool self-possession. Like Patricia. Colin's woman. He chuckled. Better never let her hear him say that.

Maybe he should've moved out, but Colin said no. Insisted he stay. And he couldn't beat the rent. Colin said she'd understand he was like a brother. *That* didn't make her like him any better. Patricia had given him the arctic treatment, almost as if he were competition.

He paced some more. *Where the hell is this woman, and how am I supposed to know who she is. All Patricia said was, "you'll know it's her."*

Patricia. Not an ice maiden, but terribly exacting, of herself and everyone else. Somewhere in there has to be passion. Colin—

Startled by the harsh rasping of a metal hubcap against concrete, he jumped back from the curb. "What the hell!" he yelled.

The car engine died in a series of coughs. It was a Sixties land yacht, a two-tone pink and white Cadillac. The passenger door swung open, and a silver shoe with a spike heel appeared, followed by a shapely leg in a black net stocking. Twisting around, the woman looked up at him.

"Hop in, sweetie." A bottle-blond with helmet hair framing a narrow face and mask of black eyeliner, thick rouge, and red lipstick. "Ya gonna get in or not?" the woman said as he gawked at her.

"You Judy Kay?" Dragging his hand along the car's tailfin, he walked up to her.

"Not me. Her." She jerked her head toward the driver. "Wanta sit up front with us?" Inching forward to get out, she hiked up her black miniskirt, showing a fringe of red lace underneath. She gave him a smile.

"Nah, that's okay," he said, staring at her legs. "I'll sit in back." Opening the rear door, he slid across the white leather seat, worn and faded but clean.

The driver, her hand still on the steering wheel, peered at him in the rearview mirror. Beyond her hand ran a hairline crack across the windshield.

"You look mighty young to be a lawyer," she said, her eyes squinting at him, her brow furrowed. A husky cigarette voice. Bouffant platinum hair.

"I'm old enough." He forced a tightlipped smile.

The other woman squirmed back into the front passenger seat and closed the door, then twisted around to shake his hand.

"Hi, there," she said. "I'm Rhonda." The hand was delicate and soft and lay limply in his palm. She had to be at least forty, trying for twenty.

"I'm Jack. Pleased to meet you, Rhonda." Always say the person's name.

58

"Judy Kay," the driver said, making no move to turn around. She reached down and twisted the key in the ignition. The beast surged to life but didn't move. Judy Kay continued studying him in the mirror.

He stared back, first at the reflected blue eyes, then at her face and her jaw working in a tight little knot, worrying a wad of gum. Except for scarlet lipstick, she wore little makeup on her smooth, pale face. *She could be Dolly Parton's twin sister*, he thought, *but maybe it's only the hair and the tight sweater.*

"Well hell," she said, jerking the gearshift into drive. "If you know what you're doing . . ."

With only a glance at the side mirror, she lurched away from the curb and across traffic into the far lane. Behind them, a car horn blared, and Jack checked for a seat belt. None. He shifted to the center of the rear seat to see where they were going and slouched forward, his hands with the court order between his knees. The sun through the back window was hot on his shoulders, raising a line of sweat along the starched collar of his shirt.

"You have the papers?" Judy Kay asked. Flashing past on either side were the glass fronts and neon signs of the bars and liquor stores, the pawnshops and hot-sheet hotels lining Main Street.

"Yeah." He waved the folder at the eyes in the mirror. "We need to get there before the D.A. changes his mind."

He stared between the bouffant platinum hair on the left and the short blond on the right. Were those wigs? The Cadillac shot through a yellow light at an intersection, and he jerked his head around. They had missed the turn.

"Uh, police lot's down that way." He pointed to the right.

Judy Kay gave a throaty chuckle. "It's okay, honey. We ain't gonna kidnap ya."

Her friend emitted a whinny and looked around at him. Judy Kay smiled in the mirror. With the blue eyes and dimpled cheeks, she almost looked pretty.

"We're goin' there, hon, but we have to do it my way." The jaw worked on the gum. "Cops wanta talk to me, so we gotta take a little ride first. Know what I mean?"

"Oh, right. Make sure you're not followed." *And what if she is*, he thought. *A chase and I'm along for the ride?*

"Yeah." Another throaty chuckle. "They're still tryin' to figure out how he got them hacksaw blades."

They were silent for a couple of blocks. Then she asked, "They still got him on death row?"

"Yeah. They won't bring him back until the trial." Jack craned his neck to look back at a street sign.

"That's pretty crappy, you ask me." She made a wide right turn, forcing an on-coming van over against the far curb. "All he did was open a damn safe."

"Least, he tried to," added Rhonda with a giggle.

"It's the escape," Jack said. "They don't want him in the county jail."

"Yep, that's Billy all right. Never 'fraid of nuthin . . . But shit, they coulda put him some place decent." She made another turn, then turned quickly down an alley and through it to a parallel street and back in the opposite direction.

"Probably best he's not back here," Jack said.

They were at a cross street, and he glanced both ways as the big Caddy slowed to a crawl and rolled through a red light. Not the best way to avoid notice. And where the hell were they? He took a deep breath.

"Deputies were pretty upset about the jailer," he said.

"Hmmm." A noise evincing some sympathy, maybe even for the jailer. "That ain't the only problem he's got," she said. Jack caught her eyes panning back to him in the rearview mirror. Worried.

"Right," Jack said. "He's looking at some long time." The car hit a bump, throwing him to one side.

"He'll deal with that," she snapped. In a softer voice, she added, "There's some down here might want to make sure he don't say much."

"They oughta know he won't talk," Rhonda said, glancing at Jack.

"They may not want to take a chance," Judy Kay said.

Jack leaned forward, placing his hand on the back of the front seat. "What do you mean? 'Some down here'—"

"I mean it ain't safe for him. Ain't *never* safe for a man who knows what all goes on in this business."

"I don't get it," Jack said. "He was caught lying in a ditch . . . what was it? A hundred yards away? He doesn't have a snowball's—"

"Don't fret about it, hon." Judy Kay was eying him in the mirror again. "I done talked too much myself. Just be careful and look after Billy. And watch out for the cops. There's things you don't know about this place."

Before he could ask what, he slammed into the back of the front seat as the car screeched to a halt several feet from the curb and a block away from the police garage and impoundment lot down the street.

"Here we are. You go on and get the car. Rhonda'll drive it."

"I sure will," said Rhonda, grinning over her shoulder.

Turning around, Judy Kay put her arm across the seat. Another smile, this one gentle, kind. "Don't let me bother you, sweetie, I'm just an ol' worrier." She held out her hand to shake, and he took it.

Now it was his turn to study her face. She didn't look so hard straight on.

"And thanks," she said, "for everything."

Chapter Eleven – Hal Goodman

THE WALK WITH RHONDA TO THE IMPOUNDMENT lot was longer and slower than he liked. Tap-tapping along beside him, she jabbered about some white-trash junkie she'd seen on the news. After killing his wife, he cooked her in a stew, then drove around half the night with a big pot of body parts in the back seat.

Ignoring as much of Rhonda's prattle as he could, Jack mulled over the conversation with Judy Kay. Why would Billy Angel think he was being set up, if that was it? And watch out for the cops? Sounds like the usual, "I been framed." But as Rhonda told about a patrolman stopping the car and a forearm and hand tumbling out onto the ground, he started worrying about Patricia and what she was getting herself into. He shrugged it off. Patricia was capable of taking care of herself.

Realizing he was five yards ahead of Rhonda, he slowed to let her catch up. Arms waving, she was telling him that they'd asked the junkie what he was doing, and he'd told them he was looking for barbecue sauce.

She grabbed Jack's arm. "Reckon he'd'a really eaten her?" she asked.

Jack gave her a sidelong glance and grunted in disgust but didn't answer. They were inside the gate now, at the front of a low building with the police shield on the door.

"Why don't you wait out here," he said. "They'll bring the car around to you . . . You have your driver's license?"

"Right here, sweetie." She held up a small black purse. "But I wouldn't leave without you." She winked at him as he turned to go inside.

The room was a low-ceilinged office with brown paneling, thin strips of which bowed out from the walls. An air conditioner chugged and rattled in the lower half of a window, below closed blinds. The only light came from bare fluorescent tubes on the ceiling. As he entered, a big fleshy woman looked up from a desk beyond the chest-high wooden counter.

"May I help you?" she asked, moving no more than absolutely necessary.

"I have an order for release of a car." Taking the order from the folder, he waved it at her and dropped it on the counter.

"Lunchtime, sonny. No one here to get it for you. Why don't you come back in an hour or so?"

The way she said it wasn't unpleasant, just matter of fact. A sandwich, chopped barbecue spilling out of it onto a wax wrapper, and a large drink cup were parked on the desk in front of her. A magazine lay open to one side.

"I don't have a lot of time," Jack said. "When will your valets or whatever they are be back?"

"I must not have made myself clear. Our whatever-you-want-to-call-them went out for lunch. May be another half hour or so. Maybe more."

"Look, I've got an order. Why can't you give me the keys and I'll go get it? It's just an old heap." Just an old Corvette, the order said.

"Ha, ha. That's good, like a self-serve lot." Her bare arms shook when she laughed. "Sorry, it don't work like that." All humor gone.

He was about to argue when the inside door behind her banged open. Beyond was a garage where cars stood in various states of disassembly. The man who came through the door was dressed in a brown suit and a beige shirt. He was big, his jacket tight around the shoulders and the sleeves too short. Taller than Jack, he looked like an ex-football player whose muscle had not gone to fat.

"Hey, Eunice, where'd all those peckerheads get to? Brought in a vehicle from homicide. Bastard killed his wife and tried to stew her up."

The man looked familiar. Where had he seen him before?

"Like I told this young fellow, Hal. It's lunch. They had a birthday gig for one of the guys and I got stuck here minding the store."

Hal scowled at Jack, then back at Eunice. "Shit!" He tossed a paper on an empty desk and fished a set of keys on a leather cord out of his pants pocket. "Just tell 'em to hurry up and go over it. Probably nothing there . . . but we're missing a foot." He slapped the keys down on top of the paper and looked at his watch. "Gotta go over to the mayor's," he said, starting for the rear exit. "I need a car. How about that Lincoln the Narcs brought in?"

"They might not . . ."

Jack interrupted her. "Uh, Hal," he said, "I'm here to pick up a car that's been released. Could you get it for me?" He faked a smile, though it was difficult under the pressure of the man's scowl. Big crooked nose, broad forehead under black hair swept back from a widow's peak. One eye bore into Jack while the other one peered off at the far wall.

Ah! The mayor's bodyguard from the cities' big energy meeting last year.

"I've got the order here," Jack said, pushing it across the counter.

Hal had paused at Jack's summons but now resumed his move to exit. "I ain't got time," he said, grabbing the door into the garage.

"Look, it's been here months. Ever since the Taco Pal robbery."

Hal stopped and turned to glare at him with one eye. "Taco Pal?" He moved the door back and forth like he was trying to make up his mind. "Okay, let me see that." He stalked to the counter and grabbed the order.

"I've got . . ." Jack paused, hesitating to mention his companions.

Hal gave the order only a glance. "Yeah, sure, I'll get it. Seeing how you're in a hurry and all." He handed the order to Eunice and, when she didn't take it, slapped the papers down beside her drink. "Give me the damn keys, Eunice, and make it snappy. I don't have time to fart around here."

Pursing her lips, Eunice shook her head, but she picked up the order and hoisted her body out of the chair. Slowly reading from the top page, she plodded over to a file cabinet and jerked open a middle drawer. After a moment, she extracted a manila envelope, peered inside, and then shook out a car key with a yellow tag. She sidled over and handed the key to Hal.

"Sign for it," she said, holding out the envelope.

"Yeah, yeah," he said and snatched it from her.

As he signed the envelope, Eunice looked over her shoulder at Jack. "You taking possession for your client?"

"Yes, ma'am."

"Then you need to fill out the receipt."

"Don't I get to see the car first?"

"You'll see it, hoss," said Hal, starting out the door into the garage. "You have a problem, go bitch to the D.A." He left, slamming the door behind him.

Eunice took a form out of her desk drawer and handed it to Jack. Behind them, the front door squeaked open, and Rhonda's head appeared in the opening along with a sliver of sunlight. "Hey, what's taking so long? It's hot out here." She stuck a bare arm and shoulder and a black-net-stockinged leg into the room.

"It's okay, Rhonda. The car'll be out shortly." Seeing Eunice eye Rhonda then him, he felt his cheeks flush. "Just wait while I do the paperwork. Okay?"

"Okay, sweetie." Rhonda's head and appendages disappeared, and the door gave a whump against the jamb.

"That your girlfriend?" Eunice asked, wobbling the few steps to reach her chair and drop into it.

"Not hardly. Friend of the owner."

He hurriedly filled in the blanks with scribbles. He was tired of being an errand boy, and afraid Hal might figure out Judy Kay was waiting for him.

"Lucky for you that detective happened along," Eunice said, taking a bite of her sandwich. She chewed and stared at him as if she were contemplating something. "More lucky he's interested in that case." The last came as a muffled afterthought.

Jack looked up as he finished writing his bar number. "Yeah, I'm lucky. He didn't seem too eager to help."

"He was there, you know."

"There?"

"At the Taco Pal . . . when they caught those crooks."

He pushed the form across the counter and looked at his watch. Fifteen minutes to finish here and go meet Fitz. Eunice started to take another bite, stopped, and peered at him over the top of her sandwich.

"Yeah, he had to go to a hearing, he told me. He was off duty . . . happened by at the end of it all." She bit into the sandwich and resumed chewing.

"Where is he? I need to go . . . It doesn't take that long to get a car, does it?"

Eunice shrugged. "May not start, you know." She smiled at him as she bit and chewed, her mood seeming to improve with each bite.

The front door opened, admitting Hal. "Lady out there wanted the key, but the order's for you, bub." He lofted the key with its fluttering tag at

Jack, who failed to make the catch. Key and tag hit the floor and slid under the counter with Jack after them, stifling a curse and trying not to fall. "Better luck next time," Hal said. He waved vaguely at Eunice. "Gotta run." He hurried behind the counter and out the door, into the garage.

The door clanged shut as Jack came up dangling the key from the tag like a dirty Kleenex.

"Drives for the mayor, you know," Eunice said, balling up the wrapper for her sandwich.

"No, I didn't know."

"Yes sir, he doesn't do regular police work—'less it's some pervert, like that man cookin' his wife." A small chunk of barbecue slipped out of her mouth, onto her blouse. "Says he likes them cases."

"That it?" Jack asked.

"What?" She held up her drink, preparatory to downing it.

"All I need to do here?"

"What else do you want?"

"Thanks," he said and added under his breath, "for nothing." He opened the door to the sunshine. Opposite him, in the exit lane by the chain-link fence, sat a classic Fifties Corvette, covered with dust but seemingly in excellent condition. Rhonda stood beside it, holding open the driver's door.

"Come on, handsome," she called. "I'll give you a lift—anywhere you want to go."

Chapter Twelve – Leon Hayes

PATRICIA DROPPED THE PHONE into its cradle and swiveled her chair around to stare out the window. In law school they didn't teach you how to handle an irate client—or how to weave your way among the obstacles and conflicting demands and obligations of a real world legal practice. She churned over the conversation in her mind as she would a dozen more times before the day was done.

Ms. Jones had demanded to know why those two old maids could chase off a cousin who was renting the house from her—and just take it over. She had grown up there, before college and escaping that awful place for New York. Why wouldn't the police just do their thing and clear those old bats out of *her* house? Patricia had explained that the sisters possessed a deed to their father, which they waved at the deputy who came to serve the eviction notice. The deed was meaningless, legally, but it was enough for the deputy. Now they had to show that Ms. Jones held the legal title. The sheriff wasn't going to do a title search, and Patricia hadn't had the time, not yet.

There followed some excoriation of Patricia's tardiness, declamations about legal rights to the rental income, of which Ms. Jones was in present need, and then a question about suing the seller or whoever made this stupid mistake in the first place. That had set off the alarm bells. The McFee firm name appeared on the deed as the preparer and a McFee company had been the seller.

As ethics required, she related all this to Ms. Jones. Then she offered that the firm, namely Patricia, would pursue the recovery of the property without charging the customary fees. Cost was all Ms. Jones would have to pay.

She hung up with a sense of unease. This didn't feel right. She had made the requisite disclosures and the client had gone along. But she didn't have the best of motives for continuing to handle the matter. To protect the firm? Win Dick's approval? Win the case? It just didn't feel right.

She reached for the phone again. A call to the deputy who handled the original eviction, or tried to, pointed to none other than Leon Hayes as the Madison sisters' lawyer. So it was Leon who had raised the "color of title" defense to stop the eviction. Maybe she could make Leon see the light. All it would take was a simple phone call.

Wrong. Leon was too busy to talk: he had a client coming in. The only way to make him see the light was to sit down across from him, and he wasn't about to come see her. So here she was, in a part of town she'd never willingly visit on her own, pulling into a gravel parking lot beside a decrepit two-story brick building with an ancient Dr Pepper sign painted high up on the wall, promising in faded block letters, "Good for Life!" The building may have been suitably downscale for Leon's business in the 'hood, but the black Cadillac in the space marked, "Reserved," exuded bourgeois prosperity and pride.

A door facing the Cadillac was marked, "NO ENTRY," so she went around to the street side of the building. Its entrance was an old storefront with a recessed doorway flanked by plate-glass windows. On each were the words, "Personal Injury, Divorce, Criminal Defense." On the door, in big letters under the name, "Napoleon Hayes, Esq.," was the promising epithet, "Honest Lawyer."

To her surprise, Leon didn't keep her waiting. A pretty receptionist with a no-nonsense manner ushered her into his office at once. Entering past her, Patricia appraised the woman's stately grace, cool efficiency, and blue pinstripe pants suit. Maybe she could work a trade with Leon—Aerial for this nice young woman. Then came a wave of guilt at the proprietary comparison she had made.

"Come in, come in," Leon said, rising from his chair behind a massive executive desk and reaching out a hand over one corner as she crossed the cavernous office. His handshake was surprisingly gentle, but firm.

"Mr. Hayes, how are you?"

Shorter than her and somewhat rotund, Leon Hayes had a round pleasant face, graying hair, and a faint, dark moustache. His wide eyes and the corners of his mouth exhibited bemusement, as if he still couldn't believe he had stumbled through the color bar to be called mister by any white woman in this bastion of the Old South.

"Fine, fine," Leon said, releasing her hand. "Expected we'd need to talk sooner or later. Appreciate you taking time out of your busy schedule over at that high-powered law firm to come out here."

She wanted to say, *Cut the crap, Leon. I'm here because otherwise you wouldn't talk to me, and you know my "high-powered" law firm is going down the tubes while I waste my time with you. And I'm not making any money to pay the bills.* Instead, she smiled sweetly at him.

"No, Mr. Hayes, I need to thank you for seeing me so promptly." They remained standing at the corner of the desk. "I am sure that we can find a reasonable way out of this, uh . . . situation. Your clients just need an explanation of how deeds are recorded."

"Why don't you have a seat and let me get you a cup of coffee? And call me Leon." He came from behind his bulwark as he spoke and went to her left, to an alcove on one side of the office. It contained a black marble countertop with a sink and coffee bar and, underneath, a mini refrigerator.

Instead of sitting, she shifted on her feet and looked around the office. It had nice paneling, a dark pine with textured grain brought out by the finish. Behind the desk was the usual lawyer decor: framed law degree, state bar admission, civic awards and photographs: Leon with various local politicians and celebrities. No windows graced the walls, and the only illumination came from the soft glow of recessed lighting in the ceiling. The door she'd seen from the parking lot was to the right of Leon's executive chair.

"No thanks," she belatedly answered to the coffee. "But—"

"Would you like cream and sugar?" Leon busied himself with the cups.

"Just black . . . uh." Now why was she embarrassed at that? Returning to the desk, he handed her one of the cups and a saucer. Gold-rimmed china that reminded her of Elroy Bell long ago in New York.

"Please have a seat, Ms. Egan, and we can talk about our little problem." He gestured toward a pair of wingchairs in front of the desk.

"You can call me Patricia," she said, depositing her briefcase and purse by one of the chairs. Then she added, "Leon," as she sat.

"Yes, Patricia." Going behind the desk, he eased into his chair and smiled at her. "This may not be as easy as we *both* might wish, Patricia." Still smiling, he held the dainty cup below his chin. "Edie and Annie Madison found the deed in their father's desk after he died. That gives the document an aura of something like, shall we say, holy writ." He paused to let this sink in.

"But my client has legal title," Patricia said.

"They think the old man, the Reverend Madison . . . he owned the house, and now it's theirs." He took a sip of coffee.

"My client lived there for years when she was growing up. That old deed doesn't mean a thing. It's record title that counts."

"You and I know that, but the sisters don't. You see, they have a deed their father kept and protected all these years."

"You can explain it to them."

"When they came to me, your client was pursuing a criminal case. I couldn't let those two women be arrested and charged with a crime."

"I doubt it would have gone that far. And it's civil now. Just get them to tell their tenant or whoever he is to leave."

"She's a she. Have you searched the title?"

"No, but I have copies of Ms. Jones' file . . . and the deeds." *This is silly*, she thought. She shouldn't have to waste her time on this. Warily, she tasted the coffee, then drained half of the small portion. It was excellent, if only lukewarm.

"Why don't you do a search and give me the chain of title. I'll try to talk to them, but I can't promise anything. We don't know what the deal was between their father and Ms. Jones' people."

"What . . . ?" She almost spluttered out a mouthful of coffee.

"They believe it's theirs, Patricia. You . . . me telling them isn't going to shake that belief. It may take a judge."

She placed the cup in the saucer and examined the desk. It was polished to a glossy sheen and empty except for a desk blotter on which rested a notepad and pen. She raised her eyes and tried to drill a hole into Leon's head.

"Surely, you can convince them—"

"They're strong-willed women. They only believe what they can see and feel and what the Bible tells them. The Lord evidently told them they own that house. Their father was a preacher. A fine one at that."

"I'll give you a chain of title. Their deed was a mix-up of some sort." She smiled and batted her eyes, something she wasn't particularly good at. "We don't want to end up in court on this."

He smiled back. "I'll show them what you come up with, but you probably need to go ahead and file your lawsuit." He pointed toward the door in the wall on his left. "You see that door?"

She glanced at the door and nodded. *What's all this about?*

"That's a divorce door. When you get an upset client or a mad husband out front, that's how you leave." He gave her a weary paternal look. "That's how you have to practice my kind of law. My car's right outside."

"I guess I better get back." Standing, Patricia searched for something pleasant to say and recalled that Leon was stepping in for the disabled city attorney.

"I understand you're going to take over some of Hector Grimes' work," she said, picking up her purse, then her briefcase.

Now Leon beamed. "Yes ma'am. It's quite an honor to help out with poor old Hector on the ropes now."

Poor old Hector! She couldn't imagine that Leon and poor old Hector had ever had anything to do with each other. If the Klan were still respectable, Hector would be a grand dragon or something.

Coming from behind the desk to show her out, Leon touched her lightly on the back, then withdrew his hand as if he had been shocked. For the first time since she arrived, he seemed flustered.

She smiled and held out her hand. "I'm sure you'll do a fine job. The city needs all the help it can get." *Ray Malloy certainly will.*

Shaking her hand, he looked solemn. "It's an honor to be called, but it won't be easy—all those scurrilous allegations going around. The stuff that gets into the papers." He shook his head. "Then that young man who started it all got himself killed."

She stopped and stared at him. "The Taco Pal robbery?" Dick had mentioned it at lunch, at Plato's. "I'm representing one of the accused."

"Yes . . . tragic, tragic. Young man in the controller's office. Hector had been . . . I understand from Raymond that Hector was handling the investigation himself." He sighed. "Guess I'll have to get into all that."

All that? *Ah*, she thought. *Ray Malloy's gossip about the mayor receiving favors from city contractors.* As they reached the door to the antechamber, another thought crossed her mind. "Won't you have a problem . . . working with Mayes and Associates, you know, while you're also representing the city?" She almost felt guilty challenging Leon's ethics—even if he hadn't helped resolve her problem. But maybe she could bollix up his collaboration with the enemy.

He gave her a smile worthy of the Mona Lisa. "We have . . . what do they call it in your high-powered firms? A Chinese wall? I won't handle any matter for the city related to the energy project. That's where I'm working with Joe and Leslie. Dick isn't still trying to get all that back, is he?" Leon's mouth dropped open in surprise. Faked, she was certain. "Surely not this late in the day?"

He grinned up at her as she fumbled at the doorknob.

"You never know," she said, giving a forced smile in return.

"No, I guess you don't." He reached past her and opened the door. "But don't you worry about my wearing two hats. I can do that just as easily as you can handle Ms. Jones' case."

The sun was slanting yellow against the old jail down the street when Jack drifted into her office. She had spent days it seemed bent over spreadsheets covered with Lacey's calculations: numbers based on estimates Patricia pulled out of thin air for billable hours and costs for legal research, drafting documents, defending lawsuits, *etc.* All so Dick could present the mayor with a credible proposal to do the Alt-Energy legal work.

"You busy?" Jack asked with only his head and shoulders inside the door.

"No, I always cover my desk with a ton of paper before I start cutting out paper dolls. What does it look like?"

He came in anyway. She watched impatiently as he moved a chair around and scrunched down in it to brace his feet against the edge of her desk.

"You should thank me for taking a wild ride with your client's moll," he said with a sigh. "Thought I'd fallen into a regular gangster movie."

"Too high class for Billy Angel." She scratched some numbers on the paper. She wanted him to leave.

Instead, he launched into his difficulties in getting Billy's car. "The guy who got it for me was a cop, detective who brought in another car. Belonged to that jerk who cooked his wife." He paused, but she ignored the bait. "Not a friendly sort. Thought he was going to stiff me, but when I mentioned the Taco Pal robbery, he agreed to get it. Seems he was there."

She had been trying to concentrate on the spreadsheet, but now she stopped and tapped her pencil on the desk. "He was there? What's his name?"

"Hal something or other. Drives for the mayor, the fat lady said." Jack shrugged. "I've seen him before . . . with the mayor."

"He say anything about the shootings?"

"He didn't say much at all. Kind of a creepy guy. Lots of muscle, one eye looks off into space. Lady there said he had to testify at a hearing."

"I hadn't . . ." She tapped the pencil harder. "What kind of a hearing?"

"Internal Affairs, I imagine. They usually do an investigation after a cop shoots somebody."

"I need to get the transcript." She started writing on a pad next to the spreadsheet. "That could—"

"Fitz didn't show up for our meeting. He called and wants me to hurry up and con those people into selling." As she finished writing, Jack craned forward to stare at the spreadsheets. "Why are you wasting your time on that?"

"Jack, would you do me a favor and do a title search? Nothing urgent, just when you're down at the Registrar's office? I need to find out what happened with the Jones property, where the sisters and their father fit in."

"I guess I could." He didn't sound too eager. "I have to check a few things for Fitz . . . I thought you were gonna get Leon Hayes to explain it all to his clients."

She laughed. "So did I, but that cagey old bastard isn't going to do any more than he has to. I've got to come up with all the documents." She paused, thinking about the conversation with Leon and getting a knot in her stomach. "You know, I'm not sure he'll explain anything to them. Damn it all!"

"How's that?"

She told him about her telephone call with Ms. Jones and the discussion with Leon. And the ethical concerns she had.

"Don't worry about it," Jack said. "Get the house back and the lady'll love you. That's what Dick would say."

She threw the pencil down on the desk. "I'm not making any money on any of this. This frigging proposal of Dick's." She swept her hand over the spreadsheets. "And now this thing with Leon." Retrieving the pencil, she waved it at Jack. "You know, he—"

"Where'd you get those?" Jack pointed to a vase of the red roses on the credenza.

"Where do you think?" She raised her eyebrows and scowled at him. "It's my birthday."

"What! Dear old Colin come out of the swamps and send his woman some flowers?"

She launched the pencil so that it hit him square in the chest.

"I'm nobody's woman, buster. And, yes, they're from Colin." She glanced at the flowers, then at Jack. "I don't know where he is, but he didn't forget. That's more than you'd ever do for any *woman*, you creep."

Jack chuckled and tossed the pencil back on the desk. "Not my thing. Look, why don't we go out for your birthday. We can raise a glass to Colin, wherever he is."

"Can you afford it, you poor boy?"

"Hey," he threw his hands in the air. "Dutch treat, okay?

Chapter Thirteen – Tale of Two Houses

THE HOUSES, LOW BRICK RANCHES with attached garages, were lined up like barracks down one side of a single street that ended in a barren avenue leading out to the Old Schoolhouse Road. Although Fitz had already bought two and had contracts on two more, almost all appeared occupied, with kid detritus scattered about several of the yards. And almost all appeared loved: neat and well maintained. The house where they pulled into the drive had a low chain-linked fence, fresh-cut lawn, and weedless flowerbeds filled with red geraniums. Only one of the houses, two doors down, looked untended and empty—except for a dun-colored Ford Pinto in the drive.

The day was gloomy, overcast and humid. It bore down heavily on Jack, even more so now that Allen, who had come along for the practical experience of extracting property from an unwilling seller, had told him he was leaving. The Mayes firm had the work he'd signed up for, and Leslie had personally called him. Jack understood why he was going, even saw it as a smart move. Still, the news weighed him down and served to highlight his own numbing inertia. He was doomed to live out his life and die in this place.

Gripping the steering wheel, he stared out the windshield at the expanse of weeds and low brush behind the houses. Grid-like indentations marked where streets and cul-de-sacs had been laid out and graded but never paved. Beyond this ghostly subdivision were long rows of young corn focused on the distant pecan grove. To one side was a field of leafy plants he pegged as soybeans. All planted by Fitz's tenant farmers. Here today, gone tomorrow.

With Allen in tow, Jack advanced up the walk and two brick steps onto a narrow porch. Why did he dread this so much? He was good at talking to strangers, persuading them to buy something—mostly shoes in his pre-lawyer days, but this seemed an especially dubious mission. Sweet-talking some ignorant, unsuspecting woman into selling her house . . . houses to Evan Fitzhugh. Without telling her who the real buyer was. Or why Fitz wanted the land. Or what it was worth. *Really* worth.

No name on door or mailbox. *Ah, crap*, he thought. *I don't know the owner's name.* In his rush to be done with this business, he'd given Aerial the file so she could type the contract, and he hadn't even looked at it.

A tall black woman answered the doorbell at once, as if she had been watching their every move. She was dressed in faded jeans and a man's loose blue shirt, both spotted with white paint. A too-large gimme cap with a Caterpillar logo was pulled down low over her hair, shadowing her eyes. From inside came a smell of fresh paint and, closer by, turpentine. Using a paint-stained rag, she carefully wiped the fingers and knuckles of one hand as she stared through the screen door, first at Jack, then at Allen, then back at Jack.

"Hi, I'm Jack Alexander. I wanted to talk to you about your house."

"'Bout my house? What's wrong with my house?" Glaring at Jack, she finished cleaning off her hand and balled up the cloth, then folded her arms under an ample bosom beneath the large shirt.

"Nothing, nothing. Missus . . . ?"

"Miss Madison."

Jack winced. This had started off all wrong. And the name, why did he know it? Behind him, Allen shuffled his feet and cleared his throat. Jack gave two downward motions of his hand for Allen to keep quiet.

"Ms. Madison, we wanted to talk to you about selling—"

"This house ain't for sale. Do you see a 'for sale' sign out in my yard?"

"No, ma'am, but I'm willing to offer you ten percent over what the house is valued on the tax rolls." He could go to twenty percent, but he'd better save that. She started to reply, but he hurried on. "And I understand you own that house two doors down." He pointed toward the untended house with the Ford Pinto in the drive. "I'll make the same deal for it."

"You're mighty young to be buying up houses, aren't you? Who are you working for? Not that slick con man with the gold medal?" She tapped her breastbone with the hand not holding the rag.

Allen chuckled, but he didn't say anything.

Jack tried out his best, most disarming smile. "I'm acting as an agent for an unnamed client, true. But who it is shouldn't matter if the price is right."

"Well, it matters to me. Who are you?"

"As I said, I'm Jack Alexander, and I do have authority to negotiate . . . within limits."

"No, I mean, are you a lawyer?" Her face came closer to the screen door.

"Yes ma'am. I'm with McFee—"

"McFee! I thought so. I got no truck with you people. You need to talk to my lawyer, Mr. Hayes. Don't you know that, young man?" To punctuate her indignation, she slammed the inside door, rattling the screen. Jack stood staring at the wire mesh, a foolish sense of clarity rising in his consciousness.

"Tough old biddy, isn't she?" said Allen.

"Jeesh!" Jack turned. "Madison. Shit! Madison. Leon Hayes. Has to be the same damn woman and her sister."

He ditched Allen at the office—no need to demonstrate any more stupidity to a law clerk, especially one going over to the other side. After getting Aerial to track down Leon Hayes, he managed to set up a meeting for three. At Leon's office, naturally. Fitz had insisted on a personal appeal.

He pulled in next to Leon's Cadillac, which was flanked on the other side by a silver Porsche. *Now who could be driving that,* he wondered, *and here, visiting Leon?* In no hurry to find out, he stared up at the Dr Pepper sign, then down at a door labeled, "NO ENTRY."

As he unfolded his legs to exit his outmatched Camaro, a short, stocky man in a dark suit came flying around the corner of the building. Faded blond hair, the look of a robust outdoorsman—Joe Mayes.

"Hey, Jack, how ya doin' pardner?" Joe yelled to him from across the parking lot. "You here takin' care of business for one of our mutual friends?" He reached out and grabbed Jack's hand. "Leon was telling me you're trying to wheedle some property off a couple of old maid clients of his while your compadre's tryin' to boot 'em outta their house. That's a trick only ol' Dick hisself could pull off." He emitted his braying laugh.

"How are you, Joe? What brings you all the way up here?" Jack nodded toward the Porsche. "And driving, too."

"Business for the cities. Meetings and a court date tomorrow," Joe said, nodding vigorously. His hair was thinning, almost tonsured on top like a medieval monk. "Thought I'd have a little visit with my local counsel. How's Dick doin'? You know, I miss the old boy, now we don't have the same clients. No opportunity anymore for us to raise a few."

"Dick's fine. And he wants his clients back."

"Well, I reckon he does." Joe showed two bright rows of perfect teeth, but his eyes had a cold, sharp look, like a cat's eyes. "What's done's done. We all need to move on."

"Like you did with our law clerk."

The grin was for real now. "Great opportunity for the boy. Lot of great opportunities these days with the energy field opening up—even more goin' on now than when Dick and I started." He paused at Jack's impatient glance at his watch. "You know, Jack, we can make a place for you, too. Leslie's always singing your praises. Not only a smart guy, he says, but a great athlete."

"Yeah, I could always kick his butt at Wiffle ball. Him and Ray."

Joe laughed. "You need to come down and whip that boy into shape . . . I'm serious, Jack, we'd like to have you on board. Always thought you should've been doin' the energy work, not that prissy lady lawyer. I bet you wouldn'a—" Joe must have caught the look Jack gave him. He sidled over to his car. "All ancient history now. Done and gone." He unlocked the door to the Porsche and opened it. "Remember, Jack, we really would like to talk to you. Give us a call." Joe gave a quick wave and ducked into the driver's seat.

Jack gave only a grim nod in return, then watched as Joe sped out of the parking lot in a rattle of gravel. Thinking, *maybe I should call Leslie. We always got along well, and they could be my ticket out of here.* He sighed and turned to lock his car. He couldn't do that to Patricia. And now he had to deal with Leon Hayes.

He never knew what to make of the old lawyer. His office was in the black section of town, not even the better area of the fermenting ghetto, yet Leon had plenty of money to go elsewhere. His primary constituency was the lower and middle reaches of society—street toughs and drug dealers at one level, working-class men and women with the usual run of working class problems at the other. He found Leon to be both affable and evasive, the jester in a mad white world, but beneath the genial words always seemed to lurk a sharp-edged meaning.

"That was Edie you were talking to," Leon said after allowing Jack to explain his mission and the send-off he had received at the Madison house.

"Did she call you?" Jack sat in a comfortable wingchair across from Leon's wide desk, a dainty cup and saucer balanced on his crossed legs.

"Nope. Just know it's her. The other one doesn't talk much, wouldn't come to the door either." He smiled. "Can I get you some more coffee?" The cup held only a pittance, and Jack had drained his.

"No thanks. I don't want to waste your time, Leon." Mainly he didn't want to waste his own time. "I'd like to buy the sisters' house."

"You said you asked her about the other house, too. The one the young lady lawyer was trying to get 'em to give up."

"I didn't realize it was the same house Patricia's client . . . owns," he hesitated, "when I went out there. When you and Patricia work that out, I'll have to talk to Ms. Jones about it." As he spoke, a thought crossed his mind: *that could be awkward. Patricia representing Jones to get the house back and me trying to buy it—before the cities' interest in the place is known to the world.*

"Now who is it you're representing?" Leon asked, making a steeple with his hands under his chin. "Is it Dick McFee? Going to start back up a development company and put in high-price country homes out there?"

"No, sir. He's working on building the law practice. The development company's all in the past."

"Thinks he can get the city back with him, eh? That's what I hear." Leon smiled and dropped his hands to the desk, running two fingers along the edge.

"He's working on it," Jack said. "I know Joe Mayes pulls a lot of weight, and he's got Leslie with the expertise, but don't count Dick out. He's smart and he has his own connections."

Leaving both hands lying flat and relaxed on his desk, Leon didn't respond for a few long beats. "Yes-s-s," he said finally, stretching the word out in a sigh. "Dick and Allie have always been good to me, treated me right. Old school liberals who wanted justice for people of color when it wasn't too popular down here. Still isn't, but . . . well, no use dwelling on all that."

Jack nodded and squinted at a pair of black and white photographs on the wall behind the old lawyer. In one, Leon stood with Dick McFee and Mayor Fisher, one of them, probably Leon, receiving an award of some sort.

After a long silence, Leon continued. "It's up to the city fathers—Mayor Fisher, the council and their friends—on who gets the city's business. I just hope Dick isn't hurt too much by what comes about." He tilted his head to one side. "For my part, I gratefully accept what scraps they're kind enough to offer."

Right, thought Jack. *Why you?* He knew Allie had pushed for a minority law firm to handle the city's work, but was there something else behind Leon's selection? And Joe Mayes could have his pick of law firms for local counsel. Why Leon?

Leon pursed his lips before resuming his usual smile. "So who are you representing? Is it Mr. Fitzhugh?"

Jack gave a slight start. *The old fox knew all along. His question about Dick was a rabbit trail he wanted to run for some reason.*

"Yes, sir," Jack said as coolly as he could. "It's Mr. Fitzhugh. He's putting together a large agribusiness operation." Sort of true.

Leon chuckled and ran the tips of his fingers along the polished top of his desk in front of the empty blotter. Looking at his hands, he said quietly, "Mr. Fitzhugh doesn't cover his tracks very well. He's already bought a bunch of dirt out there, and he made a run at the Madisons some time back." He looked up at Jack. "Not much going on by way of farming, except those few old tenants who've been there forever. Doesn't take a smart man to put two and two together." His smile was benign. "I know a little bit about land myself, you see . . . and what can be done with it."

"Yes, sir," Jack said, not smiling and not happy about the drift of the conversation. "I'm sure you do."

"That Mr. Fitzhugh, he's a slick one. Plays it a lot of ways. House of mirrors . . ." He stopped, still smiling. "Well, Mr. Alexander, I'll talk with the Madisons about your offer, but I don't think they'll sell. At least not at this time. Don't you think it might be best for them to wait and see what develops out there?" He pushed his chair back from the desk.

Ignoring the last question, rhetorical he knew, Jack stood and walked to the alcove, trying to figure a comfortable way out of this. He placed the empty cup and saucer to one side of the coffee service and turned back toward Leon, who was coming from behind the desk.

"If you want me to put the offer in writing, I can," Jack said.

"That won't be necessary. I'll let you know if there's any interest."

Back in the parking lot, next to Leon's Cadillac, Jack stopped to stare up at the Dr Pepper sign and the words "Good for Life!" What was he going to tell Patricia about all this with the two houses? He couldn't keep it secret. Allen knew, though he was good as gone. And Leon was bound to let it slip, intentionally. So he'd have to tell Patricia, and she'd tell her client that Fitz wanted to buy her house—once Ms. Jones got it back and had clear title to it.

He unlocked the car door. Instead of getting in, he hit his fist on the roof. Had he let anything slip to Patricia about Fitz's grand scheme? Buying up the land out there so he could sell it to the cities for the Alt-Energy project. If he told her, she might tell her client, her client might talk, and she would certainly hold out for a higher price. From the cities. And so would everybody else. Then there would be the scandal.

No "might" to it. Patricia would tell her client.

Chapter Fourteen – In the Exercise Yard

IN ALL HIS VARIOUS PRISONS, federal and state, he had never been in a place like this. Locked in a small cell, no exposure to daylight, nary an opportunity to shoot the shit with some other human being. They didn't even let him go for meals, instead bringing them to his cell. Only real break he got was when he faked an ailment and wrangled a trip to the infirmary. After the third time, the guards started ignoring him.

Today, finally, he had fifteen minutes in the exercise yard. Walk and smoke. He'd have time for two, maybe three, before they herded him and the others back inside. None of them made sense about anything. Retards and perverts were all they were. He circled the track, eyeing the walls, the razor wire, the towers. No way out of here.

He walked fast, keeping well away from the others. To stay in shape, he exercised in his cell: push-ups on the floor and against the wall, leg lifts, sit-ups, isometrics, and all that Charles Atlas stuff. Now all he wanted to do was walk and look at the sky. Not blue, but even the low gray clouds were a pleasure to see.

They let him read, mostly old magazines, but those only took so long, and he couldn't get the professional journals he wanted. Since his first correspondence course in the federal pen, at eighteen, the wardens hadn't been too wild about furthering his education. That first course he'd put to good use when he got out, opened a little locksmith business, but after the second B&E on his rap sheet, they'd taken his license away.

So now he was learning the law; they even allowed him all the law books he wanted. He'd sure as hell need them, with that baby lawyer. She seemed smart, but book–smart and ignorant of the real world, the down and gritty of the criminal law—not like some of the courthouse hacks he'd come across.

She was a sweet kid, though. Played hard-nosed and tough, but she was just an earnest young girl, a good-hearted sort who took her lawyer gig seriously. And she wanted to win; he could tell that. She was used to winning. She'd even gotten his car back, according to a letter from Judy Kay's sister.

But if she couldn't manage it, with all the problems in his little case, he might have to take care of things himself. He didn't want her to get hurt, but she might be able to help him out, in a pinch.

Passing a guard, not a bad sort this one, he asked for a light for his second cigarette. Maybe the last before they forced him back inside. The wiry little guard, a black welterweight no bigger than he was, gave him a smile when he struck his lighter and stuck it up under the cigarette tip. Billy thanked him and moved off again, round and round the yard, avoiding the others.

What a bucket of shit he was in.

Fish-eye made it sound easy. He knew the place: back from the road, no one around, and it opened late in the morning. Said he ate there all the time. Said he'd seen the office after they had a break-in. Safe hadn't been messed with, but it had lots of cash in it. Fish-eye had gotten his nephew a job there, and the nephew said lots of money went through the back room. Not just fast-food money. Nephew was a little snoop, a worthless little punk.

Then Lazlo had wanted to learn the trade and needed the practice. So he'd agreed to pull the safe and take it back to the warehouse.

It hadn't been like any other he'd come across. They'd gotten started late when Goodman and the kid didn't show up on time; then the safe was anything but easy to remove from that block of reinforced concrete.

Something fishy going on there with Fish-eye and his nasty stare. He usually just provided the tips on where to hit, kept the cops away, and helped move the goods. This time had been different. He wanted to come along. With a lot of money in the safe, he wanted more'n his usual fee, and maybe he wanted to make sure Billy and Lazlo didn't make any early withdrawals before they got back to the warehouse. Looked like more cover, having a cop at the door, keeping a lookout with his nephew out by the road.

The safe was a bitch, and he'd lost track of time. Then the cops showed up—unfriendly cops. Goodman took off, and bang, Lazlo was dead. Poor, dumb Lazlo. A loveable puppy, Judy Kay called him.

He hadn't seen any newspapers, but Judy Kay told him about the other man being killed—when she came to visit with the hacksaw blades.

In the last months, he'd had plenty of time to figure it out.

The man worked for the city. In city hall. Didn't take Einstein to put two and two together and come up with Goodman shooting him to keep him quiet. He'd probably seen Goodman hightailing it out of the woods, maybe even recognized him. Or Goodman was afraid he'd recognize him since he was around city hall all the time.

He was the only one alive who knew Goodman was there and probably killed a man. Except the kid, and he didn't count. Judy Kay only knew that a crooked cop tipped them about the safe, but she didn't know a name or what happened, except what she read in the papers.

He finished his cigarette, threw it down on the bare earth, and twisted his shoe on it. "Two minutes," the guard called. He walked faster, passing a multiple rapist and child killer who babbled all the time about Jesus coming to carry him away from this place.

He'd never squeal on nobody, and Fisheye ought to know that. Or would he? He was careful about his business, very careful and very secretive. He'd ordered Billy not to tell anybody about him. And Billy hadn't—until they planned for the Taco Pal. And then only Lazlo, when Goodman came along.

He'd been watching them the whole time from the door, making sure they didn't slip any cash out and into their clothes before removing the safe. Yeah, Goodman really didn't trust him. Wise on Goodman's part, since he probably would've taken a little up front. There was honor among thieves, but Goodman wasn't one of them. He was nothing but a crooked damn cop.

Maybe Goodman was the one who made sure Lazlo didn't make it. And maybe it was him who took a shot at Billy, 'cause somebody sure had.

The guard yelled at him to hustle his ass inside.

He needed to find out how Lazlo died. The lady lawyer could help him there. If Goodman did it, he might have to even things out.

Maybe Goodman was thinking the same thing.

He shuffled through the door and into the short hallway, where two guards lined them up for the march back to death row. Not a long walk and no chains. Nowhere for them to go, but run around inside here, like rats in a cage.

If Fisheye was afraid of him, of his breaking and talking, maybe even trying to place a hit on him, Fisheye would move first.

Here he was safe. Down there, he had to worry about the jailer and his friends as well as Goodman. Anything could happen down there. He needed to be careful, *real* careful.

Chapter Fifteen – Dick's Plea

IT WAS ONLY FIVE THIRTY, but the lowering clouds had already darkened the tinted windows of the City Club. Soft lounge lights produced an eerie twilight and cast a yellow glow over black leather furniture and black marble tabletops. Weaving through the maze, Dick led the way to a squat table barely large enough to hold their drinks and a bowl of mixed nuts. On the far side of the room, the piano player labored over an amorphous melody.

Patricia settled onto an overstuffed love seat, her purse at her feet, while Dick took a leather armchair to one side. Almost at once, the mayor appeared at the club's entrance. A tall, beefy man in a brown suit that glistened in the light accompanied him. The beefy man headed for the bar, and Mayor Fisher sauntered over to them.

Jumping up, Dick extended a hand over Patricia's head, followed by a noisy greeting that drowned out the piano and the conversations of the other patrons. The mayor patted Patricia on the shoulder as he slipped past to a kitty-corner chair.

"You look lovely today, Miss Egan. Just lovely."

She drew away, then felt chagrined at her reaction to such a harmless gesture. "Thank you, Mayor. Nice to see you." Still, she didn't like it.

The waitress appeared. A saucy blond in a short black skirt and white sweater, she drew the mayor's appraising gaze and an order for a double scotch on the rocks. Dick, already infused with a handcrafted martini back in the office, summoned another—extra dry, two olives. As the men fell into conversation, Patricia ordered a glass of white wine, then idly watched the waitress retrace her steps to the bar. She was almost there when the mayor's beefy companion stopped her and leaned over from the barstool to whisper close to her ear. Giggling, she tapped him on the chest, then jotted something on her pad.

Patricia remembered Jack saying the mayor had a driver or bodyguard, but she'd never noticed him before. She studied the man. Dark face, hard features. A cop's face. Sitting sideways to the bar, the man poured liquid from a coke can into a tall glass of ice. Beside her, Dick was piling on the usual sycophancies, preparatory to making his pitch. In his hand, he held a folder with the five-page proposal she had spent days drafting.

The drinks appeared and she took a quick, satisfying sip of wine. *Why does this seem so distressing? Dick will present the proposal, the mayor will take it with him, and we'll win or lose. Most likely lose.*

The preliminaries over, Dick fished an olive out of his empty glass and launched into his spiel, harking back to the genesis of the Alt-Energy project. The mayor nodded and clinked the ice in his glass, still half-full. Without pausing, Dick waved to the passing waitress for another martini.

"Anthony," Dick said, handing the mayor a copy of the proposal, "this shows how we can do everything for you, better than Mayes."

The mayor dropped the pages in his lap and reached for a bowl of nuts on the table.

Unfazed, Dick continued. "We'll cap the total each month, say sixty thousand dollars, no matter how many hours we put in. Joe can't do it any cheaper, and it's a built-in incentive not to run the meter, which I've never stooped to doing." He paused as he fished for an olive. "Though Leslie Sharp, I can't speak for. He always seemed to get in twenty-hour days, charged for his time in the shower and on the shitter, stra-te-gizing or something. None of that here." He gestured at the pages resting precariously on the mayor's knee.

"I don't know, Dick," the mayor said, riffling through the pages without looking at them. "It's a bigger project now than when we started. Far more complicated, more players—"

"Tony, Tony, that's all the more reason to keep me . . . us on as legal counsel. Mayes is nothing but a political hack. Never had an original thought in his life. And Leslie, everything he knows, I taught him. You're just getting leftover cooking with Leslie."

"That's not what you used to tell me, Dick," came a loud voice from behind Patricia. She looked up to see Evan Fitzhugh looming over her.

"Fitz, Fitz! Come join us," said the mayor. Popping up from his seat, he reached over Patricia to grab Fitz's outstretched hand. "We're just having a friendly chat here."

Ducking her head, she scrunched up her nose. The cloying smell of aftershave was enough to make her gag. Dick half stood and reached past her to shake Fitz's hand. A quick glance up showed that Dick's face exhibited no pleasure at the interloper's arrival. Fitz lightly grasped her upraised hand as he went around to the other side of the table.

"So nice to see you, Mr. Fitzhugh," she said. *You and the Boston strangler.* He eyed her as he dragged a chair over from an adjacent table.

"And you, dear, you're looking absolutely gorgeous," he said, settling into the chair. "Like your hair like that." He touched his own well-coifed pompadour.

Not answering him, she self-consciously brushed several strands aside and behind her ear. *I need to finish my wine*, she thought, *and go wash that unctuous bastard off my hand.* She glanced over her shoulder. At the bar with the mayor's driver was the local bond advisor for the Alt-Energy project. Had he arrived with Fitz? But he made no move to join them at the table.

The mayor addressed Fitz: "Dick was just showing me a little proposal he has for the Alt-Energy business." He gave the sheets representing her hard work a limp wave, then dropped them on the table in a sheen of water left by his glass. "I was telling him it's a far bigger project now. Whole new ballgame."

"Well, that's for sure . . ." Fitz started, but Dick interrupted him.

"Legal work's the same. Why . . ." Dick stopped as a tall glass appeared at Fitz's elbow, held out by a large, hairy hand.

Patricia looked up and into the face of the mayor's driver. He was paying more attention to her than to where he was placing the glass so that only Fitz's quick grab saved her work product from further insult.

"Thanks, Hal; I appreciate that," Fitz said, taking the glass.

"No problem," Hal said, one unblinking eye fixed on her, the other directed to her left. She returned the one-eyed stare with a scowl, and he swung around and stalked off. Beside her, Fitz took a long swallow of the cloudy drink and placed the glass squarely on top of her proposal.

"I know all the players," Dick said, leaning over the table. "I can run the traps, work with the engineers and bankers like no one else—not Mayes, not Leslie, not anyone." He started to pound on the table, but couldn't find an empty or dry spot. "No one at all," he said, his voice rising.

The mayor examined his hands, folded together in front of his chest. Across from Patricia, Fitz was staring intently past the table, at her legs. She pulled her skirt down with both hands and shifted to one side.

What are you doing here anyway? Can't be just a coincidence.

She looked at him, her eyes hooded, trying not to glare. He smiled back and took a swallow of his drink.

"Dick," said Fitz, replacing his glass on the proposal, "Mayes has a bigger firm and more experienced people. You always bragged on how smart and hardworking Leslie is. You need to let go of the past, look to the future."

"Who the hell's side are you on?" Dick spluttered through the dregs of his martini. "We all used to be friends, but those two stabbed me in the back; nothing but a pair of traitorous bastards, goddamn-it-all. They can't be trusted."

The mayor was silent, but Fitz uttered a congenial, "Now, Dick." But as Dick waved to the waitress, Fitz changed his tone. "Maybe you should stop now—lay off the sauce for the evening."

"One more won't hurt a goddamn thing," snapped Dick. He kept his hand in the air as the waitress approached. "Give me another, darlin'."

The mayor frowned, and his feet moved back and forth in front of his chair as if he were preparing to bolt for the door. Patricia fumbled for her purse. It really was time to go to the ladies room. But she didn't, and she left the purse where it was. She hadn't uttered a word other than the greetings. Maybe she should interject her own plea, a solid bit of advocacy based on the spreadsheets she'd put together. But she couldn't think of anything positive, effective . . . and honest. Not with Dick like this.

As the waitress left, Fitz started over in an amiable voice. "I'm using your firm for some pretty big land deals, Dick. We'll all do well when this thing gets going and the financing kicks in. Mayes can handle—"

"What's your role in all this?" Dick asked, his voice calm and deliberate. "What are you getting out of it?"

"The property out there y'all are helping me buy is gonna be worth—"

"Hold on, Fitz." The mayor's hand went up. "Let's not get off track here."

From watching Fitz, she switched to the mayor. The mayor's eyes were narrowed, his forehead wrinkled in a frown under his silver mane. *Ah-h,* she realized. *Fitz has stepped out of line; he's headed off somewhere the mayor doesn't want him to go, not in front of us.*

"Okay, Dick, I'll take the proposal," said Mayor Fisher. "Run it by some of the other folks. Maybe there's something we can do."

Fitz lifted his glass so that the mayor could pick up the pages of her proposal, wrinkled and damp in the middle and thoroughly wet in one corner. Rolling them into a tube, the mayor held it gingerly by the dry end.

"That's mighty good of you, suh," said Dick, gripping his newly delivered martini like a life buoy. "I look forward to continuing our long asso-o-she-a-shun for the energy freedom of this grea-at na-shun." He lifted his glass in a toast. The others followed suit—the mayor's and Fitz's glasses now empty except for the diminished cubes of ice.

She finished her wine and stared away from the men, at the dark window. *There's a subtext here*, she thought. *Something else is going on.* But Dick was smiling, lost in a gin-laced fog.

They stood and shook hands all around, Dick giving effusive thanks to the mayor and complimenting Fitz on his business acumen. As Dick finished his martini and Patricia searched her purse for lipstick, the other two departed. In her compact mirror, she watched the big man in the polyester suit join them at the exit. Followed by the bond advisor.

Chapter Sixteen – Ray Malloy

"CAN YOU BELIEVE IT? Dick's on my case about suing the city. That damn dog." Jack plopped down in the chair facing Patricia's desk. "Says it could complicate getting the client back. Shit! I thought you said they stiffed him?"

With an impatient grimace, Patricia looked up from an open file on her desk. "They put him on spin cycle and hung him out to dry. He was just too martini-ed up to know it."

"This is fucking absurd. Now I've got to get rid of it." He threw his hands up. "He *said* do what Allie wanted. What Allie wanted? She wanted me to sue." He rammed his feet against the corner of her desk. "I've already served the city fifty interrogatories."

"Why don't you go talk with Ray Malloy? He may hate Leslie, but I don't think he's got anything against us."

"What good's that gonna do?"

"He might be willing to cut you a deal. The pound screwed up and he knows it. You'll be a hero."

"Yeah, in doggie circles. You know what else? Dick wants me to take Allie to lunch. Sweet-talk her on giving him the business back. She's not that dumb. I'm—"

"Jack! Billy Angel's trial is next month, and I need to get started on his file. I wasted too much time on that stupid proposal."

Without knocking, Kitty stuck her head in the door, then slipped inside and leaned against the doorjamb. Showing off her new sleeveless top. Blue with sparkles.

"Jack, you have a call from Mr. Fitzhugh," she said.

"Tell him I'll call him back," Jack said over his shoulder. "Tell him I'm in a meeting or something. I'm tired of jumping every time he calls." Kitty's plucked eyebrows went up in a questioning arch. "Wait! Don't tell him that."

"Sure thing, boss. Gotcha covered." She grinned and gave him an exaggerated wink. As she slid around the doorjamb, he gawked after her, the thick red hair and smooth complexion, the body of a centerfold.

"Whew," Jack said, then looked sheepishly at Patricia. "Maybe she's the answer to my prayers." He wiggled his eyebrows.

"She may be the answer to your prayers," Patricia said, a touch of acid in her voice, "but she works for you, and you're ten years older. You'll treat her as off limits if you have half a brain. Or do you?"

"Jealous?"

"Ha! Why would I be jealous, and *you* of all people? You philandering, egotistical narcissist."

"Oh-h-h, big words."

"Go call your client. And tell Aerial to lose the sunglasses. It's getting old, seeing her in those all the time."

"Yes suh, boss." He gave her a sarcastic smile.

"Out! Before I throw something." She turned back to her file. "I've got to figure out how to convince a jury that putting two hundred stitches in a man's head doesn't show any intent to kill him."

He took her suggestion and called Ray Malloy. Ray was pleased to have him come over and talk about their big case. Ray was pleased to talk about almost anything, especially if he found it humorous.

Ray's office in city hall was as cluttered and disorganized as his old office at the McFee firm. Filling the credenza and plastering the walls were all sorts of sports memorabilia: autographed baseballs, high school trophies, photographs of baseball and basketball teams. Except for a picture of his wife and three young children in one corner, his desk was covered with law books, loose papers, and files. Topping out a jumbled stack in the center were Jack's complaint and discovery requests in *Ex rel. Princess v. City of Carrville*.

Red-faced and stocky, Ray was the apotheosis of the hail-fellow-well-met: garrulous, jovial, and solicitous to a fault, at least to those he deemed his social peers or betters. His once lush hair had grown thin and his hairline had receded, but the first thing one noticed was his wide grin and Santa Claus cheeks.

He greeted Jack as a long-lost comrade-in-arms. "How's good old Dick doin'? Still flyin' high?" Ray asked once he had settled into his low chair. He tilted it back and rested his feet on a stack of papers at the corner of the desk.

"He's fine. You know how it is," Jack said with a shrug. "He's fighting to get the city's business back." He shunted a cracked-leather chair to one side of the desk so he could see Ray past the stacks of papers and books.

"Yeah, yeah." Ray looked like he was bursting to say something and swallowed it instead. He reached out, doubling his body over his substantial middle, and grabbed the lawsuit papers off the pile. "Great set of interrogs you have here. Gonna save 'em for my form file."

"Are you going to tell me why they gassed Millie's dog? You remember Millie, don't you?"

"Sure I remember Millicent. Lovely old colored lady, works for Dick. Too bad about the dog, but shit happens, my man. No need to file a lawsuit over that." He tossed the papers back on the desk. They slid off and fell to the floor.

"Had to," said Jack, giving another shrug. "But we don't need to be wasting our time with this case. Millie's upset; she lost her dog. And the pound screwed up. A thousand dollars would make the bereaved feel a whole lot better about her government's misfeasance. Save the city money in the long run."

"The dog was a mutt. It bit a lady."

"An almost pure German shepherd, and the lady was drunk."

Ray guffawed. "I didn't know you had so much bullshit in you." They grinned at each other, and then Ray's face grew somber. "What do you hear from Leslie?"

Jack had to think a bit before answering. "He's with Joe Mayes down in Atlanta. They're representing the city now on the energy stuff."

"Yeah, yeah, I know all that." Ray scowled and gave a dismissive wave of the hand. "I work for the city, you know. But Leslie, how's he doin'? He gettin' married? Seen him lately?"

"No, I haven't seen him, and I don't know anything about his personal life." Jack hesitated, then added, "I doubt he's losing sleep over any of us."

Ray's joviality was gone. He looked away, staring out the window before turning toward Jack again. "None of that bunch is. They walked all over us, you and Patricia, too." His face brightened. "How about that little secretary I hired for you? You been pumpin' her?"

"You mean Catherine Simms?"

"Hell yes, I mean Kitty. I sure didn't mean that black hustler with the nose ring."

"Stud. It's a gold stud."

"Whatever. Looks silly as hell. Bet Miss Priss dudn't like it at all."

Jack rolled his eyes and looked away. Sometimes Ray's humor wore on him.

"You know those bastards are just stringin' you along." Ray brought his feet down and sat up, propping his elbows on the edge of the desk. "Dick ain't got a pissant's prayer in hell of getting any legal work from the cities. Whole different scam now, and he'd just queer the deal. Sell the bonds, buy the land, maybe bulldoze around some dirt. A sure moneymaker for them that's in on it." He grinned at Jack. "But Dick ain't one of 'em."

"He gave the mayor a proposal—"

"Ah shit! The mayor's a shit, and poor ol' Dick, bless his heart, is a fucking patsy . . . On that, anyway. What they're doin' ain't gonna go any-damn-where—'cept for the mayor and his friends. Including your boy Fitzhugh."

"He's my client." Jack felt the blood rise in his face. This wasn't the jovial Ray talking—still voluble, but not joking. Jack leaned forward in his chair and placed one hand on the desk. "If you think it's a scam, why don't you do something about it? You're practically the acting city attorney now, with Hector out."

"Ha, ha. Hector was a doddering old fool even before his heart attack . . . You know why they hired me? The old goat couldn't find his own ass from one day to the next." Picking up a pencil, Ray leaned back and placed his feet on the desk again. He waggled the pencil between two fingers. "Suited the mayor just fine, but after Hector started slipping gears in council meetings, Allie McFee insisted they get me involved. Those two hack lawyers down the hall," he pointed out the door with the pencil, "they only handle nuts and bolts stuff."

"Was Hector in on the scam, as you call it?" Jack asked.

"Hell no. Decent a guy as you'd ever wanna know, loyal to a fault. Only started that fucking investigation 'cause he got a complaint." He flipped the pencil back and forth across his knuckles. "He's been left out of all the energy crap for some time. Bills all go to the mayor's office . . . get paid by the mayor." He gave a wide grin. "Spread around different accounts, of course."

"Investigation? You mean, of the mayor?"

"Yeah. Guy in auditing started it." The pencil shifted to the other hand.

"The guy killed in the Taco Pal robbery?" Throw Ray a bone and he'd talk forever.

"Yeah, yeah, guy named Royale."

"That's been a while back. What's happened since then?"

"Nuthin. Hit a dead end, to the extent Hector could remember anything about it. He interviewed Mister Royale, then the fellow up and died. Can't even find a file on it." He tapped the pencil on the side of his head.

"Did it . . . did it involve Alt-Energy? Or my client?" Something he needed to know before he got deeper in the muck.

"It was before all that—before Leslie bailed and I came over here. Had to do with the mayor and his contractor buddies . . . Hey, all that's confidential. I can't be telling *you* about it."

"You didn't answer my question."

"I said it was *other* stuff." He rocked back and forth in his chair.

"Look, Ray, if you think this energy project is a scam, are you going to do anything about it?"

"I got a wife and kids." He dropped his feet to the floor and reached across the desk to pivot the picture toward Jack. "Not my job to be hall monitor here, and any-damn-way," he nodded his head for emphasis, "I'm goin' over to the D.A.'s office." He leaned back, a smug look on his face.

"So you told me . . . it was in the works. Congrats."

"Next week or two. Better pay, more respect, less crapola."

"Your leaving, that why Leon Hayes is getting the city's business?"

"Yep, that's partly it." Ray winked at him. "That nigger lawyer's in fat city now."

Jack cringed and made a face, which Ray ignored.

"Hacks here'll do the routine and Leon'll get the honey. Two dips, too."

Jack stared blankly at Ray. Leon wasn't his concern, but Fitz was. If Fitz's plans got screwed up, if he couldn't sell his land to the cities, they would all lose. "Do you really think Leon and the Mayor, they're into some . . ." he gestured loosely with one hand, "some kind of scheme to bilk the city?"

"How would I know? All politicians are out to bilk somebody somewhere." Ray sneezed and reached behind him to grab a Kleenex. Turning back, he spoke through the tissue. "I'm not the type to repeat scurrilous gossip."

Bullshit, thought Jack. Yet, he wondered, *Should I get out now. But how? The firm needs Fitz. And his money.* He stayed silent while Ray finished wiping his nose and kept talking.

"I just handle the city's business. What's confidential stays confidential, and it ain't appropriate for me to get involved in spreading rumors."

"As an assistant D.A., won't you have some duty to stop any shit that's going on here?" He had to smoke Ray out on this, figure out his exposure.

Ray leaned on his desk and stared at him. "It's just rumors, Jack," he said quietly. "Not even that . . . plain speculation. No evidence of nuthin." He shook his head. "Projects always get studied and started, contractors get paid . . . and the lawyers. And the work goes on and on. Nothing illegal about that." There was no humor in his eyes.

Jack sighed. "How about the dog case?"

"I'll give you fifty dollars. Full release."

"A hundred."

"Done."

Chapter Seventeen – The Title Search

KITTY'S SWEATER JIGGLED LIGHTLY under Jack's gaze as she hurried to keep up with his long steps. It was a lovely afternoon for the walk, cool weather for late August and a clear blue sky. When she came by after lunch to ask if he needed anything, she looked so nice in the clinging white sweater and mini-skirt that he impulsively asked if she wanted to learn how to search titles. You'd have thought he invited her to a day at the beach she bubbled so.

What was she talking about? Aerial's pissed over the sunglasses and won't speak to Patricia? Aerial had given him only a stony stare when he told her to leave them off in the office, and in a few hours, she reverted to her old self. With him. Maybe he shouldn't have told her the order came from Patricia.

As they went up the steps to the registrar's office, Kitty touched his arm. "So, who are you seein', Jack? I'm not takin' any messages from the girl in Atlanta these days."

"God, that was last year. She's long gone so I'm available." He flashed a wicked grin at her for emphasis.

"Aren't you and Patricia, uh . . . more than just friends? I mean, you are living together."

Surprised, he gave a snort. "I live in that old house because her fiancé rented me some rooms—upstairs. Just because he took off and we're still there—different floors and all—that doesn't mean there's anything between us."

"Hey, you're male, she's female. She could sure use some lovin' to loosen her up." Nudging his arm, she gave him a big grin. "Bet you're just the man to do it."

Moving away, he returned her grin with a scowl. *God she's forward*, he thought. "How about you and Allen? You two were pretty hot there for a while, or was that someone else I saw you with in the parking lot?"

JAMES GARRISON

She kept grinning, her eyes holding his, and shrugged. "You know what they say: absence makes the heart grow fonder—of someone else."

Jack laughed but didn't reply. They were inside now, and he set about showing her around the document room, pointing out the giant folio-sized volumes that listed real property grantors and grantees and the smaller indexes of lawsuits and liens. While the main purpose of this outing was to check the title on land Fitz was buying, he'd promised Patricia he'd run the title on the house involved in her case. That the Jones house was on Fitz's hit list made him uncomfortable, but he wasn't about to let Patricia in on his client's plans. Better him nosing around the property records than her. And figuring out more than she should about Fitz's land deals.

With Kitty beside him taking notes, he quickly determined that the old farmer selling Fitz twenty acres of farmland had inherited it almost sixty years before and had a clear chain of title. Explaining what he needed and where to go, he dispatched Kitty to get copies of documents and after that to search the probate records and check the registrar's intake log for any new filings that might affect the land or its seller.

With her out of the way, he went to work on Patricia's case. A quick search confirmed that her client, Agnes Jones, was indeed the owner of the disputed lot—but with a conflicting claim asserted by Edie and Annie Madison. Then he pulled a plat of the entire area to check the property lines and owners of record. Fitz owned most of the vacant land in and around the old McFee subdivision, as he expected, but one large tract to the west was in the name of a corporation: The A-E Land Company. That he hadn't known. How was Fitz going to get his hands on that land? Surely, he'd want it, since it projected into the area he already owned—and it could be essential to the Alt-Energy project.

Alt-Energy? A-E Land Company. If that was what A-E stood for, there were more people than Fitz in on the cities' secret plans.

Still puzzling over this, he saw what he was looking for on the plat. The two McFee subdivision lots causing Patricia's little conundrum were four and six, lot six owned by Agnes Jones and lot four owned by Bettina Madison. The plat was not up-to-date, but recent enough.

Going between the grantor and grantee indexes, he found the property and the paterfamilias through whom Ms. Jones and the Madison sisters

98

were asserting their claims. He wrote the transfers and their dates on his legal pad.

> ~July 2, 1965 - deed from McFee Developers, Inc. for <u>lot 6</u> (property at issue) to Hudspeth R. Jones (father of P's client).

> ~June 22, 1965 - deed from McFee Developers to Reverend Ernest R. Madison <u>for lot 6</u>.

> ~July 2, 1965 - deed from Rev. Madison to McFee Developers, <u>lot 6</u>.

> ~July 2, 1965, McFee Developers to the Reverend Madison, <u>*lot 4.*</u>

Aha! *Lot 4.* Someone had simply put the wrong lot number on the first deed to Madison on June 22nd, discovered the mistake, and corrected it by having him convey the lot back to the McFee company, which then gave Madison the deed to lot four and gave Mr. Jones the deed to lot six, Ms. Jones' disputed house. Problem solved. All Patricia had to do was show Leon the chain of title.

Easing down in a chair at an empty desk, he studied his notes. *Something isn't right.*

He retrieved the microfilm rolls he needed and brought up scanned copies of the actual deeds, one after the other, on a viewer. *What's wrong here?* He examined the parties and the signatures. The Reverend Ernest R. Madison was sole grantee on the first deed for lot six on June 22nd and the sole grantor on July 2nd reconveying the lot to the McFee company to correct the error.

But he must've been married.

Finding an old microfilmed plat of the subdivision, Jack skimmed over it quickly. Ernest and Bettina Madison were listed as the owners of lot four. So why wasn't Madison's wife on the lot six deed back to McFee

Developers? Maybe they had married after the mistake in the deeds. Fat chance.

He easily found the old marriage record he expected to find. Not bothering with the divorce records, he went to the file on death certificates and after that to the records on wills and estates. Bettina Madison, the sisters' mother, still owned lot 4—and she might be able to claim a statutory dower interest in lot six, Patricia's client's property. He leaned his forehead against the back of his hand. *Shit, shit, shit! What a mess.*

Kitty came up behind him and dropped a pile of copies on the table. "Nothing in the log." Placing her hand on his shoulder, close to his neck, she gave a gentle squeeze, then another. "You okay, Jack? Got a headache from looking at that microfilm?"

Jack raised his head, and without thinking, he leaned the side of his face against Kitty's hand. Down the row of tables, a stern looking woman holding a stack of files glared at them. He reached back and grabbed Kitty's hand.

"I'm great. Want to go for a drink?" It was almost five, and he didn't want to go back to the office. And have to tell Patricia about this little wrinkle.

"Sur-r-re." Kitty said, kneading his shoulder.

Chapter Eighteen – Kitty

AT VICENZO'S LITTLE ITALY, they sat side by side in the bar, on a bench seat facing a narrow rectangular table. Light from an opaque window next to Jack gave a black gloss to the scarred tabletop and its interlocking pattern of faded rings. A room at the back held a dozen tables with red-and-white checked tablecloths. In the bar, it was only them and a couple of permanent fixtures paying homage to the bartender.

He swilled half a Heineken almost as soon as it appeared while Kitty took a first, tentative sip of a margarita. "They never check ID here," Jack said after another long draft of beer.

"Why should I care?" She gave him a puzzled look over her margarita.

"You're only nineteen, aren't you?"

"Who told you that? I'm twenty-two."

"You are? Patricia—"

"Patricia!" She laughed and elbowed him in the arm. "Sounds like she wants to put me off limits." She gave an impish grin. "She likes you, sweetie."

"Ha! I'm her favorite punching bag."

"So why'd you come here, Jack? To the firm?"

Catching the bartender's eye, he held up his empty beer bottle. Then he told Kitty why he had come. Colin, his best friend, was here; the McFee firm offered a golden opportunity; he wanted to make money and have the things he never had before. The new Heineken arrived and he accepted it with a smile.

"But Patricia does . . . or did all the exciting stuff, didn't she?" Kitty gave him a quizzical look, eyebrows knitted.

"That happened later, after . . ." He bristled at the question. "I don't know. It just happened."

"Don't you resent her?"

"Of course not." He paused. "Yes . . . but she's good. And that's all over now. We're both doing stuff we don't want to do."

"Lacey says Dick'll get the work back." Kitty licked a few grains of salt off the side of her glass, then held the glass out as if addressing it. "We only got two-thirds of our pay last week, but she says he'll make it up. Double."

"Oh God!" Jack smacked the beer bottle down on the table. "I didn't know that." He stared at her. "I'm sorry—"

"That's alright, we trust you. Aerial. Lacey. We all do."

"Lacey worships Dick." He managed a grin. "Kitty, I don't know what's going to happen. Maybe you should look for something else."

Studying her drink, she scraped some salt off the rim with her index finger. Touching finger to lips, she licked it off with the tip of her tongue.

"I need the job," she said, fixing him with a steady, unblinking gaze. "I live with my mother. A trailer park out on the River Road. Not the best area, you know." Her voice took on a hard edge. "When I was growing up, she used to turn tricks and—"

"What! You mean—"

"Not often. Soldiers from the base. She was sick a lot, played hell trying to support me and my little brother." She took a deep breath and let it out in a long sigh. "My uncle helped us out, and she had a boyfriend. A cop. He beat her some, but . . ." Kitty looked down and closed her eyes. When she opened them, she looked at Jack and said softly, "My uncle's dead, my brother's gone, and the boyfriend left her. She doesn't look as good as she used to."

"Ugh," Jack grunted. "I'm sorry, Kitty. I didn't realize you had it so bad . . . You seem like a smart kid. Why didn't you go to college?"

"Hey, I'm taking classes at Carrville Tech." She sighed and took another sip of her drink. "Mom hurt her back, and I had to go to work."

"You have a job now—even if the check's late sometimes."

"Jack," she said, turning toward him. "I need to ask you something."

Half-listening, he stared at her reflection in the mirror over the bar. The light coming in the window from the street gave her face in profile an eerie, ghostlike pallor. There was a strange beauty in the loose, flaring hair, the prominent nose and round chin, the smooth curve of her neck.

"... Henry's death wasn't an accident."

That brought him out of his mental wanderings. "What's that? What did you say?"

"You weren't listening to me." She pushed out her lower lip in a pout and swung sideways on the bench.

"Sorry. Go back over that, will you? What you were saying?"

She expelled her breath sharply through her lips. "I was *saying* that my mother believes my uncle being shot ... my Uncle Henry, you know, there at the apartments ... when he was getting into his car—"

"Wait!" said Jack. "The Taco Pal? Henry Royale? But your name's Simms."

"My mother's brother."

"You never said anything about that."

"I told you, you and Patricia both, when she got the safecracker's case."

Jack only vaguely remembered but nodded anyway. "Okay . . . just tell me again what you were saying."

"When the Taco Pal was robbed and my uncle shot . . . my mother doesn't think it was an accident."

"Not an accident? Why would she think that? There was a police shootout for Christ's sake."

"I don't know, really. Something somebody said to her. She's not real clear anymore. Her breakfast's usually a couple of bloody mary's and a banana." She paused. "Uncle Henry was supposed to go before a grand jury . . . you know, the kind that investigates stuff. She's paranoid I know, but since I told her that you . . . Patricia was working on the Taco Pal thing, she's been buggin' me to try to get some dope on what happened. The cops just said there'd be an investigation. That was it. Nothing after that. Mom even called her old boyfriend, the guy I told you about. But he and Henry never got along, and he wouldn't help. He was even there. I don't know." She sighed.

He shook his head, trying to sort this out. "Was there an investigation?"

"They told her it was *de-termined* Uncle Henry's shooting was an accident and everything was confidential. See what I mean?" She stared at him, her eyes moist, sad.

"Yeah, I see," he said, nodding slowly. He finished his beer and signaled for another. She continued to eye him fixedly.

"I *can't* ask Patricia," Kitty said. "She thinks I'm a ditz. She'd just brush it off. Say it's crazy."

"I don't know about that," Jack said. She was right, though.

"Jack," she said, "you will try to find out . . . for me, won't you? What really happened?"

"Sure," he said, not sure about anything. "Don't worry about what Patricia thinks. Dick's the one that counts—he and Lacey, and she'll do what Dick wants." He placed his hand on Kitty's forearm and squeezed it lightly. "He likes you."

"Yeah, he's a nice old man." She shrugged. "Only he always bends too close to talk and rubs my arm." She giggled and, moving closer, rubbed Jack's arm with hers. Jack laughed and rubbed back. She stayed there, close against him, as he finished his beer and she drained the margarita down to the quarter of lime in the bottom of the glass.

"You have plans for dinner?" he asked.

"Just with you."

"Why don't we get a pizza to go?" He nodded toward the kitchen in back. "We can pick up some beer on the way . . ." He stopped. "Fu-u . . ."

"What's wrong? Then her face lit up. "Oh ho-o-o. Patricia."

"Yeah. That could be awkward."

"Afraid to bring another girl into your little love nest?"

"Cut it out. It's . . . three's a crowd. And she thinks you're too young."

"But you know better, right?" She grinned at him and placed her hand on his forearm. "It's okay."

His disappointment must have shone. She picked up her purse, a smallish leather pouch, and placed it in front of her, on the edge of the table. Fishing inside, she pulled out a key and held it up.

"I may live with my mother, but I have a friend with an apartment in town. I stay there sometimes." She closed her fingers around the key and shook her hand toward him, knuckles forward, as if she were knocking on a door.

"My friend's out of town."

Chapter Nineteen – Post Kitty

HE DIDN'T SEE PATRICIA UNTIL AFTER LUNCH. When he went home to change, she was long gone. When he arrived in the office mid-morning, she was in court, another appointed case: an armed robbery, first offense. First time the kid got caught, Aerial said.

Staring out the window, Jack tried to deconstruct the bollixed deeds that had led the Madison sisters to take over Patricia's client's house. He hoped the puzzle would push any other thoughts out of his mind, but every time someone went by, he looked up to see if it was Kitty. It wasn't—only Lacey or Aerial, and Aerial always stopped to ask if he needed anything. Finally, he got up and closed the door.

Back at his desk, a call to Millie, who seemed to know everyone in the black community, revealed that the Reverend Madison's wife of more than fifty years was still living and in a nursing home outside town. She had "old-timers," Millie said, and her daughters took care of things for her.

Next, he researched the common law of dower, which he only vaguely recalled from law school. Abolished and replaced by a statutory spousal right: an automatic claim to a third of any real estate the other spouse obtains during the marriage. *Any* real estate, however briefly. It was a mistake. None of them, wife or daughters of Reverend Madison, should have any legal *right* to the Jones property. Yet Bettina Madison's failure to join in the deed back to the McFee company would give a specter of validity to the Madison family's claim.

A slightly more tedious search of the law firm files turned up the old plat for the moribund McFee subdivision. He stared at the lot numbers, then located a more recent plat of the whole area in Fitz's files and stared at it. Ready to escape this morass, he started to put the plat away, but a passing glance at the adjacent properties stopped him. Evan Fitzhugh in several blocks and the A-E Land Company in three tracts adjacent to Fitzhugh. More than he'd noticed before.

More and more curious about the A-E Land Company, he called the secretary of state's office to check the records of incorporations. As usual, there wasn't much detail, and the acronym could represent several different names: Agri-Enterprises and two others beginning with "American." But one, the clerk said, was listed as the plain A-E Land Company, nothing else. The business purpose was land development and such other ventures as deemed appropriate by law. The incorporators—Joe Mayes and Hal Goodman, the only two names listed.

Well, goddamn! he thought, hanging up the phone. *The shit gets deeper and deeper. Mayes and Goodman. They'd be only nominal parties, fronting for the real owners.* He leaned back in his chair and stared out the window. *Does Fitz know about this?*

He ate by himself at the counter at Cisco's, a greasy spoon on Main Street. A bowl of chili and a Budweiser, no imported beer in this joint. The onions he left off since he had to talk with Patricia. It was well he did.

"You didn't come in last night," she snapped, still scratching away on a legal pad in front of her. "No stomping around upstairs. No car."

"How did your case go?" He braced his feet against the corner of her desk.

"Pled to one count. Probation." The pencil lead broke, and she reached for a pen in a holder to one side of her desk. "You had me worried. I thought maybe something had happened to you."

"It did." He grinned, exuding far more self-confidence than he felt. "I should've called."

"I'm not your mother. You—" She stopped as Aerial went by the door, slowing to peek in. "Shut the door," Patricia said, loud enough for Aerial to hear. He shut the door, first giving Aerial an apologetic grin. As he turned, Patricia asked, "You wanted to talk to me about something?"

"I did the title search on the Jones house, and it ain't good." Dropping into the chair again, he propped his feet against the corner of her desk and told her about the problem with the reconveyance of the lot. He concluded with, "The Reverend Madison's wife is still alive."

"Fuck!" said Patricia. "I'll never get those old bats out of there without a fight. Leon'll think he can extract some cash out of this."

"Go lay it all out to him. Any interest the old lady or the daughters can claim is meaningless."

She gave him a sour look.

"You think Leon's even figured this thing out?" he asked.

"Of course the old fox has figured it out. He sees dollar signs."

"Ms. Jones may be seeing some dollars from somebody, too. Like us."

"Damn!" She hit her desk with her fist. "I'm not going to let Leon Hayes get away with this. I'll add a claim for damages—fifty grand, a hundred."

"What for? Lost rent? And those old birds don't have a thing you can touch. All you need to do is clear the title. It was a mistake."

Patricia jotted notes on a yellow legal pad. "Maybe trespass, wrongful conversion, something like that," she muttered as she wrote.

"I learned a couple more interesting things," he said, letting his feet slide to the floor and sitting up.

"What's that?" She ripped off her page of notes and, not looking at him, started on a blank sheet.

He watched as she scribbled furiously on the pad. A strand of hair fell across one eye, and she brushed it aside. Examining her downturned face, he thought, *Should I tell her about Joe Mayes and Hal Goodman and the A-E Land Company?*

"Well?" she asked, without looking up.

"Nothing," he said, still thinking. *There's only one person Mayes and Goodman triangulate on: the mayor, Joe' golfing buddy and Goodman's boss. Why would Mayor Fisher and his cronies buy up land out there? The A-E Land Company? Why else? Like Fitz, to sell it to the cities for the energy project.*

She stopped writing and squinted at Jack over her raised pen. "I want to get this complaint drafted. Can't we talk later?"

"Another thing." He hesitated. He couldn't mention the A-E Land Company—or anything else that might involve his best-paying client.

"What is it?" Patricia asked in a sharp, impatient tone.

"Kitty's uncle was the guy killed in your client's little caper."

He thought he had outgrown blurting out things that sounded guilty in the extreme, even if he was avoiding something else.

Patricia held her pen in midair and stared at him, her mouth open. "You stayed with *her* last night?" She slapped the pen down on the pad.

"You *spent - the - night* with that little redheaded . . . *ditz*?"

He winced. "What I'm trying to tell you—Henry Royale, the guy shot at his car, was her uncle, and her mother—"

"Jack, she's only nineteen." Patricia was glaring at him.

"Wh-h-at?" It was his time to smirk, once he understood what Patricia meant. "She's twenty-two. She told me."

"She's lying. She's nineteen. It's on her application."

"I don't care, damn it! Listen to me. There was a police investigation."

"I know that already," Patricia said, leaning back in her chair.

"And Kitty's mother couldn't get beans out of the cops about it."

Patricia's eyebrows knitted in thought. She flicked the errant strand of hair away from her eye again, and an idle thought floated into Jack's mind. *She's really quite attractive.* He'd seen her in running shorts and a tank top, and he knew she had a nice shape, not a lax muscle anywhere, the only woman he knew with real biceps. Her face was a bit angular, with high cheekbones, and it made her seem cold and aloof.

"Oh, yeah," Patricia murmured, the hostility in her eyes and voice gone. "I meant to check on that." She made a face and bit her lower lip. "Probably closed to the public."

"Royale's own sister couldn't get in."

"Doesn't matter." Patricia waved her hand. "There has to be a transcript, and the D.A. will have to turn it over . . . for the trial." She squinted at him again. "Billy asked me to find out how his partner died."

"So I can tell Kitty you'll check it out? What happened?" He felt he owed the girl that much.

"You can tell Kitty any damn thing you please. But you better watch yourself." She shook the pen at him. "She works for you, and you're almost ten years older than her."

Chapter Twenty – Firestorm

PATRICIA WAS FINISHING HER FINAL CHANGES to the *Jones v. Madison* complaint when the phone rang. The interoffice line. Lacey.

She picked it up, and before she could utter a sound, Lacey said, "Two detectives are out here. Say they need to talk to one of the lawyers."

"They say what it's about?" Her first thought was Billy. *He's escaped again.* "They didn't ask for me, did they?"

"No on both counts. Just one of the lawyers. Said it'd be best they wait and tell you."

Patricia was silent, thinking. *That's strange. It must not be Billy or . . .* A shiver of fear ran through her entire body. *Last time anything like this happened, it was her brother Sid. But it couldn't be anything to do with her personally.* *"Just one of the lawyers."* Hmmm. *Maybe they caught Aerial selling drugs.*

"Is Aerial in yet?"

"Making copies for Jack."

"How about Kitty and Dick? They here?"

"Dick's in Atlanta, and I haven't seen Kitty since day before yesterday."

"What? She didn't come in yesterday?"

"Well, she *is* part time, and there's not a lot going on. Jack said she had to go see about her mother or something."

"He's here, right? He'd better not—"

"Hard at work."

"Okay," she said, "bring them back . . . What are their names?"

"Detective Reese and Detective Goodman."

"Goodman?" She remembered him, his creepy stare when she and Dick met with the mayor at the City Club. "Wait! Take them to the conference room—and get Jack to meet me there . . . No, offer them some coffee; I'll go get Jack."

Jack was as puzzled as she was, and he looked just as worried. He did remember Goodman, though. Especially the man's size and the stray eye.

In their few minutes talking in Jack's office and their walk to the conference room, they covered a lot of speculative territory: Billy and his girlfriend and Billy's car, Aerial, Fitz—even Dick and the firm. They decided it couldn't be about any of their clients—the D.A. would've called them—or about Dick and the firm. Only concern there was old Gladys McFee's trust and the IRS, but that wouldn't be the local cops.

When they opened the door, they found the detectives on the far side of the conference table, facing Dick's full-length portrait, each with a plastic cup of coffee in front of him. Patricia had her own mug, a fundraiser giveaway from the local classical station. With cold coffee. She also had a legal pad and a pen in case she needed to take notes. Jack was empty handed, as usual.

Goodman remained seated, leaning back in his chair and reaching out to grab his coffee as they entered. The other cop stood and stretched forward to offer his hand across the table.

"Gilbert Reese. I'm with the Carrville PD, and this is Detective Goodman." He motioned to Goodman, cradling his coffee in two big hands close to his chest.

She tried not to stare at Goodman. He wasn't so much ugly as hard looking. His one eye canted to the left away from her while the other seemed to scan her like an x-ray. She wondered how it happened. At birth? A savage fight? Not something the man could help, but it gave her the creeps. Or was it the way one gimlet eye stayed focused on her?

Detective Reese was a study in contrast. Fair skin, fair hair thinning above a high forehead, and a face that was benign and non-threatening. More overweight than solid like Goodman and a bit plodding in his movements.

Once the introductions were completed, Patricia pulled out a chair, and Jack dropped into the one beside her. The blinds behind the detectives were open, and the light coming through made her squint as she warily scrutinized the two across the table.

"We need some information about one of your secretaries," Goodman said, placing his plastic coffee cup on the table.

"Catherine Simms," said Reese.

Patricia glanced at Jack and saw him biting his lower lip. But he didn't say anything.

"She in some sort of trouble?" Patricia automatically jotted "Kitty" at the top of her legal pad. Then she scratched it out and wrote "Catherine Simms."

"When's the last time she was at work?" Goodman asked.

"Day before yesterday, I think. She didn't come in yesterday . . . did she, Jack?" Patricia swiveled her chair to look directly at Jack.

"No." Jack's face was scrunched up, concerned. "Is something wrong, Detective? She missing or something?"

"Not exactly," Goodman said.

"Do you folks know if she lived with her mother?" Reese asked. "Jimbo's Best Trailer Park, out on the River Road, west of town?"

"I think she did," Jack said. Then, shaking his head, he added, "I don't know where or the name of the park. What's this about?" Jack shifted in his chair, leaning over the table toward Reese.

"Her mother's trailer burned—"

"All the way to ground," interjected Goodman, "nothing but a metal frame and ashes—"

Jack gave a sharp intake of breath as Reese talked over Goodman. "They found two bodies and we're trying to figure out who they are."

Jack expelled his breath in a low moan. Patricia swung her eyes from Reese to Jack. His face was so pale it almost matched the wall behind him. She glanced back at Reese and Goodman. They were also staring at Jack.

"You have some reason to think one of those bodies might be your secretary, Mr. Alexander?" Goodman's face gave no hint of sympathy or any other emotion. Like he was asking a stranger for directions.

"They were both women," said Reese, his tone softer, falsely compassionate like a funeral home director.

"Oh, God!" Jack slumped back in his seat, his hands gripping the chair arms.

"We know . . . we think one was Margaret Simms," said Reese, "because it was an older woman, and it was her trailer. Medical examiner told us—"

"Why do you think the other might be Kitty?" Patricia asked. A sulfurous taste of boiled egg from breakfast welled up in her throat at the thought of the two people in the trailer. She didn't want anything to happen to the girl, especially something like that. She willed herself to stay calm. Jack certainly didn't look in any shape to deal with the situation.

"Neighbors said a young girl stayed there some," Reese said. "Thought it might be the woman's daughter. Nice looking. Peppy sort."

Goodman was still staring at Jack with his one eye. "You think it's her, don't you?" he asked.

"No!" Jack almost shouted, going forward toward Goodman over the table. Then slumping back in the chair, he added in a low voice, "I don't know."

Patricia placed a hand on his arm. His hands, no longer gripping the chair arm, were shaking. Her own stomach was doing back flips.

"When . . . when did it happen?" Jack asked, pulling his arm away from Patricia. "The fire?"

"Last night about eleven," said Reese. "Actually, there was a big explosion, neighbor told us. Burned the trailer to the ground. One beside it was empty, and it got singed pretty bad, too. They're at the end of the road, out next to the river, only a big field behind 'em. Me and a couple of others spent a long time interviewing people 'round there last night. Sounds like a gas leak and . . ." he shrugged, "all you need is a source of ignition. Fireman found the bodies—"

"So why are you coming to see us?" Patricia asked. Reese's sheepish tone and his shifting glances between them and the door gave her the impression he didn't want to be here, that he thought this was a waste of time.

"Just trying to ID the bodies, and Hal," he twisted a thumb at Goodman without looking at him, "suggested she worked here and we ought to—"

"Lady in the registrar's office told me she'd seen her with Mr. Alexander." Goodman's voice came out in a low growl. "Couple of days ago. It's an open investigation and we have to check all the angles."

An alarming thought occurred to Patricia. "You don't think somebody set the fire, do you . . . caused the explosion?" She addressed the question to Reese.

"Like Hal said, it's an open investigation. But we haven't found—"

"Arson team's going over the site," Goodman said. He scowled, his face and one eye directed at Jack. "You still haven't answered my question. You have any reason to think one of 'em was young Miss Simms? The daughter?"

Jack gave a long sigh and shook his head. "Not really." The rest of his body was still, under control. "She lived with her mother. Or I thought she did. I've never been out there."

"I didn't . . . I don't know anything about her private life," Patricia said. The sun had shifted, and the glare from the open blinds was becoming unbearable. Getting up to go close the blinds, she added, "She was only part time."

"When's the last time you seen her?" Goodman asked Jack as Patricia reached the window.

"God, I don't know," said Jack.

She turned and stared at Jack from behind the detectives. The only glare now was emanating from her. *You don't know?* She almost said it out loud. *My God, is he going to lie to them?* He was quiet, looking off like he was thinking. *Probably searching for a way to get out of this without revealing his little sleepover with the girl.*

As he looked back at the detectives, she caught his eye and fixed him with a searing glare intended to bore a hole through steel. Pursing her lips, she gave her head a small shake. Jack's eyes went down to his hands.

"I . . . I guess it was breakfast . . . yesterday."

She wrinkled her nose when he came out with "breakfast." Turning away as if to finish closing the blinds, she thought, *That must have been some breakfast. More than your usual cereal.*

"You met her for breakfast yesterday?" said Reese.

Jack was quiet, nodding slowly, while the detectives waited. On her way back to her seat, Patricia touched Jack lightly on the shoulder, thinking, *courage, boy, courage.* Putting on her poker face, more like her trial face when things weren't going well, she slid into her chair and clamped her mouth shut. Let him do the talking. She was interested in seeing what he had to say.

"Wasn't really breakfast," Jack said. "More like . . . coffee."

"Was that the last time you—"

"Where'd you meet her?" Goodman interrupted Reese. Patricia glanced over at Jack. *He almost skated free. Reese was ready to leave it at coffee.*

Jack took a deep breath. *Aha*, thought Patricia. *Now the truth?*

"Actually," said Jack, "I spent . . . we spent the night together."

Leaning way back, Goodman looped an arm over one corner of the plush chair, which groaned in protest. "Oh-h-h?" He paused, his one eye still fixed on Jack. "And *where* was that?"

Reese had taken a small notepad and a gold pen from his coat pocket and was opening the notepad on the conference table. His face had changed from bored impatience to intense interest.

"Look," said Jack, "I'd rather not talk about where we were with . . . with Miss Egan in here. It's personal." He held his hands out, avoiding even a glance in Patricia's direction.

She shook her head and grabbed Jack's arm. "Jack, you should have a lawyer present if you're going to talk to the police." Her reaction was instinctual: *Cops, a strange death, and one of the last people to see the victim. I want to hear what he has to say, make sure he doesn't have any exposure.* She stopped mid-thought. *He can't have any exposure.*

"What do you mean?" Jack pulled his arm out of her grip and turned sideways in his chair to face her. "Why do *I* need a lawyer?"

"I just thought—"

"We don't know there's a crime," Reese said. "And no one's said Mr. Alexander's suspected of anything."

"Do you have some reason to think he needs a lawyer, Miss Egan?" Goodman asked. His face held a tight grin, almost a leer.

"No, of course *not*." Patricia raised her voice, spitting out the words. Then thinking better of antagonizing these two, she returned to a normal, measured tone. "And I can vouch for where he was yesterday." *Well, except for the early morning.*

"And last night?" said Goodman."

"Yes, absolutely." She brought her hand down on the conference table next to her coffee mug but caught herself in time to soften the blow.

Jack had spent the night at the house. She'd heard all the usual stairs and floor creaks, along with water running and the toilet flushing. And his car hadn't moved—she would've noticed since hers was parked in the drive behind his.

Reese was giving her a funny look, his pen poised over his notepad. Both detectives were silent, waiting.

"Jack has the apartment above mine. I know—"

"Somebody gonna vouch for where you were, Miss Egan?" said Goodman. He jerked his thumb toward Jack. "Other than him?"

Reese gave Goodman a sour look. "Hal . . ." he started, but Jack interrupted him.

"This is nonsense. I don't need a lawyer." He had turned from Patricia to face the two detectives. The pallor in his face was gone, replaced by a crimson color that extended from his white shirt collar all the way up to his blond hair. His clipped words and angry stare were directed at Goodman.

"Patricia," Jack said without looking at her, "let me handle this." Then, addressing Goodman, he said, "I'll tell you exactly where we were last time I saw her . . . I'll tell you everything, and I don't need a lawyer or anybody else here." He glanced over at Patricia. "That okay, Patricia?"

"Fine. That's fine, Jack." With both hands, she pushed away from the table. "Just let me know if you *should* need anything." She looked back and forth between Jack and the detectives.

"This won't take much longer," Reese said, then cut his eyes over to his partner. "No one's suspected of anything. We're just trying to identify victims of a fire." This he said with some irritation—directed at Goodman.

"She told me she was going to see her mother," Jack said almost to himself, his voice low. He was shaking his head, his mouth set in a grim line. "I thought she'd be in later. God *damn*, I should have called . . . or something. Checked on her."

Patricia was almost to the door, but she came back to stand next to Jack.

"Was there a car?" Jack asked.

"Two," Reese said. "Both registered to Margaret Simms. An old Chevy that looked like it hadn't been moved for months and a little Gremlin—"

"Ahh-h." Jack groaned and twisted his head down and to one side.

"—next to the trailer. The gas tank must've gone."

Patricia felt a cold wave of despair—and anger—course through her body. The same agony she had felt when Sid died. Not the screaming outrage and crying or pulling her hair and pounding on the wall, but the same kind of emotion.

What must Jack be feeling? His head was still down; one hand covered his face. She placed her hand on his shoulder.

"Jack," she said softly. "It'll be okay." Knowing that it wouldn't be.

Jack nodded but didn't turn to look at her.

"Come see me when you're done. We—"

"Miss Egan," Goodman said, "we need to move along. We got other people see."

Patricia glowered at him over Jack's head; then she gave Jack's shoulder a squeeze and started out. As she opened the door, Reese called to her, "Tell your head secretary to come down here. We'll need to talk to her."

"She can wait outside 'til I leave," Jack said, casting a quick backward glance at Patricia.

Patricia closed the door and leaned against the wall. She couldn't hear anything from inside, not even the murmur of voices. *This is terrible. Horrid. Horrible for Kitty, her mother. And for Jack. He spent the night with the girl—how long ago was it? Twenty-four hours, a little more? Their flesh as close as . . . And now she's nothing but cinder.* Patricia gave a shiver. *How long has this been going on, and I didn't know a thing about it?* Standing motionless in the hallway, she closed her eyes and thought back over the past few weeks. *Allen was here . . . No, this had to be the first time. The idiot.*

Tapping her thigh with the notepad, she moved slowly down the hall toward Lacey's office. *What kind of feelings could he have for her? What was he thinking? She's only nineteen. What am I thinking?*

The sound of the Xerox machine came from the workroom next to Lacey's office. *Aerial? Should I tell her? Maybe she'd know something.*

A sharp pang of sorrow shot through her mind, displacing her calculating how to tell the others. Sorrow for all of them, for everyone who lives and dies. But especially for Jack. She had no reason to judge him. Or Kitty.

And she had work to do. A trial she had to prepare for.

Chapter Twenty-one – Billy's Trial (Act One)

THE INTERVIEW ROOM ON THE FIRST FLOOR of the old courthouse was nothing but a broom closet with a sixteen-foot ceiling and a single opaque window three quarters of the way up the outside wall. All it held were two folding chairs and a rickety piece of furniture no bigger than a television tray table for her to write on. Only the window and an ancient transom above the door kept it from feeling like a jail cell.

Dropping her briefcase and purse on the floor, she sat at the table—facing the door—and extracted a legal pad from the briefcase. With no more than a quick look around, she set to work on her "to do" list for the trial. By the time the jailer shoved Billy inside and shut the door, she was writing out points to argue for a plea deal.

He was dressed in an orange prison jumpsuit, no handcuffs, and the leg shackles allowed him to move at a shuffle. At least they'd heeded her plea not to load him down with chains. He shuffled forward to shake hands over the table.

"Thanks for coming, Miss Patricia."

Was that sarcasm? She held his hand for the briefest possible moment.

"Sit down," she said. "I thought we should talk before I go see the D.A." Actually, the new assistant D.A., Ray Malloy. She jumped immediately to the final point she had written on her list. "Your chances of beating the charge on escape are zero and even less on assault with a deadly weapon. The only thing we can argue is that you had no intent to kill. That'll save you ten years."

While she spoke, Billy maneuvered into the folding chair across from her and began looking around the room. He finally craned his neck to examine the high window.

He's looking for a way out of here, she thought, feeling a frisson of alarm. Her apprehension must have shown when he brought his eyes back to her.

"I'm not going anywhere, missy. But I could if I wanted to." He grinned at her, showing his crooked, yellow teeth, gaps and all.

"That didn't work out so well last time." She intentionally pursed her lips to show her disapproval.

Undaunted, he continued grinning. "If I could get outta here, I'd go get my stash. Pay you a little something for your services."

"Your stash?"

"A little something I put away for a rainy day—a little postal work that paid off real good."

"Look, I'm here to represent you in a pending criminal case, not help you with . . . with your other endeavors. I'm paid by the state."

Billy dropped his head and stared at the scribbling on her legal pad. "Yeah, I know. Just wish I could pay you . . . But I'll go with the flow." He looked back up at her. "Downstairs they got me in solitary, watching me like a hawk." He gave her the Steve McQueen smile.

"You need to cool it, Mr. Angel." She felt increasingly uneasy.

"Call me Billy."

"We have to try for a plea deal. You told me you could've killed the jailer if you'd wanted—"

"That's right, I coulda."

"That's your only defense. But you can't testify."

"I know that."

"If it's okay with you, I'll try to convince the D.A." Looking off, she practiced her argument. "The *fact* you didn't kill him, or do more damage as long as you two fought . . . and with that iron bar, shows your lack of intent."

"I was only tappin' him with it. Trying to talk him into giving me the keys." Billy made a tapping motion with his left hand moving in a small arc.

"So is it okay if I use that argument?"

"Sure, missy. I got nothing to lose by it." He smiled at her.

She grimaced back. Looking down and opening her briefcase, she dropped the legal pad inside.

"I'd like to see Judy Kay while I'm down here," he said.

She almost laughed out loud. Closing her briefcase, she stood and stared down at him. "I don't really think that's possible, Mr. Angel. Do you?"

Pushing back his folding chair, he clanked to his feet and moved between her and the door. A thoughtful expression crossed his face. "Yeah, guess you're right . . . Can you get a message to her?"

She looked at him askance, tempted to tell him she wasn't a courier for jailbirds.

"Just let her know I was here," Billy quickly added. "And I'm okay. You have the number where you can leave her a message." He smiled at her like a small boy begging politely for ice cream. "I'll be back at Central before you even have to call her."

"I'll see about it," Patricia said, going past Billy to the door.

"Thanks for getting' my car back," Billy said, turning with her.

"No problem."

"You find out anything about Lazlo? How it happened? We didn't have guns, you know."

She pulled the door open without answering him. A husky, overstuffed deputy rose from his chair and filled the doorway. Another deputy leaned against the far wall, his hand on the black gun in its holster. The husky deputy grabbed Billy's arm as she slipped to one side.

"I'm getting a transcript of the police inquest," she said.

"Guess that'll have to do." Billy held out his hands, and the deputy snapped on the cuffs, then locked the chain to the leather belt around Billy's waist.

Her appointment with the new Assistant D.A. wasn't until after lunch so she went back to the office. Exiting the elevator, she spied Jack in the hallway, coming toward her. He was wearing his suit coat and carrying a file. Head down, he looked anxious, distracted. Had he lost weight? He didn't appear in her office as much anymore and it had been weeks since they shared a dinner. But he hadn't stayed out all night since the time with Kitty—except when he went off somewhere with Fitz, golfing or whatever—and they both avoided mentioning Kitty when they crossed paths here or at the house.

"You have time for lunch, Jack?" she asked, stopping in front of him. He came to an abrupt halt.

"Sorry, I can't. Date with Fitz. Upstairs at the City Club." He raised his eyes to the ceiling. "He wants me to set up a partnership for him, some kind of energy venture. He's angling on getting money from the city," Jack gave a skeptical wag of his head, "using industrial development bonds."

"He is? Who are his partners?"

"Some people on the west coast." He shrugged. "I don't know 'em, but they must have a lot of money. One's from Vegas, I think."

She squinted up at him. "Nothing in it for Dick or the firm, is there?"

"Well, we are drawing up the documents."

"That's a one-off deal. The mayor's never gotten back to us, and we need more paying clients."

"I don't know, Patricia. I just run and fetch when I'm told." He looked at his watch. "Gotta go." He hurried on past her to grab the elevator door before it closed.

The dynamic between her and Ray Malloy had definitely changed since the days they worked together. Now she had to kiss up to him, when before she could skewer him with impunity. She didn't like the change a bit.

Extracting a legal pad from her briefcase, she asked about his wife and kids and how he liked being in the D.A.'s office. He asked about the firm and Dick and shot a few barbs at Leslie. Nothing about how she was doing.

"Terrible, Kitty dying like that," he said, "a terrible waste, such a beautiful body." Patricia cringed and gritted her teeth.

Normally, she wouldn't let that pass without a biting riposte, but Ray quickly added that Kitty was a lovely person and he didn't know any more about the fire than Patricia did. The cops were still investigating it.

"I'm damn glad to be out of that rats' nest over at city hall," he said as he settled behind his desk, already piled high with papers and books. The furniture and file cabinet had seen better days, and the floor was worn and scuffed, but the walls were freshly painted, institutional green.

"You wouldn't believe how screwed up that place is over there," Ray said. "Can't trust nobody."

"Leon Hayes seemed to be pleased to have the business."

"Leon!" He rocked and twisted in his chair. "That ol' darkie's belly will be so low to the ground, they'll be lucky not to step on him. He's got it dicked."

"Can we try to get a plea deal before tomorrow?" she asked, searching in her purse for a pen. "My man will go for escape and assault. Ten years max."

"You guys need to stop wasting your time on that Alt-Energy shit." Tilting back in the chair, he put his feet on the desk.

"Ray, I'm here to talk about our case. Can we work out a plea? . . . Ten years?" She sat stiffly in the chair, her knees together, the legal pad in her lap.

"Ha!" An exaggerated guffaw. "He escaped and tried to kill the fucking jailer. That's good for thirty. Then we'll jack it up to a hundred for all the other shit. You want to go ahead and plead to that, too?"

"That one goes to the jury. Tomorrow the only issue is whether he intended to kill the jailer when he hit him." She explained Billy's defense, and Ray listened, looking up at the ceiling. He shook his head before she finished.

"You don't expect a jury to buy that crap, do you?"

"Indeed I do. Because it's true, and it's the only *logical* explanation for why he didn't do more damage than he did." She leaned forward and tapped the front of Ray's desk with her pen. "Why waste the taxpayer's money?"

"I can't do a deal unless I talk to Steve." Steve Finnegan, the D.A. Ray rocked in his chair. "He might buy it, since we can lock the bastard up for good on the other indictment. We're looking at felony murder, too." He raised his eyebrows. "But he'll have to take twelve years on this one."

She was surprised at his mention of felony murder, but she didn't want to dignify it by arguing the point, now. On the escape and assault, it was about what she expected. Hoped for. She gave him a tight smile. "Can you let me know this afternoon?"

"I'll see," Ray said. He dropped his feet to the floor and sat up. "No promises though."

She stood, remembered her briefcase, and stooped to pick it up. "By the way," she said, bracing the briefcase against the desk and dropping the legal pad inside. "I want a copy of the inquest on the shootings. You can get that for me, can't you—for next time?"

"Maybe." He leaned over the desk and made a note on a ragged legal pad. "Wasn't an inquest," he said as he wrote. "Internal investigation of some sort."

"Whatever it was, it's pertinent to the alleged crime my defendant allegedly committed. Part of the *res gestae*."

"May be confidential."

"What's confidential about it? The cops trying to hide their fuck-ups?"

Ray grinned up at her. "Fuck-ups, Trish? I—"

"Just get me a copy of the transcript. Please, Ray."

"I'll see . . . When you getting out of that mess over there?"

She ignored him. "And, Ray, please don't make me stay up all night preparing for a trial when we don't need one."

Chapter Twenty-two – Billy's Plea

BUT OF COURSE, RAY DID. Long past midnight, she was still researching evidence issues, reviewing the rules of procedure, and outlining her cross-examination of prosecution witnesses. She arrived at the courthouse lugging an accordion file bulging with papers and a full briefcase banging against the skirt of a new black suit. As she maneuvered into the courtroom, a huge khaki-clad deputy reached over her head and pushed the door open. Removing his hat, he followed her in. Six-foot-four or better, he had a round, red face and a basketball head. A completely *bald* head. With multiple crooked and intersecting seams.

Uh-oh. The jailer.

Giving her an anemic smile, he moved to one side and stood by the wall, his hat by his leg. Patricia slid onto a bench seat farther down, to one side of the counsel tables where Ray Malloy and another lawyer were winding up their arguments on a motion. When they finished, Ray bounced over to the jailer and, gesturing toward her, said a few quiet words, then laughed. The jailer didn't crack a smile.

She felt the color rise in her face. Two hundred stitches in the poor man's head. Billy would do hard time for that, whatever she did.

"Plea's fine," Ray said, coming over to her. She stood to greet him.

"Why didn't you call me?" she snapped, resisting the urge to add, you dim-witted turkey. "I had to work all night." Not far from the literal truth.

"Didn't see any hurry." He shrugged. "Only talked to Finnegan this morning. He's not too happy about it, but he says we got better things to do."

You shit, thought Patricia. She managed to conjure up a benign smile. "So how do we present this?" she asked.

"We'll offer up the deal to his honor and see if he goes along. He may want to hear some testimony—"

"My client won't have to take the stand, will he?"

"That'd be nice." He gave a sarcastic grin. "But no, just the jailer, maybe a cop. The one who caught him."

"No more than twelve years?"

"That's what I'll ask for—what's in the statute for the escape and assault. No deadly intent."

That was how it went. Even the jailer's testimony tracked what Billy had told her—except in more detail. An open question as to where the hacksaw blades had come from. The iron bar sawed from the cell and applied to the jailer's baldpate weighed close to seven pounds. Ray handed it over to her so she could feel how heavy it was. Billy was telling the truth—at least on that. If he had meant to kill the man, he "woulda done it."

The best part was the cop who caught him. A stocky little guy for a cop, he had exited the front door of the old jailhouse in time to see Billy climb out of the bushes and start running—more like limping away, he conceded. But he'd left his gun inside, so he held out a long flashlight and yelled, "Stop or I'll shoot." And Billy stopped.

Twelve years was the sentence, the best they could hope for, but Billy didn't seem particularly pleased. He kept looking off, fidgeting beside her and twisting around, almost as if he were hopped up on something. *How could he score any drugs in here*, she wondered, *with the way they're watching him?*

Once the bailiff had instructed them to rise and the judge left the bench, two deputies ushered Billy out of the courtroom, and she wandered over to exchange pleasantries with Ray. No matter what she thought of his churlishness, she'd have to deal with him again. She was chatting amiably with him when someone called to her.

"Miss Egan, your client insists he needs to see you." A white-haired deputy who looked long past his pension date stood at the half-opened side door. "He's out in the hall, and we already got him changed and ready to go. You'll have to make it quick."

Billy was leaning against the wall, apart from the other prisoners, all shackled together in a line, except for him. Down the hall was the outside exit where the transport van was parked.

As she approached, heels tapping on the marble floor, the guard standing with Billy moved to the other side of the hallway. Billy was dressed in his orange jumpsuit with shackles on his legs and wrists. She stopped in front of him.

"What is it, Mr. Angel?"

"I wanted to thank you, missy," he said.

"I did the best I could with what I had." She stared at him. His eyes looked wild, shifting from her to the deputy to the hallway past her shoulder.

He lowered his voice. "Is there any way we can get my trial moved? You know, on the other thing?" His eyes darted about and he licked his lips. "Somewhere else, away from here?"

Setting her briefcase on the floor, she held the accordion file in front of her with her arms crossed over it. Between her and Billy. "Moved? On what grounds? Why?" Her voice was louder than she intended, and it echoed under the high ceiling.

Billy grimaced, and his head jerked side to side. "It ain't healthy down here," he said in a hoarse whisper, edging his face closer to hers. She could smell the stale breath of tooth decay, jail food, and tobacco. She drew back but dropped her voice to a whisper.

"What do you mean? Are you afraid of the jailer? His friends?"

"Nah, that ain't it. Jailer's a big dummy . . . I had a visitor." Looking around, Billy bit his lower lip. "Not someone I wanted to see."

"Who was it?" she whispered, bringing her face a little closer to his.

"Never mind that. I'll be okay so long's I'm not down here." He shifted his weight, rattling the chains. The guard on the opposite wall glared at him.

"They're not going to be in any hurry for the next trial," she said, edging back a step, "since they already got you tucked away. And we don't need to push it. That'll give things time to settle down, if it's the deputies . . ."

Billy's face became somber, and he moved closer to her again. She hitched the big file a little higher, to keep him out of her face. "Why don't you find out who killed Lazlo?" he asked. "How it happened . . . And that other fellow."

"I'm going to get the transcript on the investigation, like I told you. That's all I can do."

"Ma'am, we have to take him now," came a voice from down the hall.

A tall, good-looking deputy strode toward them. "Gotta hook him up to go outside." Billy's personal deputy pushed off the opposite wall and sauntered over to him.

"Okay," said Billy as the deputy clasped a hand down on his shoulder. "But you be careful—"

"Come on, boy," the deputy said, shoving him toward the other prisoners.

"Just find out about Lazlo, okay?" Billy said over his shoulder. "And let her know I was here. Talk to her . . . Judy Kay. You said you would."

She watched him join the line of prisoners. Several times he tried to look back, but a deputy pushed him forward. Picking up her briefcase, she turned and started off the other way, walking slowly and staring down at the marble floor's black-and-white squares, still puzzling over Billy's requests.

Who could have visited him down in the basement cell? She was sure she couldn't get a change in venue, and she was worried that all *this* was just another ruse by Billy, trying to use her to no good purpose.

Part IV

Chapter Twenty-three – Docket Call

JONES V. MADISON WAS NUMBER ELEVEN on the docket. Patricia had been preparing for trial, but the lawyers in two cases ahead of hers had told her they'd definitely go to trial this week, and a couple more were likely to as well. Taking a seat in the back row of the jury box, she doodled on a legal pad and half listened to motions the judge was hearing before docket call. Christmas was only three weeks off, and she was going to see Colin for the first time in over six months. Days of sun on the beach and nights of loving in a cool sea breeze off the Pacific. The gentle caress of his hands, his almost-luminescent blue eyes, his confident smile. And his mood swings.

What a contrast to Jack—poor Jack, although he had nice eyes, too. He must still be dwelling on Kitty, but she wasn't sure. The media interest had moved on to the next story within days, and the police investigation had seemingly tailed off to nothing. No evidence of arson or wrongdoing, according to Ray Malloy. Of course, there wasn't much left for the police or the coroner to examine in the end.

She cringed at Judge Davis' bark, berating the plaintiff's lawyer. A gravelly, whiskey voice. *What an ass, even if he is a friend of Colin's family. With that large, square face and iron-gray hair, he must've been installed here along with the mahogany railing and podium a hundred years ago.*

Another motion, this one for sanctions in a deposition. She looked at her watch. First, she had to get through this, then the dreaded Christmas party at Allie McFee's, and then she'd see Colin. Billy Angel would come later, after the New Year, maybe not until spring. He'd called twice—both so carefully monitored that his questions were cryptic, some sort of jailhouse lingo. He wanted to know what she'd found out about Lazlo. *Mental note—check on transcript.* And he asked if she had seen "Dolly Parton." Meaning Judy Kay. She might do that, but closer to trial. She'd made some inquiries about Billy's visitor at the holding cell in the basement, but none of the deputies or bailiffs knew anything, or cared to tell her if they did. And Billy had clammed up about it.

Ignoring the hum of voices, she stared off into space, at the high ceilings and portentous gray walls bearing pretentious portraits of the tyrants who had ruled this fiefdom. Long-shuttered windows. Polished, dark-auburn wood everywhere. Behind the railing were hard benches for spectators and all the way at the back, two heavy doors with tiny windows to peer through before entering.

The door on the right swung open, and Leon Hayes slipped in, hanging onto the door to make sure it closed noiselessly behind him. *Shrewd, Leon. Don't piss off the judge before you even reach the counsel table.*

No hope of settling this case with Leon. She wasn't about to pay good money in the Madisons' little extortion scheme—especially since it would probably end up being the firm's money. Money they didn't have.

Leon smiled at her as he took a seat in the gallery. She cut him a quick smile back, then looked down at her doodles.

What a mess. This, everything here. Dick had made no progress in getting the Alt-Energy group back. A complete dead end, at least for the McFee firm. But not for Leslie and Joe Mayes. Just last week, the *Times-Herald* had an article about the project. The state Supreme Court would hear the declaratory judgment case—originally *her* case; the Mayes firm was confident of success, and the cities were forging ahead, appropriating funds to pay consultants and attorneys, doing engineering studies, even investigating sites for the research complex. Municipal bonds would be issued in the spring. There would be industrial development bonds for private ventures, "to promote energy independence," according to Mayor Fisher. What the ventures would be and who the owners were, the article didn't say. Maybe Jack's rich client would land some of that money and help pay the bills.

She slashed her felt tip pen across the names she'd written on the notepad. She had to get out. Find another job. But not now, after Christmas. And Colin.

Judge Davis was almost finished flaying the lawyers on the sanction motion. Handing the file to the clerk, he rumbled, "Bring this court a petty dispute like this again, and I'll sanction you both into the next county."

Quickly gathering their papers, the lawyers scurried for cover. Before they were through the gate, the judge began his docket call.

To her consternation, he bounded through the first cases. Contrary to their earlier bravado, the lawyers she'd counted on for trials announced settlements; then his honor entered a default judgment for the plaintiff on a failure to answer and referred another case to mediation. The next four cases were continued or settled.

Now she was focused and paying attention. Her case was third in line for trial. First ahead of her was a personal injury claim, a jury trial. It would take two, three days, if it didn't settle midway.

She listened carefully to the lawyers in the following case, the one right before hers: *Goldstein et al. versus John E. Scales and Carrville Bank.* A fraud claim by four homeowners against an appraiser and the bank to which they owed money. Sitting next to the lawyer for the appraiser was a little man in a too-large suit. John E. Scales. He and his firm did a lot of business in town, including appraisals for mortgages handled by the McFee Savings Bank. Scales looked like a riverboat gambler: thin moustache, small sharp eyes, dark, combed-back hair. Nixonian, but with a small face and no chin.

She tried to remember. Hadn't he done appraisals on some properties Jack's client had been buying? She'd seen Scales somewhere with Fitz. The country club? Where the local honchos hung out and played golf.

Two empty seats down from her, a pale woman in a trim business suit and a white blouse with a floppy bowtie was furiously taking notes while the judge quizzed the attorneys on how long their trial would take. Patricia slipped into the seat next to her.

"You know anything about this case?" she asked in a whisper.

The woman slowed her scribbling but didn't stop and only glanced at Patricia. "Owners tried to sell their houses," she said in a low voice, "found out they couldn't get anywhere near what they paid, and what they owed the bank . . . Claim the original appraisals were too high. They're alleging fraud by Scales and the bank. The bank's cross claimed against Scales."

"Well, they agreed to the price they paid and the loan amount, didn't they?" Another frivolous case, to her mind.

"That's what we think," the woman said, giving Patricia a tight smile. She stopped writing. "I'm here for Commerce Savings in Atlanta. We have some of the same issues. What complicates things is that the plaintiffs are second buyers in a real estate flip by speculators. The builder's bankrupt and long gone. We're trying to figure out if there was some sort of appraisal scheme going on."

"Any chance they'll settle?"

"No way. Too much at stake. The appraiser has to maintain his credibility, and the owners are going to lose their houses. The bank . . ."

Patricia's concentration on the woman's words was broken by a heavy silence around them. No one else was talking. Not the judge, not the lawyers. She looked up to see Judge Davis' eyes riveted on her and the woman.

"Are you ladies ready to join us now?" the judge asked. He peered at them from behind rectangular glasses perched on a big, red-veined nose in a face marked with more lines than a city map.

She felt the blood rise in her face. *I'm screwed*, she thought. Small beads of perspiration popped out on her forehead and along her neck, under her hair.

"Sorry, your honor," she said, mustering a bright smile and more vim in her voice than she felt. The bank's lawyer gamely echoed her.

"If we're all back in court now, we'll continue," Judge Davis said, looking down at the clerk below the podium. "The Scales case is second for trial. I'm reserving a ruling on the bank's motion for summary judgment, though I do see merit in it."

Like a bulky buzzard in black robes, he hunched forward over the podium and straightened his glasses to stare at the docket sheet.

"Next case is *Agnes Jones versus Edie, Annie, and Bettina Madison*." He looked up. "Mr. Hayes, Miss Egan, are you ready for trial?"

"Ready, your honor," said Leon, coming forward through the gate in the railing.

Patricia stood, holding her legal pad in front of her chest. "My client lives in New York, your honor. I need—"

"You're on the docket, Miss Egan. You need to be available *with* your client *when* your case is reached."

In a one-sentence ruling, the judge had already denied her motion for summary judgment: "Issues of fact remain for trial." Now he was subjecting her to an onerous requirement that her out-of-state client appear at a moment's notice.

"Yes, your honor," was all she could respond with.

The judge nodded, giving her the hint of a smile, like an executioner taking satisfaction in his trade. "*Jones versus Madison* is third in line. Trial to the court. Shouldn't take more'n a day or two. You agree, counsel?"

She and Leon answered together. "Yes, your honor." Leon was grinning.

"Next case . . ." the judge started. No longer listening, she grabbed her briefcase and headed out the side door with her legal pad clutched in her other hand. The lawyer for Commerce Bank had already fled.

Going down the hall, Patricia did a quick calculation. The first case could settle, but the second would take a few days. That gave her until . . . when? Thursday, at the earliest. Still, she needed to find Ms. Jones and what . . . ? Tell her to come to Carrville for a trial that might not take place for days?

At eleven thirty, a little more than an hour after she got back to her office, she answered the phone to the voice of the court clerk. Be ready for trial at two thirty. The insurance case settled before the lawyers began their *voir dire* of the jury, and the judge referred the Scales case to a special master as soon as he heard the plaintiffs' opening statement.

Chapter Twenty-four – The Trials of Judge Davis

STANDING AT PLAINTIFF'S COUNSEL TABLE—sans plaintiff, Patricia laid out the heinous violations of her client's property rights to a judge who seemed no more receptive than a hunk of granite. She could perceive no flicker of life behind the reflection in his glasses. But once she finished her description of the mistake in the deeds and its correction, acknowledging that a further mistake had been made in the omission of the Reverend Madison's wife from the deed back to McFee Developers, Inc. (a name she used as infrequently as possible), a deep rumble rose from the depths of the monolith.

"Call your first witness, counsel."

"But your honor, I haven't given the legal arguments—"

"I know 'em all. I did read your motion before I denied it, Miss Egan. We don't need to waste the court's time with all that mumbo-jumbo." He gave an exasperated sigh. "Just call your witness."

Flushed, her palms sweaty, she glanced at Leon across the narrow space between the counsel tables. He was grinning up at her, his hands folded comfortably across his belly. *Like he's done this a million times*, she thought. From the other side of Leon, Edie Madison, stiff and school-marmish in a neat gray suit, glared at her as if trying to impose a hex. Next to Edie was Annie, dowdy, fidgeting, and avoiding all eye contact.

Patricia picked up a transcript from her table. "I offer the deposition of Ms. Edie Madison as an adverse party. My secretary will read the answers to the questions." She motioned to Aerial on the first bench behind the railing.

Before Aerial could do more than stand, the judge held up his hand. "This isn't a jury trial, Miss Egan. Just give me the deposition and tell me what you want me to read. You have any objection to that, Mr. Hayes?" The judge's glasses shifted toward Leon.

"Not at all, your honor. Proper procedure in a non-jury matter like this."

She was panicking. Her heart raced. Her first delaying tactic had failed, and Ms. Jones hadn't appeared. Aerial had tracked her down in the Charlotte airport, traveling on business as a buyer for a big clothing retailer, but who knew how long it would take her to rent a car and drive here.

"My client's still en route, your honor," she blurted out, clutching the deposition with both hands

"You have other witnesses, don't you?"

"A clerk from the registrar's office . . . to prove up the property records. Mr. Hayes refused to stipulate . . ."

Judge Davis' eyebrows arched up and he scowled at her. "He has that right, doesn't he? You don't think you can come into court and have opposing counsel just stip-u-late your case for you? Save you the trouble of learning the practice of real law—not like what they teach you at that *fancy* law school."

She felt like crying. Her plan had always been to ask for a bathroom break if that emotion ever came over her in court. She looked around. Leon was solemn now; his face even exhibited some sympathy. Edie Madison, arms crossed, was nodding at her with a smug, satisfied expression.

Patricia glanced back at Aerial. The secretary's jaw was clenched. Almost imperceptibly, Aerial's hand came up above her waist in a tight fist, which she pumped up and down. It was like a thought flashed between them. "Don't let the bastards get to you!" Patricia slipped from behind the counsel table and, holding out the deposition, walked toward the judge's bench.

"Just give it to the clerk," Judge Davis said with a backhanded wave toward a woman seated below and to one side of his dais. "Mark the page numbers for the record."

"I have a list of pages."

"Fine. The deposition of Edie Adams is part of the record in this case, and the pages designated by counsel are accepted as evidence, subject to any objections. You may state those after the break, Mr. Hayes."

As Leon rose halfway to his feet without speaking, she handed the deposition to the clerk, then quickly found the list of pages and gave copies to the clerk and to Leon. She didn't say anything, still afraid she was going to cry.

"Call your witness, Miss Egan," the judge rumbled.

Back at the table, she stood erect and cleared her throat. *Fuck you*, she thought.

"Mrs. Becky Brown has been designated by the registrar to prove up the records, your honor. In response to, uh, my subpoena. She's here."

"Glad you got somebody here . . . Don't just stand there; get her on the witness stand." The last part a barking command.

Mrs. Brown, filling the witness chair and beaming genially at all, was sworn, and Patricia began going through the recorded deeds, one by one.

"Is that all there is, Miss Egan?" the judge growled after a couple of minutes. "I can take judicial notice of public records. Mark 'em as exhibits and hurry up with it. Mr. Hayes, you have any problem with that?"

"No sir, your honor." Leon popped up and back down. His grin was making her furious.

"I have a plat showing the two properties and—"

"You have any objection, Mr. Hayes?" the judge asked, looking at a deed the clerk had handed him.

"None, your honor." Up, down.

"That it, counsel?" The judge's glasses shone at her again.

"Pass the witness, your honor." Still no client, and it was almost four.

"Any cross, Mr. Hayes?"

"No, your honor." Leon bobbed again.

The judge looked at the clock. "I have a quick conference," he said. "We'll recess for thirty minutes. Be back here at four fifteen, ready to proceed."

As soon as the judge, followed by a pair of out-of-town lawyers, made his exit, she headed to the bathroom. *They got a good laugh out of that*, she thought. Her face was flushed, her hands clammy, and her stomach churning. Avoiding Leon, she charged to the back and lunged out the swinging doors, almost bowling over a middle-aged black woman hurrying to come inside. Patricia didn't have to ask who she was.

"Ms. Jones! Thank God you're here." The words came out as if she were regurgitating lunch, which was what she felt like doing.

"I got here quick as I could." This with a note of umbrage. A robust woman with an unforgiving face and straight black hair, Ms. Jones was dressed in a green, silk blouse and a brown business suit that looked a size too small for her.

"You're on next," Patricia said. "Let me get to the ladies; then we can go over what we need to cover. It's not a lot . . . just what we talked about on the phone." Not waiting for an answer, she almost sprinted down the hall.

By four ten, lawyers and clients were all back and seated at their separate tables: Agnes Jones with her eyes straight ahead, her face stoic and implacable, and Edie Madison glaring at Patricia. But no judge. Finally, at four forty-five, he reappeared to the bailiff's cry, "All rise!"

"You ready to proceed, Miss Egan?" Judge Davis asked, adjusting his robes and hiking up his sleeves, then leaning forward over the high podium.

"Yes, your honor." She had remained standing. "I call—"

"Mr. Hayes, you have any objections to your client's deposition . . . the pages Miss Egan submitted before our break?"

"None worth the court's time, your honor."

The judge managed a brief smile. "Proceed, Miss Egan," he said.

"I call the plaintiff, Ms. Agnes Jones, as my next witness."

"Good," the judge said. "We'll start with her tomorrow morning, nine sharp. Court's adjourned 'til then."

"All rise!" bellowed the bailiff as the judge marched past and out the door.

By ten after nine the next morning, Ms. Jones had been sworn, taken the witness stand, and identified herself for the court. At the first question, she launched into a tirade about the manifold wrongs done to her. Directed by his honor to "just answer the questions," she settled down to doing so with only a few digressions into the injustice of it all. Things were going smoothly, Ms. Jones talking about growing up in the house with her father, never any doubt about him owning it, when Leon fired a broadside.

"Your honor, I object to the relevancy of this entire line of questions," he said, standing and pulling aside his coat to reveal a long gold watch chain across his vest. "There's no proof here that this lady's father *owned* the house in question or that it's even the same house."

"Sustained," grunted the judge. "What proof do you have this *is* the same house, Miss Egan?"

"Your honor." She winced. That had come out like she was whining. "If you look at the plat and deeds admitted yesterday, you can see—"

"Just get your witness to give the address and identify it on the plat. Won't that match up with the lot number on the deed?"

"Yes, sir." She reached for her copies of the deeds and walked Ms. Jones through identifying the house without further interruption. Until she slipped and asked, "Isn't it true . . ." and Leon was on his feet again.

"Objection sustained," the judge said before Leon could open his mouth. "Miss Egan, can we move this along any faster?"

"I'm just wrapping up, your honor. Ms. Jones, did your father ever tell you—?"

"Objection, hearsay," said Leon, only half rising.

"Sustained."

She opened her mouth to respond, but the judge lifted his hand. "I know you want to argue an exception, but that's really not necessary."

"I need to make a proffer for the record, your honor. In case of appeal."

The judge made a noise that could have been either a stifled chuckle or a harrumph of disgust. "Go ahead. But whatever the plaintiff's father said to her is irrelevant to who has what interest in this house."

Her whole body felt like an electric current was running through it. *Am I going to lose this stupid case because the judge can't see what's going on here? Am I going to have to surrender to Leon's extortion?*

She made her offer of proof and, prodded by the judge, hurried through the rest of her direct examination of Ms. Jones. Taking a cue from his honor, Leon had no questions on cross, and Patricia rested her case. Without asking for dismissal, Leon launched into an opening statement, the brevity of which brought a pleased look to the judge's face.

"So," Leon concluded, "we leave it to this honorable court in its manifold wisdom to decide the rights of the parties and see that justice is done." He turned to his client. "I call Miss Edie Madison."

The judge nodded but said nothing. Stern and erect, Edie Madison marched confidently to the witness stand.

With the ease of an experienced trial lawyer, Leon guided his client through her testimony. Somehow, he had convinced her to speak politely to the judge in answering the questions—and not glare at Patricia. Expertly tamping down a couple of outbursts, he introduced the deed the sisters had found after their father died, followed by a letter from McFee Developers that came with it. The letter congratulated Reverend Madison on his purchase of a new home at 1534 Meadow Lane. Ms. Jones' house.

Patricia jumped up. "Objection! I've never seen this letter, your honor. Defendant's counsel failed to produce it."

"I feel sure we did, Judge," Leon said. "Counsel must've missed it."

"I did not!" In response to her request for documents, Leon had coughed up no more than twenty pages, mostly garbage.

"The documents are admitted into evidence," Judge Davis said.

"I . . ." Patricia started to tell about the sparse document production.

"Any error's harmless, Miss Egan," the judge said. "I don't see it adds all that much anyway."

Oh God, thought Patricia. *The letter complicates matters even more.* She slumped back into her seat. Now it was her own client glaring at her.

To the rest of Leon's direct, she posed only a few objections, all of which were overruled, one with the admonition that the court knew the rules of evidence and could disregard any hearsay without her help. In her cross-examination, she managed to elicit several displays of hauteur, but no admissions, only a stubborn insistence by Edie Madison that the property had belonged to her father.

Leon and Patricia presented their closing arguments, hers a methodical recitation of the property records and legal arguments, Leon's a submission to the court's sense of fairness and equity—ten minutes each with no rebuttal ("this isn't a jury trial, Miss Egan"). With Leon's spiel done and everyone seated, Judge Davis leaned back in his big leather chair and made a temple of his hands.

"Are we all finished, counsel?" He aimed the reflection in his glasses first at Patricia then at Leon.

"Yes, your honor," Patricia said.

"That's it," Leon said, bobbing up like a cork.

"Good." Staring down at them for a long moment, the judge rocked back and forth in his chair. "I'll give my ruling then." He turned his gaze to the court reporter whose hands were poised above the keypad in front of her knees.

"Judgment will be entered for the plaintiff on all causes of action." Then came a gruff, rapid-fire staccato of words that Patricia couldn't believe she was hearing.

"Title to the property in question will be cleared and vested exclusively in plaintiff. Further, plaintiff shall recover all lost rental income and related expenses for the time defendants have denied or otherwise interfered with plaintiff's usufruct of her property. Defendants Edie and Annie Madison shall bear the costs of this proceeding." He fixed Leon and the Madisons with a gimlet stare. "You all got that?"

Leon looked stunned. From the gallery came a not-quite stifled, "Yeah!" from Aerial. Patricia felt like shouting too—and jumping up and down. Instead, she maintained a deceptively demure demeanor as she gloated.

"Mr. Hayes," continued the judge, "your clients are fortunate that I can find no basis to award additional damages and attorney fees. This case is one of the most unreasonable proceedings to ever reach my court, leastwise where a legally educated lawyer brought it forward. I view your participation in this travesty to be either incompetent or unethical, or both. I can understand your clients acting out of ignorance. But you, sir, should not have allowed this matter to proceed." He cleared his throat and leaned forward as if to get closer to Leon. "I'm reporting you to the state bar for disciplinary action, *counsel*," he said with an edge of sarcasm. He turned his stare on Patricia. "Miss Egan, I'd appreciate a complete write-up on how this case came about."

By now, both lawyers were standing. Leon looked like a fish out of water, gasping for air. He started to say something, but the judge waved him off.

"Tell it to the Ethics Committee . . . Miss Egan, please bring me your report tomorrow morning. Eight thirty, in my chambers." He pushed back in his chair. "This court is adjourned."

Chapter Twenty-five – Saving Leon

PATRICIA SPENT THE REST OF THE DAY dictating and then proofing and rewriting her report. By six thirty, she had finished and cornered Jack into reading it. A fitful night followed.

Her client was not happy. Ms. Jones viewed the win as no more than her just due and the entire exercise a travesty, as the judge himself had called it. She was unlikely to recover a penny from the Madison sisters. Jack ran a quick check of their assets and found none other than their own house, which was covered by an exemption. Ms. Jones departed without a word of approval or thanks.

At eight fifteen the next morning, Patricia was already pacing outside the judge's chambers when his secretary, Mrs. Donnelly, a grandmotherly sort who was pleasant to everyone and ran interference for his honor without giving offense to any, appeared with a cup of coffee in each hand and disappeared inside. Moments later, the judge stuck his head out and beckoned for Patricia to enter.

"And how are you today, Miss Egan?" he asked, ushering her past Mrs. Donnelly's desk and back into his private chamber. "Glad that one's over with?" He motioned her to a leather armchair in front of his desk.

"I'm fine, thanks," she said and then rushed to get to the reason for her being there. "Here's the report you asked for." Handing it to him, she sat on the edge of the seat and placed her briefcase and purse next to her leg.

"How's Colin?" the judge asked as he went behind his desk. "He doing okay, wherever the hell he is?"

"Yes sir." She should've known he'd ask and prepared herself.

"I've known that boy all his life, or thought I did." He eyed her over his glasses. "I'll never understand why he threw it all away like that." He shifted her report back and forth on the desk and shook his head. "What it did to his father . . . It beats the heck out of me." He stopped, his eyes never leaving her. His face lacked the hardness from the day before.

She looked down at her hands in her lap but didn't respond.

The judge sighed and picked up the memo. "Okay, let's see what we got here." He leaned back in the chair and, holding the pages out in one hand, began reading.

Feeling numb, she let her eyes wander around his chambers: heavy black desk, dark-stained paneling, white diplomas and awards, thick Persian carpet filled with rich indigos and reds. On the credenza behind the judge was a row of photographs: wife, children, friends, grandchildren; on horses, in sailboats, next to cars. A younger version of Colin and another teenage boy stood beside an old MG sports car in one of the pictures. But it was a large painting on the wall above the credenza that dominated the room. The judge's grandfather: a Confederate officer on a white horse, both man and horse with lots of gold braid and brass. Behind the figures, in the smoke of a battlefield, waved a huge red Confederate battle flag. Her eyes came back to the big oak desk and the nameplate in front of her: Judge R.E.L. Davis.

The judge cleared his throat. "Not exactly what I had in mind," he said, staring at her over the top of his glasses.

"I just set out what happened. As I see it, your honor." She shifted back on the seat.

"You make Mr. Hayes' case rather well for him." He looked down at the paper. "You say here he got involved defending against a criminal complaint. He told you, quote-unquote, he had no choice but to defend his clients, make sure their interests were protected, and they weren't going to be satisfied until a court told them who owned the property."

"That's about it, your honor." He continued to stare at her. "In a nutshell," she said, nodding and smiling sheepishly at him.

The judge took a deep breath and let it out. Removing his glasses, he rubbed his eyes. Stiffly perched on the chair seat, she waited in silence.

Finally, the judge dropped the three pages on his desk. "I appreciate your candor, Miss Egan. And your generosity. Next time, Mr. Hayes may not be so lucky." A knock came at the door, and the judge's secretary stuck her head in.

"Call for you, Judge. Lawyer wants a TRO. Something about picketing and rock throwers over at the meatpacking plant. The usual."

"Thank you, Elaine." Patricia stood to leave. "Tell him to bring over his order—and don't bring that idiot manager again."

"Yes, sir." The secretary closed the door.

"No hurry, Miss Egan." The judge waved for her to sit down. She did. "I'll keep this little paper here . . . let Leon fret a bit." He smiled at her, a real smile, and she felt a weight lift from her shoulders.

"I'm glad it's over—unless there's an appeal," she said.

"Oh, Leon won't appeal, and those ladies won't find anyone else stupid enough to take their case." This time he gave a devilish grin. "The record's appeal-proof. I made sure of that." His grin softened to a smile. "That's why I was so hard on you. No court's going to find any errors there."

Chapter Twenty-six – The Christmas Party

THEY ARRIVED TOGETHER IN JACK'S decrepit Camaro. Greeting them at the door, Allie McFee swept Patricia away to deposit her coat and purse in a back bedroom while Jack, left alone in the foyer, surveyed the expansive, sunken living room with its sparkling Christmas tree and seasonal finery. Guests milled about the wet bar on the far side, near a liveried bartender juggling liquor bottles and pouring flutes of champagne.

Lena Fisher's piercing laugh rose above the noise of the other revelers. An almost empty glass held high, her backside brushing against the district attorney, she was talking to his underling, Ray Malloy. Her free hand rested on Ray's arm.

What a funny guy, Jack thought as Lena erupted again. Ray wore a Santa Claus hat angled over one eye and a bright red vest stretched tight over his paunch. A champagne glass in one hand, he held an Alvin the chipmunk puppet in the other, making talking motions at Lena's chest. Her slinky black dress showed svelte lines for a woman of forty-five—svelte except for the breasts. They bulged out the top of the dress in raised half-moons below a white string of pearls, both flesh and pearls bouncing and swaying as she cackled at the puppet.

Cutting his eyes from Lena's breasts, Jack checked out the other guests, most of whom he knew only as acquaintances, none as friends. All nine of the city council members were here—naturally, since Allie was one of them. Sitting on a couch near the television was Judge Davis and another state court judge, their wives in chairs opposite them across an oval glass coffee table. Nearby were the city controller and Leon Hayes and his wife, a couple of assistant D.A.s and their spouses, then the city manager and various business people from the town.

Shoving his hands into his pockets, Jack started down the steps from the foyer. A hand seizing his upper arm halted him mid-stride.

"Jack, Jack! Just the man I want to see."

"Hiya, Fitz. I was just going to get some champagne." He pointed to the bar, while glancing around at Fitz. Behind Fitz was the open door of the study—and the silver-maned mayor. Moving past them, the mayor gave Jack a brief nod and a "Merry Christmas" as he headed toward his wife's raucous laugh.

"Jack, I need you to do something." Fitz tugged at his arm, pulling him back up the steps to the foyer. "I'm on my way out. Come on; walk with me."

Jack made an about face, and they went up the three wide steps together.

"I've got more properties," Fitz said, opening the outsized front door. "And some refinancings for you."

"Why are we . . . ?" Jack started to ask, but Fitz hurried on outside. Stopping on the porch, Fitz gave a shiver inside his suit coat and looked around.

"Getting chilly out here. Glad I'm goin' someplace warm."

Jack was feeling the chill as well. He mumbled his agreement and hunched his shoulders against the night air. White Christmas lights festooned the Grecian columns and high portico roof above them.

"Now here's what I need you to do," Fitz said, poking a finger at Jack's chest and fixing him with a grin. "Set me up another limited liability partnership; we'll call it 'Star Energy.' Do it the same as the last one." He talked fast, glancing around toward the drive and his Jaguar. "And the new properties, my secretary'll send over the files tomorrow. You know, usual stuff. I'm getting new loans on some of the land; then we'll transfer it to the new partnership. Also I got a line on that house your lady friend won back for the Jones' woman." He nudged Jack's arm. "How you like that?"

"Why are we doing a new partnership?" Feeling confused, he was trying to sort out what Fitz wanted. "We're only moving the property around—"

"Money. Leveraging the investment. I've got new appraisals, and we can get more loans. Use the partnership as a platform for a new energy venture. Once the cities announce their project's out there, that land'll be worth more'n ever. Sell it to cities, pay off the loans, pocket the difference."

Jack stared up at the lights draped along the outside of the portico. "You're refinancing, and then you're transferring the properties to the partnership and getting more new loans, higher loans. More money. That right?"

"Smart boy!" He slapped Jack on the back and started down the steps. "We leverage it up and everybody makes money. You and Dick'll make a tidy fee out of it."

"We can use it." Jack pulled his coat tighter, wondering if *any* of it was ever going to come his way.

"Maybe a little bonus for you," Fitz called over his shoulder. He stopped at the bottom step and looked up at him. "Be gone 'til next month. Once I'm back, we gotta move fast, and I mean *fast*. Cities are gonna make *their* move soon." He swung around and, crossing the drive to his car, waved goodbye over his shoulder. "Just thank good ol' Saint Nick!"

At the top of the steps, Jack shook his head and shivered.

Back inside, he paused once more in the foyer. Before him was a bank-vault full of diamonds, pearls, silver, and gold—even a gold ankle bracelet he admired on one attractive woman. Thousand-dollar suits and dresses clad the pampered bodies of youth and the timeworn flesh of their elders.

These functions discomfited him, their sharp contrasts to his upbringing, to his relative poverty and his struggles to get here. His envy of all this bothered him, as did the taint on the money it would take to make him a part of it. Frowning, he stepped down into the room. *Who in this crowd is involved in Fitz's grand design? The mayor was talking with him in Allie's study. The D.A., the police chief, Leon Hayes—now the de facto city attorney, the city council, the city manager, and the controller are all here, along with two judges. Are they all rising on Fitz's bountiful waters?*

He got his champagne, one glass, a second, and a third—while circulating among those people he knew and didn't know, making conversation with some he didn't care for and with most about subjects in which he had no interest. He followed his usual rule: ask questions and let them talk about themselves.

Coming to rest in front of Allie McFee, he found the tables turned. She kept asking questions about him and his work at the firm.

"Patricia tells me you're the real money earner now that Dick no longer has the city to tap for his . . . needs." She wore a calf-length sheath dress, white with a bright red sash tied around her waist and a red scarf at her throat, just low enough to reveal a thick gold chain. *Christmas decoration*, Jack thought,

145

staring at the gold chain and trying to decide how to answer.

"It's mostly Evan Fitzhugh and his land deals," Jack said. He had dispensed with the champagne and now held a beer.

"Just so long as Mr. Fitzhugh pays his bills," she said with a smile. "That's what Dick always used to say."

Jack leaned closer, his beer at his chest. "Fitz should be able to pay. He's working on a nice deal with the city."

Allie's smile flickered and disappeared. Her face froze in a look that brought Jack up short and caused him to back away.

"What do you mean—nice deal with the city?" she asked. "There's no *deal* between him and the city."

Uh oh. She isn't in on it, and I've stepped deep in doo-doo. Jack took a breath. "Well, he bought all that property out on the Old Schoolhouse Road—"

"He bought *that* property. Why, those . . ." She gave him a curious, uncertain look. "Which property?"

"A lot of the old McFee development and a bunch of farm land around it . . . You know it?" he asked.

"Damn right I know it. Tony just gave us . . ." She stopped and downed the rest of her champagne in one gulp. Her eyes narrowed as she searched his. "What else is he up to out there?"

"Uh," Jack hesitated. "I'm not sure I . . ." He shrugged.

Letting her empty glass dangle in one hand at her side, she moved closer to him, so close that he could smell her perfume, understated and seductive.

"I'm on the council, and I still have an interest in that law firm you're with. Tell - me - what's - going - on." Her usually genteel face and relaxed frame had transmuted into that of a Greek statue. Her eyes bore into Jack's as he weighed how to answer. "I want to know," she said.

"He has a couple of ventures I'm doing the legal work on. He . . . I think, he plans to use 'em to get into the alternative . . . fuels business."

"And get bond money from the city to fund them and his high-flying lifestyle?" She glared up at him as if he were to blame for Fitz's scheme.

"I'm sure he'd like some help with the funding," Jack said, moving back a step. "But he's got some partners . . . a couple from the west coast."

"I bet I know who one or two of those partners are, and they damn well aren't anywhere near the west coast."

"Allie! You keepin' this handsome young man all to yourself?"

Lena Fisher swung up against him, grabbing his arm and giving it a hard squeeze, then slipping her arm around his waist. Instinctively, he reached around her waist to keep from bowling over. Lena's free hand held a tall water glass sloshing liquid down the sides. He caught the scent of champagne, mixed with Lena's sweet perfume.

"You *are* gonna leave some of this hunk for ol' Lena, aren't you?" She let out a cackle that resounded across the room. The police chief and D.A. and their wives steered past them and stopped next to Allie.

"I need to see my guests off," Allie said, her face frozen in an inexpressive mask. She glanced at Jack. "Thanks, Jack."

Allie took the D.A.'s arm and walked her guests to the foyer as Jack stared after her. A slim woman, statuesque and handsome. She reminded him of Patricia, an older version. The piercing laughter in his ear caused him to wince.

"Did you see that cute puppet Ray Malloy has . . . Kept trying to look down my dress."

"Enjoying the party, Mrs. Fisher?" Jack asked.

"It's Lena, dear." With her glass extended out in one hand, she swept around in front of him, forcing him back. Her low-cut dress had slipped to one side, and he kept glancing down to see if the woman's ample left tit was going to pop out against his shirt.

"Fitz's been telling me about you," she said, swinging her glass to her lips and back out to the side.

Now how does she know Fitz so well, he wondered. *Another lover? Same social circles? The country club? Isn't she on the board for McFee Savings, where Fitz gets some of financing?* Ding, ding went the cash register—Lena tapping her glass against his beer bottle.

"You're going places," Lena said, backing him up to the wall. "Stick with Fitz, and you'll all be richer'n Cro-shus someday." She threw her head back in a boisterous laugh. Placing a hand on his chest, she rubbed gently back and forth. "Too bad poor ol' Dick's been left out."

Jack lifted his face away from hers. "He'd like to get the city . . . all the cities, back."

Lena shook her head and gave him a mournful look. Now leaning against him, her breasts soft against his abdomen, the sad look became a smile. "We all have to move on some time, Jack," she whispered. "Maybe you should talk with Joe."

"Joe?" Not but one Joe she could mean.

She caressed his shoulder with her free hand, then pushed back, giving a one-two stagger before righting herself, her hand on his chest. "Judges are leavin'," she said, casting a glance over her shoulder. "Gotta say goodbye to the big boys." She tacked to the right, then paused to shriek at Jack, "Merrrry Christmas! And a *rich* New Yearrrr."

Jack wanted to leave. He found Patricia in a corner, under siege by Alvin the chipmunk, and she readily acquiesced to Jack's request. While Patricia retrieved her coat, he drifted back to say goodbye to Millie—and to beg her for some cookies to take home with him. Hand raised against the swinging door to the kitchen, he stopped dead. Harsh voices were coming from the other side. Allie's was the one he distinguished first.

"I can't believe we've been friends all these years, and you'd do something like this. We trusted you; I trusted you. We defended you against those accusations . . . Were those true?"

"Of course not. A damn bunch of lies." The mayor. He was close to shouting.

"You misled us, Tony. You're trying to make money off the project."

"Allie . . ." The mayor's voice was quieter, pleading.

"What Jack Alexander *told* me made me see it. You've got your hands . . . dirty . . . in the business side of this thing. I know it."

Jack cringed and moved back from the door. What had he done? The mayor's voice was so low that all Jack could make out was his own name and something like "shouldn't have."

Allie's voice was rising again. "I'm not going to let it happen. There's already been one investigation and—"

"Allie . . . !" There was a bump against the swinging door, and it opened a couple of inches. Jack stepped back, glancing over his shoulder. The door to the hall bathroom stood open only a few feet behind him.

"Don't, Allie—"

"Let go of my arm . . . After I get through with you, none of you'll ever be able to show your face here again . . . I said, let go!"

Jack started through the kitchen door, but it swung open, and Allie charged out. She gave him a surprised look, followed by a tight smile. She kept going as Jack slipped into the bathroom. He shut the door and leaned against it, waiting. For a few moments, nothing happened; then he heard the kitchen door open and steps go past, down the hall to the sunken living room.

With Lena stumbling and clinging to the mayor's arm, the two of them made their hearty farewells to all, including Allie, who stood holding the big front door open for them to leave. There were no kisses on the cheek for the mayor, but there were for Patricia and Jack. As Allie raised her face to Jack's, she held onto his arm and looked him squarely in the eyes, then placed her cheek next to his with an air kiss.

"Do the right thing, Jack," she said in his ear. Pulling back, she smiled up at him and took his hand briefly in both of hers.

"What was that all about?" Patricia asked as he opened the car door for her. "You adding the boss's ex to your conquests?"

"Ha, ha," Jack said in a deadpan tone, but thinking that Patricia could be a bit caustic, especially after Kitty. Slipping into the seat, she pulled her coat over her lap and looked up at him as if expecting an explanation.

"I'll tell you on the way home," he said and closed the door.

He told her almost nothing. Only that Fitz had cornered him about more work and he'd overheard an argument between Allie and the mayor—but he didn't know what it was about. Patricia was so quiet, he thought she was asleep.

"You awake?" he asked.

"Yeah, barely." Her sigh turned into a deep yawn, and she slumped farther down in the seat. The haloed lights of a few streetlamps flashed past, and they both were silent. Near their house, the streets were empty and dark. Pulling into the drive, he was struggling with whether to tell her more, whether he could avoid telling her more, since he'd already told Allie more than he should. *How long will it take for this to get out, and back to Patricia? "Do the right thing, Jack."*

"Patricia," he said, as he turned off the ignition. He glanced over at her. She was asleep. Going around to her side, he opened the door and shook her awake. As she roused, he helped her out and closed the door.

"Too much champagne," she mumbled, leaning against him.

Together, they crossed the lawn and went up the steps to the porch. She clung to him, her arm around his waist as he unlocked the door. Once inside, she broke away and shrugged off her coat, dropping it onto the floor in a tangle with her pocket book. Kicking off her shoes, she stumbled sideways and almost tripped over an end table.

"You okay?" he asked, catching her.

"A little . . . disoriented, that's all." She snuggled up under his arm.

"You need help getting to bed?"

She remained pressed against him, her head turned to one side, strands of hair tickling his lips. Then she stiffened. Pushing away with both hands, she straightened up. "I'm fine." Her fingertips remained pressed against his chest. "But I appreciate the thought."

"I'm . . . I didn't . . ." He held his hands out as she turned away.

"That's okay." She threw a hand up over her head. "Let's just leave it . . ." She was walking straight and steady now.

"Well, good night." He stood watching her from the bottom of the stairs.

She stopped and did a half turn in the hallway. "What was that . . . about the mayor and Allie?" She yawned.

"We can talk about it tomorrow."

"Okay. G'night, Jack."

Loosening his tie, he watched her bedroom door close softly behind her.

Chapter Twenty-seven – Allie

UNABLE TO SLEEP AFTER THE FIRST alcohol-induced slumber, Jack tossed in his bed until he was sure that the Main Street Grill would be open. When he arrived at the office after downing scrambled eggs and grits, the world outside his window was still a dark void dotted with electric lights. Sipping his third cup of coffee, he went through the file on Fitz's partnerships and compiled a list of documents for the new venture. His eyes and fingers moved on autopilot, but his mind was whirling through the nether reaches of Hades. He kept returning to the party and Allie's parting words: "Do the right thing, Jack."

She'd certainly made it clear to the mayor what *she* was going to do. What did she want *him* to do? He had no evidence Fitz was into anything illegal. Fitz might have inside info, but there was no law against that. Or was there? What Fitz did with the land was none of his business; he wasn't certifying a damn thing to anybody else. All covered by the attorney-client privilege.

An hour or so of work further suppressed his nagging doubts, and he soon had a pile of marked-up drafts ready for Aerial. Then Lacey appeared at his door.

"Didn't know you were here," she said. She handed him a stack of papers, divided into separate packets and held together by a heavy rubber band. As she leaned forward, he caught the strong scent of cigarette smoke not yet stale with the sliding past of the day. He took the stack of papers without saying anything.

"Messenger brought these over," she said. She was staring at the file and draft documents on his desk. "That a new company you're setting up?"

"You read upside down?" Jack asked, separating out the different packets. They were the four properties Fitz was refinancing. Nothing on any transfers into Star Energy, the new venture. "Anything I need to do with these?" he asked.

"Nope. Just wanted you to see what we got. His secretary called, said there's more on the way. We're gonna be busy."

Lacey would prepare the documents and he would check them, like tapping the deck in poker; and she would coordinate with the lender, the title company, and everybody else involved in the deal. At the closings, he merely waved the legal wand bestowed on him by the state bar and gave the event an air of gravitas.

"Jack, you finished with those? I need to get busy with stuff for Dick. He'll be here after lunch."

"Oh, yeah." Lost in thought, he had been gazing at a page. He handed the packets back to her, along with the draft documents. "Give these to Aerial, will you? We've got a while; Mr. Fitzhugh's away until the middle of January."

"Still has to get done . . . Where's Patricia? It's past nine."

"Big party last night."

"Oh, that." Her nose and chin went up. No secretaries had been invited. "I'll get to Mr. Fitzhugh's business soon as I can," she said, and left.

Jack sighed and looked out the window. It was a gray December day without hope of snow or even rain. He stood and stared down at the tinsel decorations and holiday lights stretched across the street at even intervals. *Without Fitz, I have to leave*, he thought. *I can't just dump him, move on to something else. He's the biggest part of the firm's income. My income. He's the only hope for making this place pay and . . .*

"Jack, take a look at this!"

Startled, he pivoted around. Cynthia, the new temp, stood across the desk from him. He'd persuaded Lacey to hire her when Patricia was busy with the Jones case. She wasn't Kitty, but she had all the right qualifications, dressed in black tights and a molded red sweater with large white snowflakes on the front.

"See my ring!" Leaning forward, she thrust her left hand across the desk. Jack pretended to examine the stone and its setting. "Where'd you get this?" he asked, looking up.

"I'm engaged! Larry . . . Captain out at the base." She bounced on her toes. "Isn't that exciting? I gotta show Aerial." She scurried out the door.

"Congratulations," Jack murmured to her back. So much for that. But he was thinking about Kitty. He stared out the window again and shook his head. *How could such a thing happen? A gas leak?* He'd met her brother at the funeral, and he said it was an accident. Friends, Lacey and Aerial, and only one other relative, a cousin, were there. Her Uncle Henry also died a violent death. *What had Kitty said—her mother didn't think it was an accident?*

He tried to work, returning phone calls about an estate he was settling and from a woman who wanted to go back to her maiden name while she was still married. The court clerk had denied her petition and she wanted to appeal.

"Heart broken, lover boy?" It was Aerial this time, leaning against the doorframe, her hand high above her head. She was wearing black stretch pants and a tight red sweater with white snowflakes to match Cindy's.

"Huh?" said Jack, arrested by the secretary's attire when he looked up. He wasn't going to ask.

"Saw Cindy's big ring. Doesn't look like you'll be gettin' any there." She winked at him and swayed in the doorway. Then she was gone, too.

Where the hell's Patricia, Jack wondered. *Maybe I should talk to her about this thing with Fitz and Allie. Maybe she'll go out for lunch.* He pushed back from his desk and started to get up.

"Jack, Jack!" Lacey came sprinting in the door. "I need to find Dick. Are you meeting him for lunch?"

"Why—?"

"It's Allie . . . There's been an accident . . . Her daughter called from the hospital." Lacey flapped a hand in front of her face, trying to catch her breath. "It's serious. She wants us to find Dick."

"No. He's . . . I don't know—"

Patricia stuck her head in the door. "He's at the airport. In Atlanta . . ." She slipped inside and stood next to the bookcase. "Talked to him ten minutes ago. I heard you in the hallway. What happened?"

"I don't know," said Lacey. "Sally wasn't making a lot of sense. Let me go check when Dick's flight gets in." She whipped around and out the door. Patricia came over and stood beside Jack's desk.

"Maybe I should go meet him at the airport," she said in a low voice.

"I was just talking to her last night," Jack said, shaking his head.

"Why don't you go to the hospital? Her daughter . . . what's her name?"

"Sally."

"Sally may need some help until Dick gets there. Jeesh, who knows what condition he'll be in."

"She was arguing with the mayor . . ."

"Let's hope she's okay." Patricia turned to go, but stopped to stare at him. "Snap out of it, Jack. We need to help . . . Jack?"

Not answering her, he stood. Face grim, he rattled the keys in his pocket. "I need to find out what hospital she's in."

It was McFee County Memorial. As he jogged up the steps to the main entrance, he spotted a large man on the level below, crossing the wide drive in front of the emergency room. Swinging around, Jack leaned over the stone ledge by the steps and squinted down. Hal Goodman. The big cop was hurrying toward the parking garage, his long overcoat flapping in a sharp wind that had brought in dark clouds. Jack shivered and bit his lower lip. *What the hell is he doing here? Some cop errand?*

Goodman disappeared into the garage, and Jack continued across the veranda and into the lobby. The receptionist checked a list, made a call, and told him that Mrs. McFee was in surgery. The waiting area was in the new wing on the second floor. Was he a member of the family? Ignoring her query, he strode off down the hall to the elevators.

The waiting room was worse than he expected, not outwardly unpleasant so much as functional and depressing. Of the several people there, he recognized Sally McFee at once; she was the only one younger than fifty. Dressed in faded blue jeans and a boyish green shirt, hair pulled back in a ponytail, she didn't look like Dick or Allie. According to Lacey, she'd just arrived home for the holidays.

She sat in a straight back chair, plastic with aluminum legs. An open magazine rested on her lap, her hands on the open pages.

He hesitated. Maybe he shouldn't have come. He didn't like doing this. He really didn't know these people. He swallowed hard and moved across the tile floor. He did know them, as well as he knew anybody in this place, and Sally needed his help.

At his approach, she looked up. Her face was solemn and showed traces of rubbed-off makeup. Her eyes, red and bordered by smears of mascara, had a soft, pleading look, like she wanted him to be the bearer of good news.

He held out his hand. "I'm Jack Alexander. Uh, I'm with the firm. I know your . . . I'm a friend of your mother's."

She took his hand and stood, letting the magazine drop to her side. His forward motion almost shoved her back into the chair.

"Mother's mentioned you," she said. Despite the distress in her voice and face, a small smile flickered at the corners of her mouth. "She keeps . . ." she hesitated and dropped her eyes, "kept saying I needed to meet you."

"How is she?"

Sally made a choking noise that stopped short of a sob and shook her head. Not speaking, he lightly touched her arm, and they sat down side by side in the plastic chairs. She leaned forward and placed her hands over her face.

"I only got to see her for a couple of minutes, before they took her into surgery, again." Now she did sob. "They cut away half her hair." She cried softly while Jack self-consciously put his arm around her and patted her shoulder.

"I'm sorry," he said.

"Everyone's trying to help. The mayor sent someone over to ask about her already." *Ah,* Jack thought, *Goodman. The mayor is ever the politician.*

"How did it happen?" he asked.

"I don't know." She sat up, pushing aside hair that had escaped from the barrette holding it in a ponytail. He withdrew his arm and stared at her profile. Lean, pleasant features. A straw-colored blond, what Allie must have been at one time. She pulled her hair back and cinched it with the barrette, displaying a slight but noticeable figure.

"Her car went off the road, the patrolman said. A one car accident . . . It turned over." She shook her head, gyrating the ponytail and releasing more hair from the barrette. "She'd be out there still, if some old farmer hadn't come by."

"An old farmer?" he said sharply, leaning away from her. "Where was she?"

"Out on the Old Schoolhouse Road."

"Old Schoolhouse . . . what! Why was she out there?" Even as he asked, he knew.

"I don't know." Sally took a deep breath and gave a long sigh. "Millie said she got up early this morning and went out by herself." She slowly shook her head. "She hadn't even had breakfast."

155

Chapter Twenty-eight – What the Transcript Shows

"IT DIDN'T TELL ME *ONE* THING I didn't already know," Patricia said, dropping the stapled copy onto Jack's desk.

The cover was green with a large caption: "Investigation of Incident and Deaths at Plantation Road Taco Pal."

"What a waste. I paid five hundred dollars and the judge'll probably refuse to reimburse it. That's what Ray Malloy says." One hand on her hip, she leaned her opposite thigh against the desk. "He told me *that* after I paid him for it. Damn him."

"Have you read it?" She noticed his eyes glance at her hips and cinched waist on the way up to her face. "You look nice," Jack added, smiling up at her."

"Just skimmed it." She ignored his comment. "Why don't you take a look? I've got to go clean out my inbox." Pushing away from the desk, she stood sideways to him and stretched to her full height. She was dressed casually for travel. Tailored gray slacks, crisp blue shirt with white stripes, three-button white sweater she would shed on the plane. "You *are* taking me to the airport, aren't you?"

"Flight's at two, right?"

"We need to leave by twelve. I don't want to rush."

"You're not going to see your parents over the holidays?" he asked.

"My mother's off to the Bahamas or somewhere. I'll go see my father when I get back. Are you going home for Christmas?"

"Do I have a choice? My mother sticks to me like gum to a shoe, and just as aggravating."

She started to the door, then checked her motion and turned back to him. "You hear anything about Allie?"

"Lacey talked to Dick this morning. He says she'll be good as new soon." Jack gave a wan smile. "You know Dick . . . She's still unconscious, head injuries, broken leg and pelvis. They have to keep a watch on her." He grimaced. "They don't know how long she'll be out."

"Do they know what happened?" She glanced at her watch.

"She was in her little sports car. Patrolman told Dick there were traces of green paint along the left front fender."

"God!" Patricia gave a quick intake of breath. "You mean someone ran into her and left her out there?"

"The old farmer who found her said a car passed him, going fast, four or five minutes before he came up on her. She flipped on a curve so who knows what happened."

Patricia shook her head in disgust. "How could anyone do that?" Starting out again, she paused in the doorway. "Any idea what she was doing out there? The Old Schoolhouse Road, right?"

"None." Jack hesitated and then added, "She didn't tell anyone."

"I know the road. The Jones house is out there." She checked her watch again. "Isn't that where your client's doing his big land grab?"

"Yeah . . . it's a popular place." Jack shrugged, but his face contorted into a frown he got only when he was vexed about something.

"Look, come get me at twelve." She hurried out, worrying that she couldn't finish everything by then—but pleased that Jack liked how she looked. So would Colin.

Jack swung the car out of the parking garage, then almost immediately braked for the stoplight at the circle around the old Slave Market. He glanced over at her.

"What did you pack in that bag? Taking your law books along?"

"Ha, ha, smart ass. I got all I need for ten days in one suitcase."

"Not to mention that giant carry-on."

"Did you read the transcript?" she asked.

"Sure." He gave her a sheepish grin. "Some of it." A horn honked and he accelerated through the light and around the circle.

"You saw who was on the panel," she said, looking away, into the shadows inside the old Slave Market, ominous even in the bright sunlight. "The police chief, a union rep, and Hector Grimes, the city attorney."

"Regular kangaroo court."

"The cops who fired their weapons testified . . . mostly what you'd expect." She checked her watch. "They got there first, two of them," she added. "There was also a deputy sheriff and Hal Goodman. You get that far?"

"Not quite. Who else testified?"

"The coroner. Lazlo died from a shotgun blast to the back, Henry Royale from a bullet wound to the head. The entry was behind the jaw; it came out his right temple."

"Thought you only skimmed it," Jack said.

"Read parts closer than others . . . Ray says he may go for a murder indictment. The shit."

"Really? He could have a problem there, couldn't he? It's not clear who killed Royale."

"Felony murder," she said, shaking her head. "Doesn't matter where the shot came from. And the cops say they found two guns . . . Didn't you read that?"

"Didn't get that far." He gave her a quick, "Sorry, but not really" smile.

Finally entering the interstate, they dove into noon traffic flowing like molasses. Patricia craned her neck to peer between the lanes ahead of them.

"We're okay," said Jack. "What about the guns? Where'd they find 'em?"

She settled back in her seat and closed her eyes. "Lazlo was running; cop told him to stop; he didn't, so the cop blasted him. Says he found a gun on the ground—next to Lazlo's hand."

"The ever-ready gun."

She sat up. "Just drive down the shoulder and get off at the next exit."

"Patience, patience. It's speeding up. What about the other gun?"

She groaned, then closed her eyes again and tried to go over in her mind what she'd read. "The cop who went after Billy . . . who went after the second perp said he thought there were two people he was chasing. Another cop joined him, and somebody took a shot at them. Second cop testified there was only one man, or that's all he saw . . . heard actually."

She sighed. "It's all pretty confusing."

"So Billy was found later—in a ditch?"

"Near the road. He claimed he took cover because of all the shooting." She laughed and turned to look at him. "You find that believable?"

"Maybe."

"There must've been a crowd of cops by then . . . Can you please hurry up?" The traffic was moving, but Jack had fallen back several car lengths.

"And the other gun?" Jack asked, eyes straight ahead.

She grimaced and fell back in the seat. "When the cops lost Billy . . . the second perp, they started crisscrossing the woods. That's when Goodman showed up. He's the one who found the second gun."

"Where was the kid?"

"Jenkins. A deputy caught him all the way on the other side of Plantation Road. It wasn't too long after the shooting started."

"And Henry Royale? Where was he during all this?" Finally, they were moving smoothly, approaching the exit to the airport.

"In the parking lot at the apartments. The cops found his body when they were doing their search."

"But what direction? How far from the Taco Pal?"

"Umm . . . Not real clear that I remember. I have to read it again, do a diagram." She shook her head. "But the apartments are back beyond the drive-through for the Taco Pal. And there are woods back there."

"Still, if Billy or Lazlo fired at the cops, they could've hit Royale."

"Even if they did, the bullets would have to go some distance, and through the trees." She scrunched up her face, puzzled. "Isn't that strange?" They were turning into the circle leading to the terminal. She looked at her watch. "Just let me out here, will you?"

Jack drummed his fingers on the steering wheel as they crept forward behind a line of cars. "What kind of guns did they find?" he asked.

"A .357 magnum and an old .22 pistol, a Beretta."

"The .357 might've done it. Maybe you need an expert."

"And who'll pay for that?"

"Did Goodman fire his gun?

"He was off duty and he didn't get there until the shooting was over." The car slowed to a stop, and she swung the door open.

Tugging her carry-on and purse out of the back seat, she met Jack at the trunk. After some shoving and grunting, he managed to remove the suitcase and drop it onto the tarmac. As she waited, she had a thought.

"Jack, will you do me a favor?" All sweetness. "Will you find Billy's girlfriend while I'm gone? I sort of promised him I'd talk to her."

"Dammit, I'm not your errand boy," he said, straightening up.

"Hey, you're practically friends with the woman." She grabbed her suitcase and moved close to him. "She's probably holed up down on Main Street, *dear*, and I can't go down there by myself."

"Okay, we'll go when you get back," he said, as she started toward the entrance, suitcase in tow. "When *do* you get back?" he called after her.

"After New Year's." The sliding door closed shut behind her.

Chapter Twenty-nine – License Plates

NOW THAT HE HAD AN ACTUAL SENTENCE to serve, Billy was off death row and in a regular cell. His cellmate, Clovis Henley, was an artist who made his own money. They both worked in license plates, Billy in stamping and Clovis in reflective coating. He had cigarettes and regular exercise and other professionals to chew the fat with; you just had to steer clear of the weirdos and gang toughs.

Clovis was the quiet type, until he got to know you, and he minded his own business, unless something sparked his curiosity. Billy volunteered nothing to him or anybody else. You never knew what could come back to bite you in the ass, even if your cellmate wasn't a snitch.

It was their third week together and right before Christmas. They were back in the cell after a long day in the shop and the evening meal, when Clovis asked him if he planned on hanging around long.

"No way outta here," Billy said.

"Heard you were pretty good."

"Good ain't good enough without opportunity. You know something I don't?"

"No," said Clovis. "With good behavior, I'm out in two." Clovis looked like a timid accountant: thick glasses, slight build with no muscles, and a funny little paunch. He did terrific metal work, and the warden, Clovis said, let him engrave the last supper on a silver platter—for the warden's wife.

Billy dropped to the floor and started his nightly routine with a hundred pushups, and they were silent. Then he did two hundred sit-ups. Thirty minutes to lights out and he didn't want to read. He'd given up on the law books, but he had an MBA embezzler, an expert on the law, to advise him now.

"Why would anyone want to steal a safe?" Clovis asked as Billy finished his leg lifts.

Billy wiped his face and neck with a towel and grinned at Clovis, who was lying on his bunk. "Why would anyone want to print five-dollar bills?"

Clovis smiled back and shrugged. "If you were going to leave, how would you do it?"

"Not from here." He turned and hung the towel on his hook.

"Maybe you could make a run for it at your trial."

"You reckon they bug these cells?" Billy asked, giving him a hard look.

"Cost too much, and it's too random. May not be legal anyway."

"I'll ask Sammy." The embezzler, his in-house legal adviser.

"If you had to, would you take someone with you . . . you know, for safe passage?"

"Your best shot's when you have someone outside to help you."

"But if you had to?"

"Clovis, I ain't going nowhere so quit worrying about it."

"Just curious."

When I go back down there, I may just be desperate enough, Billy was thinking as he stood peeing into the open john. Even if it wasn't for Goodman, he didn't plan to spend the rest of his life in this place. He zipped his pants. On the top bunk, Clovis was reading a thick book with no picture on the cover. Billy lay down on the bottom bunk and closed his eyes.

Down in the basement of the McFee County Courthouse, it was like being out in the deep woods when all of a sudden everything goes still and you know something's out there watching you, something you can't see, but you can feel. All of the other cells had been quiet. A light was always shining into the cell so they could watch you, while out in the corridor the lights were dim even during the day, so it was hard to see them. Late at night, the corridor in the courthouse basement was as dark as the tunnel he once got stuck in.

"My angel," a voice had whispered from outside the cell. "Looking fit. You gettin' plenty of exercise up there?"

Billy had strained to see him, but all he saw was a dark form where the bars ended and the concrete wall began. But he knew who it was: the low gravelly voice, the menacing sound of it.

"I have a system," Billy said, sitting up. He went over by the bars in the corner. "You gonna help me get outta here?" he whispered.

"Not that easy. You gonna keep your mouth shut?"

"You know *me*." Billy grasped a bar with one hand. "I'd never squeal." He still couldn't see Goodman's face.

"I'm wondering if I can take that chance."

A chill ran down his spine. He'd seen Goodman crush a man's throat while the man flailed at him. They never found the body.

"My lips are sealed," Billy said. Then he had a thought. "Did you kill Lazlo? Have him killed?"

"Fuck no. Just a bit of luck."

"You sorry bastard."

Goodman's face, or half of it, came out of the shadows and into a seam of light a little above Billy's head. The face was blank, a pale carnival mask topped by thick black hair, with a red-veined eye and fathomless black pupil.

"You haven't told that lawyer of yours anything, have you?"

"'Course not. She's as green as collards."

"You better not. That'd be bad for both of ya. Your girlfriend, too."

"She don't know a thing about you."

"Don't let me catch so much as a whisper out of you, or any of 'em. You got me?" A big hand closed over Billy's hand on the bar and squeezed. Billy fought the urge to cry out. Then the pressure let up, and a slash of light moved across Goodman's face and caught the other eye, looking vacantly off into space.

"Believe me," Billy gasped, still trying to whisper, "I'd never—"

"That's right; you sure as hell better *never*." Then the hand disappeared and Goodman was gone.

A voice came over the intercom, bringing him back to the present. "Lights out in two minutes. Get ready for beddy-bye, boys."

Billy stood and stripped to his underwear and placed his prison clothes on top of his work shoes under his bunk. He lay down and pulled a sheet over him. Clovis had already shoved his book aside and turned to the wall. The lighting, except the low ones for the cells, blinked off. But he couldn't sleep.

When he'd finally gotten to his new cell and had a turn at the prison library, he came across an article on Carrville and its mayor, something about an energy project. One short paragraph said a man they called a "whistleblower," an auditor in the Carrville Controller's office named Henry Royale, had started an investigation of the mayor, but it had died with Mr. Royale. He was the bystander killed in a robbery at the Taco Pal. *Shit!* Billy thought. *Did Goodman set up the whole thing so he could plug a snitch and make it look like an accident? Or make it look like I did it?*

The bastard was perverse enough. He'd latched onto Billy one night when Billy was solo and Goodman nabbed him for B&E and possession of safecracking tools, even though he wasn't even in the building yet. Goodman took his picture and fingerprints right there by an unmarked car, Goodman and another dirty cop. They let him go with an offer he couldn't refuse. Goodman had the tips and the outlets and a few well-placed associates in the police department, names Billy never knew, just like he never told anyone about Goodman. Until Lazlo. Judy Kay knew, but not his name.

He always suspected Goodman was working more than one angle. The mayor's driver and bodyguard. He'd never suspected the mayor was a crook—though with him having Goodman around, it made sense he was.

How could they have used the Taco Pal as a cover to kill Royale? They'd have to know the man's habits, his schedule, and make sure they were there when he came out for work. And the gun battle would have to be a setup.

There were small noises all around—coughs and grunts and murmurings in the night, and Clovis' snoring on the bunk above him. On the far side of the cellblock, the porpoise began barking, but the guards shut him up quicker than usual. After that came only the haunting night sounds of eighty people crowded into one big bay, two to a cell, men with dark secrets and multitudinous demons.

Billy turned onto his side and curled up, placing both hands under his head. *It wasn't a setup*, he decided. *Too many things needed to be arranged and come together all at once. It was just a matter of chance. Fate. The man must've seen Goodman running from the back of the building, and Goodman shot him dead, to shut him up. Goodman would do that. He wouldn't even have to believe the man recognized him or could identify him.*

Billy straightened out and flipped onto his back, hitting the wall with his hand. That still left a big problem for Billy Angel. He was the only living soul who could pin the murder on Goodman, and Goodman wasn't the type to leave witnesses—not those he didn't trust. He wouldn't take the chance of having someone, anyone, left alive who might put him in here—with a bunch of people who hated cops.

"You okay, Billy?" Clovis whispered.

"Yeah, I'm fine."

Clovis didn't say anything else, and soon he was snoring again. Billy took a deep breath and willed himself to relax—and to suppress the rising fear in his gut. He had to head Goodman off, but he didn't have anyone to help him. He couldn't ask Judy Kay, even if he could reach her.

His muscles began to loosen up some. He was okay down in Carrville for his next trial, so long as he stayed in a solitary cell or he was with the lawyers or in court. Or maybe he wasn't. Maybe he wasn't even okay here, with Clovis.

He had to get away. Until he could, he had to watch everybody and everything. Watch for his chance, his opportunity. Maybe on the way back to McFee County. Then again, his best chance would be during the trial. Maybe the lady lawyer would help him—whether she wanted to or not.

Chapter Thirty – Food for Thought

IT WAS THE DEAD TIME OF YEAR when depressions deepen, suicides soar, and life's inevitable progress slows to a crawl. Jack went home for an unsatisfactory visit with his mother, highlighted by Christmas dinner at the Holiday Inn and her inane gifts—an ugly green sweater and a cast-iron fireplace set. He was sure he'd told her the old house had gas logs in the fireplace from back when it was a boarding house—that they even had to use matches to light it.

Any opportunity to escape the social vacuum was welcome, even if it was an invitation from Leslie Sharp. They met for lunch at Otto's Butchery, ten miles out of town—and not one of Dick McFee's regular haunts. The reason for the invitation: a job offer.

"I'm prepared to give you fifty percent over what you make now and a nice office in our building off Peachtree." Leslie waved his fork over his plate. "As this thing progresses, there'll be bonuses—*good* bonuses."

Jack glanced up, then back down, thinking, *That's a lot of money, a lot more than I'm making now. Even with Fitz.* "I need time to think about it," he said and speared a piece of steak.

"You are interested, though?" Leslie folded over a stalk of asparagus and ingested it in one bite.

"I'm interested." But his next thought was Patricia. He'd be leaving her alone here in Carrville, still trying to make a go of the firm—or trying to find something else while she waited for Colin to come back. "What about Patricia? You have an opening for her, too?" he asked.

"Only room for one. Can't handle twins." Leslie laughed his too-loud laugh and then got serious at Jack's blank stare. "She's a bright young woman, but she lacks the flexibility we need for this work."

"I wouldn't know about that," Jack said. "She—"

"The clients are still pissed off about Dick, and she was working with him on the litigation."

"It wasn't her fault."

"She should've dealt with the issue—him three sheets to the wind and arguing a big case like that."

"Dick's argument was brilliant, and Joe Mayes was there, too . . . lit up like a penny arcade." Now it was Jack who laughed, but quiet and mean. "Patricia told me."

"Joe didn't argue the case and insult the judges, like they were all in kindergarten." Another hollow, too-loud laugh.

Jack toyed with some carrots and pushed them aside. He stared at Leslie. "Joe could've stopped Dick. Patricia couldn't; she was his subordinate."

"Then they went to the wrong courthouse. How they did that, no one could ever figure out."

"The court of appeals was doing some experimental thing. Sitting in different places around the state."

"That's no excuse. Dick missed the argument, and they had to submit the case on briefs . . . and they lost."

Jack sighed, feeling defeated. And glad Patricia wasn't hearing this.

"The mayors are *not* forgiving people," Leslie said. "They stand for election, get pilloried by the press. You only screw up once with them."

Two days later, Jack sat in his office, alone, thinking. Slumping down in the chair, he stared at the dull finish on his desk. New Year's Eve and no plans for the evening, except to go home for a frozen TV dinner and empty bedroom. Last year there had been a firm party with laughter and glitz and glitter. There had been a bright, prosperous new year in the offing. Now he was torn between wanting to leave and fearing it. The unknowable future.

He turned and stared out the window. The sky was leaden, and the mercury vapor lamps in the parking lot across the street gave off sparkling halos in the mist.

He was drawn by Leslie's offer. Yet, working with the Mayes firm might not differ too much from representing Fitz in his land deals. Joe Mayes had set up this curious A-E Land Company and helped with—with whatever it was doing. He closed his eyes. *I'm making too much of this A-E Land Company. There's no connection with my client . . . that I know of. Fitz's just using good business sense to make a bundle of money. He was smart enough to figure out what land to buy and shrewd enough to pull the right levers to make the deals come together. How the mayor plays it isn't Fitz's problem—or mine. My duty is to my client, not to the city. As long as I don't know about anything that violates any law. And I don't.*

He examined his diploma and bar admission mounted on the wall beside the desk. *Patricia will be pissed if I leave.* He pounded on the desk with his fist. *Fuck it all! She has Colin; she doesn't need me for anything. Everything here, every bit of our business, except Fitz's deals, comes from clients who've been with the firm for years. From back when Dick was always sober and still the sharpest lawyer in town.*

He reached for his ancient wooden inbox. *Maybe I should stay. There are a few more walk-ins and appointed cases these days. Come to think of it, Lacey's no longer late in paying the bills—or the secretaries. And Dick has a family fortune to fall back on. What does the man do with his time anyway? And what does he know about Fitz's schemes? And the mayor? Not something I can ask about. Hey, Dick, you have a piece of Fitz's land deals out there on the Old Schoolhouse Road?*

Then Allie's accident. And Kitty dying like that. He tried not to think about either of them. *But what if someone—the mayor maybe?—had tried to shut Allie up. And Kitty?*

That's insane, he thought with a shudder. *This isn't New Jersey and the mafia.*

He pulled out the files Lacey had left in his inbox. On top was a new collection case, then three real estate closings, and at the bottom, in an expandable folder, the documents for Fitz's new partnership. He spread the files out in front of him and stared at them. *Why am I still here? It's a dead end. Why ...?*

"Jack, why are you still here? It's New Year's Eve!" Dick's voice boomed out as he strode in. He wore a gray overcoat and a gray fedora, appropriate for the weather outside but twenty years out of style.

"Just finishing up," Jack said, gathering the files. "What brings you here? How's Allie?" He dropped the files back into the inbox.

"Sally and I were just going up to the club. Lacey said there was a letter for me from the city, so I came by to pick it up." He started to leave, then stopped. "Why don't you join us? Sally's already up there."

"I don't know—"

"She needed a break from the hospital." He started out the door, motioning with one hand for Jack to follow. "She'd love someone her own age to talk to."

In the elevator going up to the City Club, Dick read his letter, his face blank, his eyes hidden behind his glasses. He volunteered nothing, but before he folded the single page and deposited it inside his coat, Jack saw the mayor's letterhead. From the grim look on Dick's face, Jack could tell it wasn't good news. When he asked, Dick shrugged and said he'd just received a nice New Year's note from the mayor.

Chapter Thirty-one – What Lacey Sees

JACK ROCKED BACK IN HIS CHAIR and stared out his office window. A cold front had swept away the clouds and left the sky a rich, fresh blue, divided by a spreading white contrail. His malaise had deepened with the New Year's Eve dinner in the City Club. The only thing good about it was Sally. And the chateaubriand and nice wine, of which he had partaken too much.

Patricia had returned from her holiday—in a black mood. She didn't say what happened, just threw her bag in the trunk when he picked her up at the airport and refused to tell him anything about her trip. She'd left the house early this morning—for the gym or yoga—before Jack came down for breakfast.

A sharp rap behind him made him jump. He spun around to face the door.

"Jack! I *need* to talk to you." Lacey, looking more emaciated than ever, stood in the doorway. She cradled a thick stack of papers in both arms and radiated tension.

"Come on in," he said. "What you got?"

First closing the door, something she never did, Lacey started to place the stack of papers in front of him, hesitated, then sat in the armchair. An odor of cigarette smoke wafted to him across the desk.

"Have you *looked* at any of the latest for Mr. Fitzhugh?" she asked.

"You've got everything." He scowled at her. "I never check it until—"

"Let me show you this." She plopped some clipped pages down on his desk. "This came in last week. A section he's refinancing through McFee Savings . . . The new loan is fifty thousand over the old one."

"Fitz makes his payments and McFee Savings gets a percentage on the refinancing. What's the problem?"

"This appraisal looks inflated." Staring at him, she tapped the top page with her index finger. No nail polish there; chewed to the quick. "I checked the file. He bought this section no more'n eight months ago, and the valuation's a third higher than what he paid for it. I tell you, nothing's changed out there in twenty years . . . ain't nuthin there. Dick's family couldn't even make a go of a development—"

"That's been years ago." He picked up the papers and leafed through them. "Property values go up. If there's a problem, McFee Savings will catch it."

"Ha! They don't question anything we send 'em. And they'll be relying on the appraisal and the comparatives in *it*. All those are going up. All right there." She slid back in the chair and smirked at him.

"I'm not in the real estate business; I only do the legal end . . . Not our job to second-guess appraisals."

"Shouldn't we try to protect Dick if one of his *old* friends is trying to put something over on him?" Her eyebrows went up. "Bilk his savings bank?"

"It's not *his* bank. He only owns a few shares. Any-damn-way, Lacey, they know how to value their collateral, and they know what risks they want to take."

"I think that appraiser's off his rocker." She stabbed a finger at the papers. "Look at the last paragraph on the second page. You'll see what I mean."

"Who's the appraiser?" He was looking for the paragraph.

"Johnny Scales. I've known that . . . him for twenty years, and that's all I'll say about him." She folded her arms across her chest.

"You already said he's off his rocker."

"Read that. He makes it sound like Mr. Fitzhugh's gonna do more'n just grow beans out there. Like build something . . . That have anything to do with the cities and their stupid energy thing? The one Dick started. Just read it."

Jack found the paragraph and read it. As Lacey said, it described the land as part of a larger parcel designated as the site for a future research facility and related energy projects to be financed by venture capital and municipal bonds.

"Is there a deal for that?" Lacey asked. "Like what he says?"

"No-o-o," Jack said, looking at her, then past her at the closed door. "Nothing public."

"You know about something?"

"Nope." *And I wouldn't tell you if I did*, he thought, *but the reference makes sense. Fitz's Star Energy partnership.* After a long moment, he said, "It's part of what he's doing with the new company we're forming. I don't know a thing about what the cities are doing . . . It's confidential."

"Humph! Look at these others. Three different banks. Big banks—not little ol' McFee Savings." From the stack in her lap, she dropped three more clipped packets onto his desk and shoved them toward him. "These are *all* properties he bought in the last year. All the loans are ten to twenty percent more'n what Mr. Fitzhugh paid for the dirt. That Scales is the appraiser on every one of 'em." She jabbed her finger at the pages. "Those don't refer to any energy deal, but," she gave him a smug look, "the values are based on there being a *major* manufacturing facility, something that doesn't exist, not yet."

"The banks have their own appraisers. They're big boys."

"And sloppy as hell." Sitting forward in the chair, she leaned her elbows on the desk. "I know that area off the Old Schoolhouse Road. It ain't nothing but farmland, vacant lots, and those six houses old man McFee built before his building company went belly up. Only way the values have gone up as much as those appraisals say is if there's something funny going on."

"Sorry, Lacey, that's not our area." He gingerly set the three packets back in front of Lacey, on top of the first one.

"What?" She looked puzzled.

"Something funny going on. That's not our area."

"All right, smarty pants, look at this one. This just came in this morning." She plunked the final packet, save one smaller one in her lap, on top of the others. He reached over and picked up the clipped papers as Lacey railed on. "This is the contract and financing for one of the *new* properties your Mister Fitz is buying. The purchase price is forty percent over what the seller—some A-E Land Company—paid for that old farm two years ago."

His scalp prickled and he felt an electric current run up his back. This was the first time he had seen a connection between the A-E Land Company and Fitz or any of his deals.

"I looked in the files," Lacey continued in a rapid-fire staccato as he flipped through the pages. "They bought it from the trust, old Gladys McFee's, which bought it from the McFee development company, which bought it from the farmer's estate. It's all in the trust file. I remembered it. Every time the land moves, it goes up in value. Nuthin but vacant land. But never so much as this time. Forty percent. Can you believe it? Two years." She held up two fingers. "And Scales is the appraiser."

Staring down at the papers, he let her talk, her words tumbling over him as he was thinking, *What if you keep flipping property between related entities and boosting the value each time to get loans? With a helpful appraiser, trusting banks, and enough properties and buyers to keep the money flowing. Maybe the banks or their officers help, with a wink, or with closed eyes. They make money, too.*

"We're closing on these deals next month," Lacey said, snapping him out of his worrying thoughts. "What do we do?"

"Just go ahead and prepare the documents." Exasperated, he rolled his eyes, then patted the desk with his hand. "Do your usual magic."

She stared at him, her thin lips drawn in a tight line. She slapped the last item she held—a thick brown envelope—down on the front of the desk and began gathering up the other packets.

Watching her, Jack had another thought, giving rise to a question to Lacey. "Fitz's new partnership, have you got all the documents ready?"

"Yeah, they're ready. Is he going to use *that* to flip these properties again and get more money from the banks?"

"Just give 'em to me, will you. I have no idea what he plans . . ." Lacey's hooded eyes, pursed lips, and nodding head stopped him. He cleared his throat and tried to match her truculent stare. "What he *does* with it isn't *our* business. We just do the legal work."

Holding the files in one arm, Lacey jumped up from the chair. Leaning forward, she slid the brown envelope across the desk toward him. "Personal package for you," she said. "To be opened by addressee only. Feels like a book."

"Okay, thanks." He was ready for her to leave. She spun around and walked out with the packets clutched to her chest.

His mind in turmoil, he took a penknife from the drawer and slit open the envelope. Inside was a second padded envelope with his name on it. Puzzled, he slid the knife under the flap and dumped the contents onto his desk—then gave a sharp intake of breath. His heart raced. There were two stacks of one-hundred-dollar bills, each held together by a rubber band— and on top a scrawled note from Fitz: "A small down payment. Just the beginning."

Oh, shit! he thought. *I'm fucked.* He stared at the bills, then counted them. Fifty. Five thousand dollars. *If I keep the money, I'm on Fitz's payroll. It's not just a matter of benefiting as his lawyer. Making big fees. This is dirty money, under the table. What am I going to do?*

He had to get out of here. Talk to someone.

First stuffing Fitz's note in his pocket, he replaced the money in the envelopes then hid the package in a desk drawer and locked it. He was halfway down the hall to Patricia's office when he stopped and leaned against the wall.

What can I tell her? She'll never understand. She grew up with everything she wanted. It's all black and white to her.

He turned around, then reversed course again. *What will Lacey tell her? The inflated appraisals? The property flips? The tie-in to the Alt-Energy project?* He inched along the wall.

Probably not much. Patricia always avoided gossip and idle chatter with the secretaries. But Lacey, if she stayed irritated, she would drop hints here and there, even if she didn't suspect what the envelope contained. Somehow, he had to head her off, preempt the whole matter with Patricia.

Still trying to sort out his swirling thoughts, he drifted into Patricia's office with all the casualness he could muster. Her mood hadn't improved and the mail in her absence hadn't helped.

"I can't believe it," she said as soon as he came through the door. She jammed a finger with its manicured nail down on a document in the center of her desk. "Ray Malloy's got an indictment for murder. The bastard! He *knew* when he gave me the transcript. He got it back in November and waited to serve it . . . Why the hell didn't I get this before I left?"

"Maybe he didn't have the D.A.'s approval. He told you he might—"

"He could've told me for sure."

Raising his hands, he shrugged and submissively ducked his head. As she glared at him, he slumped into the armchair and placed a foot against the edge of her desk. "I . . ." he started.

"Get your feet off my desk," she snapped. "I don't want to be cleaning scuff marks off the furniture here, too."

He dropped his foot to the floor. Not the time to bring up his own problems. "How was Colin?" he asked without thinking

"Colin's a shit, like all men." Her glare was intense and unrelenting. "Is there something you want?"

"No," he said and stood. Her glower softened into a look of dismay.

"I'm sorry. Colin's not coming back . . . not here, not to practice law." Jack sat back down. "Do you—"

"Jack," she raised her hands. "I don't want to talk about it." She waved her hand over the document on her desk, then pointed to the full inbox behind her. "I've got all this to catch up on."

"Why don't you ask for a postponement . . . of the trial?"

"No way!" Her face crinkled into a scowl. "I'll be as ready as ever, and I want to get the damn thing over with . . . Did you want something?"

"No." He stood again. "We can talk later."

When he got back to his office, he found a message from Leslie Sharp. Could they meet next week, lunch, dinner?

Another loose end. And he still had to deal with Lacey and what she might tell Patricia.

Chapter Thirty-two – Colin and Jack

PATRICIA WAS LOOKING FORWARD TO DINNER. The passage of time had thawed her mood and left her eager to talk with Jack for the first time since Christmas and his return from Sniderville. He'd gone home again to see his mother, who was in the hospital.

"I'm glad your mother's okay," she said, watching him chop the stems off two artichokes. After work, she had run, showered, and dressed in comfortable slacks—and one of Colin's overlarge sweaters that still smelled of him.

"She's old and lonely." Jack hacked away at the artichoke with the knife. "By herself in that dump. Does her good to fake a heart attack."

"You left the back door open again. The Carlyles' cat was lounging on the sofa when I got home." Jack had earned the friendship of the neighbor's black-and-white cat by leaving leftovers in a saucer on the back porch.

"Why don't you get the bottle of white wine out of the fridge? And some cheese." He swept a pile of cuttings into the trash bin under the sink.

"You've been busy," she said from the refrigerator.

"The crab salad? Took me an hour to pick it." He'd bought it at the deli.

"I mean busy at work."

"Fitz's land deals." He plopped the artichokes into the water.

"You've seemed . . . distracted."

"Hmmm. Let's go in the den while these babies cook."

While she arranged cheese and crackers on a cutting board, he pulled the cork on the wine and poured it. After a long silence, he added, "I'm worried—all this crap Lacey's working on." He picked up the cutting board and the wine bottle. "I'll take these. Bring my glass, will you."

The den was a long narrow room with a fireplace, one window—blinds wedged at the top—and two doors, one to the kitchen, the other to

176

the living room. A traditional parlor when the house was built, it became a sitting room for guests in a boarding house, then a cozy den for Colin's spinster aunt when she bought the property after WW II. The Salvation Army had provided most of the furnishings: a sagging sofa, beat-up coffee table, and a pole lamp in the corner. Colin's aunt's fine antiques had been sold after she moved into a rest home and the house left vacant until Colin inherited it.

They sat apart on the sofa with the cutting board and wine bottle on the coffee table among stacks of magazines. Gas logs burned in the fireplace, the flames illuminating Jack's useless cast-iron Christmas gift on the hearth.

"Okay, tell me what's worrying you." She'd rather talk about Jack's problems than think about her own.

"Well," Jack said, his voice slow and hesitant, "Lacey put it all together . . . before I did. Oh, I suspected, when Fitz wanted this new company . . . He told me some of it. I guess I didn't understand what he was saying." Jack stopped and stared into the fire.

She waited for him to continue. He swilled his wine then poured another glass. She shook her head when he held out the bottle.

"That appraiser you saw in court," he said, settling back on the sofa. "Lacey says Fitz is using him to inflate the values on the refinancings we're doing."

"That doesn't surprise me." Patricia shook her head. "Lacey came in the other day and started telling me Fitz is a sleaze."

"She came to see you? What else did she say?" He slumped farther down on the sofa and hung his leg over the corner of the coffee table.

"Nothing that I wanted to hear. She left in a huff."

"He's using McFee Savings for one . . . one of the refinancings." Abruptly popping up again, Jack reached for the cheese. "Dick's on the board, you know . . . so's Lena."

"The mayor's wife? Dick's *bosom* friend."

"Fitz has set up these different companies," Jack said past a raised cracker with Brie. "Partnerships—gonna get into the alternative energy business . . . And maybe they will," he shrugged, "but I think he'll probably transfer the properties into them and cover his bets with some more refinancing."

"Smells fishy." She lifted her glass and stared at the fire through the gold liquid. "Guess it doesn't matter, so long as he pays off the loans."

"Yeah, that's right." Jack was silent a moment. "So long as he can get the money somewhere."

"He's got his agribusiness and he's forming these partnerships . . ." She stopped, struck by a sudden thought and vaguely remembering something Lacey said. She gave him a sideways look. "Do the partnerships have anything to do with the cities and their project?"

"I don't know." Jack let out a breath. "I'm not sure . . . Maybe they could." He dropped his chin to his chest, his eyes fixed on the fireplace. His leg went back onto the corner of the coffee table. "That's not my concern, Patricia. I just do the legal work."

"You better hope nothing funny is going on between Fitz and his friends. That whole bunch could get into *big* trouble, and you with them."

He placed a hand on her leg. "I'm okay. No way am *I* gonna get caught up in anything stupid."

Staring at him, she drew back toward her side of the sofa. "So what are you . . . ?" She started to ask what he was going to do about Fitz, but he sat up and grabbed the wine bottle off the table, interrupting her.

"Want some more wine?"

She held out her glass and he refilled it then filled his own. They were silent, staring at the fire. He didn't seem to want to talk about Fitz, and she decided not to press him.

"How's Allie?" she asked instead.

"Still out of it. She'll recover, Sally says, but they don't know how much she'll remember. She . . ." He hesitated, then jumped up from the couch. "Let me check the artichokes."

While he was gone, she puzzled over what he had said about Fitz and his land deals and partnerships. And what Lacey had said, and she ignored. The dots didn't quite connect. But she had Billy Angel to worry about.

Grabbing the cutting board, she called to him, "Let's eat in there."

In the kitchen, she watched Jack set out food and drink on the small kitchen table, then gave voice to her worries.

"How do I defend on the felony murder charge?" She said, going over to the table. "Ray claims he can tie the gun to Billy, but I don't believe it."

"Doesn't he have to produce the gun, do a ballistics test?"

"The .22 wasn't fired and the .357 is missing," she said, pulling out a chair and sitting. "I'll ask for the ballistics report, if there is one." She poked at her salad. "Ray says he has an expert . . . Ever try to get discovery in a criminal case in this state? And who'll pay for Billy's expert . . . as if there was one?"

"I'm a real estate guy . . . only do death cases for dogs." Seated now, Jack jabbed at a hunk of crab. "Find anything helpful in the transcript?"

"Nope . . . Maybe some stuff to help me with the cops. I've got to prepare cross for Jenkins, the kid who was lookout."

"No idea how he got mixed up in this? . . . Seventeen, isn't he?"

"Nineteen now." She shook her head. "I never got much out of Billy about his gang—other than he and Lazlo were buds."

"So what's your defense?"

She laughed. "Reasonable doubt, maybe? He was only trying to steal the safe? Did you know safecracking's twenty more years than grand larceny? . . . Oh, damn! I've got to find that hustler girlfriend of his." She glared at him. "You said you'd help."

Jack shrugged. "Care to tell me what happened with Colin?"

She gave a helpless wave of her hand. "Like I said, Jack, he's not coming back." She picked up her plate and carried it to the sink.

"Is it his father?" Jack came up beside her and placed a hand on her arm.

"I should've known," she said, shaking her head. She resisted the temptation to let herself go, start crying, and to lean against Jack. She edged back a few steps. "No, Jack . . . I'm not going to talk about it. It's over. The engagement, everything."

"Why . . . ? What?" He moved closer again, his eyes searching hers.

"Maybe I need to start looking." She accidentally hit him in the chest with her hands and quickly jerked them away. "I should move out."

Jack's face became serious. "I can't stay here by myself. You go, I go."

She slipped past him, then stopped and turned. "Look, Jack, I'm sorry."

"Do you mean leave the firm . . . leave town?" His face had a bleak look.

"I don't know . . . Yes . . . Maybe." She smiled halfheartedly at him. "You okay with the dishes? I'm going to bed."

Chapter Thirty-three – Judy Kay

AERIAL TRACKED HER DOWN. The phone calls and messages didn't
work, so Aerial went alone to the Patriot bar, a redneck enclave on Main
Street. She drew stares, she said, but the only hostile ones were from the
other girls.

"I dress for success, honey," she told Patricia, who was sitting straight
and stiff at her desk. "Wasn't nobody 'bout to give this lady any lip."
Standing in front of the desk, she wiggled her torso.

I bet, thought Patricia, eyeing Aerial's blond wig, low-cut white tank
top, and bronze-leather mini skirt.

"What's the story?" she asked. "Will Judy Kay meet with us?"

"You're on for tomorrow. Took me a bit of twisting on the hunky
bartender—he thinks we have a date Friday." She gave a, "Heh, heh," and
grinned at Patricia. "He slipped out while I watched the bar for him. When
he came back, he said to have the lawyers there at four."

"I think we can manage that." Patricia tapped her bottom front teeth
with her pen, thinking about all she needed to do in the next week.

"You're to get a table back in the corner," Aerial said. "Away from
the front door. You takin' Jack with you?"

"That's the plan." This was beginning to sound like an espionage plot.

"Better keep an eye on him 'round all them big-titty dancers." Aerial
raised her eyebrows. "Did you know there's a whorehouse—"

"No! And I don't care."

"They call it Jenny's." The eyebrows again. "Jack—"

"Jack wouldn't be interested." Patricia's eyes were slits.

"You know that, huh?" Aerial chortled, finally starting out. "I'm
thinkin' the boy's been needin'—"

"Thanks, Aerial. I appreciate your help." *Like hell. Not on Jack's
activities.* She turned to pick up a pleading from her inbox.

"A regular pa-rade, out the back door and back in again." Aerial laughed. "I was beginning to think they were takin' numbers. You know, like the meat counter at the A&P." Still chuckling, she disappeared out the door.

Patricia shook her head and stared out the window at the gray January day. She'd miss Aerial when she left this place.

A half dozen town toughs and a couple of GI's were already shooting pool and soaking cocktail napkins on the bar when she and Jack arrived at 4:00pm. As Aerial had said, there wasn't a dark skin in the group. Both GI's had close-cropped brown hair, long faces, and intense looks, like twins. One was drawing a bead on a red-striped ball as she and Jack tripped past while the other leaned against the wall next to a cue rack.

Beyond the game area was a long narrow stage lit by yellow spotlights. A dancer, naked except for a G-string, gyrated about a silver pole, her body glistening with perspiration or oil, or both.

She caught Jack eyeing the girl. *A blond, fake*, Patricia guessed from the exposed roots, and not especially pretty: angular face, skin by tan-basting, a dull vacant look. Until the girl noticed Jack. A spark of interest appeared, and she gyrated her jiggling flesh over to a metal pole closer to where they were passing.

"Move it, champ." Patricia gave Jack a push toward the table in the corner. "You can do better than that."

"Just window shopping." He grinned at her over his shoulder.

She already felt self-conscious in her business suit and starched white shirt buttoned to the throat, and now this naked dancer. She wondered if her companion was doing a mental comparison. The clod.

The rear of the bar faded into smoky darkness under a low ceiling of once-white acoustic tiles. One hung down at an angle over the farthest table—where they were headed. The place reeked of tobacco, beer, and testosterone; the air compressed by the too-loud music: "Come on, let me see you shake a tail feather . . ."

Almost as soon as they sat down, a woman wearing a formless Tar Heel sweatshirt, tight jeans, and a Red Sox baseball cap appeared from a door in the back. *She must have been watching for us*, thought Patricia, gripping her purse in her lap. The woman made a beeline for them.

"Hey, good lookin'," she said as Jack stood to greet her. He held out his hand, and she took it, tilting forward to give him a hug. Her hair, no longer the bouffant Jack had described, filled the Red Sox cap, except for a few platinum strands drizzling out around the edges.

Jack tentatively returned the hug and said, "Hi."

"Rhonda's gonna be so-o-o jealous," the woman said, stepping back. "She'd sure like to take another ride with you." She winked at him, then at Patricia.

"Uh, Judy, this is my colleague, Patricia Egan. She's representing Billy." Jack took off his suit coat as he talked and hung it on the back of his chair.

Without standing or releasing her purse, Patricia held out a hand, which Judy Kay seized as if she were grabbing a doorknob. Her hand was small but she had the grip of Wonder Woman.

"Pleased to meet you, Miss Egan." Holding onto Patricia's hand, she patted it with her free one. "We're countin' on you to see justice is done . . . or injustice if that's what it takes." She gave an exaggerated wink.

"We'll do our best," Patricia said, grimacing and squinting up at the figure framed by the halo of lights. She could see why Jack was impressed.

"Hey, Barry," Judy Kay yelled as she pulled out a chair between them. She waved to the bartender. "Bring us some drinks over here."

They ordered—Jack a Budweiser, since Heineken was alien here; Patricia a club soda on ice, with lemon; and Judy Kay, a Shirley Temple, which Patricia vaguely remembered her mother ordering one time when she was on the wagon. While they waited, she set her purse down between her feet and eyed Judy Kay against the lights.

"Miss-s-s . . . ?"

"Smith." Judy Kay gave a deep full-throated laugh and poked Jack's arm. She leaned back, looking from one to the other. "Just call me Judy Kay, sweetie."

"Have you heard from Billy?" Patricia said, not smiling.

"Not much way he can call me, now is there?" She leaned closer to Patricia. "You hear me okay with this gawdawful music in here?"

"I can hear you." And smell your perfume and coconut body cream, too. With a hint of eau d'cigarette. "So you've heard nothing?"

"I didn't say that." She paused as Barry arrived with their drinks and placed them on the table. Jack paid him in cash—with a twenty-five percent tip.

The music volume subsided and the dancer perched herself on the edge of the stage. Wearing only a thin peignoir-like wrap, she sucked on a straw in a red drink while she talked to a townie who looked like he'd ridden in on a Harley.

"I got two letters," Judy Kay said, sipping on her Shirley Temple. "Could be he sent more, but that's all I got. He sends 'em to my sister in Cleveland. They read his mail, you know, so he has to be careful. He said to talk to you, sorta in code and all. I can't get nuthin into him, 'less it's through you."

"You staying around here?" Jack waved his hand toward the bar.

She stared at him a moment, then cut her eyes to Patricia. In the background played a melancholy, "Hey there lonely boy . . ."

"I reckon you won't turn me in," she said after a few lines of the song. "I'm stayin' at Jenny's, back there." She grinned at the look Patricia gave her. "Don't worry. I'm not a worker." She chuckled. "Have my own business, but I need a place to hang my coat when I'm in town."

"Don't want to know this," Jack said, addressing his beer. He took a long swig from the bottle.

"You two must be a pair—just look like you go together." Judy Kay laughed and gave Patricia another wink.

"Judy," Patricia said, "the prosecutor has indicted Billy for murder under something called the felony murder rule. He won't seek the death penalty, but he will go for life or long years."

Judy Kay nodded, her face somber, her big eyes with a sad, lost look.

"I've got a transcript of the investigation," Patricia continued, "an internal affairs hearing on the deaths. Legally, it doesn't matter if Billy fired the shot that killed the man at the apartments, but it may make a difference with the jury, and on the sentence." She paused. "Billy told me he didn't have a gun—"

"Lord, no!" Judy Kay leaned forward, almost knocking over the half-empty Shirley Temple. "He'd never take a gun on a job. Too dangerous."

"How about Lazlo?" Jack asked.

"Not Lazlo. He was a creampuff. He did what Billy told him. Just learnin' the trade."

"The kid? Jenkins?" Jack eyes stayed on her.

"Ha!" Judy Kay threw her head back. "That pothead. He wasn't nuthin but a lookout. Wanted some thrills." Her expression became hard and bitter. "Well, he got 'em."

"The cops found two guns," Patricia said.

"They always do," was Judy Kay's quick, tight-lipped retort. "They gotta cover their asses. They was just shootin' at each other and poor ol' Lazlo's as dead as that thing there on the wall." She twisted around to point at the head of an eight-point buck above the mirror behind the bar.

Patricia sighed. "So-o-o, what do I do?" she asked. Using one foot, she shifted her purse under the chair and waited.

Judy Kay merely shrugged and stared at her.

"Tell me what Billy's afraid of." She fixed Judy Kay with what she hoped was a penetrating look while squinting into the lights and ignoring the dancer, who was seductively removing her wrap in front of the biker.

"Billy ain't 'fraid of nuthin."

Pushing aside the club soda can and glass, Patricia leaned over the table. "When he was down here last time, somebody came to see him, so he told me. He seemed afraid to me."

Judy Kay was pensive. Her voice was soft. "I didn't know about that. When was it?"

"Just before he left." Patricia's sleeve was soaked from the wet spot where her glass had been, but she ignored it. "He asked me to find out what happened to Lazlo. I—"

"Shit!" Judy Kay hit the table with her small fist. "I should've known."

"What is it?" Jack asked, shifting his gaze to Judy Kay from the dancer. Her friend had gone, and the music was revving up again.

"You need to tell me what's going on," Patricia said. "Is it the jailer? His friends?"

Judy Kay shook her head, her eyes narrowed, her mouth in a tight line. Placing an elbow on the table, she put her forehead in her palm, pushing the cap up and allowing her platinum hair to fall around the sides of her face.

"No, no," she said, shaking her head. "That's not . . . that's . . ." She continued shaking her head. "I can't say."

"You can't say!" Patricia spread her hands out wide in front of her. "For God's sakes, I can't do anything to protect him unless you tell me *what* I'm protecting him from. I need facts."

"God, oh God." Judy Kay held her head with both hands on the cap. "There had to be another man," she said softly.

The dancer was gyrating and twirling to the blaring music.

"What?" Patricia asked, moving her chair closer.

Judy Kay dropped her hands to the table and leaned into Patricia, her mouth next to Patricia's ear. "There was another man." She placed a hand on Patricia's shoulder. "He'd wanta make sure Billy keeps quiet. Goddamit!" She struck the table with her fist again.

"Billy's visitor, right? Who was it? Tell me." Patricia waited, her eyes fixed on Judy Kay, but Judy Kay didn't answer. "How did he get to see him? He was in solitary. You can tell me. You have to."

Rocking back and forth in the chair, Judy Kay shook her head. "I can't." She glanced away, then quickly back at Patricia. "I don't know his name. What I know . . . I can't say 'less Billy tells me to."

"You have to tell us," Jack said, leaning toward Judy Kay from the other side and raising his voice over the music.

Staring at the table, Judy Kay was silent. Then lifting the Red Sox cap, she crammed her hair back under it and stuffed stray curls up along the sides. "There's the code. No matter what, you don't rat somebody out." She sighed and slumped down in the chair, like a collapsed balloon.

"Judy, I need . . ." A scream stopped Patricia mid-sentence. A woman in a biker's jacket and jeans had leaped onto the stage and was swinging a flashing blade at the dancer.

"You bitch! Thought I didn't know!" The knife arced downward, but missed its target. Bedlam broke loose as some of the patrons grabbed for the attacker—but not before she left a long red slash across the dancer's chest.

Judy Kay stood, then hesitated and bent back down. "See what you can do for Billy. He ain't a bad person." She gave Patricia a quick hug, then disappeared into the dark at the rear of the bar. As sirens wailed in the distance, Jack and Patricia slipped past the melee and out the front door.

Part V

Chapter Thirty-four – Billy Returns

PATRICIA LEFT HER PURSE IN THE BAR. The good news was that Barry the bartender found it, back in a dark corner. The bad news, her credit cards and cash were gone. Then she and Jack both got the flu: fever, aches, the whole bit. After two days, Jack went back to work. Not only to escape from the house and her; Fitz was back. Patricia finally limped into the office only to face Billy Angel's trial the following Wednesday.

They brought him down over the weekend and she went to see him Monday afternoon. The room was larger but no less tired and dismal than the last one and the chair no more comfortable. One plus: there was no window for him to stare at and contemplate an escape.

As the guard left, she opened her briefcase and took out a legal pad. The table wasn't much larger than the pad and Billy was no more than three feet away. She stared across at him—in his fresh orange jumpsuit with the McFee County Jail logo emblazoned on the front. His hair hung down boyishly across his rough forehead like the first time she saw him in Central Prison. Though clean-shaven, he looked worn and gaunt, yet his eyes were as limpid and direct as ever. And he still showed the gaps in his yellow teeth when he grinned.

"As I told you on the phone," she said, "the D.A.'s charged you with murder. Under something called the felony murder rule."

"Yeah, I got a copy of the indictment." He gave a Jimmy Carter grin. "I read up on it in the library," he said. "They can't make a case. I didn't have no gun."

"First of all, it *don't* matter," Patricia said, making large "Xs" on her legal pad. "An innocent man died because of your little caper." She paused to make sure that sank in. "And second, the cops found not one, but two guns, and they say one was yours. A cop may have shot Lazlo, but the D.A.'s going to contend you fired the shot that killed Henry Royale." She stared directly into his eyes. "Even if you didn't, you caused the whole mess."

"It didn't happen the way they said it did." He placed his elbows on the table and gave her a benign smile. He leaned forward, causing her to draw back. "Real smart guy inside," he said, "he studies the law books. Told me they need to prove we . . . I fired a gun. I didn't."

"Sorry, Mr. Angel. Smart guy got it wrong. That's not the way it works. It might help, if they can't prove you had a gun. The best thing you've got going is that *they* lost the gun, the one they think killed Royale."

Billy sighed and dropped his hands into his lap. "I trust you, missy. You'll do okay by me, I know."

"If you trust me, tell me what happened."

"You know it." He shrugged, giving his hangdog look. "When the cops showed up, I ran and hid. Me and Lazlo took off in different directions—like we'd agreed we'd do." He sat up straight, his eyes still on hers. "Only people shootin' at anything was the cops."

"I talked with Judy Kay. She says there was another man there."

Billy frowned, no grin now. "You didn't tell me you'd seen her."

"You asked me to . . . Some mad slasher tried to kill a dancer in that bar while we were there."

His eyebrows shot up and his eyes grew wide.

She grimaced at him. "It was a catfight. Look, we don't have a lot of time. You told me to find out what happened to Lazlo. Well, we know what happened from the transcript. But something was bothering you when you left here last time."

His head drooped, eyes down. "Guess I wasn't thinking straight. It's okay . . . now." He looked up. "We need to keep Judy Kay out of it."

"There was another man, right?"

"Ah-h-h, missy. That don't do me no good. I'm not a snitch." The hangdog look again. "Wouldn't live long if I was."

"Did *he* have a gun?"

Staring down at the table, Billy was silent for a long moment. Finally, he nodded. "Could have." He nodded a couple more times, his lips in a tight line. "Yeah, he probably did."

"Who was it?"

"Best you didn't know."

"I'm your lawyer. You have to tell me."

He looked up at her with his clear blue eyes, not blinking, and shook his head. "It'll go with me to my grave."

She sighed and tapped her fingers on her legal pad. "Okay, then at least tell me where he was."

"At the door. Outside." Billy grinned. Every positive response seemed to require a grin. "He gave us a signal . . . cops was out front. We shoulda known a lot sooner, but that little shit . . . the kid I mean, must've gone to sleep or gotten stoned or somethin'. He was out by the road, by one of them big signs. He had a flashlight to signal, but the cops were out front before . . . before the other guy told us to scram."

Billy paused and she waited without saying anything.

"Lazlo went out the back one way," Billy said, waving his hand to one side, "and me and that . . . guy," his lip curled up, "we went the other. Well, he was already gone off ahead of me. I went off through the woods, working my way back," he grinned, "to get to my car."

"Did that *guy* go toward the apartments?"

"Toward the . . . ? I don't remember."

"They're straight back. Behind the drive-through where the little call box and menu are for the Taco Pal."

"Sorta, I guess. He went more that way than I did. I was angling away from there, more toward the road. He angled the other way, and he was outta there quicker'n we was."

"And he got away." She made a face. *Lot of angling going on still.*

"He had a little secret to help him."

"What?" She cocked her head and gave him a sideways look.

Hunching up his shoulders, Billy flashed a different kind of grin, one that was silly at best. He shoved his chair back from the table, but didn't speak.

"Could he have shot Royale?" she asked, picking up her pen and drawing a few small circles on the pad.

"Does it matter?" Billy's face was solemn now.

"I don't know. I need all the facts, though." She made a few more doodles. *What's my ethical duty here? To Billy? To the court?*

Billy shook his head. "I was a long way out in the woods when I heard the shotgun. I knew it was on the other side of the place—over where Lazlo went. I just kept going. Nothing else I could do. But I wasn't trying to stay as quiet after that." He grinned at her again. "You know how it is."

She gave him a quizzical look.

"They were shoutin' stuff, then they started shootin' . . . I heard shots. Just one, then it was like the Hatfields and McCoys. Them cops doin' all the shootin'. That's when I dove in the ditch." He gave a tight smile.

"You stayed there until the deputy found you?" She doodled some more on the pad.

"Sonuvabitch like-ta stepped on me."

"You heard the shotgun. You knew Lazlo was dead—certainly afterwards. So why did you ask me to find out about Lazlo?"

Billy looked down at his hands, resting on his knees. "I dunno. Guess I wanted to make sure it happened like they said."

"Why wouldn't it have?"

He looked up, let out his breath. "I wanted to make sure . . ." he hesitated, "the other guy didn't have nuthin to do with it."

"Huh? What do you mean? Why would he?" She leaned on the table.

Billy stared at her, not answering, shaking his head, and not grinning now.

"Okay, let's try this," she said. "The kid's going to testify. Do you think he'll tell about your other . . . partner?"

"Hell no! That little rat, he'd be dead for sure. He's lucky I didn't get outta here . . ." He raised his hands, palms out, at Patricia's glare. "No, no, it's not what you think. He just—"

"Code or no code, he's going to testify. And if I ask him—"

"He'll lie."

"That's perjury. He'll get a lot more time for that . . . than under his plea deal."

Billy stared at her, a slight smile playing around the corners of his mouth.

"Right," she said, lifting her hands off the table and then dropping them back down beside the legal pad. "How do I prove he's lying? You can't testify. And who else is there?"

"They're going to come for me soon, missy. Can you get me some civilian clothes . . . for court?" He tugged at the neck of the orange jumpsuit. "I don't have any."

Through narrowed eyes, she regarded him a moment. *Am I going to have to go shopping for this clown? As well as run around in this never-ending maze?*

"Okay," she said. "I'll see if my . . . associate can get you some clothes." Good old Jack. But she wasn't ready to leave the fourth man, not yet.

"There may be another way to smoke out this other partner of yours. Maybe I could tell the D.A. his key witness knows—"

"No!" Billy came the closest to shouting she'd ever heard him. "That'd be the end of me." He was almost out of his chair and across the table. "Don't do it. An army won't be able to protect me, if you do."

Surprised, she shifted back a few inches and spread her hands over the legal pad. "You're in solitary here, aren't you?" she said. "There are all kinds of guards around you, night and day, right? And I don't think it's the jailer or his friends you're afraid of."

"You don't understand, Miss Egan." His face contorted in anguish. He kept shaking his head. "Leave it alone. An army might not even protect *you* . . . you open that can of worms."

"What can—"

A knock on the door stopped her question. The door opened at once.

"Shift change, ma'am," the deputy said from behind Billy. "We got to get him back now."

When she entered Jack's office, she found him engaged in a fierce contest to close the bottom drawer in his desk.

"You'll never believe the insane conversation I had with my client," she said, sinking down in the chair across from him and dropping her briefcase and purse on the floor.

He pulled out the drawer again and rammed it home. "So your client's insane," he said, swiveling toward her. "That's new?" He fidgeted, shifting papers about and then into small stacks at the front of the desk.

"He won't tell me who his other partner was and—"

"No surprise there."

"Yeah, but he says an army couldn't protect him if he tells, and . . . get this, couldn't protect me either." Clamping her mouth shut, she exhaled through her nose in exasperation.

Standing, Jack placed both fists knuckles down on the desk pad and frowned at her. "What does he mean by that?"

As she recounted her visit, he moved around the desk and sat on the front edge.

"When I said I could go to the D.A. . . . .well, Ray Malloy, and get the kid to tell . . . just to see what Billy would say, he came unglued. Wouldn't have it." She waved her hands in the air. "That's when he said it would be dangerous for him, and for me. Or that's how I interpreted it."

"Not something you can exactly go to Ray Malloy with."

"Don't I have a duty to report that," she shook her head, "you know, someone involved in a murder? And there's a prosecution witness who's going to perjure himself."

"Think about it." Jack went behind his desk and locked it while he talked. "Your client told you this. His defense is he wasn't there. Duh."

"Yeah," she said after a moment spent biting her lip. "Guess you're right. Blow his defense, as if he had one."

"Only one he's got. Unless he 'fesses up and just tries to beat the felony murder rap." Jack dropped his keys into his pocket.

She picked up her briefcase and purse. "It does scare me a little. What he said."

Jack was at the door, taking his suit coat off a hanger on the back. "You don't know what that joker's up to. But I'd give up on this fourth-man thing. It doesn't get you anywhere."

Jack stood aside to let her go out, and she started down the hall, then wheeled around.

"Do you think he could have killed Royale, Jack? This other guy? I mean intentionally."

"Intentionally? Why? Because Royale might identify him?"

They were facing each other several yards apart in the hallway. Holding her briefcase in front of her, bumping her knees, she edged closer to him, her eyes on the floor.

"That's one possibility." She paused. "But could it have something to do with Royale and the mayor?"

"Yeah, right . . . the mayor put out a contract on him."

"What?" Giving a start, she looked up at him.

"Just kiddin'." Jack wagged an index finger at her. "But it sure helped the mayor to have him out of the way."

"Yes," she said with a grimace, "whistleblower meets convenient end." Staring at him, she swung her briefcase out to her side and back. "Pretty farfetched, isn't it? A bunch of smalltime crooks and the mayor?"

"Jesus, Patricia, are you serious?" He shook his head. "You're way out in left field on this. And how does it help your case, anyway?"

"I need to talk to the deputies or whoever it was guarding him the last time Billy was down here. I want to find out what spooked him."

"You really think they'd tell you? He beat up a jailer, for Christ's sake." Glancing toward the elevators, Jack shook his head. "You're chasing rabbits, Patricia."

Chapter Thirty-five – Jack Backs Down

AFTER CLOSING ON THE NEW PROPERTIES in the morning, Fitz bought lunch then insisted on an outing to the country. Neither of them mentioned the envelope filled with hundred dollar bills, still in Jack's bottom desk drawer. Patricia had barged into his office the day before and almost caught him with the envelope before he locked it away.

The day was crisp with a sharp wind, and the top was up on Fitz's convertible. It was the first time Jack had been out here since before Christmas—and Allie's accident. Any one of the several curves they raced around could have been her undoing, but he didn't know which.

Fitz whipped around the corner into the McFee development. Five of the six houses were empty now, the lawns ragged with piles of dead leaves against the western walls and along the low chain-link fences.

"That Jones woman," Fitz said, looking over at him. "She's going to sell me the house your lady lawyer got back for her." He pointed to a house surrounded by dead weeds.

Fitz had hired an old oil land man after Jack's failure with the Madison sisters. That was why the parcels, mostly small farms and rural lots, had been piling up for closings like the dead leaves.

They turned at the cul-de-sac and made their way back down the street. Curtains moved in one window of the only house that appeared occupied—its lawn evenly trimmed and the flowerbeds, though empty, well-tended.

"That's the Madison house," Fitz said, pointing past Jack's nose.

Like I don't know the damn house, he thought.

"They still won't sell. Like Jews in the promised land." Fitz gave a sarcastic laugh, then gunned the car back out to the main road. The Old Schoolhouse Road.

"So, sport, you were looking for a witness, you say?" They were on the short stretch before the turn to the river. "Odd place to look for a witness."

He'd made the mistake of telling Fitz about the catfight at the Patriot Bar, not a usual hangout for young professionals. Patricia had sworn him to secrecy; they had to protect Judy Kay—but he let it out anyway.

"Patricia wanted to talk to the Taco Pal robber's girlfriend." Jack stared away from Fitz, out over the bare fields.

"Dumbest thing I ever heard." Fitz whipped the car off the pavement and down the dirt road to the river. "Robbing a fucking Mexican restaurant."

"They have a safe. Money in safe, *kemo sabe*."

"Ought to hang 'em all," Fitz said.

The car jerked to a stop at a grove of pecan trees that had been lush with greenery the last time they were there. Now the trees were bare, their limbs stretched out against a vivid-blue winter sky. Sodden black leaves and dead branches blanketed the ground under the trees. Between the car and the pecan grove stretched a carpet of long grass, brown and beaten down.

This morning was the first time he'd seen Fitz alone since his client's return from the Caribbean. For the last couple of weeks, he had found a pleasant distraction in Sally McFee. They had lunch; then he called her and they went to dinner and a movie. And shared a long goodnight kiss at the big oak doors of the McFee manse.

The property closings included the ones Lacey had harangued him about. To Fitz, Jack said nothing about the inflated appraisals, nothing about the mayor's involvement in the A-E Land Company, nothing about the cities' energy project. Jack simply blessed the transactions and gave Fitz copies of the Star Energy agreements for Fitz's partners to review and sign. The final documents and requisite filings for the venture would be completed in a week or so. The refinancings came first. Unsaid was that Fitz's properties would be resold later, at higher prices, to Star Energy.

Jack was reluctant to raise any concerns, pee on the deals that were bringing in rich fees. That was how the bills got paid and Lacey, Aerial, and the rest of them ate and paid their rent. He wasn't prepared to walk away. And what Fitz was doing wasn't illegal or even unethical. He had convinced himself of that—despite Allie. And he hadn't returned the money.

Fitz had sent flowers to Allie, who was still in the hospital. He was greatly concerned and he wanted to know the details. In telling him, Jack avoided saying anything about her fight with the mayor—or its cause. These days, there were a lot of subjects he avoided talking about with anyone.

"Ain't this great!" Fitz said, opening his door and getting out. Reaching in the back, he grabbed his sheepskin jacket and slipped it on.

"What's so great about it?" Jack asked over the black canvas top of the car. "There's nothing here."

"Goddamn right! Ain't nothing here but raw pasture and fields and trees." Sidling to the rear of the car, he grinned broadly at Jack. "Over three hundred acres we can turn into one big-ass energy park. After that comes a shitload of opportunities, my friend." He popped the trunk and reached inside. "Got a new toy," he said from the muffled depths. He emerged, pulling a shotgun from its case. "Beretta twenty gauge. Just bought it."

"Nice," Jack said, coming closer. "Looks expensive."

Tossing the case back in the trunk, Fitz extracted a box of shells and broke the action to load the gun.

"When I look out at all this empty space, I see the future," Fitz said as he stuffed several more shells into his jacket pocket. "Office buildings, research and technology centers."

Fitz started through the dead grass, then after a few bounding steps, circled back and came up beside Jack. They stood facing each other—one tall and lean, the other shorter and solid, like a middleweight fighter.

"Why do you reckon Allie was out here, Jack?" Fitz asked, staring up at him.

"No idea." But Jack drew back in surprise at the question.

"She and Dick are old friends of mine. Absolutely tears my heart out to see anything bad happen to her." He shook his head. "Such a lovely woman, too . . . You know, even though they're divorced, Dick's still devoted to her."

He swung around and stalked off toward the river. Reluctantly, Jack followed, wondering why Fitz had brought this up. After a good fifty yards, Fitz stopped near a rotting post to which a few rusty strands of barbwire were stapled.

"This is what I was telling you," Fitz said, kicking at the post as Jack came up. Jack looked down. His wingtips were wet.

"They used this as the goddamn corner instead of the tree," Fitz said, pointing to a small orange flag planted at their feet then to a gnarled red maple. "We'll damn-well fix that shit." He snapped the action shut on the shotgun, raised it to his shoulder, and fired two quick blasts at the tree. A lower branch splintered wildly in every direction and a gouge appeared in one side.

"Ow!" said Jack, covering his ear and flinching away from Fitz and the gun. "How about telling me next time."

Fitz lowered the shotgun and grinned at him. "Sensitive ears?"

He ejected the shells, then reloaded and charged off through the grass to the maple tree, where he briefly examined the damage before going on past to the other side. Jack came up behind him, and they stopped together beneath the tree's crisscrossed web of bare limbs. At their feet, exposed tree roots reached out from the crumbling riverbank. Several yards below, milky brown water swept by in swirling currents peppered with flotsam.

"This water's important for us," Fitz said. He pointed to the other side of the river. "We'll set up a filtration plant over there."

No distinction between the cities and himself, Jack thought, staring dully at the murky water. For a long moment, they were silent and everything was quiet around them, except for the rushing water.

"You know, Jack, I hope Allie isn't against all this." Jack looked up to find Fitz's eyes on him. "If she is, it could queer the whole deal. She pulls a lot of weight on the council." Fitz was staring at him as if he expected something.

"Hard to tell," Jack said with a shrug, but he was thinking, *What the hell does Fitz know about Allie and the mayor?* "It'll be a while before she gets back to work," he added.

Fitz gave him an odd, mouth-slightly-open look. "We need to get her on our side. You'll help us with that, won't you, my man?"

Jack started. He knew how Allie felt—that is, before her accident. But he couldn't tell this to Fitz. And she might not have the ability to do anything now or ever again.

"Fitz, I don't have any influence—"

"You're a family friend. You can get her to support us."

"But the city's interest in this property isn't even certain. You're—"

"Not certain!" Fitz hit the tree with his open palm. "Let me tell you, my young friend, I know how it's gonna end up. The cities are gonna buy a lot of this land, and I'm gonna develop the rest."

"Allie might not like it, you—"

"It's an open goddamn secret!" Fitz's tan didn't conceal the rising red color in his face. "There's no insider trading laws here. There's nothing that keeps me from making an informed decision on my investments." He fixed Jack with a gimlet-eyed glare. "Don't get squirrelly on me."

"I'm not." Jack shook his head and grabbed at a low branch on the tree. "It's just . . . the appraisals on these refinancings keep going up and the price for the land . . ." His words tailed off as Fitz continued to glare at him. "Well, the cities are gonna pay a premium."

"That's how the hell we make money." Fitz was bouncing on the balls of his feet. "How do you think developers work? . . . Huh, huh? Buy cheap, sell for a fucking profit. Build something, hold it—"

"I don't think Allie's going to approve."

"Don't be so naïve." He took the lapel of Jack's sport coat in one hand and tugged at it. "How do you think these fucking politicians get rich? They look after their friends and their friends look after them. These jokers don't get elected without people like me paying their way."

"I don't think Allie's like that." Jack pulled his jacket out of Fitz's grip and stepped back.

"She'll be out of it for a while, sport." Fitz stretched his mouth into a smile. "You need to get her on our side if . . . when she gets back in the game."

"She doesn't like the mayor's involvement."

"The mayor!" Now Fitz stepped back, almost against the tree. He stared at Jack a moment, then said in a low voice, "Mayor Fisher's only doing his civic duty." His voice rising, he spread his arms. "The man has vision. This place can be another Research Triangle."

"Is he profiting, personally?" Jack gestured toward the empty pastures behind him.

"Hell no!" Fitz stopped, then grinned at Jack, but with a hard glint in his eyes. "Maybe he has a little investment, you know, skin in the game.

But that's how it's done. He'll do a better job for the citizens by being involved in the outcome."

"What does the mayor's in-*volve*-ment make this look like? Especially if it's not disclosed?"

"Hell, Jack," Fitz said, emitting an exasperated sigh. "He's only got a small interest."

"Like this A-E Company?"

Fitz gave an almost imperceptible start before he answered. "He can't give up all of his investments just because he's a public servant. This project's bigger'n he is." Fitz was looking past him, toward the bare fields. "Bigger'n all of us. There'll be hundreds of millions of dollars invested out here before we're done. Think of all the jobs." He waved his hand past Jack's shoulder; then his finger was under Jack's nose. "Don't get squeamish over a few broken eggs. Not when we're gonna—"

"Was Allie a broken egg?" Too late, he wished he hadn't said it. But he was starting to believe it.

"Allie? What do you mean?" Shaking his head, Fitz walked slowly past him, in the direction of the pecan grove. Jack followed.

"She was out here," Jack said, catching up with Fitz. "And all this with the mayor, the city—"

"Hey, look at that!" Fitz grabbed Jack's arm. "Bobwhites! Covey ran out from under the trees . . . Over there." He pointed off across the field. Jack caught only a glimpse of a few brown birds scurrying into the high grass.

"I'm gonna get a shot at 'em," Fitz said in a hoarse whisper. The action of the shotgun closed with a smooth click.

"What! How you gonna do that? You don't have any dogs." Jack backed away as Fitz waved his shotgun toward the grass. "Are they even in season?"

Fitz gave him a downward shushing motion with one hand. "Gotta be in that grassy area. We just walk toward it. They'll flush; you watch."

Holding the shotgun at half-mast, he was already moving.

Jack stared back and forth between Fitz and where the birds had disappeared into the grass, then followed him. They passed in front of the pecan grove and stopped thirty yards short of where the birds had gone.

"Won't they hunker down or something?" Jack asked in a low voice.

Fitz eyed him for a moment, then nodded. "Maybe you're right. You go off to the left there," he waved his hand, "then double back across. They'll fly off to the right and I can get a good shot."

"Whoa! Wait a minute." Jack stepped back and held up his hands. "I'm your lawyer, not your bird dog."

"Come on, I'm not gonna shoot you. Never come close to my dogs." He patted the shotgun. "Been itching to see how this baby does."

Assessing Fitz with an incredulous stare, Jack wondered what the man expected of him, of everybody. Wondering if maybe he wasn't the prey.

"Look, I'm not a hunter," Jack said. "I don't know about this." Their voices had risen to more than a whisper now.

"Just do me this little favor." Fitz took a step toward him. The shotgun was across his chest, his finger outside the trigger guard.

Jack sighed and, pointing at his shoes, gave Fitz a grim smile. "You need to buy me some new wingtips."

"Sure thing—and a new suit if I get one." Fitz jabbed a hand toward the grassy area. "They should be out thata way," he called in a hoarse whisper as Jack started off. "I'll watch for 'em while you move across there."

Jack circled wide to the left, almost to the river, then cut back through the open field, walking slowly and watching his step. A slight breeze rippled the grass, patches of it up to his knees.

Looking up, he saw Fitz gesturing with the shotgun to keep moving. Eyes fixed on the gun, Jack stepped in a hole and stumbled forward. One knee hit the ground, then an outstretched hand. He scrambled to get up— only to plunge back down on both knees as the bobwhites rose in a frantic whirr, flying right above him.

The shotgun erupted with a blast, then another.

Jack heard—and felt—a whizzing mass of hornets fly over him. Whipping one arm over his head, he rolled sideways onto one shoulder to avoid flopping flat into the dead grass.

"Damnation!" yelled Fitz, bounding toward him. "Missed 'em." He came up and stared down at Jack.

"Jack, you okay, boy?"

"Shit! . . . Yeah. I guess." He got to his knees, then with Fitz's help, to his feet. Fitz held the shotgun broken over his other arm.

"That was mighty damn close," Jack said in a higher voice than he intended. He brushed off his pants, then his coat sleeve.

"Hell, wasn't expectin' them to go right over you." Patting Jack on the shoulder, Fitz gave a snorting chuckle. "All's swell that end's swell." He turned to go. "Need to get back." Without waiting, he strode rapidly away through the grass, toward his car.

Jack looked around. He was trembling. His wingtips were ruined and his pants and coat were filthy with dirt and grass.

The crazy son of a bitch had almost shot him. And he hadn't done the right thing.

Chapter Thirty-six – Billy Goes to Trial (Act Two)

THE JURY WAS A MIXED BAG—but maybe the best she could expect since it was the first she'd ever picked. If she'd had a rich client, she would've hired a jury consultant. As it was, all she had was Jack, equally ignorant but eager to offer his whispered opinions.

They were in a crowded shoebox of a courtroom, on the second-floor corner of the old granite courthouse. With the same old granite-faced judge. This time, though, he struck no fear in her heart. Still, she knew enough to be wary. The bar was higher and she'd have to work harder.

She covertly examined the twelve jurors and an alternate, shoved together on uncomfortable chairs in a makeshift jury box. Not a hanging jury, but unpredictable. Two high school teachers, an accountant, three homemakers (one insisted she was an old-fashioned housewife), a postal clerk, a couple of small business owners, and the rest city or corporate indentured servants who would enjoy a break from their cubicles or the shop floor. Seven women, six men. Ten white, three black. Not a jury of Billy Angel's peers: professional safecrackers who hadn't drawn a paycheck in years.

They had been assembled and sworn to fully and faithfully perform their duty. Not something that would benefit her client. Billy sat beside her at the small counsel table, while Jack perched, knees up, in a folding auditorium seat behind her. Aerial, when she wasn't running errands, sat next to Jack—his plan to appeal to the black jurors, at least the two males. The woman, older and impeccably dressed, had cast more than one disapproving glance at Aerial.

Ray Malloy and a new assistant D.A., who looked like she'd been hired based on Ray's usual criteria, huddled together at the prosecution table. He was still going for felony murder, maybe not the death penalty, but for enough years to put Billy on ice for good. His honor had reserved ruling on Patricia's motion to exclude any evidence of the .357 magnum the police found at the scene—and then lost, as well as the coroner's report that said Henry Royale's head wound was consistent with a bullet from a .357 magnum. When Patricia suggested a throw-down gun, the judge openly scoffed at her. Every defendant claims that.

She scribbled a note on the last page of her legal pad: "4th man?" Should she have brought up the missing crook?

The bailiffs and deputies who supervised the prisoners in the holding cells all disclaimed any knowledge of *any* visitor to Billy when he was down for his first trial. And there was nothing in the logbook they kept. One thing she was sure of: Billy hadn't imagined it. But the cops had a code, too. They'd never rat on one of their own or volunteer anything, not to a defense lawyer. With nothing more to go on, she had decided not to mention a fourth man in her motion and argument—or even in an aside to Ray Malloy. Not yet. That decision could wait until tomorrow, when the kid took the stand.

Beside her, Billy was glancing furtively at the jury and around the courtroom. He was dressed in brown slacks, without a belt (merely a precaution, the bailiff said), and a green plaid sports shirt straight out of the package. Thanks to Jack, the prisoner in the dock looked quite presentable.

She caught Billy staring past the prosecution table and the jurors, at the large church-size window behind them. It was opaque, either painted over or made that way. Was the scoundrel assessing how he could get out of here?

Noticing her watching him, he grinned and looked the other way, then back over his shoulder. As she studied the jury again, and a few of them studied her, Billy nudged her arm.

"Are they supposed to be in here?" he asked. "Back there." He didn't turn around, but kept his eyes on the legal pad she'd given him to make notes on.

She twisted around to stare between Jack and Aerial. In the back of the courtroom sat three uniformed cops and Hal Goodman, in plain clothes—an olive suit, white shirt, and solid red tie.

"See that?" she said to Jack, grabbing his leg, propped against the back of her chair. He turned to look. Without waiting for his response, she stood and bent across the space separating her from Ray Malloy.

"Ray, I'm invoking the rule. You need to get your witnesses out of here." She gestured at Goodman and his cohorts.

"Sure thing, counselor. I told 'em to come by so's we could get everybody sworn at once—the ones likely for today."

"I thought Goodman was tomorrow."

"All rise," bellowed the bailiff, a paunchy, dyed-black-hair man standing by the door to the judge's chambers. Patricia popped back in place as Judge Davis swept into the courtroom like a dark specter from the Spanish inquisition.

Ray's first witness was the deputy sheriff who had almost walked on Billy lying in the ditch near Plantation Road. A young, fresh-faced man, he drew chuckles from the jury at his description of Billy's discovery. Patricia asked him only two questions.

"You didn't see how he got there, did you?"

"No, ma'am." Ma'am? She couldn't be much older than he was.

"You would've hit the dirt, too, wouldn't you, if people were shooting all around you?"

"Yes ma'am, but—"

"Thank you, deputy . . . I pass the witness."

Ray stood. He flashed his teeth at Patricia, then at his witness.

"Did you find anyone else out there—now how long was it after the shootin' had stopped?" Ray asked.

"No sir. It was about twenty minutes since the gunfire," the deputy answered before Patricia could object. Damn Ray and his compound questions. She stayed in her seat. Never highlight a response with an unnecessary objection.

Next came the Taco Pal manager, a soft-spoken little man who had a comb-over that almost wrapped around his opposite ear. Ray's assistant, Megan Tate, did the direct. Her sharply focused questions quickly dispelled Patricia's judgment of the woman as one of Ray's typical hires.

The manager's wife, on her way to work, had dropped him off several blocks away from the Taco Pal. He needed the exercise, he said, and it was a beautiful morning.

"Must've been before six fifteen. I always unlock for the associates and do some paperwork. They get there by seven and we open at eight."

"And what did you find when you arrived?"

"I heard this tapping noise. See, I walked up the driveway and went to the front door, but I stopped to listen to this bird. In the dogwood, there in front. When he stopped singing, I heard this noise . . . tap, tap, tap." The manager's head bobbed with each tap. "It sounded like it was comin' from inside, so I looked in . . ." He started coughing. "'Scuse me," he said and took a swallow of water from a cup that Ray hurried to hand him.

"And what did you see?" Ms. Tate asked.

"Somethin' didn't look right. My office is back past the kitchen, and I saw a light back there—and it shoulda been dark. That tappin' kept on, then I heard something like a drill and I noticed the back door," he gestured to his right, "was open 'bout halfway. I knowed somethin' was wrong then, sure 'nuff. So I scooted on back down the drive, quiet as I could. Called the police from that Gulf station down the street."

Ray's assistant quizzed him about where he was when the police arrived and when the shooting started. Then she asked him what his office looked like when he finally got to see it.

"Like a hurricane had hit it, or some monster that ate concrete."

"How much was in the safe, Mr. Margoulis?"

"Fifty four dollars and forty five cents. See, yesterday, I—"

"Thank you, that's all," said the assistant D.A., closing her notepad.

From beside Patricia came a sharp intake of breath. Billy. They had never discussed what was in the safe. He must have thought there was more money.

Ms. Tate was talking to the judge. "Our crime scene expert will describe the area, so I'll pass the witness." She nodded at Patricia.

"Don't ask him any questions," hissed Jack, leaning forward and touching her arm. She waved her open palm downward, beside her chair.

"No questions, your honor," she said, smiling at the judge.

As his honor told Ray to call his next witness, she turned to the side away from the jury and scowled at Jack. He smiled back and shrugged. Aerial was gone, her purpose served.

Next up was Ezra, "everyone calls me Bud," Smith, one of the police officers who chased "the perpetrator" through the woods—the one who wasn't shot. So much for her image of cops. Officer Smith was someone who spent his days off at the gym or hanging out in the fire station weight room.

As first on the scene, Officer Smith and his partner Benny Bates had eased their patrol car to a stop in front of the Taco Pal. No siren, a quiet approach to see what was up.

"We were just getting out." He ducked his head and shoulders as if he were getting out of the car. "Officer Bates was taking the shotgun out of the rack when we heard this commotion 'round back. So we left the doors open and started to the rear of the building." His clipped police voice became less practiced and more conversational. "That's when Stan . . . Stan Gryzbowski arrived in the other car. He's robbery investigation and he—"

"What happened when you started around back, Officer Smith?" Ray asked with a smile and a nod.

"Like, there was some sort of commotion back there, then this man in a gray jacket and ball cap comes barreling past the corner. Guess he didn't expect to see us, 'cause he froze like a deer in the headlights. He took off through the woods and Benny and I started after him. We were both yelling . . . you know, 'Police! Stop!' But I hadn't gone more'n two steps when I saw something movin' on the other side of the building, like somebody trying to sneak off. So I started that way, and somebody started tearing out through the woods. Lot of bushes and small trees over there so I couldn't see much. Stan . . . from robbery, he came around the other side of the building and was ahead of me, after this guy. Benny kept on after the guy in the cap, going the other way. Stan's kind of chubby and I can move faster'n him, so I got—"

"Okay," Ray said, "so you and Stan were chasing this man through the woods. Did you get a good look at him?"

"No sir. Just saw he had on these blue coveralls. For a minute I thought there was two of 'em . . . 'cause of the noise, but all I ever saw was the one."

Patricia's mind focused on "two of 'em." Maybe she could ask this witness?

"I heard a shot," Officer Smith was saying. "Thought it zinged through the leaves higher up." He made a curved-arm, pointing motion above his head. "So I ducked. Then there was another. I don't know where it went. Stan . . . he was down on one knee in firing position, and he let off a few rounds."

"How many incoming rounds did you take?" Ray asked, his face serious.

Officer Smith screwed up his mouth in a perplexed look. "I don't rightly know. It all happened so sudden."

"Did you start back after the robber—"

"Objection," said Patricia, on her feet. "Assumes facts not in evidence."

"Now Miss Egan," said Judge Davis, "wouldn't the fact the man is *running* and shooting at the police pretty well establish he's one of the robbers?"

"That's okay, your honor," Ray said. His face was sporting a solicitous grin. "I can rephrase the question if it'll make everyone happy."

"Go ahead, Mr. Malloy." The judge frowned at Patricia then looked at the court reporter. "Strike the question, Miss Sparrow . . . and my comments."

"Will the court instruct the jury to disregard all that, your honor?" Patricia said, giving the judge a sheepish look. He smiled faintly, then turned to the jury.

"Ladies and gentlemen, you will *not* consider the question and comments on *the robber* as evidence."

As she sat, Jack gripped her arm from behind. "Bad move, Perry," he whispered in her ear.

She shook off his hand and concentrated on Ray's rephrased question.

"When the shooting stopped, what did you do?"

"We waited a few minutes; then we started forward, tree-to-tree like . . . and keeping down low. A couple more of our guys came up. Stan almost shot—"

"Just tell us what you did then, Officer Smith," Ray said.

"We conferred and decided to work a grid through the woods. All the noise out front of us had stopped. So that's what we did the next twenty minutes or so. Must've been a dozen of us combin' the woods out there. It was Detective Goodman that found the gun under a bush."

"Objection, your honor." She was on her feet again. "Hearsay. There's no evidence—"

"Well, I saw it," said the witness.

"Just a minute, Officer Smith," said Ray.

"This witness didn't find a gun," Patricia said. "That's—"

"Objection sustained. That part of the answer will be stricken. The jury's instructed not to consider it . . . Now let's move on, counsel."

She felt good. She'd won one! Then she remembered what Judge Davis had said about an appeal-proof record.

Winding up his direct, Officer Smith testified that the search ended when a lieutenant told them that two men had been apprehended and a third shot by Benny Bates, his partner. Then he described the scene inside the Taco Pal: the manager's office covered in hunks of concrete and a layer of dust that must have been a quarter-inch deep and a barrel safe almost stripped of the reinforced concrete encasing it—all as shown in the photographs Ray handed him.

On cross, she managed to elicit two admissions of dubious benefit. Before the shots buzzing over them, Smith had already heard the shotgun blast that made an end to Lazlo, and while his own weapon was a .38, Stan's was a .357 magnum. Her victory was short lived. Ray asked for a bench conference and argued that she'd opened the door to evidence of the found gun. Judge Davis seemed to agree, but he would address the whole gun issue at the end of the day—in a conference in chambers. The exchange left her with a sinking feeling as she returned to her seat.

With Officer Smith off the stand, Ray called his expert. The woman looked more like an Olympic swimmer than the college professor she was: short blond hair, tan, svelte, and erect in an expensive beige suit and low heels. As she settled into the witness chair, she gave Patricia the appraising stare of a competitor. And not just as a witness.

Her name was Dr. Henrietta Erlanger, the emphasis on the doctor, and her recitation of credentials and publications left no opening for challenge. An expert in crime scene reconstruction.

Why does he need this woman, Patricia wondered. Someone tried to bust a safe out of a block of concrete and almost succeeded before they got scared off. She examined the photographs while the woman droned on in mellow tones, slightly accented, giving her interpretation of what had happened.

All plausible and not worth objecting to, Patricia decided. *The hammers and chisels and an electric drill are still there in the photographs. Wait. Didn't Billy say they gathered up their tools? Then he dropped them in the woods.*

So what good did that do her?

The cylindrical safe stood out like a sore thumb inside three exposed iron bars. *It's a wonder they didn't awaken everyone in the apartments. Why would anyone waste time doing this?* Ray finally asked the obvious question she was thinking.

"It appears that they were trying to steal the safe," was Dr. Erlanger's answer. Some titters came from the reporters and spectators in the gallery. The jurors, though, all remained serious and several glanced over at Billy.

If only they knew, thought Patricia. Staring at the photograph of the safe, she noticed it wasn't open, and there wasn't a dent on its face or a mark on the dial. *Safecracking is thirty years, grand larceny ten.* Yet, how could she get past attempted safecracking? Her musings almost made her miss Ray's next question.

"So, Dr. Erlanger, did you make any comparisons of the cement dust from the office and that on the defendant's clothing?"

Patricia was on her feet. "Objection, your honor—"

"Sustained," said Judge Davis. "The clothes aren't in evidence nor are any samples taken from them."

"I understand, Judge," Ray said, his grin wide and understanding. "I'll fix all that, if you'll allow me."

"May we approach the bench, your honor?" She started around the counsel table and headed toward the podium.

"Looks like you're almost here," the judge said. She stopped. "But come on." He beckoned her forward. "Jury's excused. Fifteen minute break."

Before the jury was out the door, she launched her protest. "Your honor, he didn't give me notice the expert was going to compare samples from my client's clothes with the cement dust in the restaurant."

Ray chuckled and showed his even white teeth again. "Dr. Erlanger's a crime scene expert. She puts together all the parts of the *res gestae* and connects them with the accused. That's what she's doing here, counsel."

Judge Davis gave them both a sour look. Holding onto the edge of the podium, Patricia rose on her toes.

"I object to this brazen ambush. He—"

"Miss Egan, the concrete is part of the crime scene," the judge said. "I think he's making a permissible use of his expert—if he can introduce the clothes or whatever he's got."

"I can, your honor," Ray said. "I'll put on the officers—"

"Can't you stipulate they're his clothes, Miss Egan?" the judge asked.

"Only after I get a chance to cross examine the officers."

Judge Davis sighed, a long weary sigh. "I'll let you get your own expert if you want a continuance for a few weeks to do it."

"I . . . he . . . my client doesn't have the money for that, Judge." Not that it would do him any good if he did.

"You can't have your cake and eat it too, counsel. Do you want to proceed?" A sardonic look on the craggy face.

"Yes sir." Now it was her turn to sigh. "We don't have much choice."

And proceed they did. Ray brought on the officers and the clothes, and the expert returned to testify that the ingredients of concrete had fingerprints just like humans. She then linked the cement dust on Billy's coveralls and shoes to that from inside the Taco Pal.

Billy tugged at her sleeve. "Missy . . . Miss Egan—"

"Shhh," she said. "I need to hear this."

The doctor of science finished her testimony by describing how chemical analysis and microscopic examinations matched up the samples, and then Ray passed the witness. He gave Patricia a smug look as he closed his legal pad.

"Your honor, may I have a moment to confer with my client?" she asked, only half rising.

"Go right ahead. Take all the time you want."

Did she detect sarcasm in the judge's voice? Huddled with their heads together, Jack, Billy, and her, she asked what Billy had wanted to tell her.

"Them clothes and shoes," Billy said in a barely audible whisper, his face screwed up in a frown. "There's so much dust on them, that woman could never tell what come from there."

"Don't you ever change the coveralls?" Jack asked. "Or wash them?"

"Nah. not for a while." He gave a sheepish grin. "For luck."

"Your luck ran out," snapped Patricia, trying to keep her voice down, but wanting to yell at him: *That's not a viable defense.*

She turned back to face the judge. "Only a few questions, your honor."

A few questions too many. They served only to highlight the suave PhD's expertise and allow her to reiterate the connection between Billy's clothes and the debris in the Taco Pal. This elicited a low groan from Jack, followed by a slap on his leg from Patricia.

Dr. Erlanger made her exit with a slight smile at Patricia, *like a sleek panther*, Patricia was thinking, *hauling off her prey*. With the main attraction over, the judge excused the jury for the day and led the lawyers back to his chambers. Minus Jack, who left close behind Dr. Erlanger.

Once they were in the judge's inner sanctum and he was shrugging off his robes, he addressed Patricia. "I can see how you might've expected the professor only to talk about *how* the perpetrators . . . tried to remove the safe . . . from the concrete." He puffed with the effort of hanging the long robe in an armoire to one side of the room. "But Mr. Malloy said she was here for crime scene reconstruction. Isn't much of a stretch to link dust on the clothes to the concrete in the restaurant. After all, your client was found near there lyin' in a ditch."

"But your honor . . ." Patricia started, then stopped as the judge gave her a dismissive wave of his hand. He went behind his desk.

"What I want to talk about is this felony murder charge. I'm concerned about that missing gun." Still standing, he looked down at Ray, seated next to Patricia on the far side of the wide desk. Ms. Tate, Ray's assistant, sat on the other side of Ray.

"Who do you plan to offer on this tomorrow, Mr. Malloy?"

"Judge, I plan to show the gun that was found . . . well, pictures of it. And the detective who found it will testify—"

"But there is *no* gun, counselor. It was lost. By the police." Judge Davis eased down into his high-back leather chair. "I find that a mite suspicious."

"That happens, your honor. Lots of stuff in that evidence room—"

"Yeah, and some of it ends up right back on the street." The judge leaned forward and pressed a button on his phone. "You folks want some coffee . . . co-colas?"

"No thanks," Ray said. Patricia and Ms. Tate echoed his refusal.

Judge Davis settled deeper into his chair. "What's your means of tyin' this found-and-lost gun to the dead man, the one there in the parking lot?"

He held up a hand to stop Ray from answering. As if by magic, the judge's secretary appeared with a steaming-hot mug of coffee.

"You don't have a bullet," the judge said as she deposited the mug in front of him. "You don't have a ballistics test. Miss Egan made that clear in her motion, and you don't disagree."

He took the mug and, as his secretary left and while Ray and his assistant were whispering and shuffling papers, he slid a bottom drawer in his desk open a fraction. From around the side of the desk, Patricia caught a glimpse of a silver flask. His honor quickly slopped some liquid from the flask into the mug.

"So what do you have?" Judge Davis asked, straightening up and placing the mug back on his desk. He glanced over at Patricia. She suppressed a smile.

Turning from his assistant, Ray said, "The coroner's going to testify that the wound—"

Patricia was on the edge of her seat, waiting to interject her objection, but the judge struck first. "Oh, come on, Mr. Malloy." He took a tentative sip from the mug. "There were bullets flying all over the place. This whole business with the coroner doesn't mean a thing."

She settled back to listen. His honor was almost quoting from her motion, with a few twists of his own.

"I'm inclined to exclude the coroner's testimony and all that stuff about this gun that's gone missing." He took a deeper draft of his potion.

"I think you're wrong, Judge," Ray said, his face red. His pretty cohort sat stiffly beside him and kept quiet.

"You can take it up on appeal, if you like." Leaning back, the judge rested the mug on the bottom of his necktie and gourmand's stomach. "But you'll lose." A self-satisfied smile smoothed out a few of the crevices in the granite face. "You got anything else on the murder charge?"

"The young man who was lookout . . . and some more officers." This came out in Ray's normal voice, all braggadocio deflated. His assistant, who had been studying a legal pad with some writing on it, held it out in front of Ray. He looked, then added, "There was a felony in progress, and a bystander was killed. That's all we're required to show, under the law."

The judge rocked back in his chair, giving no indication of agreement or disagreement. He looked over at Patricia. "You have anything to say, Miss Egan?"

She debated raising the fourth man, decided the judge was going her way, and shook her head. "This really isn't a murder case, your honor. My client didn't shoot anybody and there's no evidence he even had a gun. Did they do a trace test on his hands?"

She looked at Ray, who shrugged.

"Of course not," she said. "They know where all the bullets came from."

"Nicely put, Miss Egan." The judge nodded. "I'm inclined to agree with you—but that may be the last time in this trial." He raised one eyebrow at her, and then he looked at Ray. "Mr. Malloy, unless you've got something more than you've shown me, I'm going to direct a verdict for the defense on the murder charge. It seemed a bit tardy in coming anyhow."

"Your honor," Ray said in a subdued voice, "we'll go talk with the police and coroner and—"

"Little late for that," the judge said, taking a swig from the mug. He leaned forward and set the mug on the desk. "Nine o'clock tomorrow, counsel. We'll hear any new motions, if they're pertinent, before we bring the jurors in."

On the way back to the office, Patricia almost danced an Irish jig down the street. Now all she had to worry about was robbery and safecracking. No more quandary about Billy's other partner.

She'd tell him in the morning.

Chapter Thirty-seven – Billy's Big Break

THE BAILIFF WITH DYED-BLACK HAIR delivered Billy to a different cell from the solo one he'd occupied for the last three days. The cells in the courthouse basement were nothing more than holding pens for prisoners awaiting trial, like him, or the overflow from the county jail. Based on what he'd seen, there was always an overflow.

The cell was empty. It had yellow stucco walls decorated with black scuffmarks and a concrete floor with chipped gray paint. There were two bunks, one above the other, a sheet and a blanket folded neatly on each. Opposite the cell door was a metal sink with a metal mirror above it and, beside it, a metal toilet without a seat.

"I need to go get your county duds," said the bailiff as he undid the last loop on the shackles. "You just make yourself right at home here." A deputy sheriff watched from outside the cell.

"Thanks for everything," Billy said, rubbing his wrists.

The bailiff made him uneasy. Any change made him uneasy, especially after what he'd heard today—just peanuts in the safe. The fuckers might make a move on him, to shut him up. Maybe the bailiff was one set of their eyes. He didn't look like much, no bigger than Billy, middle-aged with a dyed pompadour and shadows under his eyes. *I could take him*, Billy thought, observing the bailiff's slouching shoulders and paunch.

Although the cuffs hadn't been that tight, he continued to rub his wrists as the bailiff locked the cell door and disappeared along with the deputy into the dim depths of the hallway. A little farther down, an early drunk started yelling for them to let him out, ending in a screech, "God's gonna get you for this!"

Billy took the lower bunk. Spreading the sheet and blanket out on top of it, he grabbed the bedding off the one above and made a pillow, then stretched out to think. *The trial will take two, three days more at most. These young lawyers aren't going to be able to protect me, not for another week here if*

214

they don't move me back to Central right away. Goodman could do almost anything in that time. Maybe only send a message, with a few bruises, but it could be worse.

He felt in his pocket. Nearest thing he had to a weapon was the plastic pen the lady lawyer had given him to write with on the pad. He took it out, examined it, then snapped it in half. The clear plastic splintered, forming jagged pieces around the central tube of ink, which he removed and shoved under the mattress. With his thumb, he tested the ragged ends. *Not worth a shit but better than nothing.* He stuffed the pieces of the pen into his shirt pocket.

How can I get away? He dozed as the drunk down the hall renewed his clamoring for attention. The bailiff didn't return.

The cell door rattled. Starting up, he raised himself on one elbow.

Two white deputies stood outside the cell, holding onto the arms of a giant black man with a cannonball head and hooded, sleepy eyes. The man was hunched forward, his arms jammed up behind him. His left cheek was swollen, a glowering purple against his ebony skin. A long angry welt ran across one side of his forehead to the bridge of his nose.

Finally getting the door open, one of the deputies, almost as big and beefy as his prisoner, shoved the man inside and slammed the door behind him. The man stumbled a couple of steps, then pivoted easily on the balls of his feet and seized the bars with huge gnarled hands. He faced his jailers without speaking.

"Better watch yourself, boy," the big deputy said, once the door was locked. "Next time you take a swing at a cop, you'll get worse'n that."

Staring out through the bars, the black man stood silent and impassive as Stone Mountain. He continued to watch as the deputies departed, until their voices mingled with the drunk's bellowing down the hall.

Ignoring Billy, supine but vigilant on the lower bunk, the big man lumbered across the cell to the sink. He fiddled with the spigot, then placing both hands under it, splashed water on his face and the back of his neck. After rubbing his eyes and carefully testing his injured flesh with his fingers, he took a thin white towel from the shelf above the sink and dabbed at the welt on his forehead, examining himself in the metal mirror.

He stopped abruptly and lowered the towel to his chest. He turned from the mirror, his face sullen, and glared at Billy.

215

"What you starin' at?" he said in a resonant bass.

Billy sat up, eyes fixed on the black man's face, his muscles tensed and ready. Thinking, considering. *Play it right, this could be my ticket out. Or the message they've sent. Goliath when all I needed was a plain ordinary nigger.*

"I was just thinking what a stupid black motherfucker you are, takin' a swing at a white cop," Billy said. "You really do that?"

"Aw, man, I don't need no lip from a piece of white trailer-trash like you." Still holding the towel with both hands, he moved toward Billy. "Just get off my bunk and give me one of them blankets."

Billy stood and made like he was going to hand the man a blanket. Instead, he punched him hard in the chest, above the towel. A good two heads taller and a hundred pounds of muscle and bone heavier than Billy, the black goliath shifted only a step backward—not so much from the blow, but from the surprise that showed on his face.

"What you do that for?" The surprise changed to a puzzled look.

"'Cause you're a dumb-ass nigger, and I'm gonna whup your fat ass." Billy lunged at him.

Dropping the towel, the man enveloped Billy in his arms.

At first, the giant only grappled with him, while Billy aimed his fists upward at the man's mouth and the welt on his forehead. After a couple of short jabs made contact, the man let out a bellow and began pummeling Billy in earnest—in the face, in the gut, in the chest. Blood trickled from Billy's nose and from a cut over his eye. Finally, he fell down and curled into a ball on the floor. Unappeased, the giant gave him a kick in one thigh then in the small of his back, followed by a glancing blow to the ribs.

Billy worked the splintered pen out of his shirt pocket. After receiving another kick, he bolted to his feet, agile as ever despite the pain in his face, his hip, and his back. Darting under the swinging arms, he made a slash down the side of his opponent's neck, breaking the plastic into small shards, but drawing streams of blood.

With a shriek, the man grabbed Billy with both hands and hurled him against the bars. One blow of the huge fists followed another, until Billy's face ran with blood and he had doubled over, unable to breathe. Only the cell door opening saved him from the unrelenting punishment.

"What the hell are you doin'! Get back, goddamn you, get back," yelled a deputy. Stepping over Billy, he and another khaki uniform shoved the black man to the rear of the cell.

Billy lay gasping on the floor. Another deputy came in, then the bailiff, and the two bent over him. Opening his eyes in narrow slits, Billy watched them through a red haze. His hand still clutched the pieces of jagged plastic.

"This one's in bad shape, J.B.," said the bailiff to the deputy next to him. "Better get an ambulance."

"This black bastard's gonna need some stitches, too," a deputy called from the other side of the cell.

"That motherfucker started it," came a deep voice. "Didn't do nuthin to him and he just started bad mouthin' me. Then he jump me, no reason at all."

"Shut up!" yelled the deputy. The black man gave an "oomph" like somebody had hit him. There were sounds of a struggle.

"Get some shackles," shouted one of the guards. "We need to wrap this'un up, get him to the hospital."

Suddenly it was quiet. The black man had stopped struggling, but he kept up his rumbling complaints about Billy.

"Call the meat wagon," said the deputy, J.B. He still knelt next to Billy. "This one ain't gonna be no problem to nobody, not for a while."

The other two deputies dragged Billy's adversary out of the cell, then J.B. and the bailiff went off down the hall, past the still-hollering drunk. Billy was beginning to recognize the bailiff's footsteps, slow and shambling.

They'd locked the cell door and left him lying on the floor. Not even a blanket for his head or to cover his aching body. He was badly bruised. Cuts on his face and a busted nose, but no broken bones. Maybe a cracked rib or two. And another tooth gone. One thing he'd learned in life—how to take a beating and survive. He opened his eyes wider. He needed to dope this up some more.

Groaning and rolling back and forth, he worked his hand under his head, then jabbed a sharp plastic shard into his ear, but not too deep. He screamed in pain. Feeling the fresh blood running over his hand, he cast the remaining plastic splinters away from him, underneath the bunk. Then he stuck two bloody fingers down his throat and vomited. Concentrating on bearing the pain and working out his plans, he lay there in his blood and vomit until the ambulance crew arrived.

They were packed like lab rats in the back of the ambulance, Billy on a stretcher on one side and the black prisoner, sitting upright in double shackles, on the other. The bailiff and a deputy sat on two jump seats, while a paramedic knelt beside Billy. Deputy J.B. was up front with the driver.

During the time they were loading him and driving to the hospital, siren wailing, Billy played possum. Except for a fluttered peek at his surroundings, he kept his eyes shut. His breathing was fast and shallow. He responded to nothing they said, but listened attentively to the snatches of conversation.

"Cozy back there?" the driver asked through the small window to the cab.

"Shits wouldn't give us a car," came from near him. The deputy.

"Hell, they all gone off to supper." The bailiff.

The deputy gave a snort. "Gawd, this bastard stinks." He bent close to Billy's face. "You sure he's breathing okay?"

"Yeah," said the paramedic. "Nothing more we can do 'til we get there." There was a metallic sound distinct from the muffled siren and road noise. "Got an IV going." Rubber encased fingers touched his face and the side of his head. "He may have a skull fracture. Blood's comin' out his ear." A rustling as the paramedic adjusted a monitor they'd rigged up to him. "Pulse and heart rate's good, though."

Bill struggled to overcome the pain. He was sure they had given him something in the IV. He prayed it wouldn't slow him down.

The radio in front crackled. "Red rover," came a voice through the static, "you almost at your destination? I need you ASAP. We have a transfer."

"Yeah, yeah," the driver said and, after some preliminaries, added, "we're headed to McFee. But Ted and I gotta have somethin' to eat."

"Make it fast. This one's a priority."

"Okay, but give us a couple of minutes," the driver said. "We'll grab something inside."

Eyes closed tight, Billy listened and worked this into his calculation.

The ambulance swung sharply around a curve and up an incline then braked to a stop. Almost at once, the rear door sprung open. The EMTs unloaded Billy while the two deputies jerked the shackled black prisoner out and onto his feet. Billy fluttered his eyes and caught the man glaring at him. A white bandage stained red with blood covered the man's cheek and neck.

Poor bastard, thought Billy. *Hate I had to do that to him.*

As soon as the EMTs had him on the ramp, a nurse and orderly joined them beside the gurney. Together they wheeled him inside, into a large open area, where the ambulance crew promptly disappeared. All around were a jumble of voices and strange sounds and the seemingly directionless, hurried movement of people. A voice over a speaker paged a doctor, telling him to go to a room and giving some cryptic hospital code. There were pungent odors, hospital smells of sickness and antiseptic and cleaning fluids.

Trailed by the bailiff, now Billy's sole guard, the nurse and orderly maneuvered him down a short hallway and into a closet-like recess. A curtain rasped closed behind them. A bright light shone down on his face. The IV bag dangled close by his head. Moving up to the gurney, the bailiff grabbed the pole for the IV and stared down at him. Through his lashes, Billy glimpsed dyed black hair and stubble on the bailiff's cheeks. A harsh breath brought him a sour whiff of garlic.

A small, blue-suited doctor breezed into the cubicle. Owlish, balding, Ghandi-ish, he had little more than grunts for anybody. Billy kept his eyes closed, but not too tight, while the doctor poked, squeezed, and prodded.

"Get him cleaned up." A brusque, practiced medical voice. "Vital signs are excellent. He's in no danger." Judgment pronounced, the doctor did a military pivot and exited through the curtain, quickly followed by the nurse.

"Aw, fuck," said the bailiff. He had moved to a corner with the arrival of the doctor. "Have I gotta wait around here all night for this?" He pointed at Billy's still form. The still form groaned and moved his head to peer at the bailiff through bleary slits beneath his lashes.

"Go on, get a coke," said the orderly, a post-adolescent white kid with a shaved head and blue tattoos on both arms. "I gotta strip him and wash him down." He started undoing the remaining buttons on Billy's new sport shirt, bloody and wet with vomit, but only slightly ripped at the right shoulder and missing the top button.

After briefly tugging at the second button, the orderly gave it a jerk. "Shit! Best cut the damn thing off. It's covered with shit." Through Billy's lashes, the orderly appeared solid but slow—like he'd had one-too-many joints on breaks.

"Back shortly," said the bailiff. The curtain swayed. Billy sensed it was just him and the orderly now, and the orderly was off to one side of the cubicle, rummaging through a metal cabinet.

He started counting. Give the bailiff a couple of minutes, but he had to keep his shirt. The orderly returned, carrying scissors and a pan with liquid and sponges, and placed them on a rolling tray table by Billy's head. Bending close, he took the front of Billy's shirt in one hand and raised the scissors. Billy tensed. *Time to go.* Then he gave a start, which he hid with a groan.

A series of short buzzes were sounding not far above his head. The orderly reached across him and lifted a white phone off the wall.

"Yo," he said. Then silence, followed by, "Hey, man, I can't get that for you now." A pause. "Yeah, that's right. And don't call me down here." Silence. "Yeah, yeah, catch you later." Fumbling with the cord and muttering, "Dumb fuck," he hung up the phone.

Billy exploded off the gurney. Yanking the IV out of his arm, he grabbed the orderly's throat and threw him to one side, then gave him a roundhouse blow with the pole. And a second.

As the orderly crashed into the metal cabinet, Billy bolted through the opening in the curtain. With a quick glance around, he found the exit and sprinted toward it, down the hall and through the open area, past a nurse's station on one side and the admissions window on the other. The few white-clad objects in his way he dodged or bumped aside. His head, his arm where the IV needle had been—his whole body hurt, ached, throbbed, but he kept going.

The ambulance in which he'd arrived stood just outside the entrance. He was down the ramp and around to the other side in seconds. On instinct, and with only a faint hope, he peered in the driver's side window.

Hot damn! The driver had left the keys. He yanked the door open, vaulted inside, and turned the ignition. But there his luck ran out.

As the ambulance roared to life, the bailiff and Sid, the head deputy, burst through the large swinging doors to the emergency room.

"Stop, you!" one of them yelled. Billy jerked the vehicle into gear.

The deputy kept running, down the ramp and behind the ambulance. The bailiff, though, dropped to a crouch, his gun out, and fired.

The bullet shattered the glass in the passenger side window in the instant before the ambulance leaped forward. Searing pain shot through Billy's right shoulder—but he kept his foot on the gas pedal.

The ambulance tore out of the hospital entrance on the wrong side of the drive and careened into the street, where it swerved back and forth across the center white line, sideswiping a parked car before it straightened out in a lane that was empty of other traffic. No more shots followed the first.

A wet ooze covered Billy's right shoulder and arm. He felt more pain than ever—sharp, burning pain. Glancing over, he saw a slash in the darkening fabric along his upper arm and shoulder. He lifted the arm, bringing a blinding flash of pain. He could move it, but it felt like his blood was pumping out of the wound with every heartbeat. And the bullet must have hit the bone.

He was rattled. He'd never had anything like this, the uncontrolled bleeding. He needed to calm down, get back on plan. And stop the bleeding.

Two turns and ten blocks away from the hospital, on a four-lane road with strip malls and used car lots, he pulled over onto a gravel shoulder. No one was on his tail, or they would've caught him by now. The deputy and bailiff must have gone back inside to call for help.

What little light left of the day had faded and dissolved into night. Streetlights, gas stations, car lots, and neon signs spread in bright cascading streams down both sides of the wide boulevard in front of him. Headlights flared in the side-view mirror, before turning into red taillights as cars zipped past. The pulsing lights were making him dizzy.

I need to get moving. Dump this monster. First, stop the bleeding.

Gingerly lifting his shirt at the collar, he checked his shoulder in the flashing lights. Bleeding, but not as badly as he'd thought. Moving his arm brought a deep, agonizing stab of pain, but duller now, as if his body had numbed to it. Using his good arm, he searched the cab. Under the passenger's seat, he found a large metal box, white with a red cross on it.

Fighting the pain in his shoulder, he dragged the box into his lap and pried open the latches. Compress bandages, like in Nam. He tore the wrappers off two and slipped them inside his shirt, over the wound. Clumsily wrapping adhesive tape around his arm, he ripped the tape with his teeth and tossed the roll aside.

Two, maybe three minutes lost. The area looked familiar. Plantation Road. Near the Taco Pal.

Easing the ambulance back into the rush-hour traffic, he leaned against the steering wheel and eyed the multiple switches on the dash. There it was: "siren." He flipped the switch, gave it a moment, then stomped on the gas pedal. The sea of cars parted—except for one he almost had to shove aside by the bumper.

He knew where to go and he knew how to let Judy Kay know where he was. But he had to ditch the ambulance first, and far away from the warehouse.

After a long sweep of strip malls and service stations, he switched off the siren. Now he heard its mates, far to his rear, going to where he wasn't. He hoped. At the next stoplight, he whipped the vehicle to the right, down a two-lane road without all the lights and businesses.

He glanced in the mirror. Still no pursuit. Not hot, at least.

Driving slowly and checking the street signs, he found the entrance to a working-class neighborhood he remembered passing through once, on his way to a job. He made the turn and, gliding along a quiet street with overhanging trees, searched for a dark house with a car out front. At an intersection, he twisted to look down a cross street. Pain radiated in both directions from his shoulder.

Shit! No way could he hot-wire a car, not like this. He slowed down to think. Maybe he could commandeer one, with a driver.

He stopped in front of a brick house with a ragged front lawn illuminated by a blinking streetlamp and a yellow light bulb on the front porch. A child's swing set cast long shadows across the bare yard. An old Buick sat in the drive.

As he surveyed the car and the house through the ambulance's shattered side window, the front door opened and a woman peered out. Wiping her hands on a dishtowel, she stared at him from the doorway. By her legs huddled two small children, no more than cutout silhouettes under the yellow porch light.

It took only a second for him to make his decision. He eased the ambulance away from the curb and into the night.

Coasting through a warren of subdivision streets, he sought an exit he vaguely recalled as feeding into Rayland Road. From there, it was only a couple of miles to the old warehouse district. Where they stored their inventory. Where Judy Kay kept up the commerce feeding the greater economy. Where there was an empty office with a phone.

Wedging his left shoulder against the steering wheel, he managed to switch on the two-way radio and find the police band. A bulletin was out on the ambulance—a description of him, the vehicle number on the side, and the shattered window. There were checkpoints on Plantation and Rayland roads. The cross streets the dispatcher gave put him square in the middle of the search area.

He slowed the ambulance to a crawl. In front of him was a school inside a high fence. Beyond the school, several blocks to his right, a helicopter swept its search light along a chiaroscuro of houses and trees, droning in a line parallel to the street he was on, but moving away from the ambulance.

He stopped by the curb, under a wide oak and equidistant from two streetlamps. Lights off, engine off, he sat for a moment, waiting and watching as the chopper wheeled and came back in another parallel line, one block closer.

Stuffing two unopened bandages inside his shirt, he eased out of the ambulance as fast as he could without increasing the throbbing pain. His shoulder was still bleeding, but now only oozing. The first two bandages and his shirtsleeve were soaked with blood.

He stumbled and almost fell. Clenching his teeth, he trotted toward the school. Through an open gate, he spied cars and a van parked under a row of mercury vapor lights that cast a yellow haze over the vehicles and the high wall of what looked and sounded like a gymnasium. From inside came muffled shouts and the echoing thuds of feet and a basketball on a wooden floor. Glowing white windows high up on the wall seemed to bulge and shake.

He didn't head for the new model Oldsmobile or the Mustang or the Ford van. Instead, he made his way to a rack in the shadows of the gym wall. Five boys' bicycles were lodged and locked into place in the rack's grip. He selected the sturdiest one, the one with the widest tires and highest seat, and the only one with an old-fashioned combination lock. In ten seconds, he had it opened.

"Not lost my touch," he said to the brick wall. Pulling the bicycle out of the rack, he glanced up at the sky beyond the edge of the building. In the distance, the helicopter was making another turn.

Climbing on the bike, he gritted his teeth at the pain. He braced himself with his good arm, his hand gripping the handlebars. Then he pushed off with one foot and pedaled out the gate and down the street, away from the school.

Chapter Thirty-eight – Looking for Billy

PATRICIA ANSWERED THE PHONE with a curt hello. Ray Malloy's words came through sharp, clear, and irritating.

"He did what!" she yelled.

Jack was sitting at the kitchen table, the comics open in front of him. Ignoring his quizzical stare, she paced between the wall and the sink, trailing the phone cord behind her.

She understood perfectly well what had happened. It was only a matter of them giving him the opportunity. Then Ray asked if she had helped him.

"No, I did not! That's a goddamn stupid question, Ray." He tried to back off and be nicer, but still pressing. "No, not at all," she said.

Then an admonition. "Okay," she replied, "I'll let you know if he . . . anybody calls." She listened again and answered, "Tomorrow then, at ten? Fine."

Without saying goodbye, she jammed the phone onto the wall set. Jack returned her glare with a raised eyebrow.

"Billy's escaped," she said, one hand on her hip, the other still on the phone. "Somehow he got beat up by another prisoner." She sighed and released the phone. "When they took him to the emergency room, he stole the ambulance and got away."

"Ha, ha!" Jack rocked the chair back on its legs. "That's fucking great!"

"It's not funny. He's been shot. They're searching for him now."

"How bad is it?"

"Ray didn't know." She eased into the chair across from him. "They think he's someplace off Rayland Road. A woman called and wanted to know why an ambulance stopped in front of her house."

"So what was all the 'no's' you were giving Ray?" Jack folded the paper and pushed it aside.

"Bastard wanted to know if I helped him. Then he asked if I knew where the girlfriend is."

225

"What did you tell him?"

"You heard me; I don't know where she is." She grabbed the newspaper and stared at the top page. "I want to find out how he got beat up," she said, pushing the paper away. She bit her lower lip. "Ray said he was unconscious, or they thought he was, when they got him to the hospital." She looked over at Jack. "You think he could've had another visitor? Somebody threatened—"

"Or helped him?" Jack pushed away from the table, stood, and stretched. "We'll never know, unless he tells you. You want a beer?"

"No, thanks . . . You think *she* could have helped him?"

"Who knows?" Removing a Heineken from the fridge, he gave a wry chuckle. "I'll bet he made a beeline to her."

"You think—?"

"I think you best stay out of it." He took a swig from the bottle and nodded at her as he swallowed. "Stay away from that damn bar and Judy Kay."

"Maybe I could get him to turn himself in."

"Why? If he escaped, he wanted to get away. His best bet's to leave town fast as he can, go up in the mountains someplace."

Sitting in front of Ray Malloy's desk, she assumed a contrite look of sweet innocence as Ray told her about how Billy made his escape and fled the hospital with a hot lead sendoff.

"That boy's good, I'll say that." Ray grinned at her. Resting between them on top of a thick file was a half-eaten sausage biscuit in a greasy wrapper. He sipped from a take-out coffee cup.

"They found the ambulance last night. Window shot out. Lots of blood." He reached over and picked up the biscuit. "Medical examiner says it's not enough to be fatal. Probably wasn't that bad or he stopped the flow."

She watched in silence as Ray chewed, swallowed, and drank more coffee. *Be quiet and let him talk*, she thought. *Don't volunteer anything*.

"The sonovabitch was still able to steal a bike. Can you believe that? Some poor kid's bike. Boy had to walk home." Another bite of sausage biscuit. "He couldn'ta got far. Not unless somebody was helpin' him." He set the coffee cup down on the desk and leaned forward, giving her what he must have intended to be a piercing look, difficult for Ray with his fat cheeks.

"You wouldn't know anything about that, would you, Miss Egan?"

"Come on, Ray, you know me better than that. I want to know why they put him in a cell with someone else. They've been keeping him in solitary."

"Space issue." Ray shrugged, eyeing the last of his biscuit. "Not the smartest move, I guess."

"He's been afraid down here; did you know that? He thought . . . I don't know what he thought . . . someone was out to get him or something."

"Is it any wonder? He beat up a fucking jailer! . . . Pardon the French."

"I don't think that's it, Ray."

"Hell's bells, I lectured the supervisor over there to make sure he didn't fall down the stairs or slip in the shower or something . . . Shit! That's partly why I went for the felony murder rap—keep the sheriff and all his little ol' deputies happy."

"That's gone now." She gave him her demure smile.

"You think so, huh? Judge hasn't ruled yet and maybe this'll give him pause." Ray showed his white teeth, then flicked a bit of the biscuit from the corner of his mouth.

"Ray," she cleared her throat, uncertain whether to continue. "Could there have been someone else at the Taco Pal. Another man?"

"Your *man* was there." He threw his hands up and made a face in mock disgust. "Look at the evidence, Trish. No way—"

"Hypothetically, let's say the jury *finds* he was there." Placing her hand on the desk, she shifted forward in the chair. "Do you think there could have been someone else, other than Lazlo Benes and that pothead kid you cut a deal with?"

Crumpling up the biscuit wrapper, Ray tossed it at a metal trashcan against the wall. He missed.

"Why are you suggesting that?" Eyeing her, he swept some crumbs off the top of a file, onto the floor. "You have some reason for suggesting it, don't you?" he said, cocking his head to one side.

"The transcript on the deaths. Also, the cop yesterday. He *said* at first he thought there was someone else."

Ray shook his head and smirked at her. "Excitement of the chase. No one ever saw anybody else."

"Billy could be afraid of this . . . other man. Maybe that's why he ran."

"Is there something you aren't telling me?" He gave her a sideways look. "You know where he's gone?"

"No! Of course I don't." She sat up straight, indignant at his tone.

"Covering for an escaped felon is a crime, you know. Misprision or something like that."

"Don't you threaten me, Ray Malloy." She felt the heat rising all the way to the roots of her hair.

Ray rocked back in his low chair, as if he were taking refuge behind the stacks of books and papers on his desk. "I'm not threatening, Patricia, just stating a fact." He halfheartedly shook his finger at her. "You need to tell us anything you know that'll help find him. It might save his life."

"It was your jailers and that sorry bailiff who caused this, or let it happen. Putting him in a cell with some crazy black guy. Don't blame me for your clients' fuck-ups." She was angry, but her mind was also probing at whether Judy Kay or anyone else could've played a role in Billy's escape.

"Do you know where we can find the girlfriend?" Ray asked. Almost like he was reading her mind.

"No." A tight-lipped answer. Ray hadn't asked the right question.

"Well, counselor, if you find out anything, you need to tell us. He contacts you, get him to turn himself in."

"I'll do that." Giving Ray her sweet smile again, she stood to leave. She felt an urgent need to escape, herself. "Don't you think he'd want to get as far away from this place as he can?" She nodded her head vigorously at the idea.

"Maybe, maybe not," Ray said. "He may be hurt pretty bad."

Back in the office, she gave Jack the CliffsNotes version of her visit with Ray. "They think he's still around here, I know it," she said.

"Sounds possible." He took a file out of a drawer and slammed it shut. "He was wounded, all beat up. We don't know how bad."

She stood and paced in front of the desk and then over to the window, behind Jack's chair. "Do you think they know about," she hesitated, "the Patriot Bar? And Judy Kay's business back there, whatever it is."

"My guess is they don't. But that's just a guess."

Patricia continued looking out the window. The afternoon sky was clear and bright, with crystal coldness. On the horizon, gray clouds were edging into the blue and hung like slatted shutters in the west.

Jack's phone rang several times, but he didn't reach for it. When the ringing stopped, she turned from the window and moved to the side of his desk.

"Maybe I should leave a message for Judy Kay," she said.

"Don't do it." Rocking in the chair, he shook his head. "They'll keep an eye on you, maybe even tap your phone. You could get disbarred, or worse."

"I'm trying to locate my client." Folding her arms and bracing against the desk, she leaned down, close to his face. "The *idea* is to get him to turn himself in. They should thank me for that."

Jack continued shaking his head. "Stay out of it, Patricia. It took—"

A rap on the closed door was quickly followed by Lacey popping through it. Patricia jumped and moved away from the desk, back toward the window.

"That was Fitz," Lacey said, ignoring Patricia and looking at Jack. "He wants that Star Energy thing finished and ready to go by the end of next week."

Jack grimaced, but he didn't answer.

"He's sending over the signature pages. His partners signed them, but they have some revisions in the master agreements. He'll be in here Tuesday, and he wants to finalize everything then, and he wants to talk about transferring properties." One hand on her hip, she gave Jack a knowing, sarcastic look.

"Fine," Jack said. "You take care of it."

"You have to go over the papers."

"Yeah, yeah, I know." He flashed a Cheshire-cat grin, cuing her to exit. She did, leaving them to continue their debate about Billy Angel.

It was Friday afternoon, almost time for Patricia to leave, when the phone gave its low burr. She answered it on the first ring. The voice was muffled.

"Patricia, this is Melissa, your old friend from college."

She started to say she didn't have any friends named Melissa, new or old, but hesitated, thinking she recognized the voice. "Uh, yes, hello, Melissa," she said, checking the doorway to make sure no one was there. Lacey and the other secretaries had already gone, and she thought Jack had left for the gym.

"Good to hear from you," Patricia said after a moment.

"A friend of ours," the muffled voice paused. "She's pretty sick and she'd like to hear from you. You might be able to help her."

Putting aside caution and Jack's warning that they might bug her phone, she ended the charade. "Look, Judy Kay, just tell him to turn himself in."

"He's hurt bad. Maybe getting an infection or something. I think the bullet's still in there . . . He wants to talk to you."

"Put him on the phone then."

"He needs a doctor." She paused. "But I think he wants to work some things out, first."

"Does he know you're calling me?"

"Uh . . . no. But if you'll come to Jenny's in the morning . . . ?"

Patricia was silent, thinking.

"Won't you please come?" A pause. "I'm afraid for him." The husky voice tumbled the words out, the worry and fear evident even over the phone.

"Okay, but he'll have to turn himself in, right after I talk to him."

"We'll work it out . . . Come to the bar. Around ten, if that's okay?"

"A bar? You want me to come to a bar on Saturday morning?"

"Only be Barry there . . . The bartender. I'll take you to Billy." Another long pause. "Just don't bring anybody else."

"Why not my partner?" Meaning Jack.

"Billy might not talk with him there. You'll be all right." Judy Kay sighed, or sobbed—Patricia couldn't tell which. "He needs help; I don't think he can wait a whole lot longer."

"Why don't I come right now?"

"I need to work on him a bit . . . But he'll go along. You'll see." Another resonant sigh. "Thanks." And she hung up.

Patricia sat back in her chair and stared out the window. To the west, the sky was suffused with golds and reds and grays outlining slashes of pale blue.

Calling Ray Malloy crossed her mind, and departed without engaging it. Asking Jack to go with her received more consideration, but she rejected that, too. She'd go alone. Maybe she could negotiate a safe surrender and Billy would be in the hospital for real—even if back in custody—by the next sunset in Carrville.

And then what?

Chapter Thirty-nine – Jenny's Place

THE OLD MERCEDES GLIDED TO A STOP in front of Dwayne's Pawn Shop and Gun Store, across the street from the Patriot Bar. A cold drizzle streaked the windshield, and a pallid fog rising from the boggy lowlands by the river stretched long ghostly fingers past the old Slave Market and down Main Street, enveloping streetlights, storefronts, and automobiles in a pale twilight.

Patricia took an umbrella from the backseat, wrapped her raincoat tightly about her, and opened the door. Then she hesitated and closed it. *Better check out the lay of the land, case this joint as Billy would say.*

She checked the mirrors: only one car parked on her side of the street and two on the other side, none of them close. There was a fourth car across the street, but parked well beyond the bar. The bar's plate glass window was painted white with "Patriot Bar" splashed across it in wavy red-and-blue letters with white stars sprinkled in the blue. To the right of the window was a recessed entrance, and above it a tall vertical sign that said "Hotel" in faded neon lights. The no-name hotel's redbrick façade extended over the bar, with evenly spaced windows, black eyes to the gloomy day, reaching up four floors.

A movement drew her attention to her side of the street. A man in a gray raincoat and floppy hat ducked under the pawnshop awning and tried the door. It didn't open, though lights shone through the barred windows. After a couple minutes, he drifted away, down the street.

The rain had turned to a fine mist. She checked the mirrors again. No patrol cars, but she wouldn't know an unmarked one if it drove up her tailpipe.

Over the next ten minutes, two cars and several more hunched figures passed by, until finally she gave up trying to guess if any were cops. She exited the car and locked the door. Clutching her raincoat closed with one hand and holding the unopened umbrella like a club, she marched across the street. She'd stuffed her driver license, credit cards, and a twenty-dollar bill into one pocket of the raincoat and a wad of Kleenex into the other.

A sign on the Patriot Bar's entrance, a door with blue-tinted glass, said "Closed." But when she gave it a tentative push, it swung open. Barry the bartender sat on a stool at the end of the bar, head bent low over an open paper, a coffee cup and ashtray off to one side. The place reeked of stale beer, cigarettes, and Lysol.

As she brushed the mist off her hair, Barry took a draw on his cigarette and expelled a thin haze of smoke. He waved the cigarette toward the cave-like blackness at the rear.

"Through that door yonder." A quiet, no-nonsense voice. "Go left . . . knock on the first door you come to."

"Thanks," she said. Barry nodded and tapped the cigarette on the edge of the ashtray. Still staring at her, he took another drag and then released streamers of smoke from his nostrils as he looked down at his paper.

The door at back opened into a hallway that might once have been a covered alley, but bricked up long ago. A single bulb cast cubist shadows along the bare bricks and concrete floor. Turning left, she knocked on the first door she came to. It opened a few inches and a young black woman peered out.

"I'm . . ." Patricia started, then hesitated.

"You're here to see Judy Kay, right?" The woman opened the door a little more and looked Patricia up and down.

"Yes. Is she here?"

"You look like she said . . . a sophisticated white lady, so I guess it's you." She swung the door open and stepped back. She wore jeans and a dashiki, flowery with pinks, blues, and streaks of magenta. Her Afro was neatly trimmed, a red-shell comb pressed into one side. Arms crossed on her chest, she stared at Patricia.

"Why are you're dressed like a spy? And your hair's wet as a mop." Her voice had a sharp, sarcastic tone.

Jesus, thought Patricia, *I've found Aerial's sister.* Without answering, she cautiously stepped inside. They were in a large utility room with unpainted walls and a concrete floor. On one wall, a washing machine chugged away and a dryer whirred beside it. There was a fresh, warm laundry smell.

When Patricia didn't respond, the woman said, "Just joshing you," and grinned. She held out her hand. "I'm Latisha. Friend of Judy Kay's—like everybody around here. Your name's Patricia, I hope."

"That's right, I'm Patricia." She took the woman's hand and found a warm, firm grip. "Where is she? She said to be here at ten."

"She's detained . . . Come on outta here; I'll hunt her down." She made for a partially open door away from the washer and dryer. "You wouldn't believe the sheets that have to be washed in this place."

Removing her raincoat and shaking it off, she followed Latisha through the door. *I'm sure there's a lot I wouldn't believe about this place.*

"Why don't you wait in here, Pa-trish-a? Hey, you rhyme with La-tish-a." They were in a brightly lit kitchen with cabinets and appliances far nicer than the ones in Colin's old house.

"Grab you some coffee." Latisha nodded toward an industrial-size coffee maker. "One of the girls brought in sticky buns. Said it was the only decent thing about last night." She laughed, a vibrant, throaty laugh, then disappeared through a swinging door on the far side of the room.

Patricia eyed the sticky buns, and discovered she was hungry. Finding a coffee mug, she filled it, sat at the table, and picked at a sticky bun while she waited—and worried.

Did the cops follow me? I'm in deep shit if they find me here—and before I can contact anyone to arrange Billy's surrender. No explanation will be good enough.

The swinging door banged open and Judy Kay barged in.

"God, am I glad you're here," she said. "We need to get him someplace quick." Dressed in rumpled pink slacks and a loose black sweater, she had lost some of her luster, and her platinum hair looked even more deflated than when they'd met in the bar before.

As Patricia stood, Judy Kay rushed forward and almost bowled her over. "I've been . . ." Latisha's entrance interrupted what Judy Kay was about to say.

"Stop! Don't want to hear this." Latisha held up a hand as she went past and into the utility room. She pulled the door shut behind her.

"I've been arguing with him for the last hour," Judy Kay said, stepping back. "He said not to involve you. You can't do no good. But I . . . I think he'll give himself up if you talk to him."

"Where is he?"

"Come along . . . 'fore he changes his mind." Taking Patricia's arm, she led her out through the swinging door.

The hallway they entered was shabby—peeling old-fashioned wallpaper and scarred panel doors on each side and carpeting that was threadbare and stained. The only light came from a row of opaque globes spaced at regular intervals. As they snaked through a warren of narrow corridors, Patricia felt like she was in a maze. Judy Kay must have sensed her unease.

"I'm in the back," she said, "on Pine Street. This old hotel must've been expanded a thousand times since it was built."

Patricia was wondering how many of these rooms were being used—and what for. As they retreated farther to the back, they reached a newer and wider hallway with better carpeting and fluorescent lights.

"Is that woman . . . Latisha, is she one of the . . . girls?" she asked.

"Ha, ha! You think this is just an old whorehouse, don't you, honey?" Judy Kay stopped at a door that looked like a regular hotel door with a brass number in the center. She dug into the pocket of her slacks.

"This is a residence hotel—rent however you like. Jenny has the penthouse." She pulled out a key and held it up. "Girls in the rooms by the bar are mostly free lancers."

She struggled to get the key in the lock, turned it over, and tried again. Her hand was shaking.

"Latisha?" she said, glancing back at Patricia. "She's a sweetheart. Says this is where Jesus told her to come, where the sinners are."

She finally got the door open and ushered Patricia inside. The room was feminine, smelling of perfume and bath powders, and well lighted by three high windows. It contained a queen-size bed, a vanity, a sofa, and a chair. And a large television console. But no Billy.

"Stay here when I'm in town," Judy Kay said, turning on the ceiling light. The bed was made with a colorful spread and four lacy pillows, a Raggedy Ann doll cradled among them. "Try to get back here when Billy's around but I go all over the place." She closed the door and gave Patricia a forlorn look. "We both used to." She sighed. "Kitchen's down the hall and there's an entrance on Pine Street, end of the corridor."

"Where is he?" Patricia asked.

Judy Kay took her by the elbow and guided her to a closed door next to the console with the TV. "Through here," she said. She pulled the door open and pushed a matching door into the adjoining room.

"I put him in here. Didn't wanta be too obvious. All sorts of people comin' and goin', you know."

The second room was smaller, with little furniture and two small, high-up windows that were painted over. Recumbent on a single bed below the windows was Billy, propped up by a pillow on top of the rumpled covers. On a nightstand by the bed was a low-wattage lamp. An almost inaudible television opposite the bed sent flickering shadows around the room.

As they entered, Billy clicked off the TV and placed the remote on the nightstand. He raised himself on one elbow.

"Glad you could make it," he said, with only a hint of sarcasm. He was still dressed in the brown slacks Jack bought for him. Instead of the shirt, he wore a dashiki like Latisha's, except his was a mixture of blacks, greens, and reds.

Carrying her coat over one arm, Patricia edged forward. Instead of answering Billy, she let her eyes wander over the room. No decoration of any kind. A few boxes, marked with Zenith, Sears, and GE logos, were stacked against the wall on the far side of the bed. It looked like a storeroom. But like Judy Kay's room, it also had a door to the hallway, directly across from Billy and next to the stand with the television.

A mound of crushed cigarette butts half-filled a highball glass on the nightstand, and the dominant smell was a mixture of mold and tobacco. Beneath it, though, floated a sour odor of human sweat and sickness, or blood.

"You really screwed up this time, Mr. Angel," Patricia said, drifting toward the bed. She stopped in front of the nightstand and stared at Billy over the dim lamp. "How's your arm?"

Using his left arm, back, and legs, he worked himself into a near sitting

position against the pillow. His right arm lay like a piece of dead wood across his stomach, and he grimaced with every squirming movement.

"Shoulder's swollen like a melon. Can't use my arm or my hand."

"He needs a doctor," Judy Kay said, coming up beside Patricia. "I can't . . . I'm scared to move him. You should see—"

"That's all right," Patricia said, her face grim. She addressed Billy. "You need to give yourself up, right now."

"It ain't safe, missy, not in this town. I'm as apt to die back in jail as here."

Judy Kay bent over him and touched his cheek and forehead in quick succession, as if he were a child. "He's got a fever," she said, straightening up, her eyes on Patricia. "Bad. I'm giving him some Darvon, but it gets worse at night. So does the pain."

"She's a good nurse," Billy said.

"I can arrange a surrender," Patricia said. "You'll be safe with me here." Judy Kay started to speak, then clamped her mouth shut.

It hit Patricia like a slap in the face: *surrendering him here will cause a lot of problems for a lot of people. How can I do this without perjuring myself? Or be guilty of misprision of a felony or aiding an escaped convict, as Ray put it.* She took a breath.

"Maybe I could take you to the police station. In my car. Judy and Barry, or whoever, could help you out to . . . I don't know, some place on Pine Street." She gestured toward the opaque windows above the bed. "I could pick you up back there and take you to the police."

"They might not care for that." Billy's eyes stayed fixed on her, but the irises didn't seem so limpid blue now.

They? She started to ask who he meant.

"He needs a doctor," Judy Kay said. She was clasping and unclasping her hands in front of her. "Right away."

"What if I take you to the hospital? I could call the D.A., have him meet us there. He'd bring some deputies probably, and—"

"I need to talk to you, Miss Egan. Attorney, client like." He looked over at Judy Kay. "Baby, why don't you go get me a beer? That breakfast, sticky buns or whatever they were, they didn't set too well with me." The only thing he moved was his head. No gestures or motion of his good hand.

237

"I'll have to go to the bar, honey." Judy Kay wrinkled up her forehead. Her platinum hair looked almost straight, Patricia noticed, flattened and tangled. *Of course, my own hair is no fashion statement at this point.*

Billy smiled at Judy Kay. "That'll be okay—take your time. Me and the lawyer here'll need a few minutes to work things out."

"Sure, Billy. Just a beer?" She gave him a wistful look, clearly reluctant to leave.

"Just a beer. I doubt Miss Egan would want one . . . but anything you'd like?" he asked, shifting his eyes to Patricia. She shook her head.

Judy Kay left by way of her room, leaving open the door on his side and closing the one on hers. When she was gone, Billy cleared his throat.

"I got something I need to tell you, Miss Egan."

Chapter Forty – Billy Spills

PATRICIA LOOKED AROUND FOR A PLACE TO SIT. It was awkward standing here, staring down at the man. The only chair was a straight-back one, by the door to Judy Kay's room. Still holding her raincoat, she started for it. Billy stopped her.

"Would you get me a smoke?"

Making a face, she took a step toward the nightstand. "Where are they?"

"Mine are finito. She's stopped, but there's probably a pack in the vanity . . . in there." He nodded toward the next room.

"We need to make this quick," Patricia said and pivoted away from him, more and more impatient at every delay.

She almost ran into Judy Kay's room and over to the vanity, where she found a half-empty pack of Virginia Slims in a drawer. Leaving her raincoat on Judy Kay's bed, she hurried back into Billy's hideaway.

"Here," she said, extracting a cigarette from the pack and thrusting it at Billy.

"Sorry, missy. You'll have to light it for me."

"I don't have a lighter . . . or matches." Growing exasperated at his temporizing, she started to tell him to forget the cigarette.

He twisted sideways and, using his left hand, managed to open the drawer in the nightstand—but the effort caused him to wince with pain. The drawer was empty except for a crumpled cigarette pack, a paperback novel, and the requisite cigarette lighter, nesting in a loose stack of Kleenexes.

As he straightened up with a low groan, she gingerly fished the lighter out of the drawer. Rather than giving him the cigarette, she placed it between her own lips and after several tries ignited it. She took a minimal draw and, with a sneer of distaste, blew out the smoke and handed the lit cigarette to Billy.

"Okay, you've got your cigarette. Now talk." Pulling the chair away from the wall, she sat and folded her arms across her chest.

JAMES GARRISON

He exhaled a cloud of smoke and held the cigarette out to examine at it. "I can taste your lipstick." He turned his head to stare at her. "You know you're pretty, don't you. Pretty and smart."

"What do you need to tell me . . . Billy?" Seeing him try to reach for the glass with the cigarette butts, she got up and handed it to him. Holding the cigarette with his fingers, he balanced the glass on his stomach.

"If I go back, what's going to happen?"

"There's no *if* to it," she said, sitting back down. "We'll try to work out a plea deal. We don't have much choice after this," she waved her hand in the air, casting her eyes around the room, "this little escapade of yours." She pursed her lips, watching him draw on the cigarette. He was a sad little man now, sad and shriveled up, and ill in a sick bed.

He exhaled a wispy column of smoke toward the ceiling but didn't say anything.

"I think the felony murder charge is out," she said, "and maybe we can get you concurrent sentences for this new caper. But you'll have to take fifteen or so years on the robbery counts. That'll be more than thirty—when it's stacked with what you already have. That's the best you can hope for."

"I could be out in . . . what? Ten or twelve with good behavior? Take early retirement." He grinned, but not as wide.

"You'd know that better than I would. But we do a quick plea, we might be able to get you back to Central Prison quicker. After you get out of the hospital."

Billy exhaled more smoke in a sigh and studied the diminished cigarette. "Might not be quick enough," he said. "But it's pro'bly the only way. I can't run no more."

"Why are you afraid?" She leaned forward. "Is it this *other man* you keep dancing around? . . . He can't very well get at you in jail. So, who is it?"

Billy stared at her through a wreath of smoke. Then he tapped the cigarette ashes into the highball glass and chewed on his lower lip.

"Hal Goodman," he said finally, his eyes now on the glass and the ashes.

"Goodman!" She half stood.

"He was at the back door."

"The mayor's driver, or whatever he is?"

"Yeah, he has a lot of sidelines." Billy took another draw on the cigarette. "He and a couple of other cops find the jobs for me . . . Those others you don't need to know about. Then they help find buyers and get the loot out of town, what's not cash." He gestured with the cigarette to the boxes along the wall.

"Whew!" She let out her breath between her teeth and leaned back. "That's some serious business." She caught herself nervously rubbing her arms.

"See why they might like to shut me up? Like six feet under?"

"Okay, I see. But why was he . . . with you?" She pointed vaguely toward the door. "Out there?"

"Been puzzlin' over that myself. He don't usually go along, but I thought he was keeping an eye on us—or maybe it was just for kicks. He's kinda crazy like."

"We need to get this out in the open. The more people who know . . . the more they know, the safer you'll be." *And the safer I'll be,* she thought. *And the whole damn city.* Then another thought.

"Does Judy Kay know about this?"

"Not who's who. She knows there's cops, but I try to keep—"

"She knows too much, so she's in danger, too."

Billy didn't answer. He took a final drag on the cigarette, now almost down to the filter, and dropped it on top of the cluster of butts in the glass. A thin, acrid wisp of smoke continued to rise from the glass as he strained to place it on the nightstand. She watched, lost in thought. Finally succeeding in his efforts, he grimaced in pain and fell back into a sitting position on the bed.

"Goodman killed Henry Royale, didn't he?" Patricia said.

"Yeah, I know he did . . ." Billy groaned and shifted his position farther from the lamp. "The gun he found, it had to be his. One of his spares."

"Why would he kill the man? He was just up there by his car, going to work." But she had an idea why.

Billy gave a slight shrug with his good shoulder. "Maybe the man saw him . . . recognized him. He's around city hall all the time."

"The man he shot was a whistleblower. An auditor with the city and he started an investigation of the mayor. Did that have something to do with it?"

Billy stared at her, his face blank. "I wouldn't know. I wasn't in on anything like that, I swear it." He took a breath and releasing it haltingly, turned his head to stare at the ceiling. "But I started wondering. Didn't know anything about that fellow 'til after the trial, after Goodman came to see me. He told me to keep my mouth shut."

She reached her decision. She knew what to do.

"Billy, if you give up Goodman . . . and his gang, maybe we can get a reduced sentence, if you turn state's—"

"No!" Billy rose a foot or two off the pillows. "I ain't a snitch. I hate snitches." He fell back with a groan. "'Sides, they'd have a hit on my ass, wouldn't matter where I am."

"But you think they're after you anyway."

"I don't know." He settled farther down with a low moan. "I go away quiet, back to Central, maybe they'll think they got nuthin to worry about."

She stood and started pacing beside the bed. She was ready for Judy Kay to come back and Billy to have his beer, so they could get moving— on whatever they were going to do. She stopped at the foot of the bed.

"How about that kid? He knows there's another man and he's already ratted on you. Won't he talk?"

"Ugh!" A cross between a groan and a sneer of disgust. "Goodman's fucking nephew. Sister's boy. Worked at the Taco Pal." Billy's voice was halting, his breathing increasingly labored. "Told us . . . told Goodman . . . owner kept a bunch of money in the safe . . . It wasn't there."

"My God!" She walked over to the connecting door, thinking she heard Judy Kay. The other room was silent and empty. She needed to work out a plan to get him to a hospital. And arrange his surrender. She came back to the chair.

"Kid'll get probation," Billy said. "First offense . . . Uh," he groaned again. "You got any painkillers, missy?"

"We need to get you to the hospital." Eyeing him, she shook her head. "The D.A.'s your best bet. I'm going to call him." Meaning Ray Malloy.

She moved closer to Billy and stared down into his eyes. The pupils were small deep pinholes wrapped in milky blue shadows.

"Do what you need to," he said in a murmur. "Just keep her out of it."

"I'll try. Do you have a phone?" She looked around. The nightstand held only the lamp, the TV remote, the highball glass, the half-empty cigarette pack, and a small dirty plate with a crumpled napkin on it.

"One in there." Coughing, a strained dull sound from deep in his chest, he pointed loosely with his left hand toward the door to Judy Kay's room.

Hurrying through the connecting doors, she grabbed the phone off the nightstand in Judy Kay's room—then stopped at a noise. From Billy's room came the low drone of the TV. An edge of flashing color was visible through the open doors.

She couldn't remember Ray's home number. She could call Jack and have him call Ray. No, she wasn't going to involve Jack. But he could give her the number. As she dialed, she eased down on the bed and began formulating her plan. *We have to get Billy out to my car. I'll drive around back to the Pine Street entrance.* She misdialed a digit, hung up, and started over. *Maybe I should call Ray from the hospital—after I get Billy to the emergency room. But what if I'm seen, or stopped on the way?*

There was a knock on Judy Kay's door.

"Police! Open up!" The voice was loud, threatening. Another series of raps: one, two, three, more insistent this time.

She sat frozen on the edge of the bed, her finger poised above the telephone dial. *What do I do? I'll lose my license. And what about Billy?* All ran through her mind between the word, "Police," and the last raps.

With a loud crash, the hall door to Billy's room burst open. Just beyond the connecting door loomed a big man in a gray raincoat, his hands stretched out in front of him at eye level. Hal Goodman.

"Got ya, you bastard," Goodman said in a low voice.

Dropping the phone, she launched herself off the bed, toward the door, as Goodman stepped nearer to Billy.

"No, it's not . . ." Billy's voice, feeble but high-pitched.

"Police, stop!" Goodman yelled, his voice rising, then his extended arm jumped twice as the gun he held gave two loud cracks.

She reached the door as Billy's face exploded in a cloud of red spray and an ugly red hole erupted in his chest where the dashiki formed a V below his neck. His body jumped from the impact, his arms flung out to either side.

She screamed. "No! No! Goddamn you! No!" As she lunged into the room, Goodman spun around to face her, one hand held out with the gun.

Strong arms seized her from behind, stopping her advance.

"I got her, Hal," yelled a voice in her ear. Across from them, a uniformed cop ran in through the hall door behind Goodman. He bounded forward and grabbed Goodman's outstretched arm.

"He's got her," the cop yelled. Goodman's gun remained pointed at her, the arm unbending. The cop yelled again: "It's the lady lawyer, man!"

She continued screaming, whipping her body back and forth against the viselike grip that kept her from charging Goodman.

Goodman's gun drooped downward while she wailed, her eyes wide, blazing at him. "You murderer! You fucking murderer! I saw you . . . Oh, God! Why? Why? You killed him."

"Son of a bitch pulled a gun on me," Goodman growled, shaking off the uniformed cop's hand. He inserted his gun inside his coat; with the other hand, he jabbed a thick index finger toward the bed and Billy's body—the mutilated head against the wall, canted away from the bloody pillows, the arms spread wide to either side, palms up.

A silver pistol lay on top of Billy's outstretched thighs, on top of the brown pants Jack had bought. Brown pants mottled with the dark wet stains of Billy Angel's blood.

Chapter Forty-one – Entr'acte

SHE SPENT THE AFTERNOON IN A POLICE interrogation room. For her lawyer, she called Jack, and he called Ray Malloy and Leon Hayes. Through Jack's and Leon's efforts, with Ray's acquiescence, she was released by four o'clock. A trip to the emergency room revealed bruises on her arms and shoulders where the cops had grabbed her, and another dark bruise on her back where she seemed to remember Hal Goodman hitting her as he and his partner shoved her out the door, in handcuffs. The doctor had given her a sedative.

"At least they didn't strip search you," Jack said, handing her another cup of tea. He stood over her, at the corner of the coffee table in the narrow den. She sat on the sofa, legs tucked up under her, trying to draw warmth from the gas flames in the fireplace.

Dinner had been leftovers, anything edible Jack could dredge out of the refrigerator. The drizzling rain had turned to ice, and the ice pinged against the uncovered window at the far end of the den.

"Or put me in a cell for the night," she said, taking the cup of tea and blowing on it, sending coils of steam away from her face. Her hair was tangled, still damp from the shower, her second since her return home. She had dug out a set of red flannel pajamas and brought in a woolen blanket to curl up under.

"I could've been arrested if it weren't for you and Leon."

"Technically, I think you were." Jack gave a hollow laugh. "You were handcuffed and questioned against your will." Placing a Heineken bottle on the coffee table, he sat down close beside her.

"I agreed to answer the questions, once they got Goodman out of there. They didn't read me my rights, so they—"

"Did they record you?"

"I don't think so. I didn't see them writing anything down, and I didn't sign a damn thing, except a receipt to get my stuff back."

"Aerial brought your car home."

"Aerial? What . . . ?" She stopped, not wanting to ask how Aerial got involved. "Good thing the cops didn't impound it." She sighed. "It was mostly the same as when you got there. The lieutenant must have asked me what happened from ten different angles. I told him about Goodman, and that I was arranging for Billy's surrender when that wrecking crew showed up."

On the way home, she had told Jack what she learned from Billy about Goodman, about Goodman's gang of crooked cops and his killing Henry Royale. Jack's only response: he'd never liked Goodman, but he couldn't see how the mayor would be involved in any of it.

"Telling 'em about Goodman," Jack said, looking over at her, "may have made them leery of getting anything in writing."

"They kept asking about Judy Kay," she said. "I had to tell them she was there . . . she'd brought me there." She paused as the sleet swept across the window in staccato waves and the wind rattled its ancient sash. She drew the blanket tighter around her. "I'm glad she didn't come back."

"She'll go to jail if they find her, and not just because of Billy. There was a truckload of stolen shit, TV's, all kinds of electronics," he took a quick swallow of beer, "stashed in *her* rooms and in a couple of others they searched."

"How do you think they found us . . . him?" Patricia asked, leaning closer to Jack. She finished her tea and set the cup down on a magazine.

"Ray said they had a source." He shrugged. "Maybe Goodman knew about Jenny's . . . business. Or they have an informant."

Patricia was silent, watching the fire. A gust of wind whistled across the chimney, and the flames dipped and jumped in a disjointed can-can.

"Jack," she said, leaning away from him and staring at his profile in the firelight. "I thought he was going to shoot me." She shivered under the blanket and huddled closer to him, stretching her feet out on the sofa behind her. "He might have if his partner hadn't been there, a*nd* standing behind me."

He put his arm around her shoulders, and she snuggled up against his chest, feeling safer here with Jack than she had with anyone in a long time.

"What did you do to the cops," he leaned his head back to stare down at her, "that caused them to give you those bruises?"

"I was struggling, screaming . . . crying, I guess. I probably took a swing at that fuck Goodman." She paused, then added, "Wonder if I tried to bite him?"

"You're damn lucky Ray pulled the paperwork. They were ready to charge you with a bunch of shit: resisting, assault on an officer, assisting an escaped felon—"

"How about a glass of wine?" She sat up, pulling away from him.

"On top of whatever mega-tranquilizer the doctor gave you?"

"I'm fine. Tonight, I could use some wine."

While he was gone, she stared at the fire and listened to the sleet on the window. The cops said Billy had a gun, but she knew he didn't. She hadn't seen Goodman toss it on the bed, in Billy's lap, and she didn't know how he did it. But he had. He had to.

So what could she do about it? They'd make damn sure Billy's fingerprints were on it.

Jack returned with the wine. As soon as he handed her the glass, she took a long swallow from it.

"I'm not going to let him get away with it," she said as Jack settled down beside her. She leaned her forearms on her knees, the wineglass cradled in both hands. She looked sideways, up at him, and shook her head. "Not if I have to pound on every door in city hall."

"You can still be charged, you know. All Ray did was stop them this afternoon. He'll probably have to give it to a grand jury."

"Oh, shit." She made a face and, clutching the wineglass, sagged back on the sofa. She felt her bravery dissolving into fear. Taking a long draft of wine, she felt better at once.

"Listen to the wind," she said, moving closer to Jack. His warmth through the T-shirt he wore made her feel even better. His arm came around her shoulders and she snuggled up against him. The blanket had fallen away and lay on the couch behind her.

"I probably shouldn't tell you this," he said after a few minutes of silence. "Judy Kay called here—I don't know how she got the number. She called just after you phoned from the jail. I was almost out the door."

Patricia pulled away from him, but not too far. "What did she say?"

"She knew Billy was dead."

"Poor woman."

"She said you'd been hauled off by the cops. Ordered me to go help you." Holding up his beer, he looked past it at her. "She's on the run. Only thing she had, she said, was her purse and her car. She and Rhonda were leaving town . . . She was sniffling a little."

"I guess she *did* love him." Patricia finished her wine in one gulp and set the glass on the coffee table.

"They were more like business associates."

"So what? We're business associates," Patricia said without thinking.

"So, business associate, how do you feel about me?" He gave her a gentle hug.

She was still for a long moment. *I've lived with this guy for over a year. In separate bedrooms. I probably know him better than anybody— better than Colin, who I don't really know at all.*

She looked up to find his face close to hers and the beer bottle on the table. They kissed, long and deep, his arms around her and her hands clutching at his neck and the back of his head. All of the emotion that had built up since Billy's death went into her kiss and she embraced him with all her might.

The wind whipped around the corners of the house and whistled across the chimney. Conjured by the iron implements on the hearth, a Kokopelli shadow danced along the wall and up the threadbare curtains by the window.

Finally breaking apart, he caressed her hair and neck and back as she snuggled against him. She stared at the flames flickering in the gas logs while the wine and sedative worked their spell and she fell asleep.

Chapter Forty-two – Searching for Justice

IT WAS ALMOST NOON WHEN PATRICIA finally roused. She couldn't remember how she made it to bed. But she was in her own bedroom—and still dressed in her flannel pajamas. No sign in the bed of a second occupant. She didn't know whether to feel relieved or disappointed.

Shuffling into the hallway, she called out to Jack upstairs. No response.

In the kitchen, there was a note on the table. Jack's aunt had called. His mother had fallen and was in the hospital, a fracture of some sort, and she wanted him to come. So he had gone, despite the continuing mess of fog, sleet, and freezing rain.

Not long after she read the note, the phone rang. Jack had made it safely, though his old Camaro must've slid halfway there. It was the ice that had almost done in his mother. She'd slipped on the steps when she went out to retrieve Dimples, her little Yorkie. He'd have to stay a few days to take care of her affairs—and Dimples. But he wanted to make sure Patricia was okay.

Still in pajamas, she spent the day in the kitchen and on the sofa in front of the fireplace, reading and accumulating cups, glasses, and dirty plates beside her on the coffee table. Trying not to think about the last forty-eight hours and Billy and what he'd told her. Telling herself each time some part of it crept into her mind to let it go—for now. Until she could think clearly and develop her strategy.

The freezing rain ended and the wind died, but the day remained overcast and dreary, and the temperature plummeted as night fell. With another sedative, the last, she fell asleep as darkness filled the den.

Monday dawned with brilliant sunshine reflecting off a frozen landscape: grass, trees, roads, roofs, the whole world crystalline under a bright blue sky. And the usual sounds after an ice storm: tires spinning, limbs cracking, water dripping from eaves, and by evening, gushing along every channel it could find.

By the time Patricia showered and finished her first cup of coffee, she had her plan, a multi-prong attack—and she was ready to get moving. But the city offices and the courts were all closed. When she reached Ray Malloy at home, the line went dead before she could arrange to see him. Then the lights went out.

The gas logs in the fireplace continued to burn, as did the burners on the gas stove in the kitchen, so she ate hot soup and drank hot tea and thought and read some more in the sunlight coming through the window. When night came, she slept in her own bed, under five blankets.

The bedside lamp flaring on startled her awake. She checked her watch. Five a.m. By six thirty, she was at work, by eight, at city hall. Her bar I.D. gained her admission to the restricted area for city officials. In the lobby, she made a quick search of the index on the marbled wall. Chief of police: third floor. She'd met him only once before—at one of Allie's parties—but it was time she and the chief became better acquainted.

Marching down the open corridor on the third floor, she received a few odd looks. *This is more than just being out of place,* she thought as she greeted a woman she knew from the gym. The woman ignored her.

She passed through a door with frosted glass, "Criminal Justice and Enforcement" stenciled on it in large letters, and halted in front of a receptionist.

"Would you tell Chief O'Reilly Patricia Egan is here to see him," she said, standing stiff and straight, her briefcase by her side.

"Do you have an appointment?" asked the receptionist, an attractive middle-aged woman who looked and sounded over-qualified for the job.

"I called, but whoever answered said he was out. I know he's here." She gave the woman a tight smile. "Downstairs, they saw him come in." The helpful guard at the x-ray machine.

The woman responded with an appraising stare, and a look of disapproval.

"Let me check his schedule." She reached for a black binder.

"Why don't you just *ask* him if he can see me? I'm the lawyer whose client was shot—murdered by one of his detectives. Saturday morning. Maybe he'd like to talk to me about it."

The receptionist stopped with her hand on the binder. "I'll go ask," she said. She emerged from behind the L-shaped desk and minced in high heels down the inside corridor.

She was back in two minutes.

"Chief O'Reilly says he can't see you, Miss Egan. There will be an investigation and hearing." She emphasized, "will" as she went behind her desk, where she remained standing. "You'll likely be a witness."

That there would be an internal affairs hearing, she hadn't considered. Or that she would be called as a witness. But that could take weeks, months even.

"He needs to know what's going on," she said. "Now. There are rogue cops—"

"I'm sorry. He said there's an investigation. The only ones here who can talk with you are the detectives investigating what happened . . . and your involvement." She sat down and turned away, toward her typewriter, even though there was no paper in it.

"Eh!" said Patricia in disgust. "He sure said a lot for all the time you were back there." She pivoted on her low heels and stalked out.

Down in the basement canteen, she had a coffee, and thought. *The police aren't so good at investigating their own. And what happens in the meantime? They hold this over me, keep me quiet? While Goodman stays on the street.*

"Come on, counselor. Don't look so glum. It's bad, but the power's back on." Ray Malloy, a take-out coffee cup and white paper bag in one hand and his briefcase in the other, grinned down at her. He still had on his overcoat and his shoes were wet.

"You're on my list, Ray." She jumped up and grabbed her briefcase and coat off the chair beside her.

"Uh, oh." He stepped back in mock fright. "What list is that?"

"I want to see you. Let's go to your office."

"But I gotta be in court—"

"This won't take long. You just need to push a couple of buttons."

"Shouldn't you have your lawyer with you?" He gave her as near to a serious look as he ever managed.

"Don't mess with me, Ray. Let's go." She took off across the black-and-white linoleum squares to the exit. He followed.

Outside, on the short covered walk leading to the courthouse, she slowed to let him catch up.

"This isn't about me," she said. "It's about all the crooks and murderers you have working in this fucking place." She waved her hand back at city hall.

Not answering, he kept pace with her and together they entered the courthouse, passed through security, and boarded an empty elevator. Two men she knew to be detectives came in right behind them. They greeted Ray, but after a quick leering once-over ignored her.

Neither she nor Ray spoke again until they were inside his office. He set the coffee cup and paper bag on his desk, the cup on a manila file and the bag on a book of case reports.

"Ray . . ." she started as he shucked off his overcoat.

"I read the police report," he said, hanging the overcoat on a hat rack in the corner. "It ain't a pretty picture."

"It tell about Goodman?" She sat on the forward edge of a chair facing his desk, her coat in her lap.

"Says he had to shoot the *es-capee* in self-defense. Man pulled a gun on him." He slipped off his suit coat and onto a coat hanger.

"Bullshit! That's absolute bullshit . . . I know Jack told you what happened."

Ray plumped down in his swivel chair so that his head and shoulders were all that appeared above the books and files. As Patricia fought back the urge to swear at him, he opened the paper bag and, with the flair of a magician, produced two sausage biscuits in slick white wrappers. Seemingly his regular breakfast, or morning snack.

"Report said you fought like a banshee," Ray said, examining his prizes. "Took two detectives and a uniform to get you under control." He shook his head. "Resisting an officer, no less. *And* helping an escaped felon."

"Goddamit, Ray Malloy, I was trying to call *you* to arrange his surrender." She couldn't move any farther forward in her chair without landing on the floor. "Those . . . *idiots* broke in without a warrant and gunned down a sick man."

"They didn't need a warrant and he had a gun," Ray said evenly. He opened one of the wrappers.

"Goddamit, he did not! That's a lie!"

"Your word against his . . . theirs. Two detectives and a uniform. In my game, that beats your pair of deuces."

He eyed the biscuit like a grizzly bear with fresh meat. Then he chomped into it and started chewing, eyeing her at an angle.

"Ray." She took a deep breath. "Hal Goodman murdered Billy Angel in cold blood. He . . . Goodman . . . was the fourth man at the Taco Pal. He shot Henry Royale . . . Listen to me!" She leaned on his desk, staring into his narrowed eyes as he took another bite of the biscuit.

"The mayor's driver, or whatever he is," she continued, "shot the only witness against the mayor in the investigation of his . . . Goddamit, will you listen to me!" She felt like she was losing him to the biscuit.

Ray nodded and said, "I'm listening," but with a weary, uninterested look.

"The only *witness* to allegations he was taking kickbacks, getting work done on his house . . . Oh, shit! Why am I trying to talk to a fucking wall that does nothing but chew?" Throwing her hands up, she sank back in the chair.

Ray took the top off his coffee cup and took a sip. "God, it's great when it's still hot," he said. He took another sip, while she glared at him.

"Look, Patricia, I like you. You always treated me right over there, and I think you're a bright young woman, and pretty, too." He raised his eyebrows. "But that guy you're . . . you *were* representing was a crook, an *in-vet-er-ate* liar. Nobody's gonna believe anything he told you. He was just using you—"

"He was not!" She shouted, coming forward in the chair again. Her eyes were burning with tears of rage. "I know what's true and what's not," she said, dropping her voice. *Calm down*, she thought. *Don't yell. That'll only raise the hackles on his donkey back.*

"Okay, okay . . . so you say." Ray balled up the wrapper on biscuit number one and tossed it into the metal trashcan, now beside his desk. "But what are you gonna do? You've got yourself all tied up in this bucket of shit." He wrinkled up his nose, then nodded. "Jack told you the charges they want me to bring, didn't he?"

She didn't answer.

"Well?" He opened the wrapper on biscuit number two.

"Yes, but—"

"You don't have any credibility, lady."

"He was going to plead out."

Ray shook his head and focused on the biscuit.

"The judge was going to drop the murder charge," she said. "Your indictment . . ."

Taking a bite of the biscuit, Ray waved his free hand in the air. "Ancient history," he sputtered, mouth open, revealing teeth and food.

"But Goodman—"

"There'll be an investigation. *I* get to present all the evidence to the internal affairs panel." He licked his fingers, then reached for the coffee cup. "We'll get to the bottom of it," he added and took a swallow from the cup.

"Do I get to testify?" *Make it sound like I want to*, she thought.

"Absolutely." Another bite of biscuit. "You'll be subpoenaed."

"I'm going to bring it all out on Goodman." She gathered her coat and reached for her briefcase. "The mayor, too," she said, looking back up at him. "If it wasn't because Royale fingered him, it was—"

"You can try, but this board ain't gonna want to hear about *who* shot Royale or anybody else. All they want to know is about your client— whether his shooting was justified."

She stood and started to leave. Ray placed the remnants of his biscuit on the wrapper and sat up straight to glare at her above the litter on his desk.

"I may be able to keep 'em from pressing charges against you, but not if you . . ." He stopped and shook his head. "Piss off the cops, Miss Egan, and all bets are off." His eyebrows jumped, and then he gave her a fake smile as she opened the door. She looked back at him over her shoulder.

"Ray," she said, "wipe your mouth. You have crumbs all over it."

Chapter Forty-three – And Searching

HER NEXT STOP WAS THE COURTHOUSE and Judge Davis. She hadn't called for an appointment; this was far too important to risk rejection.

The judge's secretary, Mrs. Donnelly, opened the antechamber door.

"Mrs. Donnelly, would Judge Davis have five minutes to see me?" Patricia's expression was contrite, pleading. "It's urgent."

"Come on in, Miss Egan. It is Egan, isn't it?" Without waiting for confirmation, or asking what was urgent, she continued, "I'll go and see. He just got back and he has a motion to hear in a few minutes."

With a smile, she pointed Patricia to a chair and hurried across the anteroom to the judge's door. Her knock brought a low gruff response. Slipping inside, she closed the door, but almost immediately emerged and ushered Patricia into the inner chamber.

"Judge Davis, I'm here . . ." Patricia began.

"I know. You're here because of that fiasco over the weekend. What was your part in all that?" Rocking gently in his ducal chair, he didn't look pleased at the interruption. But his voice revealed some real concern—and curiosity. A thick brief lay folded over on the desk in front of him, next to a coffee mug.

Coming here, she'd decided to stick with Billy's story about the Taco Pal robbery. And his deliberate murder. Stay away from any connection with Henry Royale and the mayor, the judge's friend.

As she recounted her interview with Billy, the judge listened closely, one elbow on his desk, his chin on the back of his hand. His face was impassive—except for a hitch of the eyebrows when she related what Billy had told her about Goodman's role in the robbery. He remained silent until she reached the end of her tale and described the shooting.

"I'd convinced him to surrender," she said. "I was calling Mr. Malloy—"

"Shouldn't you have called the police, Miss Egan? Soon as you knew where he was?" Leaning back in the big chair, he stared at her over his raised coffee mug. His look was hard, accusing.

"He was my client. I had a duty—"

"That's highly debatable." He rocked in the chair. "You're an officer of the court. The crime of an escape from justice was continuing." He leaned forward. "You became complicit in it by going down there . . . And look what happened."

She felt a rising sense of dismay. And fear. This was going all wrong.

"He was afraid," she said, her voice strained. "He told me *someone* was out to shut him up. And there was." She nodded, hoping for some sign of understanding. None came. "They had access to him even inside the jail." She waited, but the judge remained silent, leaning back again, his coffee mug in both hands in front of his chest, his eyes seeming to contemplate her fate.

"He was hurt and needed help." She couldn't keep the pleading, almost whining tone she hated, out of her voice. "I couldn't let him . . . let him . . ." She felt the tears welling up in her eyes. "I was in the other room, trying to call Ray." Tugging at the coat in her lap, she fumbled in the pocket for a Kleenex. "When that man broke down the door . . . He shot my client." She stifled a sob, although tears were running down her cheeks. "In the face . . ."

"Here, Miss Egan." The judge reached in a drawer and pulled out a tissue. He handed it to her across the desk and waited while she wiped her cheeks and blew her nose. Noisily.

"I can understand why you're upset," Judge Davis said, setting his mug on top of the folded-over pages of the brief. "But you placed yourself in a dangerous situation. The man had a gun—"

"He didn't!" She stretched forward, her hand on the front of the judge's desk. "I saw everything near him. There was no *gun* on the bed, on the nightstand, anywhere . . . not until after *that man* shot him." Squeezing the tissue into a small wet ball, she gave a strangled sob. "They use throw-down guns all the time," she finally managed to say, unable to conceal her bitterness.

"Not as often as you think," the judge said, rocking back in his chair. "But I admit, it does happen." He shook his head. "However, you're the only one saying it happened here, and you are directly involved. That taints you, your perspective, you know."

"But I saw it! Billy Angel did *not* have a gun!" She half rose out of the chair, gripping the arm with her fingers.

He waved her back down with a slight motion of a raised hand. Sitting up, he assumed a judicial pose—erect, back and neck stiff.

"Miss Egan, you're smart and you have the qualities to become a fine lawyer. But you need to see the practical side of the problem." His mouth spat out "problem" like it was a piece of rotten fruit. "I've been on the bench for over twenty years. Nothing's black and white, although the law often tries to make it so." He paused and nodded at her. "We sometimes have to make things fall on one side of the line or the other, even if they don't fit," he said quietly, almost so that she couldn't hear his low gravelly voice.

Where's this going? She bit her lip to keep from interrupting, disagreeing. He gave her a grim smile and leaned back slightly.

"I can probably keep you from being prosecuted." He shook his head, his lips pressed tight. "I don't believe you're guilty of anything more than naiveté, and perhaps a bit of poor judgment and blind idealism."

Feeling her face flush, she opened her mouth to speak. He raised his hand, killing the protest in her throat.

"We probably shouldn't even be having this discussion . . . It's one of those gray areas, you see, that the law doesn't like."

He's right, she thought. Threatened with prosecution, she shouldn't have come here. But she had no choice, and no regrets. The judge was looking past her, still talking.

"The only person who says Goodman was involved in that robbery is dead . . . and not credible either. You have to realize that the police, the D.A., all those bureaucrats over there hang together." He made a loose gesture toward what she took to mean city hall. "They have potential liabilities in this. People could lose their jobs. And this man, who by happenstance was your client, was a criminal. He had a rap sheet longer than this brief." He tapped on the document under his coffee mug. "He'd already contributed to two deaths by his actions. Some might say he got what he deserved."

"I don't care what happens to me," she blurted out. Even though she did. "I just want to see justice done." She was past crying now. "Justice we claim to have . . . under a rule of law. There's a killer who has to be stopped, crooked cops running amok—"

He waved his hand to stop her, palm out, an imperial gesture. "No use getting dramatic." He smiled, an actual crumbling and refashioning of the granite visage. "You're highly principled and idealistic, Miss Egan, and I admire that." He shook his head slowly, and his smile faded. "But you need more than you *have* . . ." he paused, before continuing, "to do *anything* more. Best you let it go. This is just the way things are." He tilted his head back, looking up and displaying soft folds in his neck. "Names and faces may change, but the nature of people and the parts they play don't." His eyes came back to her, his face again adamant. "I'll take care of Goodman, *when* the time is right. Let's not go risking your career to do it."

Without waiting for her agreement or any other response, he pushed back from the desk and stood. "It's time *now* for court. We're a little late, but that's fine . . . builds suspense, makes good theater." A fleeting smile crossed the weathered face as he held out his hand

Her last stop was Leon Hayes' office. Leaving the courthouse, they had almost collided on the steps as he chugged up them and she meandered down, both with their eyes fixed on where their feet were going. She asked to talk to him, but he didn't have time. The governor had called only an hour before—Leon was being appointed to the district court bench, a vacant judgeship. As he told her, glee showed in his eyes and he did a little hop and skip along the steps. He was headed inside to the clerk's office— to pick out his vestments. But he agreed to see her in the afternoon, five o'clock sharp, at his office.

Patricia's worries pushed aside her puzzlement over Leon becoming a judge, her wonder at the peculiar swings of fortune. She had to get to her own office and check her in-box, and think through what she was going to do now.

The ice had all melted; the pavement was wet, the ground soggy. Work crews scrambled along the streets, raking and piling up downed branches, felling ravaged trees and loading dump trucks. By five o'clock, the sun was low in a hazy white sky, casting dull shadows among the shabby buildings and lighting up a single faded-red corner of the Dr Pepper sign high above Leon's Cadillac.

She had forgotten how macabrely elegant Leon's office was. The low lighting, the dark wood paneling. Like a funeral director's conference room—or maybe the chapel, and she was here for the wake.

"Coffee, Miss Egan?" he asked as he released her hand. She had gripped his hand eagerly this time, perhaps too eagerly.

"No, thanks . . . too late in the day. Please call me Patricia." She set her briefcase down next to the chair and removed her coat.

"I may have just a touch," Leon said, moving to his recessed coffee bar. *Jeez,* she thought, settling into a client chair, *instead of Leon it'll soon be "Judge" and "your honor."* She folded her coat in her lap.

"Congratulations on your appointment," she said as Leon returned to his desk carefully balancing the cup and saucer in front of him.

"Well, I'm not sworn in for another thirty days and I still have to tend to the city's business. They're looking for a new city attorney, if you're interested." He set the cup and saucer on the big empty desk and eased down in his executive chair. A new judge's chambers would be a comedown from this.

"Don't think they'd have me as city attorney now," she said. "And I don't think I have the stomach for it."

"You seemed to have a lot of guts last weekend." Leon's tone and smile removed any sarcasm she might have read into the comment.

"You're my last resort."

"I'm not surprised. The chief told me you'd been to see him and I ran into Ray Malloy at lunch. He'd heard *I've* been *anointed* to the bench." Leon grinned at her above his coffee cup. "Amazing how cordial that makes folks."

"I also talked with Judge Davis."

"Our old friend," Leon said, the grin still there

She told him about her discussion with the judge—discreetly omitting anything about his helping her avoid prosecution. Leon listened, sipping his coffee, until she finished.

"I'm not surprised Judge Davis counseled you to let it go," he said. "And Ray Malloy did, too, didn't he?" Leon set the empty cup down in the saucer.

She shook her head and sighed. "Ray talks too much."

Leon chuckled. "Ray puts his finger to the wind and sails with the tide." *As if you don't*, thought Patricia. She gave Leon a faint smile as he continued.

"The judge works in mysterious ways, like the Lord. As - we - know." Leon smiled, his fingers covering his chin and pulling at his lower lip. "But he sups at the same table as the devil. He's not going to jump in front of any train, even if it is loaded with crooks. Especially if it's people he breaks bread with."

Talk about mysterious. Leon's waxing philosophical. She kept her face frozen, attentive, a slight smile to answer Leon's.

Leon's face, despite his fifty years or so, was almost cherubic, round and smooth. *Like a shadow version of the man-in-the moon,* she thought, watching him. *A man whose experiences in life are far removed from my own.*

"The city's like a machine," Leon said, nodding his head, "a great big money machine for them that run the town. All the wheels go round and round, all the gears and cogs mesh and grind—spinning off gold and silver to relations and friends and business partners. To all those invited to the party."

He drummed on his desk, obviously pleased at the description. His round face was blurred in the shadows as he rocked back in his chair.

"And the mayor's the chief cog in the works," he said after a moment. "He's been in some sort of office over in city hall as long as Judge Davis has been a judge, maybe longer."

"How about Dick McFee . . . and Allie? Where do they fit in?"

"Old aristocracy, landed money. I guess they're sort of above it all, but they have to work to stay there. Not look too hard, not ask too many questions, just go along for the ride." He sat forward and stared solemnly at her. His face was almost sad. "You're probably thinking I'm just like Ray and the judge," he said. "I go with the flow and I don't get in anybody's way."

"I don't—"

He held up a pudgy hand. "No, no, you don't need to perjure yourself in front of this judge—who hasn't even been sworn in yet. Don't change who you are and say something that's not completely true to your mind." He gave a low, self-deprecating laugh. "As a black man in this lovely center of

Southern hospitality and culture, I've always known my place, and I keep my mouth shut. And you know, I've done pretty much all right . . . Oh, being lucky enough to be in the right places always helped, because everyone— even whites who see me as colored, or worse—they all respect money. It's just that," he said, shaking his head, "you have to be all things to all people."

"I need your help, Leon." *But I can't be your confessor*, she thought.

"How can I help you? I'm just a weary old black man. They only listen to me over there when they *want* to hear what I'm saying. Usually with money." He held up his palms. "All legitimate, political contributions." He dropped his hands on the desk with a smack.

"You . . . we've got to do something, get the truth out . . . about these people." Her voice was level and hard. "Goodman . . . the mayor." She gripped the edge of the desk across from Leon's outstretched hands on the other side. "We've got to do something about the corruption—"

"What about your clients at the McFee Law Firm? Mr. Fitzhugh? Don't you think he's tied into all this with the city?"

"I don't know . . . Maybe. But I don't care if it all comes down on us."

"And your associate? What about him? And mine in Atlanta." He sighed. "What a tangled web. You have to understand, I'm in a precarious position here, especially now, before I take the bench."

"Leon, you've got to do something. Help me with this . . . this horrible mess!" Her face contorted with her plea.

Looking down at his hands, Leon sighed again, then looked up at her. "You helped me once and I'll help you—but only to the extent I can," he coughed, "*realistically*." Nodding, he scratched the side of his head and spoke as if thinking out loud, "As acting city attorney, I'm still on the hearing panel for internal affairs. It's me, the chief, and the union rep. The union rep plays it pretty straight, though he tries to look after his people. The chief . . . well, he'll sail with the tide, like Ray." He paused, his eyes fixed on hers. "You'll have to testify, and without immunity . . . Is that okay?"

She had to think about that. Her testimony could be used against her if she were indicted . . . or she could exercise her constitutional right to stay silent, plead the Fifth. But she didn't think long. "I'll do it. Ray's going to subpoena me anyway." She slid back in the chair. *And I'll take my chances with the grand jury*, she thought. *If Judge Davis comes through, it'll all work out.*

Leon smiled. "We can get this Goodman fired, even if we can't see him prosecuted. I can't do any more than that."

Opening the door to her old Mercedes, she glanced up at the Dr Pepper sign and the words "Good for Life!" The drab exterior of Leon's building was quite a contrast to the well-appointed office she'd just left. As she stared at it, the divorce door looked a little less shabby and beaten up than before.

What Leon offered her was better than nothing, but he would always have a door through which he could escape. Gripping the steering wheel, she wished she had one, too. Should she go to the F.B.I.? The U.S. Attorney?

What credibility would she have—after Billy?

Chapter Forty-four – Jack Takes a Stand

JACK BARELY MADE IT BACK TO CARRVILLE in time for the meeting with Fitz. It had been a long miserable drive with a whimpering dog in the back seat. His mother was in worse shape than he'd expected. Not only did she break her wrist, she also managed to crack her pelvis. All for poor little Dimples. A week in the hospital, then physical therapy for six or eight more. She'd be happy with that, all the attention she'd garner. But now he had Dimples to look after.

He punched the elevator button, waited only briefly, and punched it again. Chewing on a broken fingernail, he stared at the gray metal doors. Patricia had called him after her rounds with the powers that be. He was uneasy about her testifying in any kind of hearing—certainly in one where she had no immunity. It would stir up a hornets' nest. A bizarre thought struck him. *Maybe Goodman's a hit man. An enforcer for a mafia-like machine in control of the city. That's what she said Leon called it: a machine.*

He jabbed at the button again. The floor number still didn't budge. Closing his eyes, he rubbed his forehead.

If Goodman and some other cops are working both sides of the street, who else could be doing the same? The police chief? The city manager? The mayor for sure. Maybe even Ray Malloy . . . He almost laughed out loud. *Too much effort. But what about Judge Davis? Patricia thinks Leon's right. The judge is a survivor, not a crusader. So long as the gang-in-charge plays by the rules—mainly don't get caught—Judge Davis won't interfere.*

Then there's Leon himself. An outsider to the good ol' boy gang of thieves. White thieves is the key. But how the hell did he ever get appointed to a judgeship? No question, all that land translated into money, then into donations to the right people. Can't buy me love, but it sure as hell buys a lot of other stuff.

All this was pissing him off, especially standing here waiting on an elevator that was making him late for his meeting. Which brought him back to the debate he'd been having with himself on the way here.

Fitz was part of it—and now, so was he. Buying up the land, inflating its value, and then Fitz cutting him in on the deal, if only in a small way. The deal with the mayor and his cronies, the inside information. *What would Patricia think if she knew?* He had told her only enough to deflect whatever Lacey might let slip. It had always made him uneasy, deceiving her like that, but now, after what had happened in the last week, it was tearing him apart.

He had ducked trying to buy her client's house, once Fitz hired his land man. He'd even avoided telling her about Fitz's dealings with the mayor—and about Allie's reaction to it. *Jesus. Allie. What would she think of him?*

Then there was Leslie's job offer. He sighed. Somehow he had to clear the air with Fitz. Then he'd call Leslie.

The numbers over the door started blipping down: five, four, three— and stopped. He pounded on the button, cursing it and the entire day.

He had meant to come home last night, but closing up his mother's house, then finding someone to keep the dog kept him there. After learning the cost of a kennel, he packed Dimples into the carrier and the carrier into the backseat of his car. Along with his royal highness' monogrammed bed, twenty cans of special-diet canine cuisine, and half-a-dozen dog toys.

Fitz was already in the conference room, small stacks of paper spread out like a poker hand in front of him. Lacey had performed her magic and produced the documents to complete the Star Energy partnership—and transfer a dozen or so properties into it.

"Heard about your mother," Fitz said, standing as Jack came through the door. "Hope she's doin' okay."

"She's fine. Good as anyone could expect." As they shook hands, he eyed Fitz's brown leather jacket and cerulean silk shirt. And the perennial tan.

"You have to drive all the way to Sniderville in that storm?" Fitz asked. "Must've been a real bitch." He slapped him on the back as Jack leaned down to place his briefcase under the conference table. "My flight was cancelled and I ended up in Vegas another night. Tough duty, man." He winked and grinned as if he expected Jack to know.

"Yeah, tough duty. Lacey give you all the documents?"

"I gave him everything he needs to see or sign." Lacey's voice came from behind him as she entered from the hallway. "Had to get my notary seal and book." She held them up to show him.

Jack smiled at her and received a glare in return.

"Already started making my mark," Fitz said, resuming his seat at the head of the table. An empty coffee cup sat close by his right hand. On his ring finger was a shiny gold ring with a large dark-blue stone.

"All these little red tabs, right, hon—that where I sign?" Fitz scribbled his name even as he asked. Lacey ignored him, but that didn't slow his progress.

Jack took a seat cattycorner to Fitz and facing the windows, while Lacey dragged over a chair from among those along the wall. Glancing around, Jack took in the conference room, as if for the last time. These days it never accommodated more than five or six people, even for birthday cake and coffee. Dominating it still was the George Washington-sized portrait of Dick in all the promise of his youth. A Dick McFee he'd never known.

Fitz chattered away as he skimmed the papers and signed without reading them and Lacey filled in the blanks and stamped the notarizations. He talked about the ice storm and the damage it had done, the cold dry weather in Vegas, and his next hunting trip in the spring.

Jack half listened, watching the tanned hands riffling through the documents and expertly wielding the black ink pen. Looking up from the hands, he squinted at the sunlight and blue sky showing through the open blinds. A corner of the old jail viewed at an angle across the blinds gave the illusion of an abstract painting.

Lacey must have noticed him squinting. She marched over to the windows and one by one closed the blinds until the outside light was extinguished. He watched as she crossed behind Fitz to turn on the overhead lights at the door. On the way, she gave Fitz the evil eye, then frosted Jack with another glare.

"That should do it," Fitz said, handing Lacey the final page. "Good damn work, Jack. We've made some great progress since we started this little venture." He reached over and patted Jack on the shoulder.

"I'll have to make copies," Lacey said, picking up the documents.

"Thanks, Lacey." Jack smiled up at her, only to receive a sour look. "Will you bring us coffee?" He pointed at Fitz's empty cup. Her look turned to one of disgust, making him think that the foot-high stack of papers she held was about to descend on his head. He added, "Please, Lacey," and faked an apologetic smile. But he still wanted her to bring the coffee. He needed to talk with Fitz, now, while his determination—and courage—lasted.

"When I get a chance," was Lacey's icy response. She started out.

"Oh, and will you close the door," Jack said, swiveling around in the chair. The door slammed before he could add another, "Please."

"What's with her?" Fitz asked as Jack turned back to face him.

Not answering, Jack bent down and pulled out his briefcase and opened it. He removed a thick brown envelope, then snapped the briefcase shut.

"Fitz, I don't want your money," he said, slapping the envelope down on the table, in front of Fitz. "This is the last thing I'm doing for you."

"What! What do you mean?" Fitz drew back, mouth agape.

"I'm withdrawing as your counsel. I can't represent you any longer."

"Does Dick know about this?" Fitz's face was red now, his eyes narrowed in a scowl.

"I don't think he's here, but I'll be sure to tell him when I see him. Maybe tomorrow. Or maybe I'll call him. But it's my decision."

"You can't . . . you can't do this!" Fitz rocked and bounced in the plush chair. "You'll be ruined in this town. Dick McFee, this firm, you'll all be ruined." He shook the fist with the ring at Jack. "Kaput! You hear me!"

Jack had made his decision in the elevator. No plan, no consideration of what came next. He kept hearing Allie McFee. "Do the right thing, Jack." She couldn't, so he would.

"I don't think it's right," Jack said. "The mayor's involvement in those land deals out there. This A-E Land Company you're buying property from." Fitz continued to glare at him and rock in his chair. "The refinancings. Then you . . . trying to buy me. Where does it end, Fitz?"

"Where does it *end*!" Fitz rose a foot or so out of his seat, along with the rising volume of his voice. "It ends with us making a lot of fucking money." He threw his hands out in a wide arc. "It ends with all kinds of new energy shit for this place." Settling back in the chair, he leaned away from Jack and peered down his nose at him. His teeth were clenched in an attack-dog grin.

Erect, elbows on the table, Jack returned the stare, his own face and neck taut, his mouth set in a grim line. A long minute passed before either spoke. The envelope of money lay on the table between them.

"You're still wet behind the ears, my young friend," Fitz said, sitting up straight and nodding. "These politicos . . ." He placed his hands on either side of the envelope and touched it gingerly with the tips of his fingers. "They don't do any real work and they don't get paid the big bucks." He shifted the envelope around, all the time nodding at Jack, who didn't move. "What they do . . . they have their fingers in a *lot* of little deals. Nothing too obvious. Deals they help along, get a little payoff from." Fitz's voice now bore the soft, unctuous tones of a television preacher. "And their friends—and the people they help are *al-ways* their friends—these friends give a little back to those bearing the burdens of public service. A little cash, a few shares of stock, something of value."

Grinning, he stroked the palm of his left hand, flashing the gold of his ring in the light. Then he rocked forward and hammered on the table with his fist.

"This is a goddamn important project—for the cities, the whole goddamn country." In a quick motion, he spun the envelope toward Jack. It came to rest at the edge of the table. "I . . . you . . . the mayor, we're all in this together."

"Count me out," Jack said. He shoved the envelope away from him. "I'm not in it. The whole thing's warped. I overheard Allie telling the mayor—"

"Yeah, I heard about their little . . . disagreement." Fitz's chair was still; his eyes bore into Jack's. "That was unfortunate. Quite unfortunate."

"The mayor shouldn't be making a profit off a project the city . . . the taxpayers are funding. They depend on his honest . . ." Jack threw his hand up at Fitz's sarcastic smile. "Dammit, they depend on these people standing up for the city, not acting for their own benefit. He owes a duty—"

"And he's doing it!" Fitz was bouncing in the chair again. "He . . . all those fucking bureaucrats and politicians, they're just getting a tip for a job well done . . . Shi-it! It'll come out of the bond money anyway—and a lot less than all the fees you fucking lawyers and the fucking bankers will get."

Jack slumped back. His shoulders drooped as he gripped the ends of the chair arms. *So that's it*, he realized, staring at Fitz. *The bond money.* Allie had figured it out, and he hadn't. Not until now.

"It's not just the inflated land values, is it?" he said in a dull voice. "Or the loans, or even the prospect of selling the land to the cities."

"The land's valuable only because of the project. You know that. You've known it since the first time I took you out there."

Jack continued, as much to himself as to Fitz. "The big payoff's from the bonds. The investment bankers." He paused, glaring at the other man now. "What are they giving you, Fitz? Tell me, *what* are they giving you out of the bond proceeds? That's the big money, right? You, the mayor, whoever else is in on this."

"Not a goddamn thing!" His preternatural tan turned even darker and mottled with anger. "I don't have to listen to this. Not from you or anybody."

A soft tap came on the door; then it opened. Lacey entered carrying a tray with two paper cups filled with coffee. She opened her mouth to speak, but snapped it shut when she saw their faces. As she set the tray down next to Jack's left elbow, away from Fitz, her eyes shifted to the brown manila envelope lying between them on the table, and stopped there.

"Let me know if you need anything else," she said, backing away. "Aerial's finishing the last of the copies."

"Thanks," said Jack. She left, this time softly closing the door behind her.

"You'll get loans backed by the city," Jack said as soon as the door closed. "Industrial Development Bonds or something like that, for your part of this so-called energy venture—"

"Of course! That's the whole fucking point . . . and you damn well know it. We'll need substantial—"

"For your salaries, bonuses, expenses—"

"Yeah . . . sure, somebody'll get those. Why not us? Including you and Dick." Leaning on the table, he reached past Jack and took one of the cups of coffee, sloshing some over the side and onto the table.

"Some extra . . . fees."

"All that's incidental to the project, part of the cost," Fitz said, tasting the coffee.

Jack took a paper napkin from the tray and wiped up the spill. "I don't want any part of it. Just take your money and leave me out." He balled up the napkin and tossed it on the tray. "Will anything be built out there? Someone bet me it wouldn't." Ray Malloy. Long ago.

"Sure it will." The response sounded hollow behind the coffee cup. Fitz lowered it to display a sardonic smile that served only to heighten Jack's ire.

"What if I spoil the party?" Jack said, raising his voice for the first time. "What if I spill the beans on your . . . on yours and the mayor's scheme?"

"Goddamit, you're my lawyer!" Fitz shouted and hit the table with his fist. A long iron-gray coil of hair fell across his forehead, almost to his eye. "My business is confidential, and you better damn well remember that . . . You understand me?" He leaned away and gave Jack a gimlet-eyed stare. "You'll keep it confidential, buddy boy, whether you like it or not. Even if you did go and shoot off your mouth to Allie McFee."

"Allie McFee? Is that what—"

"Don't be stupid." Fitz whipped out a comb and restored his hair to its proper place, then grabbed his coffee again as Jack glared at him.

"Keep it confidential?" Jack said slowly, thinking of Allie. "What *you're* doing?" He gave a disgusted snort. "Not if it involves a criminal enterprise."

"Bullshit!" Fitz slapped his half-empty cup down on the table, splashing out more coffee. Seizing the envelope, he jumped up, then wagged a finger under Jack's nose. "You need to think about what you're saying, sport."

"Maybe I'll go to the papers," Jack said, his voice quiet. He studied his hands, flat on the table.

"Not in this town, you won't." Fitz stormed over to a chair by the wall and grabbed a thin attaché case off it.

Jack swiveled around to stare after him. "Maybe the attorney general or the Feds would be interested." That stopped Fitz. He turned to face him. "If you go on with this scheme," Jack said, "I'll be there—in your way." His jaw worked, as Fitz glared at him.

"What d'ya mean? *In my way*," Fitz said with a sneer. "You helped put these deals together, my friend . . . Don't be fucking naïve." He stalked to the door. One hand almost on the knob, he spun around and shook his finger at Jack. "Don't think you're playing kids' games here. The mayor . . ." Fitz shook his head. "You don't know him. You don't know *me*." Still shaking his head, he took a deep breath. "Don't be a fool, Jack. I've always liked you."

He jerked the door open and hurtled out past Lacey.

"What was that all about?" she asked, looking over her shoulder as she brought the stack of copies to the conference table.

"I just did the right thing," Jack said, standing up. He gave her a wry smile. "I think."

"What do I do with Mr. Fitzhugh's copies?"

"I don't care. Throw 'em in the trash." He started for the door. "Oh, hell . . . use a courier. And make sure you put it on his bill."

Now he needed to call Leslie. Tell him what to do with his job offer.

Chapter Forty-five – Coming Together

GIVING A DEEP SIGH, Patricia settled into the passenger seat and closed her eyes. They were in Jack's car; hers they had left at the office. It had been a long day, followed by dinner with the boss at Plato's Cave. That Fitz was no longer a client didn't faze Dick McFee in the least. He seemed more concerned about Allie, whom he'd just seen at the rehabilitation center—she was making progress, he said.

Jack had also gone to see Allie after he dropped Dimples off at the house. Allie recognized him, Jack said, but she remembered nothing of the accident. When he told Allie about Fitz, that he had fired him as a client, all she did was nod, and when he was leaving, in the confusion of attendants changing out linens and other visitors arriving, she'd asked if he was worried about Fitz. Before he could answer, and tell her again that Fitz was no longer his client, she asked about Patricia, if she was okay. But Jack agreed with Dick; Allie was making progress, even though she spent most of her waking hours in a wheelchair.

Despite his preoccupation with Allie, Dick seemed attentive to their tales of woe. With Jack, he exhibited indignation at Fitz's land deals, surpassing Jack's own measured, dispassionate evaluation of the scheme to defraud the city. And he agreed: Jack had done the right thing in ditching Fitz. The McFee firm would never be a party to any illegal or unethical conduct. He was shocked that an old friend would be involved in something like that. Must've started after Joe Mayes and Leslie took over and changed the scope of the Alt-Energy project.

When reminded by Jack that Fitz had started buying land out on the Old Schoolhouse Road long before Leslie's defection, and had even bought the old McFee development, Dick didn't miss a beat in excoriating Leslie and then reminding Jack that he, Jack, had been Fitz's principal lawyer all these months since Leslie. After that, Jack clamped his mouth

271

shut and rolled his eyes in Patricia's direction. He repeated nothing to Dick of what he'd told her about Dick's other good friend, the mayor, and the scheme to milk the cities' municipal bonds for buckets of money.

That was all during the opening drinks and *hors d'oeuvres*. Through the spinach salads and entrees, and two bottles of wine, they spent far more time on her ordeal with Billy Angel and Hal Goodman, and her search for justice. With concern and sympathy, Dick expressed his unwavering support. He'd be there with her. He'd go to bat for her with his old friends. And he'd make damn sure "that miscreant" Goodman was brought to justice.

But she knew better. His words were slurred, his eyes awash with spirits. Leaving the restaurant, he refused a ride, and they left him with Plato holding him by the arm and insisting on calling him a cab. She and Jack were in a hurry. Through some silent communication, she sensed they both wanted to be free of their boss and alone with each other.

At the second traffic light, Jack broke the silence. "I had a job offer from Leslie," he said, looking over at her.

Her drowsiness dissipated in a flash, and she started up. "When was this?" Shifting in her seat to see his face, she gave him a sharp look.

"A few weeks ago . . . I turned it down." He smiled over at her. "Today, after the meeting with Fitz." Behind them, a car horn beeped.

"Why didn't you tell me?" She didn't know whether to be angry or relieved.

"I don't know." The car horn blared now, and he looked away from her, up at the green light. Then he accelerated through the intersection. "I didn't know what to do, I guess." The car behind them flashed its lights and sped past. "Maybe I didn't want to piss you off, or cause you to leave if . . ."

Watching the red taillights recede in the distance, she waited until he added, "I decided I want to stay here . . . with you."

She laughed. "And you want to stay completely away from that mess with Fitz. Who happens to be Joe Mayes' golfing buddy."

"Yeah," he said. "That, too."

How could she be angry with this guy? Guile was not in his nature.

They were silent as Jack steered the car onto the freeway and off again and onto the winding streets leading to the decrepit old house they shared on the hill above town. She stared out at the knobbed street lamps and shadowy trees gliding past. Wondering what she . . . they would do now, both tonight and tomorrow.

"So what do we do now?" Jack asked.

She spoke as much to the night as to him. "Well, I'm stuck here until the Internal Affairs hearing." She sighed and, pulling her coat around her, slumped down in the seat. "This whole business bollixes up any job search, and the D.A.'s office might get antsy if I just left." She looked over at him. "How about you? What are you going to do now?"

"I'm going to be a royal pain in the ass for that bunch of crooks," he said, as he braked to a stop. He hit the steering wheel with his palms.

"I'll stay with the firm. Dick's not going to be much help, but he won't stand in the way—especially if I push the ethics angle." He grimaced and shook his head. "What the devil *is* ethical in this business anyway? Dick's made compromises all these years, taking the fruits of his friendships, not asking any questions. Almost every-damn-body here has. Dick, bless his heart . . . he needs to win, be accepted. Wants the money, power, and he ignores all the filth that comes with it." Jack shrugged. "Maybe that's the price of success."

"Hmm. May *be* why he drinks . . ." She was growing sleepy, but she liked listening to him. She stared out the window at a filigree of black limbs etched on a gray sky. Yellow rectangles glowed in the passing houses, and decorative lights in yards and on porches cast long shadows across frosted lawns. An old neighborhood, but changing; renovated Victorian homes, newly painted, stood next to structures like their own, decaying until fit only for a wrecking ball.

"Maybe I'll stay, too," she said, musing out loud.

"Even after the hearing?" He swung into the driveway to their old house.

"You need somebody to look after you." She gently touched his arm, as he downshifted to a stop.

"Me! What about you?"

"Maybe I need you, too." She left her hand on his arm.

He parked the car at the bottom of the drive, down from the gnarled oak at the front of the house. A dog barked off in the distance. Staring straight ahead, she made no move to get out.

"What about us?" he asked, looking over at her.

"You think that, perhaps. . ." she said, slowly unbuckling her seatbelt, "we've both been looking for the right person in all the wrong people?"

"Something like that." He leaned across the center console as she reached up to him. His kiss generated a thrill and sudden warmth that pulsed through her entire body, and she clutched him tightly, desperately to her. Far down the hill, a freight train trailed a mournful whistle as it left the town behind.

After the whistle was long past and the low muttering rumble of the train had faded to silence, she broke away from him. "We don't have to stay out here, you know." She left her hand beside his neck. "We live in the same house."

"Too far apart." Slipping away, he opened the door.

She was already out of the car by the time he made it to her side. Arms around each other's waist, they shuffled through the storm debris on the drive toward the porch. As they reached the steps, a rustling noise came from the direction of the vacant house being renovated next door, and a figure smaller than the neighbor's cat hurtled out of the gloom beyond the screen of azaleas.

"Yip, yip, yip!" A mobile dust mop.

"Dimples?" said Jack, bending down and catching the dog as it catapulted into his legs. "What are you doing out here? I left you inside."

"Maybe he jimmied a window." Patricia giggled, something she hadn't done in a while.

"Here, take him." Jack handed her the wiggling dog, then mounted the steps two at time. "I'm sure I closed the door, dammit."

He unlocked the front door and went in while she was still trudging up the steps—with Dimples lunging at her averted cheek. As soon as she was over the threshold, she dumped the dog on the living room floor. She pushed the door closed behind her as Dimples darted after Jack, who was going from room-to-room to the rear of the house, opening doors and clicking on lights as he went.

She slipped out of her coat and heels and waited a moment, listening. Only silence—then a door slammed. She wandered into the den, shoes in one hand, the coat over her arm.

"Must've left the back door open," Jack called from the kitchen. "I was in a rush to get back to the office. Damn screen on the porch is torn."

There were noises from the kitchen. The rattle of glasses.

"Yeah," she yawned, "we need to fix that. What are you doing in there?"

She started for the open door into the kitchen, but almost tripped over Dimples scuttering out. He made a circle around her feet, then headed over to Jack, on his way into the den.

He held up a bottle and two wine glasses. "Let's have some brandy."

"Brandy?" she said, not sure she wanted more alcohol. "Now?"

"In front of the fire." He came up to her, his arms out, the bottle to one side and glasses to the other. "To celebrate *us*." He smiled down at her. "I don't have any champagne."

Twisting around, he used one foot to steer Dimples into the kitchen, and hitting the bottle against the door, tugged it shut behind the dog.

"A little brandy would be nice," she said, as he turned back to her. She placed her arms around his neck, pulling his mouth down to hers. His arms—impeded only slightly by the bottle and the glasses in his hands— clutched her tightly to him. From the kitchen came yips, whimpers, and scratching.

Breaking away, she held him at arm's length, staring up at him.

"Why don't you figure out what to do with your friend in there while I go change. I've got to get out of these pantyhose."

"Why don't you . . . ?" he started, but the yips and whimpers had become piercing howls.

"I'll be back." She kissed him on the cheek in passing. "Why don't you light the fire and pour us some brandy? The long matches are on the mantle."

In the hallway, she shucked off her pantyhose, blouse, and skirt, and the rest in her bedroom. She was back in five minutes. She had slipped into a silk peignoir Colin had given her—for summer. Over it, she wore a long, snuggly fleece robe. They were waiting for her, both Jack and Dimples, on the sofa across from the blazing gas logs in the fireplace. Dimples lay curled in a ball between Jack's hip and the sofa arm.

She pantomimed a sexy entrance, her robe open and the strap of the peignoir off one bare shoulder. The dog opened an eye, then tucked its nose back under its paw. Jack whistled, shrugged at the dog, and grinned up at her.

"So-o-o, is this a *ménage a trois*?" she said, pulling up the strap and closing the robe. Passing behind him, she patted his neck and ruffled his hair.

"He'll be okay," Jack said. "If it's people he knows, nothing bothers him."

"Oh-h-h, is this the voice of experience?"

She sank down on the third of the sofa they had left for her. In answer, Jack reached around her shoulders and pulled her to him. His hand in her hair, hers on his neck, they kissed. His other hand slid inside her robe. The lights were out, and the yellow and blue flames hissing from the gas logs cast dancing shadows on the wall. Dimples snored softly at his end of the sofa.

After the first long embrace and exploring caresses, Jack broke away and leaned across to the coffee table for his glass of brandy. As he took a sip, he handed her the second glass.

"I used to wonder what it would be like to make love to you," he said into his glass, his eyes on her face. Meeting his eyes, she smiled and touched her glass to her lips without speaking.

"My best friend's girl. His fiancée."

"Ex fiancée." She lowered her glass, and laid her free hand on his arm. "I always thought you were . . . too wild or something."

"What!" said Jack. "How could you think that?"

"All those different girls and never a relationship. And you disappear without any explanation." Her smile disappeared and her face grew serious. "Maybe I shouldn't tell you this, but I was really angry about Kitty."

"Ah, Kitty." He sighed. "Poor . . . sexy Kitty."

"I *was* jealous." She shoved him in the chest with her hand.

"You shouldn't have been. There was only the one time, and we won't talk about that." He took a good swig of the brandy.

"So-o-o . . . all those other nights, where were you?" she asked.

He laughed. "Bars, basketball games. Fitz gets tickets. Sometimes I go . . . well, I went with him . . . sometimes alone. I don't have to report to you."

"You jerk. You could have told me." But she giggled and gently rubbed his chest, snuggling closer against his side.

For a moment, they sipped their brandy and stared at the fire. Then she leaned her head down against his chest. Dropping his hand, Jack ran his fingers along the nape of her neck, under the collar of her robe, and onto bare skin. He tugged at the strap to the peignoir and slipped his hand underneath it and down.

"Dressed light tonight?" He dropped his empty glass onto the floor.

"You just noticed?" Her hand played along his stomach, undid a button, and slid inside his shirt. With the half-full glass of brandy, she made small circles along the inside of his thigh.

Jack pressed his cheek to hers and whispered, "There's some things I need to tell—"

"Yip! Yip! Yip!" Dimples sat up and bounded over the top of the sofa. The dog sniffed along the bottom of the closed kitchen door and growled.

"What's wrong, pooch?" Jack said, releasing Patricia and rising from the sofa. "Smell a rat?"

As she sat up, he went to the door and pushed it open. Dimples slipped through ahead of him.

Jack froze in the doorway.

With a series of high, keening yelps, the dog flew past his feet and into the den. Feeling behind her to place her glass on the coffee table, Patricia stared anxiously over the back of the sofa. Jack's hands went out to his side, and he slowly raised them above his head.

"Back in there," came a low gruff voice from the dark beyond him.

Jack inched backward into the den. "What are you—"

"Turn around and shut up."

She rose from the sofa, one knee on the cushion. Pulling her robe closed, she peered into the gloom, deepened by Jack's undulating shadow.

"Who *are* you?" she yelled. "What do you want?"

Alternately barking and growling, Dimples bounded back and forth at Jack's feet.

"Get that damn dog." The voice sharpened in pitch.

"It's okay, I've got him." Turning, Jack scooped up Dimples, then moved slowly back into the den. Following him was a large figure in a dark raincoat, a black gun extended in one hand. The jagged flames from the fireplace played across the man's face, as on a pale screen.

She gasped in recognition and leaped up, clutching her robe even tighter. Hal Goodman.

Jack was at the end of the sofa, his back to Goodman, the dog squirming in his arms. His eyes were trained on hers, and a mutual thought flashed between them: nothing they could say would save them; they needed to act, and they needed to do it now.

She made a slight dip of her chin. Jack twirled and thrust the dog in Goodman's face, then grabbed at the gun and shoved the big man away with his other hand.

Flipping the airborne dog over his shoulder, Goodman shook off Jack's hand and gave a downward chop with the gun butt. Jack's cry of pain ended with an "oomph" as Goodman's fist sank into his stomach, followed by the thump of the gun barrel on his lowered head. Beyond them, the dog thudded to the floor and yelped off down the hall.

As Jack fell, Goodman swung the pistol barrel again, this time against Jack's left temple, followed by a hard chop to the side of Jack's neck.

She heard a sharp crack from the blow. She had watched in horror, but now she lunged around the sofa, screaming,

"You bastard! You bastard!"

Stumbling past Jack—hunched forward, on his knees—she rushed at Goodman. He seized her outstretched arm, then spun her around and brought her arm up behind her in a hammerlock. His gun hand reached over her shoulder and he secured a chokehold around her neck.

She clawed at his arm with her free hand. She kicked back at him with her bare feet, stretching to reach his groin, but he lifted her off the floor and she connected only with his hard shins and thighs, or flailed empty space, as he dangled her in front of him. She struggled for air.

Then everything went black.

Chapter Forty-six – Torn Apart

WHEN SHE CAME TO, she was half sitting, half lying on the sofa, facing the coffee table. Her wrists were trussed behind her with something silky. She bent her fingers to tug at the fabric. Her discarded pantyhose. She squirmed farther onto her side and tried to stretch her bindings. Instead, they tightened around her wrists.

It was dark, no fire in the fireplace. The only light came from the window at the end the room, light from streetlamps in town and the car lots and strip malls along the main roads, reflected on the sky and filtered through the trees. In the middle of the floor, just beyond the coffee table, she could barely make out her fleece robe.

The room was cold. She was cold under the silky fabric of her peignoir—what little of it covered her torso and thighs. She shivered. Twisting and craning her neck, she managed to look down at her feet. They were bound by a leather belt looped twice around and tied in a hard knot against her ankles.

She lifted her head higher, straining to see in the dim light from the window. Jack was at the other end of the sofa, his head down, his body sagging forward and away from her. He was breathing, but the breaths came shallow and halting, labored.

"Jack," she whispered. He didn't answer or move.

"Jack!" she said louder. "Are you okay? Jack? . . . Jack!"

Twisting her body upright on the sofa, she managed to slide closer to him. She stared at his face. A vicious dark welt marked his temple where Goodman had hit him. A dark stain ran down his cheek and darkened his shirt collar.

Falling back on her side, she struggled at her bonds, first trying to loosen her hands, then her feet, then her hands again. Working her arms back and forth, tugging and twisting, she managed to stretch the pantyhose and pull her wrists apart a few inches, but the effort left her fingers numb and the snarl of fabric only tighter on her wrists.

A noise in the kitchen stopped her.

Entering through the open door, Goodman came around the sofa and stood over her. She closed her eyes, hoping he wouldn't see that she was conscious.

Pulling her legs forward, he ran his hand up to her buttocks under the peignoir, then lowered himself onto the sofa, between her and Jack. His hand slid down to her thigh. A hand encased in a thin rubber glove.

She felt his hot breath on her neck. The strong odor of onions and beer and cigarettes penetrated her nostrils. Then he pinched her hard on the thigh.

"Ow! You bastard!" She jerked away from him and started to struggle.

Grabbing her by the throat, he lunged forward and pinned her to the sofa as she writhed and flailed her legs. Then he thrust his free hand beneath her and gave her bound arms a vicious downward twist.

She shrieked in pain.

One eye gleamed down at her while the other gazed off in the distance. A big crooked nose flattened by a fist somewhere. A forehead sloping back from deep-set eyes to swept-back dark hair. A big man who weighed more than twice what she weighed.

"Awake, my pretty one," he whispered, a harsh sibilant hiss. But he relaxed the pressure on her throat.

"You can't get away with this," she said, gasping and straining against him. "The mayor . . . you . . . you bastards—"

"The mayor? Ha! That pussy's got no balls." Releasing her throat, he rammed his fingers, sheathed in the surgical glove, into her mouth. "We keep havin' to bail him out."

"Hop hit!" she screeched, whipping back and forth and trying to bite him.

His rough hand pried her jaws open. A thick cloth was forced in, past her teeth. Gagging bile swelled up in her throat, joining the pungent taste of the cloth. Her nostrils filled with a smell of damp, dirty laundry. Jack's sock.

Goodman's full weight pressed down on her, sending a wave of pain up one arm and into her shoulder. She strained to escape from beneath him, but succeeded only in making the pain worse.

"This time we get two birds," Goodman said and jerked her head forward. Extracting a roll of duct tape from a bag beside the sofa, he roughly wrapped three swaths around her head and over her mouth. Her efforts to scream ended in gagging coughs as he ripped the tape with a long carving knife.

"Don't vomit, bitch!" He was breathing hard from his efforts, enveloping her face in a noxious wave of foul odors. Releasing her head, he dropped the knife and tape on the floor.

She stopped coughing, but continued to struggle against the oppressive weight and the suffocating gag. In the struggle, her feet had stretched out against Jack's thigh. She strained her head back and away from Goodman's face, but kept her eyes, full of hate and loathing, fixed on the one eye glaring down at her.

He reached to the side of the sofa and lifted a fluffy white pillow— one from her own bed—and held it inches from her eyes. She stopped struggling. Her breaths came in irregular sniffles, shallow and fast.

"You cause me trouble, *bitch*, and we can always do this." He lowered the pillow onto her face.

She felt the world closing in. She couldn't breathe. She tried to swing her head back and forth. She shrieked, "No, no, no!" The words came out only as a muffled, "Unh, unh, unh!"

He lifted the pillow and grinned at her, a mirthless, malevolent grin. "No, don't think you want that. Relax. We got a little change in plans, and I need to think about it."

Her head back, she breathed hard through her nose, trying to fill her lungs with fresh air and avoid his odor. But his smell clung to every molecule and invaded her senses.

"Damn dog . . . but that's okay." He sniggered, a nasty nasal sound. Rising slightly, his head directly above hers, he reached behind her and seized the pantyhose at her wrist and pulled them tighter. She strained to counter the pulls, trying to maintain the little space she'd gained.

"You see, my meddling little cunt," his voice rasped in her ear as his upper body pressed down on hers, "I'm good. I'm really good."

She went rigid, fearing what came next.

"A gas leak late at night, a little spark, and bang! You're gone."

She lay still. She willed him dead, and herself killing him.

"Too bad I don't have time to play," he said. He sat up and, with his hand grasping her shoulder, canted his head toward the coffee table. She tried to follow his one eye. He was staring at the fireplace.

"I'll fix it up for you. So you look natural. You and your lover."

She writhed and screamed, emitting muffled howls of rage.

Shoving her hard against the sofa, he stood, towering over her in the dark. "I'll be back and you'll still be warm." He patted her hair.

She watched as he went over to the fireplace. Going down on one knee, he fiddled with something, but she couldn't see what. Then he stood and slid an object into his pocket. The gas hissed among the logs.

Understanding, she shook her head wildly back and forth and tried to shout at him through the wet sock.

"Don't worry," he said, coming back toward her. He stopped to pick up her robe. "There's no fire, but this'll keep you warm—for your little nap." He tossed the robe over her, covering her shoulders and hips.

Going to the far end of the sofa, he grabbed Jack by the hair and jerked his head back, then forward, then back again. Jack gave a high keening groan, and his chest heaved.

"He's done," Goodman said, moving to the door.

She continued shaking her head, trying to yell, to scream, as he went into the kitchen and closed the door behind him. A key clicked in the lock.

When the old place was a boarding house, there had been a lock on every door. Most of the keys had disappeared—except those in the bathroom and bedroom doors. Goodman wasn't taking any chances.

Edging up on the sofa arm, she saw a sliver of light appear at the bottom of the door. On the other side, there was movement, a shuffle of feet—and the light at the floor disappeared as something was stuffed in the crack.

She looked around. The door to the living room, to the left of the fireplace, was also closed. The den already felt like a dark tomb, the only light the cloud-reflected city lights from the one window.

Jack was breathing, a dry wheezing snore followed by quick, shallow breaths. Then she smelled it. The odorant in the gas.

She tugged at the pantyhose binding her wrists. No more give. But he hadn't pulled them tighter.

What's that bastard thinking? Still be warm? She groaned. *I'll still be warm.* Not even her worst nightmare matched this. *Where's he gone?*

While the thoughts ran through her mind, she continued to struggle, pulling her wrists apart and working them farther down her back. The fleece robe had slipped off, onto the floor. Shivering and out of breath, she paused. The pantyhose had stretched some, but her hands were numb. She jerked her arms back and forth, up and down.

How had Houdini done it? How would Billy do it? Billy.

Scrunching up on the sofa, she slid her wrists down to her hips and tried to force her body through the loop formed by her arms. The loop was too short. All those years in gymnastics and dance, and now her yoga, and she still couldn't do this. They were going to suffocate. He would arrange them to look like they were making love—when they died from the fumes. But who would believe that? The odor should have alerted them. But with alcohol and sex? And fire—or explosion. That was it. It would obliterate the evidence. Like with Kitty?

Struggling to pass her bound arms underneath her, she tumbled onto the floor, squeezed between the sofa and the coffee table. She rested there, her hands almost but not quite beneath her hips.

The thought hit her. *The fumes will be worse down here, won't they?* She couldn't remember, but she had to keep at it.

Twisting and turning, worming her way along the floor and banging into the coffee table, she managed to get up on the balls of her feet with her knees against the sofa. She hunched over, closer to Jack. Listening to his wheezed exhalations, she tried again. She'd always been double-jointed, able to slip her hands back and forth over her head while grasping a stick. Her hands, squeezed tight against her buttocks, were still too close together.

She leaned forward and nudged her forehead against Jack's shoulder, then his cheek. He groaned. She felt a wet smudge on her head.

"Hold on Jack." She struggled to whisper into the gag. "I can do this. We can make it."

Wedged against the sofa, she worked at the pantyhose, pulling one-way, then another, then twisting her wrists back and forth at harsh angles. The strands loosened a bit. With all her might, she shoved and jerked her tied hands under her buttocks—pitching her back against the coffee table. Something popped in her left shoulder. An excruciating pain swept through her arm and neck. Only the sock kept her from crying out.

Falling to the floor, sobbing in pain, she sawed and yanked and tugged with an urgency and desperation like none she'd ever felt before—until her hands, straining against the stretched pantyhose, slid all the way underneath her thighs. She sat up, back against the couch, hands beneath her, and rested. Then leaning forward, tightening into a ball, she forced her bound feet between her wrists, and then her legs through the loop made by her extended arms and the pantyhose—and her hands were in front of her.

She ripped the tape from around her head, pulling out strands of hair, then jerked the saliva-soaked sock out of her mouth and threw it as far as she could with both hands. Another jab of pain shot through her shoulder. She muffled a scream.

Her neck and back ached. Pain throbbed from her left shoulder down to her elbow, and her hands were so numb they felt dead. Her peignoir was torn; not even its filmy silk covered one breast and most of her back. She felt shivering, icy cold. But she had her hands in front of her.

Ignoring the pain, she tugged at the pantyhose with her teeth, but her struggles had pulled the tangled knot even tighter. She couldn't undo it.

Bending her knees and reaching past them with unfeeling fingers, she concentrated on the belt around her ankles. The knot loosened, then after several jerks and tugs came undone. She unlooped the belt and tossed it on the coffee table.

Struggling to her feet, she painfully twisted her arms up and pulled the peignoir strap back onto her shoulder. Her head, her entire body, felt light, as if she were floating in an ocean. All she wanted was to sleep.

Through the haze came Goodman's voice, but only in her mind. *The mayor's a pussy. Hasn't got the balls.*

Then who?

It was all muddled, spinning over and over in her thoughts. *Mayor, balls, who, who?* She needed to clear her mind, concentrate on getting out of here. She twisted her head back and forth and kneaded her eyes with her fists.

The gas. The low hiss from the fireplace. She didn't know how fast it was coming in or how much oxygen it displaced or how quickly and where. *Down low*, she thought. *Or high?*

She sank down on the sofa and, reaching out to touch Jack's face, rubbed his cheek with the back of a bound hand. He moaned, but his eyes remained shut, his breathing faint and irregular.

She had to move, and fast. But she couldn't. *This is a dream*, she told herself, *a nightmare. I'll awake from it. Soon.*

As if in a trance, she glided around the coffee table, to the fireplace, and dropped to one knee at the recessed opening in the floor for the gas valve. The T-shaped tool to turn it off was gone. In Goodman's pocket.

She thrust the fingers of one bound hand into the opening and twisted at the valve nut. It refused to budge. She twisted again and again, frantically looking about for something to make it move. The low hiss of the gas beckoned her to lie down and sleep.

Air. I have to have air. She was near to collapsing.

Goodman. He'll be back.

My robe!

Staggering to her feet, she stumbled to the coffee table, leaned across it, and picked up the robe. She stumbled back to the fireplace.

Stop the flow. But the gas will seep through. Slow it down. She threw the robe on top of the logs. Still in a dream, she sailed to the sofa and collected two seat cushions and, sailing back, stuffed them in the fireplace, on top of the robe.

The hiss was fainter, farther away, but it persisted.

She found herself by the window, her bound hands propping her up against the wall. A whisper of cold air touched her face and right arm— from somewhere around the sash. Not enough. She took a deep breath and shook her head; free it of the fog.

A frisson of horror ran up her back. *What had he said? Gas leak. A spark. He's coming back. To arrange us.*

I have to do something. Save myself, save Jack.

Air. Oxygen. On the plane, your own mask first. Gas is heavier, right? Maybe if she got higher up. But Jack needs air. I need air. She was thinking in circles.

Whining and scratching came from the door to the living room.

Dimples. There would be fresh air in there. Moving past the fireplace to the living room door, she tried to open it. Locked. *Of course. Goodman had locked both doors.*

The window. Unopened since the fall—when Jack painted the room. And the window sash. I have to try it.

Confronted by a pale, ethereal reflection in the quartered panes, she pounded and shoved, until finally she had to rest her head and a silk-clad breast and bare shoulder against the cold glass. She couldn't budge it. Panting for breath, she twisted to one side and leaned against the wall. *What now?*

I can break it. I can break the window.

Her eyes rested on the fireplace, with its slow, interminable hiss of gas. On the hearth stood the fireplace set Jack's mother had given him for Christmas. Shovel, brush, and cast iron poker.

I can break the window with the poker.

Dimples' scratching stopped and a low growl replaced it. From the kitchen came the sound of the outside door opening. Closing. Not surreptitiously, but as one would normally enter.

She froze as heavy steps moved toward the door to the den. From beyond the door came Goodman's gruff voice, muttering, humming: "We all live in a yellow submarine, yellow submarine . . ."

A wave of panic swept over her. *It's too late! What can I do?*

The footsteps receded out of the kitchen, down the hallway, away from the den. Another door opened—followed by the creak of stairs. The basement. *He must've been down there, making his preparations, then waiting and coming up quietly when we were on the couch. He's down there now making the final arrangements.*

Feeling lightheaded and gasping for breath, she swam across the room to the fireplace. If she had slowed the gas, she hadn't stopped it, and her oxygen was less and less minute-by-minute, second-by-second.

Dimples whimpered softly on the other side of the door to the living room.

Her bound hands were sufficiently separated by her struggles that she could grip the iron poker with both hands. She tugged it out of the stand. Pain swept over her upper body from her shoulder.

I mustn't scream. Not a sound.

Hefting the heavy poker with both hands, she weaved across the room, past the coffee table and sofa, and stationed herself to the left side of the door to the kitchen. Dropping the poker's pikestaff end to the floor, she paused to catch her breath—but even breathing as deep and fast as she could, there was no catching it. She wouldn't last much longer.

Stop gasping, she told herself. *No noise, no noise.*

The stairs creaked again and footsteps sounded in the hall.

She lifted the heavy poker, sending pain slashing through her arm and shoulder. *No sound*, she thought, clinching her teeth. *Make no sound.* Slowly, she raised the poker with its curved, sharp hook and pike high above her head. And waited.

Rattling the key in the lock, Goodman pulled the door inward, into the kitchen, and entered the den. His long coat was gone, and he wore a dark pullover and wool cap. A fireman's mask covered his face, and a small oxygen tank hung on his back. Using both hands, he adjusted the straps to the mask. No gun in sight. He stopped just inside the door, and the facemask shifted its angle toward the end of the sofa where she should have been—and wasn't.

With her last bit of strength, she slashed the poker down, in a long arc, ending with a dull thunk, like a sharp stake puncturing a watermelon. Twisting toward her, Goodman staggered under the blow and fell forward, dislodging the curved hook and pulling the wool cap off his head. Except for a loud grunt, no sound came from the mask.

He stopped his fall with one knee and a hand on the floor. The insect eyes of the mask twisted around and stared up at her. His hand clutched at the gun on his belt.

Fighting overwhelming pain and fatigue, she struggled to raise the poker. She wanted to scream curses at him, but she couldn't muster the breath. In one last effort, she swung the poker again, propelling the hook into the glass eye of the mask. Blood blossomed out of it and over Goodman's face. Then he fell forward, facedown onto the floor, pulling the poker with him.

Releasing it, she fled. Through the open door into the kitchen, bumping into the table and knocking it aside, and then out the back door onto the screened porch, all the way gasping for air, she fled. Through the broken screen door and down the cinder block steps and into the yard, her peignoir clinging to her chilled body, she fled, sucking cold, deep drafts of air into her oxygen-starved lungs.

She collapsed onto the dead grass and, still gulping the untainted air, crawled away from the house. Shivering in the cold February night, she rolled onto her side and brought her knees up to her chest. She hugged them to her with arms still bound at the wrists, the shivering uncontrollable, her breath coming in choking sobs and gasps.

I have to get control, flashed through her mind, *get Jack out of there.*

Taking a deep breath, then another and another, she settled into a steady, measured rhythm. She sat up in time to see Dimples wiggle through the tear at the bottom of the back screen door. He bounded up to her and she caught him in her arms as he leaped to lick her face.

"Oh, God," she murmured into the dog's fur. "I've got to go back . . . I've got to go back in there."

She hugged Dimples to her chest. Her head was clearing; her breathing no longer a violent, desperate pant; yet her pulse raced. She couldn't stop shivering.

Move! she told herself. *There's not enough oxygen in there—not even with the door open. And he's hurt, badly hurt. Oh, God, he's dying.*

She pushed Dimples aside and struggled to her feet. She stumbled, went down on one knee, then stood again.

I can run next door. No! Too much time—getting someone, convincing them, their insisting on waiting for the police or firemen or somebody to come.

She could get him out—even as heavy as he was. Drag him. She could do it. She knew she could do it. She had to do it.

Even as she debated, she staggered across the lawn toward the back door. She could see it in her mind, visualize it. *Up the steps, inside the kitchen, into the den, over Goodman on the floor; grab Jack under his arms, tugging at him, pulling him off the couch.*

The absence of air and she was panting. Jack's legs moving, and they were moving together, floating through space.

The world around her became a long blur, an out-of-focus movie in which time slowed almost to a stop, then looped and speeded up again. The sun erupted around her, and then everything went black. The night and the house were a great weight bearing down on her, pushing her forward and to the ground.

The first blast knocked her down. She rolled over and over to get away from the heat. The second, larger explosion blew out a section of wall on the side of the house screened by the azaleas, dropping part of the roof into the debris. Flames snickered and flicked in the shattered windows, until rising and licking at the wood, they began to devour it.

She turned and crawled frantically toward the back porch, still free of flames. She sobbed and rose on one knee.

"Jack! Jack!" she wailed, stretching out her bound wrists toward the house, now ablaze everywhere but in the very back, at the kitchen. *Please God, don't let him be in there,* she prayed.

Had she only imagined going back inside? She couldn't remember. *I started back. I was at the porch.*

Struggling to her feet, she stood, facing the conflagration.

Her face and back and arms burned like the most horrible sunburn she'd ever suffered. Her mouth tasted of ashes. Not only her pulled shoulder, but every muscle and bone in her body ached. The back of her peignoir clung to her skin as if it had been pasted on.

A giant red tulip of flames engulfed the back porch, and the door to the kitchen disappeared inside it.

Driven by the scorching heat, she turned and stumbled away from the inferno, dragging her feet through the dead grass, clutching the peignoir to her chest with her bound hands, until she fell to her knees, then her hands, and getting up, fell again and started crawling on her knees and elbows. She curled into a ball in a corner of the yard partly shielded by bushes, her back to the fire, and sobbed.

Dimples came out of the dark and licked her face. Reaching out her hands, she drew the dog to her, his fur on one side singed and crumbly to her touch, and pulled him inside her cocoon. Her breath came in long sobs. She shivered violently—then she heard a low moan.

She lifted her head and, rising on one elbow, stared back at the flaming house. There in front of her, to one side, was a human body. A hand reaching out toward her.

Chapter Forty-seven – Patricia

SHE WAS MEETING SALLY MCFEE for lunch. They had crossed paths in the lobby of the McFee Savings Building, she on her way into the office and Sally on the way out from visiting her father. Sally suggested it and Patricia had agreed, if reluctantly. In the last weeks, there hadn't been many people she wanted to see socially. Or privately. Her mother had come and gone, to her relief.

Colin had called—from a Mennonite store somewhere in Central America. He was concerned about her. Angry about what had happened to Jack. But he hadn't offered to come. And she didn't want him to.

So here she was. On her way to meet Sally McFee, whom she didn't really know. They'd talked at any length only once before, at the hospital, when Jack was in intensive care.

Other than the McFee firm, they had few things in common, Sally and she. But another was Jack. She wondered how Sally knew so much about him, why her comments sounded so intimate, why her eyes glistened as they faced each other in the drab hallway of the hospital.

She had felt self-conscious then. Her hair still showed black tips and broken strands and gaps she covered as best she could with combing and fluffing. She had considered buying a hat, but only briefly: that was too much like her mother. A few places on her arms and neck were still blistered then or peeling, and she had to wear sunglasses to hide her singed eyebrows and lashes. Even with her arm in a sling, her shoulder had ached, and every appendage was stiff and sore, her free arm so stiff she could barely hold on to Dimples when she handed the dog, no longer struggling to escape her, to Jack's mother.

She had forced herself to stop crying all the time and she cried not at all now.

Allie had come to visit her in the hospital, in a wheelchair, maneuvered into her room by Sally and accompanied by Millicent, Allie's now constant companion. Allie had taken Patricia's hands in both of hers.

"He's a strong young man," Allie said, looking up at her. "We're all pulling for him." The apparatus holding her jaw in place distorted her words, but her eyes spoke recognition—and memory.

"He sure is, best lawyer I know," chimed in Millicent from beside Sally, who was preparing to turn the wheelchair.

A full cast of Jack's friends and acquaintances had gone to the hospital after he got out of intensive care, even though he was barely conscious most of the time. Lacey and Aerial and Dick McFee. Judge Davis, Leon Hayes, and Ray Malloy, Ray with his wife and oldest kid. Leslie and Joe Mayes flew up from Atlanta, but left Jack's room quickly when Patricia showed up.

Fitz came by, shaking hands, lamenting the accident, consoling Jack's mother and giving Patricia a hug before she could back away.

Lena Fisher came with Fitz. Her husband, the mayor, was detained, urgent business, Lena told the nurse, who told Patricia. Something to do with the Alt-Energy project.

The infernal alternative-energy project. Patricia had heard it was unraveling, verging on collapse. Some of those standing to benefit were unnerved by Goodman's attack and Jack's near death. Her near death. And possibly afraid of what the investigation might reveal. What she might say. Suspicions were even directed at the mayor, suspicions that he might bear some responsibility for his aide-de-camp's activities.

But Allie said the project would go on, although the board would, at the very least, move it away from Carrville. Jettisoning Mayor Fisher. And Fitz.

That was a ray of sunshine.

Locking the door of her old Mercedes, she stopped to stare up at the sky, clear and blue. *Ha!* She thought. *Fitz's and the mayor's land deals are all in the toilet. All that land out there on the Old Schoolhouse Road, all it's good for now is to grow soybeans and corn. Just farmland, like some greater power intended it to be.*

Lost in thought, she dodged a car speeding into the takeout lane and crossed the parking lot to the restaurant. The mayor and Fitz still had the municipal bonds and their private ventures. What could she do about that? Jack had vowed to stay and fight. But she wasn't. She was leaving.

Pausing at the entrance, she stared at the name and winced. *Taco Pal. What if Billy Angel had never set foot in here?* She hadn't, herself, set foot in here, not even to prepare for Billy's trial. Maybe she should have.

When Sally suggested lunch, it just popped into her head. She didn't dislike Sally, but she wasn't eager to do lunch with her, either. Having accepted the invitation, though, the Taco Pal seemed fitting.

Sally greeted her just inside the door, away from the counter. A sweet-faced blonde wearing designer jeans and a mannish white shirt, open at the throat one button lower than Patricia would have dared. Seizing her outstretched hand like an old friend, Sally stepped forward and hugged her tightly. Two women bonded by caring—or was it love?—for a man who was only half-alive.

They both ordered chicken taco salads. As she waited by the counter for her order, she stared past the cashier, toward the back, toward a door barely visible through the array of ovens and deep fat fryers and stoves and silver countertops. *Why would anyone rob this place?*

She watched another customer, a small Hispanic man in a laborer's dusty work clothes, count out wrinkled dollar bills and coins to pay for his meal. *Why not a bank or jewelry store? Too difficult, perhaps. But surely there were better targets. Why spend hours chipping away at a block of concrete to steal a safe he could open in minutes? Not even a lot of money in it.*

The whole idea was ludicrous. It had to have been a set up by Goodman. To get Royale. To get the mayor out of an embarrassing mess.

But why steal the damn safe? To help Lazlo learn the art? A small safe on which he could practice? Maybe Billy didn't tell me everything, or maybe they were all spaced out on drugs.

"My father really hates to see you leave," Sally said, interrupting her thoughts. They were carrying their plastic trays to a table by the front window.

"He told me," Patricia said. "Suggested I could become a partner in the firm." She resisted rolling her eyes. *A very junior partner in a two-lawyer firm. Unless . . . until Jack recovered and—*she didn't want to think about it.

"He says you're a brilliant lawyer."

That he didn't tell me. She placed her tray on the table and stared out the window without answering Sally.

"I wish you would stay," Sally said, sitting down across from her.

"Nice of you to say that," Patricia replied, her mind elsewhere.

Using her plastic fork, Sally sorted through her salad as if she were searching for something edible. "I know Daddy has his problems, but with you and Jack, we could make this a real law firm again."

Real law firm? What did she think we were doing all these months, Patricia thought. *Jack and I. Selling encyclopedias?*

Patricia shook her head. "I've lost too much here and I have an offer in Atlanta. A bank." Giving Sally a tight smile, she dug her fork deep into the bowl of greenery and broke a tine on the plastic fork.

Disappointment showed on Sally's face.

"Someone tried to kill me," Patricia said, standing. "Excuse me. I need to get another fork." She held up the broken plastic utensil.

When Patricia returned and before she was even seated, Sally said, "He's dead, you know. That man Goodman. You don't have to worry about him."

I know he's dead, you blond bimbo, Patricia thought. She sighed and renewed her attack on the salad, one leaf and chicken nugget at a time.

"I need a change in scenery," she said, trying to hide her irritation.

Sally was poking at the salad, her eyes down. "I'm sorry," she said. "I'm making a fool of myself." She looked up. Her previously smooth forehead wrinkled in concern. "I feel terrible about what you've been through."

"That's all right. I didn't mean to make you feel bad."

"I have a lot of respect for you. That's why I want you to stay and help me do something with Daddy's firm. When Jack can—"

"You need to understand that Goodman may be dead . . ." Patricia stopped and took a breath. "But he was just the sharp edge of a hard instrument."

"Mom told me about the mayor . . . and Mr. Fitzhugh."

"Oh?" Patricia gave her a quizzical look.

"The only thing my mother doesn't remember is the accident. We thought it might be best not to advertise her . . . recovery. Not yet. She'll still be in a wheelchair, but she'll be back at work in a few weeks, and she's going to fry the mayor on a hot griddle."

Patricia smiled now. "Good for Allie. I'm glad to hear it. Both her recovery *and* that she's *not* going to let the mayor get away with . . . his scheme, whatever it is."

"I'm going to help her . . . well, as soon as I pass the bar." Sally reached across the narrow table and placed her hand on top of Patricia's, curled in a loose fist beside her tray. "We want you to stay and help us. You can't give up the fight now." Eyes fixed on each other, they were silent a moment. "And Jack may be able . . . may be back to help someday . . . soon."

"I don't know. I'll think about it." Patricia turned her hand over and squeezed Sally's, then quickly withdrew her hand into her lap.

Sally smiled at her and changed the subject. "Your hair looks nice."

"It should. I paid enough to cover the damage." She laughed, then paused, thinking a moment. Her face became rigid, serious. She had aged twenty years in the last month. "You know what that bastard was trying to do?"

"Goodman?" Sally said, looking up from her salad.

"He turned Kitty's . . . her mother's trailer into a fire bomb, and he . . ." She grimaced at a piece of chicken. "Dimples caught him . . ." She trailed off and deposited the chicken in her mouth, chewed quickly, and swallowed. "They told me he would've finished us off, then blown up the house. Our bodies would've burned . . ." She stared at Sally and shook her head. "The perverted bastard was warped. He wanted to play games with me, like a cat with a mouse."

Sally, who was watching her intently, bit her lower lip and looked away.

"One of the investigators . . ." Patricia paused. "He knew Goodman . . . said he was like that. Mean, perverse." She stared down at her hands, then took a deep breath. "He came back to . . . to . . ." she stopped, feeling like sobbing again, "to rape me."

"He *was* a pervert," Sally said. "At least he's dead now."

"And Jack's in rehab, who knows for how long." She looked up and met Sally's eyes. "I don't know how he got out of there. I don't remember anything," she shook her head, "after I started back in." She felt a catch in her throat and coughed several times, her napkin over her mouth. Lowering the napkin, she added, "I'm not the same person I was."

"I'm sorry."

"I want to help you, Sally. I want to see that bunch out of business . . . You know what that rat Fitz did? He handed Jack's mother a check for five thousand dollars. At the hospital. Down on one knee beside her in her wheelchair." She gave a small laugh. "Salving his conscience."

She stopped, remembering what Goodman had said. *"The mayor's a pussy" or something like that. "We have to bail him out."*

Fitz, damn it. It had to be Fitz. Protecting the mayor. Cleaning up his messes. Putting all the scams together—like one of his goddamn companies. He was behind it all. Well, most of it, what Goodman wasn't freelancing. Allie's accident? Maybe even Kitty. It had to be Fitz.

"Mother'll see that he's excluded from any of the contracts," Sally was saying, "and the bond funds."

Patricia nodded slowly, still going over the realization that had come to her. "You mean Fitz," she said, staring fixedly at Sally.

Sally moved her tray aside and leaned forward. "Yeah, Mr. Fitzhugh. And the mayor's out of the project—for good. Mother will make sure he doesn't get a penny, not even under the table. I swear it."

"I hope Allie can do that. I really hope she can." Patricia shook her head and sighed. "But she needs to be careful." Her eyes searched the face of the woman across from her. She didn't have enough evidence to point a finger at Fitz. Not yet.

"I hate to say this, Sally, but lightening *can* strike twice." She hesitated to add, *Whether it's Allie or me or anyone else, including you*. Instead, she said, "The mayor isn't the only one trying to ride this Alt-Energy horse to riches."

"Mother and I talked about that. We're not going to let them scare us."

Patricia was forced to smile at the young woman, still a law student. So young and untested. And brave. Like she once was.

She nodded. "I'll think about staying. I really will. But no promises."

Maybe I will stay. Jack would have. And he's still here. She felt herself tearing up and her smile vanished. Sally gave her a puzzled look.

"Are you okay?"

"I'm fine . . . feeling better all the time." She resurrected the smile and forced back the tears. She wasn't going away and leave Jack *alone* here with this naïve young girl. He needed her, needed her to help him get well and join the fight.

She stared down at her hands, still red from the fire, thinking, *In life, there are only pauses and choices to make and then getting up and going on with whatever it is. The only true ending is death, and even then, the living go on living. And sometimes maybe you get a second chance.*

Made in the USA
Columbia, SC
22 January 2020